TAME ME

HEIDI RICE

NATALIE ANDERSON

MILLS & BOON

First published in Great Britain 2024
by Mills & Boon, an imprint of HarperCollins*Publishers* Ltd,
1 London Bridge Street, London, SE1 9GF

www.harpercollins.co.uk

HarperCollins*Publishers*, Macken House, 39/40 Mayor Street Upper, Dublin 1, D01 C9W8, Ireland

Tame Me © 2024 Harlequin Enterprises ULC

Revenge in Paradise © 2024 Heidi Rice

My One-Night Heir © 2024 Natalie Anderson

ISBN: 978-0-263-32012-1

06/24

MIX
Paper | Supporting
responsible forestry
FSC™ C007454

This book contains FSC™ certified paper
and other controlled sources to ensure responsible forest management.

For more information visit www.harpercollins.co.uk/green.

Printed and Bound in the UK using 100% Renewable Electricity
at CPI Group (UK) Ltd, Croydon, CR0 4YY

REVENGE IN PARADISE

HEIDI RICE

MILLS & BOON

To Amanda Cinelli, a fabulous author
and an even better friend, who helped me
brainstorm this story with the immortal line:
'Why don't you just have her steal his boat?'

CHAPTER ONE

MILLY DEVLIN HIKED up the borrowed designer gown—
which had cost ten times her current monthly income—
and raced down the steep stone steps in the moonlight…

She was running away again, this time from the stunning Capri palazzo—perched on the clifftop above, overlooking the azure sea—and the site of her latest disaster.
Because having a public spat with her sister in front of
an audience of stupidly rich, ludicrously beautiful people supping vintage booze and nibbling priceless caviar
on the marble terrazzo had not been her finest hour. And
certainly not her intention, when she'd agreed to accom-
pany Lacey to the launch party for her husband Brandon
Cade's new Italian subsidiary.

Milly cursed as her heel snagged on one of the cobble-
stones but managed to grab the iron balustrade before she
pitched headfirst into the Gulf of Naples. Which would
have put the final bow on this evening's entertainment.

She took a steadying breath, and kicked off the cursed
shoes, which her sister had lent her too—because designer
footwear was not in Milly's wheelhouse any more than
lavish social events.

Lacey hadn't wanted her to feel out of place in the world
where Lacey and her daughter, Ruby, now lived—courtesy of her billionaire husband, Brandon Cade, Ruby's dad.

Mission so not accomplished.

Milly scooped up the shoes, and bit her bottom lip to stop it quivering.

She glanced back, at the exclusive party still in full swing above her, and recalled the whispers she'd overheard as she pushed through the crowd on the terrazzo looking for the nearest exit. If only she didn't speak such good Italian.

'Can't imagine why Cade and his wife put up with her, the woman is an ungracious ungrateful brat.'

'She's a liability, and a complete nobody. I heard she's been backpacking around Europe like a homeless person.'

She ignored the ripple of embarrassment. She didn't care what any of those people thought of her. She had no desire to be part of their world. She'd only agreed to come to show Lacey she was perfectly okay. But as she rushed down the steps, her bare feet warmed by the stone, it was a lot harder to dismiss the anxious look on Lacey's face when they'd argued twenty minutes ago…

'Why can't you come home to London, Milly? Ruby misses you. I miss you. Brandon's worried about you and so am I.'

'It's not his job to be worried about me. Is that why you invited me here? To ambush me again? I'm happy in Genoa, Lacey.'

Except it wasn't entirely true. Because Milly's grand plan to make a living out of her art hadn't exactly been a roaring success… Yet. The truth was, she never had time to draw, or develop any of her ideas, because she had been too busy working in a string of minimum wage jobs first in France, then in Italy, which barely kept her head above water.

But she could not bear to return to London a failure. She couldn't let her sister and her new husband support her.

It didn't matter how wealthy Brandon Cade was, her life was her responsibility. Nor did she want to be a spectator in her sister's blissfully happy, loved-up new marriage.

She swallowed, hating the trickle of envy. Her older sister had worked so hard for so long, becoming a single mum at only nineteen, and being a stand-in mum to Milly too. She deserved to find happiness with the billionaire media mogul who had got her pregnant.

If only Milly didn't feel so hopelessly displaced. Milly and Lacey and Ruby had been a unit, once. A tight, close, strong, unbreakable family unit. Until Brandon Cade had discovered Ruby was his daughter... And had swooped into their ordinary, unassuming lives eighteen months ago and insisted on marrying Lacey and becoming Ruby's daddy for real. And changed Milly's family for ever.

She did not fit in their exclusive world. And the sooner Lacey and Brandon figured that out, the better off they would all be. As for her adorable niece Ruby...

Milly cursed as she reached the private dock below the palazzo.

Low blow, Lacey, low blow.

Milly spoke to her niece every weekend on a video link. But Rubes was busy these days spending quality time with her daddy, training her very naughty dog, Tinkerbell, and adjusting to her new baby brother, Arthur.

If you only knew how much I missed Ruby, Lacey. But she doesn't need me any more, and neither do you.

She had to make a future for herself, which didn't depend on the Cades. Why couldn't her sister understand that? And butt out of her life?

And yeah, maybe Milly was making a great big hash of said life, but Lacey and Brandon's overbearing concern was not helping.

The tremor of irritation fortified her as she paced along the dock where a parade of shiny oversized super-yachts and motor launches were crowded so closely together they obscured the shimmering, moonlit water.

It took her less than two minutes, though, to realise she'd screwed up again. The private dock was a dead end. She could not get to the ferry terminal to get a boat back to Sorrento from here without swimming past the rocky headland in her sister's designer gown or scaling the cliff face.

Fabulous. Ms Screw-Ups-R-Us strikes again.

She swore. The sound bounced off the cliff walls and returned to her. Because it was going nowhere fast either.

Of course, the other option was to retrace her steps and exit through the palazzo in her sweat-stained dress, smudged make-up and what was left of the hairdo Lacey's personal stylist had constructed at their hotel in Sorrento, which had started to list like the leaning tower of Pisa during her madcap escape.

No way. I'd rather swim a mile in designer couture than face those judgmental snobs again.

She strode to the end of the wooden platform built into the rock wall—to make sure there were no other viable exits from the Dock of Doom—and spotted a gleaming motor launch tethered at the far end.

Wasn't that the boat she and Lacey had arrived on from Sorrento?

She scoured the deck—but it was empty and dark, there wasn't even a light coming from the half-doors that led to the cabin.

The old fellow who had driven them here was probably getting his supper with the other staff up at the palazzo—ready to escort her and Lacey back to Sorrento when the event ended after midnight. She pulled out her phone to call him. Then swore. No service.

She shoved the phone back in her evening bag.

The Cade Launch Ball was due to go on for at least another two hours. The elegant event she would rather die than have to return to this century.

But... Why not just borrow the launch? She knew how to drive it, because she used the same make, if a much older model, to ferry tourists around the marina in Genoa, one of the two jobs she was currently juggling. Once she got back to the luxury hotel in Sorrento where she and her sister were staying, she could get one of the Cade staff to return the boat to Capri and pick up her sister later?

Fireworks exploded in the sky, the cheers of the crowd on the terrace above reminding Milly of all the reasons why she did not want to go back.

The sparkle of blue and green lights glittered over the bay.

She took a staggered breath and slung her heels on board. Tucking the hem of the gown into her panties, she leapt over the railing.

The boat swayed as she tiptoed towards the console. And grinned. Because there was the key, stuck in the ignition. That had to be a sign. Surely?

She rushed to untie the anchoring lines.

As soon as I have service, I'll let them know I've borrowed it.

Getting back to Sorrento early would also mean she could be packed and changed and at the bus station before Lacey returned to the hotel. She did not need another tortuous conversation tonight about her independence, to go with all the others she'd had with Lacey over the past year.

She would send her sister a text as soon as she was on the

bus, apologising and telling her not to worry before Lacey took the Cade jet back to London tomorrow morning.

Milly returned to the console and fired up the boat. The engine purred as she steered the launch round the other bigger vessels and out into the bay.

As the tidal waters from the Gulf of Naples tugged the hull, she scanned the horizon, her vision adjusting to the milky darkness. The water was clear as far as the eye could see, the fishermen and tourists having gone to bed hours ago.

A triumphant laugh popped out as she slammed back the throttle. Adrenaline hurtled through her system as the boat reared, skipping across the surf as if it were flying.

Free at last.

Of the obligations and anxiety that had dragged her down ever since Lacey had invited her to the event. And she had felt obliged to attend.

She let out a rebel yell—the endless frustrations of her overprotective family and trying to figure out her future lifting off her shoulders as the wind slapped her face.

But the whoop strangled in her throat as the cabin door burst open and a man charged out. Dark and dishevelled, in a black tuxedo jacket and trousers, his feet bare and his white dress shirt undone to the waist, this guy was not sixty-something Paulo who had driven them to Capri three hours ago.

Awareness shot through her as she got an impressive eyeful of his bare chest sprinkled with hair and spotted a tattoo of crossed cutlasses over his heart.

A marauding pirate in a designer tuxedo... Am I dreaming or hallucinating or both?

'Who are you?' she demanded of the apparition, so shocked the words came out on a high-pitched squeal. 'And what were you doing hiding down there?'

His staggeringly handsome face contorted into a furious scowl.

'I wasn't hiding, I was sleeping, until you woke me up,' he growled in a deep voice loud enough to be heard over the hum of the engine—and the heartbeat now punching her eardrums. 'And this is my boat. So, what the hell are you doing stealing it?'

The truth dawned, like the fireworks still bursting in the sky behind them.

Oh, fabulous... Miss Screw-Ups-R-Us just borrowed the wrong boat!

Roman Garner starred at the girl steering his boat barefoot, her toned legs displayed by the glittering gown hooked into her panties and a clump of her hair sliding down her head on one side.

He'd just been tossed across the cabin and woken from a perfectly sound sleep.

But the jet lag and fatigue—which had driven him down to his boat to take a nap and escape the boring spectacular of the Cade Launch Ball in the first place—had disappeared. He grabbed the rail as the boat skipped over the waves, glaring at the girl, whose wide eyes were now the size of saucers.

'I… I wasn't stealing it,' she said, having regained the power of speech.

'Oh, yeah, does it belong to you?' he snarled, determined not to be amused by her horrified expression. Or turned on by the way her breasts pressed against the jewelled fabric of her dress and seemed to be sparkling in the moonlight.

His head hurt and it was all her fault.

'I was borrowing it,' she explained.

'Usually, when someone borrows my property, they ask me first,' he pointed out and rubbed his forehead, where he was pretty sure he'd just lost a sizeable portion of brain-cells after headbutting the cabin floor. 'So I can tell them to get lost.'

'I thought the boat belonged to my brother-in-law.'

A likely story. Did she think he was an idiot? 'Yeah, right.'

She opened her mouth to say more, when the boat smacked a rogue swell. Her hands were yanked off the steering column as the boat wheeled to one side.

Her scream split the night as he lurched to catch her before she went headfirst into the Tyrrhenian Sea.

They went down hard on the deck together. He managed to roll just in time to take the brunt of the fall, instead of crushing her body beneath his much larger one. But it cost him. He grunted as pain radiated through his hip.

The boat's engines cut out instantly. Thank God, the kill cord was already engaged.

He lay dazed on the deck, staring up at the night sky with his arms full of the little boat thief—who it turned out was soft in all the right places.

It had clearly been far too long since he'd had a woman on top of him, if he was noticing the girl's lithe figure and abundant curves.

Something to remedy another time, Roman.

His wayward libido quickly got a clue, though, thanks to the throbbing pain in his backside—and his all-round fury at being inconvenienced to this extent.

She scrambled up, managing to recover a lot quicker than he did, her face a picture of anguish and shock… But not nearly penitent enough for his liking.

'I didn't mean to steal your boat,' she protested.

'Yeah? So, whose boat did you mean to steal?' he snarled, lifting himself up on his elbows.

But then the full moon appeared from behind a cloud and he got a proper look at her features.

Her make-up was almost as much of a mess as the rest of her, but the smudges of eyeliner, the dregs of mascara and the lipstick she had chewed off did nothing to detract from her unusual face—wide eyes, a stubborn chin and a slight overbite accentuated her surprising beauty. A small gold ring in her left nostril added to her quirky, unorthodox appearance.

The girl was striking…

His eyes narrowed. And vaguely familiar.

How did he know her? And then it hit him. She had arrived with that bastard Cade's wife, Lacey. If he'd known Cade wasn't going to be at the launch himself, he would never have bothered to attend the event—even though it was less than a mile from the island retreat where he was supposed to be starting an enforced two-week break.

'You work for Brandon Cade, right?' Was she the wife's assistant? If one of Cade's employees had tried to steal his boat, he would find a way to use it against his rival.

Perhaps a little industrial espionage? Or better yet, a major lawsuit to humiliate the man.

'What? No…' she said. 'Do you know Brandon?' she asked, sounding wary now, but still not sorry.

He climbed to his feet, ignoring the pain from his slam dunk on the deck.

Brandon, was it? Was she one of the Cades' inner circle, then? A mistress, perhaps? Was that why the wife had been having that whispering altercation with her much earlier in the evening? Although it seemed odd to bring this girl to the Cade Ball if she was sleeping with her husband.

But whatever way he looked at it, this situation could have potential. Unless, of course, it was some kind of a set-up. His usual cynicism kicked in. Because what were the chances this girl would have chosen to steal *his* boat? And why the hell was she such a mess, when she'd looked pretty hot earlier…?

Whoa, boy? Hot? Seriously?

He admonished his unruly libido for the second time in one night. Which was a record. He *definitely* needed to get laid if he was finding one of Cade's cast-offs hot.

'Yes. I know of Cade,' he said, cryptically. 'We share similar business interests,' he added, although he and Cade shared a whole lot more. The familiar resentment twisted in his gut. But he let it go.

That Cade had always refused to acknowledge their connection was Roman's strength now, not his weakness. After sixteen years of hard work, Roman was now a major player in the same field the Cade family had ruled for generations in the UK. But unlike Cade, who had inherited everything he had, Roman had earned his position.

'Who…? Who are you?' she asked again, as if she didn't know.

He scowled. *Cagey.* No question about it.

If this girl worked for Cade, she *had* to know exactly who Roman was—because he'd made it his business to get on Cade Inc's radar and headhunt their best staff, just to annoy the man. But even in her dishevelled state and with her inclination to boat piracy, she did the innocent look very well.

'As I'm the injured party here, I demand you identify yourself first,' he said with his best Captain of the Universe voice. He had given her more than enough information already.

She was on his boat, in the middle of the Gulf of Naples, without his permission and she'd just given him a sizeable bruise on his arse thanks to her antics. There was a major power imbalance here—which she seemed to be wilfully ignoring with her ballsy attitude.

Annoyingly, he found himself becoming intrigued by her stubborn expression. Why didn't she want to tell him her name? And why did it only make her seem more… hot? Because he didn't usually find antagonism and inconvenience a turn-on.

'Injured, how?' she demanded, because she clearly had not got the message who the captain of this universe was. Another new experience for Roman, who was used to having women do exactly what he told them.

'Okay, that's it.' Roman yanked his phone out of his jacket pocket—resolutely refusing to be impressed by her attitude problem. 'You've got two seconds to tell me who the hell you are, what you are to Cade and why you stole my boat, or I'm calling the Polizia Municipale and having you arrested for piracy and assault.'

'Piracy and…' She huffed out a shocked breath—which made her breasts bounce, distractingly. 'You have got to be kidding? And how exactly did I assault you?'

He tapped a contact on his phone—to call Giovanni, his estate manager on Isola Estiva, not the cops, but she didn't need to know that. 'That'll be one second now,' he said, lifting the phone to his ear.

'Ciao, la polizia?' he said, when Giovanni picked up on the second ring.

And at the exact time that Giovanni said, 'Signor Garner, is that you?' his uninvited passenger threw up her hands.

'Okay, wait. My name's Milly Devlin, I'm Lacey Cade's sister.'

She was Brandon Cade's sister-in-law? So not his mistress...

Relief washed over him. Then he frowned. Why on earth was he pleased the girl wasn't his rival's extramarital squeeze, when that would have made a much better tabloid exclusive?

'*Va bene, signor...*' he said into his phone, cutting off Giovanni, who was still trying to establish what the hell was going on. That made two of them, he thought ruefully as he ended the stunt call and shoved the phone into his trouser pocket.

'That's more like it,' he said, but was careful not to lose the frown.

He was much more intrigued now than mad. But he had no plans to let her off the hook—because her family connection to Cade could only enhance the potential of this situation.

So that explained why she and Cade's wife had come to the event together. But it did not explain the argument he'd witnessed. Not that her domestic situation interested him per se. Families were not his forte—he knew nothing of their dynamics and he did not want to know. But if there was trouble in the Cade paradise he might be able to use it to his advantage. Cade's much publicised marital bliss—ever since the man had finally deigned to recognise his own child and marry the mother, four years too late—had not convinced Roman in the slightest. Roman had bought Drystar to break the story, and had then had his tabloid journalists looking for another juicy exposé ever since. But, annoyingly, Cade had managed to turn the revelation of his secret love child to his advantage, by marrying the girl's mother and then pretending to be in love with the woman.

Getting to know Cade's sister-in-law might help him get to the truth about that. Of course, he didn't usually bother doing any of the dirty work himself, that was the job of his editors, reporters and columnists. And he had also stopped caring about Cade—because he had decided it was not good for his mental health to be so focussed on the guy… But this scoop had landed in his lap. Like, literally. And he had the bruises to prove it.

'Now tell me why you stole my boat,' he demanded.

The girl wrapped her arms around herself, a gust of wind slapping the hull. The tissue-thin dress didn't give her much protection against the night air. If he were a gentleman, he would have offered her his jacket. But he wasn't.

She looked away, a shiver running through her. '*Borrowing* your boat was a stupid impulse that I now deeply regret. But I genuinely thought this was the Cade launch,' she offered, her tone a tad more contrite.

Progress.

'And I needed to leave the party,' she added. 'Is that enough of an explanation for you?' she finished, but the stubborn tilt of her chin and the direct stare totally ruined the almost contrite effect.

'Not hardly,' he replied. It had to be the oldest cliché in the book, but when her back straightened, and those huge eyes narrowed, he had to admit, she was even more attractive when she was staring daggers at him. 'I'll need a much more specific explanation of why you climbed aboard my boat and tried to pinch it,' he added.

She looked so mad, she couldn't speak—and he was actually starting to enjoy himself, more than a little.

Although he wasn't sure what was more satisfying, having a Cade family member at his mercy, or the way her face looked even more stunning when she glared.

'That is,' he continued, 'if you don't want me to have you arrested.'

She hissed something under her breath that sounded like 'rich people' and not in a complimentary way.

'Fine, arrest me!' She threw up her arms in exasperation. 'But you'll end up getting charged yourself with wasting police time when it turns out this was all a massive misunderstanding.'

'Perhaps I'll settle for slapping you with an enormous lawsuit instead, then.' He rubbed his sore backside, pointedly. 'Fifty grand for every bruise ought to make you think twice before *borrowing* anyone else's boat without their permission.'

'Sue me, too, then.' The daggers became broadswords as the last of her fake regret went up in smoke. 'But I have a grand total of one hundred and sixty-two euros in my account. So a ten-second call to your lawyer will cost you more than you'll g-get out of m-me.'

The threat would have been more convincing if her teeth hadn't chattered right at the end.

'A pauper who wears designer couture and is Brandon Cade's sister?' he scoffed. 'I think I'll take my chances.'

He knew what poverty looked like—because he and his mother had lived on the thin edge of it during most of his childhood—and she wasn't it…

'This dress isn't mine,' she said. 'I borrowed it from Lacey. And I'm not Brandon's sister, I'm his sister-in-law and I'm certainly not his responsibility. If you sue me, you'll be suing complete nobody Milly Devlin, who is about as far from being worth suing as you are from being an ugly humble pauper without a gargantuan ego.'

He had to bite his lip to stop from chuckling at her outrage. And her back-handed compliment. So, she didn't think he was ugly. Good to know. He'd take the hit about his gargantuan ego, because she wasn't wrong about that. Yes, he had a very healthy ego—which he had nurtured from a young age, to see him through the deprivations and humiliations of his childhood.

Her comment about Cade was also illuminating. It seemed she was not one of the man's acolytes and didn't enjoy his largesse. But he knew enough about Cade to know he was fiercely protective of anyone he thought 'belonged' to his family, and his wife's sister would no doubt qualify. Even if she didn't seem to think so.

She shivered again, dramatically. And he sighed.

'Here…' He dragged off his jacket and dumped it onto her shoulders—no point in having her freeze to death before he'd got any useful information out of her.

'I didn't ask you for your j-jacket,' she said, still shivering.

Her fierce expression made it impossible for him to contain his amusement any longer.

'What are you smiling at?' she asked indignantly, which only made his smile widen. Her snarky attitude was actually rather refreshing. Who knew?

'You,' he said. 'You're incredibly ungrateful for a boat thief.'

'For the last time, I'm not a boat thief, I'm a boat *borrower*.'

'Whatever…' He stepped to the console and fired up the boat's engine. He wasn't ready to let her go yet, but he also did not want to give her pneumonia, which left only one option.

She grabbed the console when he wheeled the boat around and headed towards Isola Estiva—the coastal island he had bought two summers ago, but had rarely had the time to use, until now.

'Where are you taking me?' she asked, gazing longingly at the lights of Sorrento, which were disappearing in the distance at a rate of knots as he drove past Capri and out into the Gulf.

He gave her a quick once-over. 'To my private island, where I plan to sleep on what the hell to do with you. Because I'm too tired to decide a suitable punishment tonight...' Which was not untrue. A decent night's sleep had eluded him for months now, as he pushed himself and his business to the limit. And he hadn't taken a proper break in over a decade—which was precisely why he'd been so deeply asleep when she'd woken him up.

'But you can't! That's kidnapping!' she shouted over the wind and the slap of the waves on the boat's hull.

'Kidnapping, huh? That's rich, coming from a boat thief...'

'I'm not a flipping...' she yelled back then swore as she was forced to grab the console again. 'Oh, for Pete's sake, I give up.'

'Sit back and relax,' he said, enjoying her exasperation, almost as much as the sight of her body draped in his jacket. She was a petite little thing, the jacket reaching almost to her knees.

'It'll take us about half an hour to get to Estiva,' he said jauntily. There was something so perfect about having Cade's prickly sister-in-law in his boat, he was not about to give up the buzz just yet. Holding her hostage and needling her might even make this enforced break more amusing.

'I'll scream,' she declared, pointlessly, because they both knew no one would hear her.

'Go ahead,' he said, calling her bluff.

Her glare became radioactive, but her lips remained firmly shut, probably because she was no fool.

She dropped onto the bench seat that surrounded the deck, the kick of the waves in the open sea becoming choppier. She looked dejected for about a nanosecond, then she whipped out her phone.

'How about *I* call the *polizia*?' she said, brandishing the smartphone like a lethal weapon. 'And tell them I've been kidnapped?'

'Good luck,' he replied. 'Don't forget to mention Roman Garner is kidnapping you, for stealing his boat,' he supplied helpfully. 'And taking you to Isola Estiva for punishment. They can pick you up tomorrow, if you'd rather be arrested.'

He pursed his lips to hold onto the laugh that wanted to burst out at her confused expression. Then turned back to the console, to concentrate on navigating the boat.

'Roman Garner?' she murmured, behind him. 'I think my sister, Lacey, might have interviewed for a job with you. I'm sure I've heard that name. She's a journalist.'

'Possibly,' he said as it occurred to him she really didn't know he was her brother-in-law's biggest rival. Either that or she was an award-winning actress. 'Although I wouldn't know anything about your sister's job prospects,' he added. 'I don't involve myself with the day-to-day operations of the business.'

Which wasn't entirely true...

He hated himself for the small white lie. Why should he care that Lacey Carstairs—the byline she had used before her big reunion with Cade—hadn't accepted the job at *Buzz* online magazine. Breaking the story of her hasty marriage to Cade after Cade's 'surprise' discovery he was the father of Lacey's four-year-old daughter had been just one of Roman's attempts to humiliate the man over the years. The offer of a job had been a way for Roman to keep tabs on what he suspected was a fake marriage. But it hadn't surprised him when Cade's new bride had turned it down. After all, the woman would surely have realised keeping the pretence of a happy marriage to Brandon Cade was a much better meal ticket than an opportunity to become *Buzz*'s main celebrity correspondent.

In the early days of Garner's growth, when it had still been called Blackbeard Media, Roman had made it his business to get on Cade's radar and annoy the hell out of the guy. And having Cade's new wife working for him would have been quite the coup. But Garner Media Group had more important things to concentrate on these days—such as taking over Cade Inc's top spot in the world of media conglomerates.

'I can't believe I accidentally borrowed your boat,' she mumbled. 'Lacey and Brandon are going to be so unimpressed.'

He glanced round, to find her staring out to sea, but where he had expected to see contempt—because he knew Cade despised him as much as he despised Cade—what he saw on her face was dejection. As if the person Cade and his wife would be unimpressed with was her... Not Roman.

So, Cade had never mentioned their feud to his family? Or the real reason for their mutual animosity? Why did that not surprise him? He'd always been the Cade family's dirty little secret, after all.

'Why don't you ring Cade and tell him whose boat you just tried to steal tonight?' he goaded, all his old resentments against the man resurfacing—as well as that vague feeling of being not enough, which he'd thought he'd banished a long time ago. How irritating to realise those feelings were still there in some hidden corner of his psyche. 'That should really make his night.'

'No thanks,' she said, but her glare had downgraded

considerably. 'I'll take my chances,' she added, sounding a lot less sure of herself.

Interesting... He'd given her a chance to call her brother-in-law to come to her rescue, and she hadn't taken it. Why?

Tonight, surely, had the potential to be very fortuitous for him. Once he figured out how to use this woman's connection to Cade. But somehow the thought only made him feel more exhausted. He turned his attention back to the console. Perhaps he should concentrate on getting them back to Estiva in one piece, first.

Luckily for Milly Devlin, he didn't take advantage of defenceless women. But she still owed him.

After all, she'd just tried to steal his boat and given him a head injury and a bruised arse in the process. And for that he would require payback.

Of all the boats, in all the docks, in all the world, why the heck did I have to accidentally steal the boat of another flipping media mogul?

Milly stared in dismay at the rigid back of the man standing at the controls of the motor launch, and handling it with consummate ease, as they shot through the night towards who knew where.

Roman Garner.

She'd heard Lacey mention him before... And she wished she'd listened more carefully. All she really remembered from when Lacey had been offered the job at *Buzz* was that she hadn't ended up taking it. She'd also described Roman Garner as a 'playboy'. And she could vaguely remember Brandon once describing his business practices as ruthless. But then, didn't that go with the territory, if you were a billionaire media baron?

From what she'd seen of him so far, Garner certainly seemed to be the perfect fit as a 'ruthless playboy'.

Except...

Shivering violently, she wrapped his jacket tighter around herself—which was still warm from his skin—and inhaled a lungful of clean soap and sea salt and a delicious sandalwood cologne.

Delicious? Really, Milly?

Still... Why had he given her his jacket? Because the chivalrous gesture was so out of keeping with his threats of punishment and the fact he was currently kidnapping her.

Not only that, but he'd saved her from falling off the boat and taken the impact of the fall when they'd hit a wave and she'd nearly capsized them both.

A completely inappropriate kick of awareness made her shiver again as the white tails of his shirt flapped around his torso—revealing a band of tanned skin, and another tattoo on his lower back. Was that an elaborate skull and crossbones to match the crossed cutlasses on his left pec?

Clearly, he was big on pirate iconography. Which was somewhat ironic, given that he had accused *her* of being the pirate.

She huddled on the seat, to get out of the wind, and snuggled into his jacket, tired and confused and wary... But also not scared. Or not as scared as she probably ought to be. Because she was definitely being kidnapped.

But as her eyelids drooped, all she could picture was the dancing light in his eyes while he'd baited her—which had infuriated her a moment ago... But now only confused her more. Why did she get the impression this was all a big joke to him? And why had their argument been more exhilarating than upsetting? Was it because she had seen the blast of admiration in his expression when she'd challenged and provoked him?

Or had she totally misinterpreted that? Frankly, she

knew next to nothing about flirting, because she'd never even had a proper boyfriend. It was one of the things her European jaunt had been supposed to remedy… As well as her plan to take the art world by storm, she had been on a mission to finally have some fun, to hang out with people her own age and lose her blasted virginity. But she hadn't had the chance, because she'd been far too busy staying solvent to get up close and personal with any fit guys.

Yet another example of how Milly Devlin's grand plan to kick-start a new life over the past year had been a complete and utter disaster.

She tucked her hands under her cheek, blinking furiously as she tried to stay awake. To stay alert. Forget about his charms, Roman Garner might be fit beyond her wildest dreams and exciting to spar with, but she also doubted she could trust him.

And not just because he was an arrogant billionaire kidnapper with a gargantuan ego. But also because he had a naughty, and undeniably hot, twinkle in his eye, which she had no idea how to handle.

Well done, Milly, never screw up small when you can screw up big.

But as the boat bounced over the waves, her eyelids became heavier, and her mind couldn't quite get to grips with the unprecedented and unfamiliar awareness making her exhausted body feel different somehow, as it melted into the butter-soft leather seat…

CHAPTER TWO

ROMAN STEERED THE launch against Estiva's dock and cut the engine. He rubbed the back of his neck, as the familiar exhaustion that had been bearing down on him for months made its presence felt again after the brief shot of adrenaline caused by his boat thief. Added to that was a dazed feeling, courtesy of the newly acquired bump on his forehead.

One of the boathouse staff grabbed the line he threw and began tying it to the dock as his estate manager, Giovanni, appeared and climbed aboard.

'We did not expect you to return so soon tonight, Signor Garner,' the older man said, then blinked as he spotted the prone figure of Roman's uninvited passenger, who was curled up on the bench.

'You have a guest?' his estate manager added, with a commendable lack of surprise. But then, Giovanni was nothing if not the soul of discretion.

'Not a guest, a prisoner,' Roman announced, while staring down at her, too.

She looked remarkably peaceful for a kidnap victim, he thought, cocooned in his jacket. Her bare toes peeked out from under the hem of her gown. Her face was serene and innocent in sleep, the smudged cosmetics making her look like a cross between an urchin and a trashed supermodel.

He frowned. Although she was too short to be a supermodel. In his experience, and he'd had quite a lot of experience with supermodels, they were always tall and undernourished. This girl's body though had curves.

A memory flash of her pressed against him on the deck had something warm and fluid flowing through him. Annoyingly.

'A prisoner, *signor*?' Giovanni said, carefully. 'She is here against her will?' he asked politely, but there was enough of an edge for Roman to know his estate manager would rat him out to the police in a heartbeat if he thought there was anything untoward going on. Giovanni had four grown-up daughters, and was not above showing his disdain for Roman's revolving door policy with dates. Which was one of the reasons he liked the guy.

Having never had a father and after being brought up without any boundaries whatsoever, Roman had a bad habit of employing only people he could respect. Unfortunately, that usually meant they were more than prepared to challenge him on his behaviour, despite the fact he was paying them a generous salary.

But right now, Roman was way too tired to deal with Giovanni's disapproving frown or his passive-aggressive questions.

'She tried to steal my boat… So stealing her right back seemed like a good idea at the time,' he explained, although even he was beginning to see the flaw in that logic. 'Plus, she has a phone, so she can call and let her family know where she is at any time.' The fact said family included his nemesis Brandon Cade didn't seem like quite such a boon either any more.

'Except she is asleep?' Giovanni said.

'Which just goes to prove she's not afraid of me,' he argued, and scowled. Why was he defending his actions to a member of his staff? He certainly hadn't had any wicked intentions when he'd brought her here. The swell of warmth as he stared at her, though, told a slightly different story...

Giovanni clicked his fingers at the young employee who was securing the gangplank. 'Marco, carry Signor Garner's guest to the pool house.'

But as the young man leapt aboard, Roman thrust out his forearm. 'Leave her.'

The surge of possessiveness—at the thought of anyone but him having his hands on her—was almost as disturbing as the hot ache in his groin, which he didn't seem to be able to shake...

'I'll carry her,' he said. As he scooped her into his arms, she stirred slightly, forcing him to stand still. But then she snuggled into his embrace, making herself comfortable. He ignored the hot ache in his groin.

He hadn't had anyone in his bed for months, he simply hadn't had the time—or the energy—for sex. Which had to explain this unprecedented reaction.

One thing was for sure, though, he'd brought her here, so she was his responsibility. Until he decided what to do with her. But he was definitely going to have to sleep on that.

She wasn't quite as light as she looked. But as she moaned, then shifted again, her soft hair nuzzled his collarbone, and the ripple of arousal sprinted into his abdomen and started to pulse. He gathered a hasty breath and got a lungful of her scent—which was fresh and flowery but also unbearably erotic, and only made the pulsing pain worse.

Still ignoring it, manfully, and Giovanni's judgmental frown, he stepped over the side of the boat. Walking fast, he strode along the dock, across the torchlit path past the beach and headed through the grounds to the large villa he'd renovated two years ago. But as he took the stone steps through the olive groves, the old citrus orchard and past the tranquil pool terrace—he wasn't feeling all that tranquil.

He marched past the pool house—which was actually a luxury two-bedroom guest villa—where Giovanni had suggested leaving his uninvited guest for the night and kept on going.

Giovanni followed behind him, saying nothing. But Roman could sense his estate manager's disapproval, boring into the back of his neck, as he entered the main house through the open French doors, and took the stairs up to the villa's second level.

He hesitated on the landing, to stifle the powerful urge to turn left, towards his own suite of rooms.

Quit it, Garner, you did not bring the boat thief here to seduce her.

Taking a decisive turn to the right, he headed down the long hallway to the guest suites on the east side of the villa—as far as it was possible to get her away from him, while she was still in the house.

As they entered the main guest room, Giovanni rushed forward to turn down the summer quilt, so Roman could place his cargo gently on the bed. Bright moonlight streamed into the room, but the sea breeze was doing nothing to cool the ache in Roman's groin when his jacket fell open, revealing the twinkling bodice again and her enticing cleavage. She moved on the bed, and he noticed the clump of hair that had been listing during their argument detach from her head completely.

What was that? Fake hair?

The shorter cap of real hair framed her heart-shaped face, accentuating her delicate bone structure. Then her eyelids fluttered open, and he found himself staring into warm whisky-brown orbs—which really were exquisite, despite the trashed make-up—the rich amber highlighted with gold shards.

Her face flushed a dull pink and her breath caught—and for a moment he thought he saw his own vicious awareness reflected in her expression.

He stepped away from the bed, stunned by the fierce desire to press his mouth to hers and hear her moan again, this time for him.

Where had that come from?

She blinked, and murmured, 'Where am I?'

Giovanni took Roman's place at the bedside. 'You are at Isola Estiva, *signorina*. I am Giovanni Mancini, the estate manager. You are a *guest* here,' he added pointedly. Roman didn't correct him. 'If you wish for anything, you must let me or my wife Giuliana know by calling the house phone beside your bed.'

The girl nodded. '*Grazie mille*, Giovanni,' she said, but then she stared past Giovanni's shoulder, to where Roman stood, ramrod straight in the corner of the room.

'Leave us now, Giovanni,' Roman muttered.

The man had done his job and put Milly Devlin's mind at ease. But he would be damned if he'd let her get too comfortable. Because she was still a thief who had caused him no end of trouble tonight. And a close relative of the man he'd had good reason to hate his entire life.

The estate manager bowed his head, then sent Roman a quelling, paternal glance—which was probably supposed to be a warning of some sort—before leaving the room.

As Giovanni's footsteps disappeared down the hallway, Roman's head started to throb, along with his groin. The cheek of the guy. Did he know who was paying his damn salary? Roman Garner didn't take orders from anyone, and certainly not his own staff. Plus he did not take advantage of women… Despite any appearances to the contrary tonight.

'I like your estate manager.' Her soft voice floated towards him, drawing his attention back to the problem at hand.

A smile twitched on her tempting lips—and amusement twinkled in those whisky-coloured eyes—only annoying him more and not helping much with his headache. Or the throbbing in his groin.

Terrific.

'That makes one of us, then,' he said, his tone sharp with irritation.

He didn't know what the hell he'd been thinking bringing her here—but the idiotic notion he could use her relationship to Cade to his advantage was beginning to appear more and more misguided. Because the inexplicable desire—which he had refused to acknowledge on the boat—had a volatile feel to it, which had the potential to backfire on him.

She opened her mouth, but then the loud buzz of the phone in her bag interrupted them.

'Answer it,' he commanded. 'If it's your family, tell them they can pick you up first thing in the morning.' The sooner he was rid of her, the better.

He headed towards the door. Staying in this room, with her, was not smart—because it would only stoke that inexplicable attraction.

'Preferably, before I wake up,' he finished.

He heard the phone's ringtone cut off as he walked out, and her soft voice answering the call. But he didn't hang around to hear more.

He needed to sleep now. And hope she'd be long gone by morning.

* * *

'Milly, where on earth did you go? I've just got back to the Grande Palazzo in Sorrento and the staff say they haven't seen you…' Her sister's panicked voice had the slither of guilt—from the moment Milly had spotted Lacey's name on the phone—turning into an anaconda, which promptly wrapped around her throat.

'I'm okay, Lacey,' she whispered, cupping the phone to her ear as she rolled over on the enormous bed and stared out of the open window. She could see the lights of the Amalfi Coast glittering in the distance. The aroma of lemons and sea salt hung on the breeze, accompanied by the lingering scent of Roman Garner's sandalwood cologne. She could still feel his arms around her.

Her stomach swooped down to get jammed in the hot spot between her thighs. Funny she'd known instinctively it was him holding her—her efforts to wake up the rest of the way during their journey to the villa hampered somewhat by the delicious sensation of being cradled so securely.

'Where are you?' Lacey asked, the concern in her voice forcing Milly's mind back to her sister, who clearly thought she wasn't capable of looking after herself, even though she'd been doing it for over a year.

She understood Lacey's concern, because Lacey was a mum, not just to Ruby, but also to her—ever since their own mum had died when Milly was fifteen, Lacey was eighteen and their deadbeat dad had basically washed his hands of them for good, more than happy to concentrate on his 'new' family.

But as Milly stared at the sparkle of Sorrento's lights on the horizon, and imagined Lacey sitting in the luxury hotel suite there, the determination to be independent, and accountable only to herself, kicked up another notch.

'Lacey, I'm okay. You need to stop micromanaging my life,' she said, deciding going on the offensive was the best approach. Mentioning she'd accidentally borrowed the wrong billionaire's motor launch and been spirited away to his private island probably was not going to calm Lacey's nerves.

'I'm sorry for causing a scene at the ball,' Milly added grudgingly.

She heard Lacey give a hefty sigh. 'No, *I'm* sorry,' her sister said, surprising her. 'I didn't mean to put you on the spot like that. It's just, I worry about you. Ever since you had to leave your job at the school you've been rootless…' The words trailed off.

But Milly could hear the misplaced guilt in Lacey's voice.

'Lacey, will you please get it through your thick head that it's not your fault or Brandon's fault the paparazzi wanted to get shots of me? And were prepared to ignore the privacy of the kids to do it. That's on them, not you. Okay?'

'I know, but you were happy there and they were only interested in you because of me and…'

'Lacey, I was a teaching assistant. I liked that job, but I wasn't planning to make a career out of cleaning up after five-year-olds and listening to them read. I'm really enjoying getting the chance to work on my art…' Or she would have been, if she could actually find the time to do it.

'Okay,' Lacey murmured, sounding as tired as Milly suddenly felt—probably because they'd had this argument almost as frequently as the *why-don't-you-come-home-so-we-can-mollycoddle-you-to-death?* argument. 'Let's talk about it tomorrow morning,' Lacey added, going into proactive mode. 'How about I send a car to pick you up now and we can have breakfast together at the hotel before I leave?'

'Um…actually about that…' Milly mumbled, frantically trying to get her exhausted brain to work out some semblance of a convincing excuse as to why she did not want to be picked up. 'I'm already on the bus back to Genoa,' she blurted out.

'Wait… *What?*' Lacey sounded shocked and even more concerned. 'But all your stuff is here.'

Oh, yeah, right! Rats.

'It was a spur-of-the-moment decision,' she rambled on, busy trying to dig herself out of the massive lie without giving away her real whereabouts—or looking like even more of a reckless nitwit than was necessary. 'I spotted the bus leaving when I got back to Sorrento and just jumped on board. Could you send my stuff care of Signora Cavali, my landlady in Genoa?'

'I suppose so, if that's what you would prefer,' Lacey said slowly, the sadness and confusion in her voice making Milly feel like a bitch. Because she could hear what her sister wasn't saying… Had Milly really been so desperate to get away from her sister, she had jumped on a bus in the middle of the night, without even picking up her luggage, or saying a proper goodbye?

'I think it's for the best,' Milly said, all but choking on her guilt. But what else could she say? She didn't want Lacey to know where she really was, or how she'd got here. Because that would send Lacey's mother-hen instincts through the roof.

Instincts that would probably have the Cades sending the SAS to storm Roman Garner's private island to rescue her. Which would turn her little *faux pas* into a headline-grabbing catastrophe… The boat-stealing incident would be blown even more out of proportion, Garner would definitely sue, and Milly—and her wayward spoilt-brat ways— would become the darling of the tabloid press for the rest of her natural life.

Worst of all, she would have only herself to blame for it. She frowned. Herself and Roman 'Gargantuan Ego' Garner.

She shouldn't have accidentally borrowed his boat. But he really shouldn't have kidnapped her—even as a joke.

She rolled over to stare at the ceiling of the lavish room. But then again, he hadn't looked quite as pleased with himself once they'd got to the villa. A smile curved her lips at the memory of his startled expression when she'd opened her eyes and caught him staring at her lips, his rapt expression making sensation sizzle, everywhere.

Even though he hadn't taken advantage of her.

The hot spot between her thighs hummed. Almost as if she were disappointed about that.

'You need to stop worrying about me, Lacey,' she said carefully. 'And give me space to get on with my life. You know I love you and Ruby to bits. I also like your husband quite a lot,' she added. 'Even though he has a bad habit of trying to tell me what to do all the time.'

Lacey gave a weary laugh. 'Join the club,' she said. 'Brandon is the definition of overprotective, it drives me nuts on occasion, too.' But then her voice sobered. 'I love you too, Milly. But I guess you're right, we need to lay off and let you find your own way.'

Milly felt the tightness in her chest ease. *Finally.*

'I'll get my assistant to courier your stuff to Mrs Cavali tomorrow, if you want to text Cassy the details. But you promise to let us know if you need anything… At all…' Her sister sighed again. 'Ever.'

Milly nodded. 'Of course.'

'And you will still come to Artie's christening next month in Wiltshire, won't you? Ruby will be devastated if you don't. And so will I. And I'd love to see the work you've been doing...'

'Of course, I'll come, Lace,' she said. 'I'll be desperate for a fix of my niece and my new nephew by then. And I'll show you all my work.'

If I can find the time to produce any worth showing you in the next sixteen days... And counting.

'Fabulous,' Lacey said, sounding relieved. 'Why don't I send you some money to pay for the trip...?' she added. Clearly her sister hadn't quite given up the ghost of watching over her. 'Or we could send the jet to Genoa to pick you up.'

'Please don't send any money. Or a jet! I'm perfectly capable of getting there under my own steam, Lace,' Milly said, trying to control her irritation at the ludicrous suggestion. 'I'll be there, I promise. Trust me, okay?' How the heck she was going to find a suitable outfit for the swish society event, not to mention have some actual work to show for her long absence, she had no idea. But she'd figure it out. She could get Lacey's dress dry-cleaned and eat and sleep less so she could finish some of the work she'd barely started since arriving in Genoa four months ago.

Lacey sighed again. 'I do trust you. I'll see you then. I love you, sis.'

After saying her goodbyes, Lacey finally hung up the phone.

Milly dropped the mobile on the bed and stared out at the night. Her heart throbbing painfully in her throat.

She was finally free of the mollycoddling—for two and a half weeks at least.

Ironic, though, that she'd got her sister to let her stand on her own two feet—after *actually* having been kidnapped. Sort of.

Now all she had to do was figure out what the heck she was going to do about the wildly handsome and far too arrogant billionaire who had brought her here. But as she pulled the quilt up and left his jacket on to stay warm—and wallow in his compelling scent—she couldn't quite kick the thought that waking up on Roman Garner's private island tomorrow did not feel nearly as problematic as it should.

In truth, it felt exhilarating—the same way that arguing with him on the boat had been. Like being trapped in a pirate's hideaway—if the pirate were extremely hot and compelling and contrary, and he had a secret chivalrous streak that everyone else was unaware of. Except her.

CHAPTER THREE

BRIGHT SUNLIGHT SCALDED Milly's retinas as soon as she opened her eyes the following morning. It took her several seconds to adjust to the daylight, and several more to figure out where she was. Then everything came rushing back in lurid Technicolor.

She still had Roman Garner's jacket on, except now the designer fabric was hopelessly crushed, along with the jewelled material of her sister's dress. One look in the mirror of the bespoke stone bathroom attached to her bedroom had the last of her misplaced excitement and confidence from the night before—when she'd had some daft notion of seducing her uber-hot and arrogant host—evaporating in a rush of cringe-worthy memories.

Garner could even now be calling the police. Had she imagined the hot look in his eyes last night? Probably. It seemed highly unlikely a playboy billionaire would be interested in an unemployed teaching assistant-cum-wannabe-artist with panda eyes, grubby feet, a borrowed designer gown and a collapsed chignon.

Make that *certainly* not interested.

After a long hot shower, to revitalise her decimated ego and wash away the evidence of last night's shenanigans, it occurred to Milly she didn't have a lot of sartorial options after putting on the guest suite's complimentary bathrobe.

Not only did she have no make-up with her, she had no clothes either, other than Lacey's wrecked designer gown and Garner's oversized jacket—even Lacey's uncomfortable heels had been left on the launch.

Thoughts of Lacey brought back memories of their midnight chat. She blinked back the emotion threatening to destroy what was left of her confidence.

She had sixteen days to prove she wasn't a total screwup to Lacey and Brandon, and most importantly herself. Now all she had to do was get off this island—while naked and barefoot—before the police arrived, use her meagre savings to buy a return coach ticket to the UK for Arthur Cade's christening, and find the time to do enough artwork in the meantime to have a viable portfolio to boast about when she got there in between doing two jobs.

No biggie, then.

First things first though, she needed clothing. She eyed the house phone, remembering a vague conversation with the very nice estate manager. Depending on the kindness of strangers wasn't her usual vibe, but she didn't have much of a choice.

A friendly voice answered on the second ring. 'Signorina Devlin, you are awake. I hope you slept well,' the estate manager said in perfect, if heavily accented, English.

'Yes, thank you, the bed is very comfortable.'

'Would you require breakfast?' he asked, as if she really were a guest, and not a thief.

'Actually, I'd really like some day-clothes. If you have any—that might fit me,' she said, as embarrassment heated her cheeks.

'I will send up my wife Giuliana with some options for you.'

'Oh, thank you.' Milly's relief was palpable—escaping in a bathrobe had always been a tall order.

'Is there anything else you require?' he asked.

'Could you…could you tell me if the police are coming?' she managed around the thickness in her throat. How much time did she have to work out a convincing defence for attempting to borrow Garner's boat without his permission.

'La polizia?' The man sounded shocked, but then he laughed. 'Signor Garner did not contact the police, Signorina Devlin—this is not his style,' he added. 'And also, he would have some uncomfortable questions to answer about why he kidnapped you.'

She huffed out a nervous laugh at the man's amused and paternal tone—apparently, Giovanni at least thought last night's antics had been a joke.

Good to know someone found them funny.

After thanking him and hanging up the phone, she felt some of the impending doom lift off her shoulders. But the acute embarrassment remained.

It was still there half an hour later, when she ventured out of the bedroom, now clothed in a pair of shorts and a tank top and trainers, which Giuliana had told her belonged to one of her daughters.

Giuliana—the estate's housekeeper and head chef and also the very nice estate manager's wife—had also been a font of knowledge about her employer. Apparently, Roman Garner had bought the island two years ago, rebuilt the villa, and kept the place fully staffed all year round. Although Garner had only visited the island twice in total— once to host a lavish team-building event for his executives and once with one of his dates for a weekend rave, complete with two hundred specially selected guests, and entertainment provided by world-famous DJs, chart-topping bands, a roster of celebrity chefs and fitness and health gurus. But he'd been at the rave for only one night before he had returned to work in London and left the date behind.

It hadn't taken much more probing for Milly to discover Signor Roman—as the housekeeper referred to her employer—was well liked by the staff, because he paid them all a very lucrative salary and never made unreasonable demands, but his celebrity friends and dates not so much.

Giuliana had also supplied the information Garner was spending a fortnight alone on the island this time, on doctor's orders, because he was burnt out. But despite being exhausted when he had arrived yesterday afternoon, he had insisted on attending the Cade Ball, then woken this morning at dawn and left to swim to one of the hidden coves on the far side of the island over two miles away.

Giuliana was concerned about his safety. Milly wouldn't care if he drowned.

Then again, Milly couldn't deny the prickle of disappointment—that she wasn't going to see Roman Garner again—as she made her way down to the dock after the delicious breakfast laid out for her by the very talkative Giuliana on the villa's sea-facing terrazzo.

That the staff seemed to have decided she was a guest, not a prisoner was also good news. So why did Garner's apparent indifference to her this morning feel so deflating?

Because you're a fool, Mills. Who clearly needs to lose her virginity pronto, before she starts getting inappropriate crushes on arrogant burnt-out billionaires.

Garner had brought her here to teach her a lesson. But, of course, he'd lost interest as soon as they'd arrived. That hot look last night—and the flirty nature of their boat altercation—had all been in her head. The well of anticipation, the ripple of awareness and the sizzle of attraction a result of the fact she'd spent so much of her life convincing herself she didn't want male attention—thanks, Dad. So, when a man like Garner paid her the slightest bit of attention, even in a back-handed way, she totally overreacted.

It would be ironic, if it weren't so excruciatingly pathetic.

At the dock below the villa's lavish gardens, she found the motor launch, alongside a beautiful hand-crafted sailboat, while an enormous super-yacht was anchored in the bay.

Her conversation with the dockhand, Marco, soon added a nice thick layer of frustration to her embarrassment.

'I am sorry, *signorina*. I cannot take you to Sorrento without the permission of my employer. And he left no instructions this morning.'

Probably because he's totally forgotten about me!

'Can you contact him? And ask him?' she said, desperate to leave. She did not want to still be hanging around when Garner got back.

The young man shook his head. 'He does not have a phone with him, he is swimming.'

'Do you know when he's likely to return to the villa?'

'It is a long swim. He asked for the dinghy to be left at La Baia Azzurra, which is at the opposite end of the island.'

Right. So, he would be a while, then.

And she was stranded here, until he deigned to return.

She could ask Giuliana or Giovanni to help, but she'd inconvenienced them enough. And, while they seemed relaxed about their relationship with their employer, she did not want to make things difficult for them, or any of his other staff.

As she turned to trudge back to the villa through the

groves of olive and lemon trees, though, she spotted an old bike propped against the boat shed.

'Marco, is that your bike?' she asked.

He nodded.

'Could I borrow it? Just for a little while?'

The boy smiled. 'Of course, yes, you are a guest, *signorina.*'

She stifled the prickle of guilt. She wasn't really a guest. But she didn't know *what* she was any more—which in some ways was almost worse, because now she felt like an inconvenience, and a forgotten one at that… Which was exactly how her father had always made her feel.

Garner hadn't kidnapped her precisely, because he really hadn't put that much thought into last night's 'abduction'. And after his parting shot when he'd left her in the guest bedroom, she suspected he had changed his mind once they'd arrived on the island.

But her phone had died during the night, so she couldn't get anyone to come over from Sorrento and collect her, even if she had the funds to pay them, which she did not. So she was basically an accidental prisoner here, until she got Roman Garner's permission to leave.

The arrogant, entitled egomaniac.

She jumped on the bike, and took the coastal path past the dock, heading in the direction Giuliana had mentioned. As she pedalled down the bumpy island tracks, past the ruins of fisherman's cottages, and the collection of secluded beaches and rocky coves, the cliffs decorated with rambling bushes of bougainvillea, she was struck by the island's natural, unspoilt beauty—and how much she would have loved to capture some of the landscape in pen and ink and acrylic, if she weren't here under duress.

But as the sun rose higher in the sky, and she began to

sweat, she found herself scanning the deserted cliffs, trying to locate the Blue Cove Marco had mentioned, or a lone billionaire swimming in the sea. She needed to find out where Garner was hiding, apologise again for borrowing his boat, thank him for the bed for the night and the delicious breakfast, and then ask him, ever so politely, to let her off his blasted luxury island, *pronto*.

Roman ploughed through the water, the soft waves buffeting his aching limbs and the tide dragging his tired body back into the surf.

Where was the damn Baia Azzurra? Because it felt as if he'd been swimming towards his favourite cove for days, even with the fins he'd slipped on when he'd set off at the dock just after dawn. He had not slept well last night, again, thanks mostly to sweaty erotic dreams of his uninvited guest—aka the boat thief. If the beach wasn't around the next rocky outcrop, he might have to attempt a cliff climb, in his swimming shorts.

He cursed the decision to venture out on this marathon swim before he'd really woken up properly for about the thousandth time as he finally cleared the headland.

The sight of the translucent sea, calmed by the rocky bay, its stunning azure waters lapping lazily onto the white sand beach less than fifty feet away, pumped renewed vigour into his leaden arms. He powered towards the shore, letting the waves carry him into the shallows, sending up a prayer of thanks that his staff had left the sailing dinghy anchored on the sand as requested.

No way was he swimming back.

But as he stood in the thigh-deep surf, his knees shaky from the one-and-a-half-hour swim, he spotted movement beneath the trees near the cliffs.

He swept his wet hair back, and stared, as a figure—dressed in perky shorts and a sleeveless T-shirt—jumped up from the rock and walked barefoot across the sand towards him.

Her.

Shock came first, swiftly followed by annoyance.

What was the star player in last night's X-rated fantasies doing in his favourite cove?

The denim cut-offs moulded her butt like a second skin, while the figure-hugging vest made her lack of a bra all too obvious. Holding a pair of worn running shoes, she looked fresh and young and appealing, and as beautiful as the trashed socialite boat thief he'd met the night before.

He swore under his breath, unable to detach his gaze from her figure as she strolled across the beach as if she had every right to be there—invading his downtime, again. And sending inconvenient pheromones firing through his exhausted body.

He scowled. Maybe he was hallucinating, courtesy of the nightmare swim that had nearly drowned him—and which he had only embarked on in the first place to forget about her.

No such luck.

'Hello, Mr Garner,' she called, waving, the tone sweet and accommodating. He stood like a dummy, aware of the heat he had hoped to freeze out coursing through his system all over again.

She used a hand to shield her mesmerising golden eyes from the dazzling sunlight.

'Are you okay?' she asked. 'I spotted you swimming around the point from the clifftop. For a minute there, I thought you weren't going to make it.'

He tugged off the flippers and shoved them under his

arm, annoyed she had spotted him struggling. He hated to show a weakness to anyone, especially women—but showing a weakness to *this* woman was even more galling.

He trudged out of the water, gratified when she backed away as he arrived on the sand. No doubt she could guess from the frown he could feel turning into a crater on his forehead he was not pleased to see her.

'What are you doing here?' he demanded.

She propped a fist on her hip and glared back at him. So much for the sweet and cheerful act. That didn't last long. The surge of adrenaline only irritated him more. He would not be aroused by her snotty attitude again, because it was infuriating, not intriguing. He wanted her gone now. What was she still doing here? Ruining his break and stopping him from getting the rest he so desperately needed?

If she hadn't got him all riled up last night he wouldn't even have been here, he would have been lying comatose in his suite!

'*Really?* You want to know what I'm doing on your private island?' she snapped, misunderstanding his perfectly reasonable question deliberately, the little minx. 'I'm stranded here,' she said, her voice rising with indignation. 'Or did you forget already you kidnapped me last night?'

He dragged in a furious breath, and a lungful of her delicious scent—flowery shampoo and musky female sweat—got lodged in his solar plexus.

The heat rose. Along with his anger.

'I know why you're on my island. I want to know why you're *here*, in this cove.' He strode to the fibreglass sailing dinghy beached on the sand and grabbed a towel from the supplies his staff had left for him. 'Perhaps I should add stalking to the ever-growing list of your misdemeanours,' he added. But as he rubbed his hair, he could hear her soft footsteps following him.

'I'm here because I can't leave Estiva without your say-so, according to Marco.'

He swung round to see her standing behind him. But the belligerent expression dissolved as her gaze dipped to his bare chest. Her throat contracted as she swallowed. The heat in his groin flared as the whisky colour of her eyes darkened...

The same vivid awareness he had noticed the night before, when she had stared at him in his guest bedroom, made her look a little dazed.

'A-and...s-stop pretending you're going to call the police,' she managed, although her voice had lowered to a husk, her gaze still anchored to his chest. 'B-because we both know you're not,' she finished, struggling to sound outraged, when all he could hear was desire.

She wanted him... And he wanted her.

Damned if he knew why that was, she was hardly his type. Not elegant and sophisticated and compliant, but feisty and fierce and quite frankly a complete pain in the backside since the moment he'd set eyes on her.

But he couldn't deny the surge of heat any longer.

He tucked a thumb under her chin, tilted her face up.

'Stop staring at my chest,' he said.

She blinked, a vivid blush firing across her cheeks and highlighting her exceptional bone structure. She really did have the most compelling face, the gold nose ring adding to her funky appeal.

'I—I'm not,' she said, but the protest was weak at best. And didn't fool him for a second, her expression as transparent as her desire.

'You know, I'd have a lot more respect for you if you

admitted why you *really* followed me here…' he goaded, enjoying the way the fiery blush spread down her neck to explode along her collarbone. And those expressive eyes lit with a combination of desire and confusion.

Why did her dazed arousal only make him want her more? The chemistry between them made no sense—she was a complication, her connection to Cade only making his knee-jerk decision to bring her here more problematic. But after an hour and a half spent attempting to drown the spark she had created, he was through fighting it.

'I—I don't know what you mean…' she murmured, but he could see the lie in her eyes. She knew *exactly* what he meant, because she felt it too, even if she was unwilling to admit it.

He swept his thumb across her bottom lip, the last of his anger releasing in a rush of longing when she shuddered and stumbled back.

He let his hand drop, but he kept his gaze locked on hers and embraced the surge of awareness that had driven him here in the first place.

The long swim was supposed to have controlled this incessant, inexplicable desire, and ensure she was gone when he returned to the villa—because he'd decided during the night, when he woke aching for her, that he had no intention of pursuing this inconvenient attraction. But she'd ruined his best-laid plans. So now, they would both have to deal with the consequences.

'Stop playing the clueless virgin, Milly,' he murmured. While he found her confusion intriguing, he wasn't fooled by it. She was as drawn to him as he was to her, last night's arguments had been foreplay, so why not see exactly where this would lead? 'We both know why you really followed me here.'

She stared at him, dazed and wary, but not denying the obvious any more.

Then her tongue flicked out to moisten dry lips, and his gaze zeroed in on her mouth. The plump bottom lip, the slight overbite, the cupid's bow at the top that had tempted him beyond bearing the night before, although he'd been too damn mad to admit it.

He didn't feel mad any more. He felt vindicated. By the answering awareness in her eyes.

'Now that you've gone to considerable trouble to track me down,' he said, spotting the bike on the sand behind her. 'What do you want to do about it?' he asked, goading her, deliberately.

They were both consenting adults, and they wanted each other. Sometimes it was just that simple. But he'd be damned if he'd do all the work. Or if he'd let her play the kidnapped virgin sacrifice.

He hated those kinds of games. And despised the women who played them.

This chemistry was vibrant and volatile enough to be extremely rare. But if she wanted him to take this further—and the delicious quiver of her bottom lip would suggest she certainly did—she would have to tell him so.

Her head rose, her gaze meeting his. His lips quirked at the slight frown on her brow. And the brightening hue on her cheeks.

Her throat contracted. And he wondered if her mouth was as dry as his. Lifting his hand again, he cradled her cheek, and felt her shudder of reaction—as her eyes flared with need.

She didn't draw back this time, though. And he knew he had her.

'You're going to have to ask for what you want, Milly,'

he murmured, struggling to keep things light, even as his own control hung by a single torturous thread.

The need pounded in his groin as he waited, the chilly exhaustion of the long swim incinerated by the volatile, visceral yearning, to discover where their extraordinary chemistry would lead.

Her frown deepened. But then her gaze snagged on his mouth. She seemed to consider his proposition for a moment, but when her eyes rose to his, he could see she had made a decision. Need fired through his torso, and down into his trunks.

'I think... I really want to kiss you,' she said, her voice barely more than a whisper. But he could see the delicious combination of determination and arousal turning her whisky eyes to gold.

He clasped her cheeks, angled her face up to his, her scintillating shiver setting fire to the last of his control.

'Snap,' he murmured.

But his determination to take things slowly, to tease and tempt, to savour the experience, exploded in a rush of desperation when his mouth found hers and he felt her jolt of response. She gave a sob of surrender and her hands grasped his waist.

He thrust his tongue deep when her mouth opened to let him in. And proceeded to take what they both wanted.

This is nuts... But I don't care!

Milly clutched Garner's waist, dragging him closer, until his hard, warm naked chest pressed against her unfettered breasts barely covered by the thin vest. The heady rush of adrenaline turned to the deep, visceral throb of desire as his lips claimed hers. She writhed against him, desperate to ease the ache in her nipples—both of which had become torpedoes ready to launch as soon as she'd got a good look at those spectacular pecs.

Roman Garner wasn't just fit, he was seriously gorgeous, his long lean physique bulging and flexing in all the right places. His skin was soft, and yet firm, toned and tensile as she let him take control of the kiss.

He sucked on her tongue, then probed deep into the recesses of her mouth, claiming her in a way she had never been claimed before.

She probed back. She didn't want to surrender to his moves. But it wasn't easy to focus, when the man was a seriously good kisser.

Determined to be bold, the way he seemed to be so effortlessly, she let her hands explore as she lapped up his addictive taste. Salt and musk and man, with the hint of his morning coffee.

She caressed the smooth skin of his lower back, found the band of his wet trunks and edged her fingers underneath, tracing his spine, and finally landing on the bunched muscles of his glutes. She squeezed, brutally aware of the ridge of his erection, thickening in his trunks—and pressing into her belly.

His harsh shudder had triumph hurtling through her, before he dragged his mouth free. And yanked himself back, dislodging her eager palms from his phenomenal backside.

Fire leapt in his eyes—turning the vivid sea green to a rich emerald—before his sensual lips, reddened by their ferocious kiss, quirked in a challenging grin.

'Now, really, Milly. I don't remember giving you permission to grab my arse,' he said, the faux outrage contradicted by the wicked glint in his eyes.

She cleared her throat. Then forced an obsequious

smile—determined to flirt back, and pretend he hadn't just overwhelmed her with one phenomenal kiss.

If he had any inkling about her body's ferocious reaction, the need pulsing and pounding at her core, and making every single one of her erogenous zones beg for mercy, he would know exactly how inexperienced she was, and how far out of her depth.

'Please, Mr Garner,' she said, fluttering her eyelashes for all she was worth. 'May I have permission to grab your arse?'

His eyebrows shot up to his forehead, but then he choked out a rough laugh. Not cynical this time, but rich and husky and surprised.

'Damn,' he murmured. 'You're quite the little ball-buster, aren't you?' But he was still smiling as he took her wrists in his and returned her hands to his backside. 'Permission granted.'

Before she could let her new-found power go to her head, though, his thumb stroked across her collarbone, then dipped to circle her breast through the loose cotton.

She gasped, the nipple drawing tight, her hands rising from his butt to cling to him as his mouth landed on her neck. He nipped and sucked at the pulse point as those devilish hands found their way under her vest to cup her naked breasts.

A low groan escaped her as she bowed back, thrusting her tender flesh into his palm. He played with first one nipple then the other. Her guttural moans echoed around the quiet cove. She might have been embarrassed, but she couldn't think about anything but the sweet, vicious darts of sensation arrowing down to pound heavily at her core.

Eventually, he wrenched himself away, leaving her panting.

'Damn it, I need to see you…' he demanded, the mocking tone replaced by impatient demand. He wrestled her top off and threw it onto the sand, exposing her to his avaricious gaze.

The warm sea breeze rushed over far too sensitive skin, making her breasts feel heavy and tight.

No man had ever seen her naked to the waist before, and had certainly never studied her bare breasts with such concentration and entitlement. But what she saw in his gaze wasn't judgement or disdain, it was pure unadulterated lust.

'Offer them to me,' he groaned, part plea, part demand.

She cupped the swollen orbs, lifting and caressing them, doing instinctively as he asked. Passion flared in his eyes, before he brushed her hands aside and leant forward to capture one turgid tip in his lips.

He worked the pebbled flesh with his teeth, then trapped it against the roof of his mouth and suckled hard.

She grasped handfuls of his damp hair, held his head to her, pressing into his mouth. The warm weight became heavier between her thighs, the drawing sensation reaching all the way into her abdomen.

He transferred the exquisite torture from one breast to the other, while he plucked at the buttons of her shorts with his other hand. The fabric released and dropped to her ankles, then those demanding fingers delved into her panties.

She bucked against his hold, her body a mass of throbbing, aching, painful sensation now. His thumb circled the swollen folds, touching and then retreating, teasing her with a titanic release, which hovered so close, but just out of reach.

She gasped, panting, unable to draw a full breath, riding his hand, desperate for relief. She wanted to demand more, but was unable to speak as the coil at her core tightened, and twisted, becoming painful, and all-consuming.

'Please...' She moaned.

'Please, what? Ask my permission, Milly...' he coaxed, his voice raw now, no longer teasing, the exquisite unfulfilled desire torturing them both.

She grasped his wrist, rubbed herself against those talented fingers. 'Give me more.'

He chuckled, but then his thumb centred at the heart of her at last.

With one flick, two, exactly where she needed it, the wave barrelled towards her.

She cried out, and crashed over, plummeting into a huge vat of molten pleasure as the fire raged through her.

As she came down, her knees dissolved. And she heard him grunt as he lifted her into his arms.

Her eyes fluttered open, to find him studying her. Embarrassed heat washed away the afterglow. His fierce expression became hooded, but then he grinned.

He carried her to the small boat, perched on the sand, and deposited her onto the seat.

She sat on the bench, aware of her naked breasts, and the visceral rush still making every inch of her glow. Then her gaze took in the thick ridge in his trunks, which were at her eye level. She assessed the impressive size and girth of his erection.

Her throat dried to parchment. *Again.*

He'd given her an incredible orgasm, but he hadn't found release.

She reached out and traced a finger down the length of him through the damp shorts, suddenly desperate to return the favour. Desperate to make him beg, too. And fascinated by the evidence of his desire he couldn't hide.

Having exposed herself, she needed to regain some of the power. To make them equal somehow, even though she knew they weren't.

But when she reached up to tug the waistband down, revealing the swollen head of his erection to her greedy gaze, he grasped her wrist and dragged her fingers away.

'I don't think so,' he said, stuffing himself back into his trunks. 'Not here.'

'Why not?' she asked, the throb of need painful again as he covered himself.

'Because I want to be inside you,' he said. 'And for that we need condoms and a bed. Plus, this sailboat is too small to get comfortable on and sex on a beach tends to get sand in all the wrong places—trust me, I know.'

The bold statement was full of arrogance and entitlement. But the husky desire in his voice, and the feral gleam in his eyes, had a raw laugh popping out.

'I'm not sure what's so damn funny,' he said, his gaze narrowing. But his pained expression made her feel impossibly powerful all of a sudden.

He doesn't know that you don't have a clue what you're doing. And he doesn't have to know. If you play it cool.

The ache at her core began to throb again, her gaze returning to the thick outline in his trunks.

His erection looked… Enormous. Disconcertingly so. But it didn't dim her desire in the slightest. She wanted to feel him inside her, too. Stretching her tight, aching flesh—and taking her to places she had always yearned to go.

And, surely, he was the perfect person to finally lose her virginity to. Not only was he super fit, and beyond hot, and a phenomenal kisser, but he seemed to know just how to touch her and caress her to make her want him. And he

was a playboy, which meant he didn't do commitment…
So she could use him with a clean conscience.

The endorphins fired through her system again, like
toddlers on a sugar rush.

She wanted someone who knew what they were doing
for her first time—but she did not want to risk making
the classic mistake of thinking great sex meant emotional
intimacy.

This could never be more than a one-off. They knew
next to nothing about each other. But one thing she did
know, they came from totally different worlds. After all,
he moved in the same circles as her brother-in-law. And
those were circles where she had never belonged.

He had opened her eyes, though, to what she had been
missing for so long. One of the things she had been searching for.

She grinned up at him, determined to fake a confidence
she didn't have.

'I suppose I could give you a rain check,' she said. 'If
you ask me nicely.'

He tilted his head to one side, rueful amusement making him look even more gorgeous. Her heart bobbled in
her chest when he smiled.

'I suppose I can ask you nicely,' he said, the goading
tone not exactly conciliatory. 'Given that you begged me
for release so nicely a moment ago.'

She clasped her arm across her bare breasts. Aware of
the light breeze on her over-sensitive nipples, still damp
from his kisses.

'I didn't beg…' she said, indignant. 'Precisely.'

He clasped her chin, then leaned down to press a provocative kiss to her lips. She groaned, the molten need
throbbing at her core again, when he finally released her.

'Sure, you did,' he said. 'But I promise not to hold it against you.'

She wanted to be outraged at the hint of condescension in his tone. The man was nothing if not full of himself. But she felt too good to be annoyed. And too excited.

So she sat and watched, with what she was sure was a hopelessly smug smile on her face, as he strode back across the beach to collect her clothing.

He flung the garments to her, before pushing the boat into the surf.

'You better cover up. I wouldn't want you getting sunburnt nipples on the journey back, because I have all sorts of plans for those later.'

She chuckled, she couldn't help it, his over-confidence as attractive as his wicked sense of humour. She scrambled into her vest and shorts, the pulse of excitement and anticipation flooding into her chest as he jumped aboard the boat and wedged himself behind her on the bench seat.

The canvas sail caught the breeze, as he tugged her securely into his lap, before steering the boat into the wind. Her heart bounced with the boat as it bobbed over the incoming surf.

She caught sight of the word Blackbeard inscribed on his wrist, in an ornate piratical font, and wondered about the significance of all the pirate-themed tattoos...

She'd have to examine him once she got to see him naked. And find out how many others he had.

Potent desire unfurled in her abdomen, and she ignored the clutch in her heart, to drive away any lingering doubts. She might be a virgin but, thank goodness, she'd never been a romantic. And she certainly had no illusions about men.

Seeing her mother struggle with cancer when she was

still a teenager—while their dad had ignored them to concentrate on his new family—had seen to that.

Spending a few glorious hours in bed with Roman Garner to finish what they had started on the beach was reckless and impulsive. Just like her decision to leave the safety of her family and find her own way a year ago now had been... But at least this experience promised to be fun.

And she'd had precious little of that in the past twelve months.

She turned into the wind, lifted her arms and whooped as the boat gathered speed.

'Hold that thought,' he shouted above the rush of the sea, his rough chuckle a vindication. Then he tightened the arm he had banded around her waist. 'But don't fall out of the damn boat!'

CHAPTER FOUR

'HEY, MARCO, TIE up the boat for me.'

Roman threw the line to the dockhand, then leapt out of the dinghy, so eager to get to the villa, he was fizzing with energy for the first time in months.

'Yes, Signor Garner,' the young man replied as he caught the rope and tugged the boat alongside the dock.

Adrenaline charged through Roman's veins as he grasped Milly's hand and hauled her out. He was semi-erect, thanks to having Milly wriggling in his lap the whole journey—which had felt as if it had taken five times as long as the swim to the cove.

As soon as she climbed onto the dock, he placed his hand on her lower back, intending to direct her to the villa. He wanted her alone and naked, asap, before he exploded.

But before he could apply any pressure, she sidestepped his controlling hand to turn and address the boy. 'Hi, Marco. I'm so sorry, I left your bike at the cove. I can go get it later, before you take me back to Sorrento.'

Roman frowned, his impatience turning to frustration.

And no small amount of irritation. Why was she arranging to leave, already? And how come she was on a first-name basis with the kid?

The boy blushed. 'I will be happy to collect it, *signorina*. When do you wish to leave?'

'In an hour or so,' she said.

An hour? What was she talking about? No way were they going to be through with each other in an hour. Was she mad?

But while he was still trying to get his head around the preposterousness of her putting a time limit on their booty call, she added: 'If that's okay with you, Marco,' speaking to his employee with a deference she had never shown him.

The kid nodded and smiled, the flush on his cheeks becoming radioactive. 'I am at your service, *signorina.*'

What. On. Earth?

'The *signorina* is *not* leaving tonight. And certainly not with you,' Roman barked.

Milly and the young man both spun around to stare at him, clearly startled by his outburst. Although he had no idea why. Was she playing some kind of game with him? Because they'd come to an agreement on the beach, and now she seemed to be reneging on it—and flirting with his boat boy to boot.

'*Sì*, Signor Garner.' The boy bowed, looking suitably chastened, and shot off to secure the boat, which was his actual job.

From the sharp frown on Milly's face, though, he knew she was not going to be anywhere near as compliant. *Quelle surprise.*

'Roman...?' she gasped. 'You mustn't talk to Marco like that, or me either.'

'Save it,' he said, aware of the young man listening to their every word as he grasped her hand and proceeded to head up the path towards the villa.

Having Milly Devlin question his authority was nothing new. In fact, up to now he'd found her ballsy attitude towards him refreshing and... Well, hopelessly hot. But he'd be damned if he'd have a negotiation about the duration of their fling in front of an audience. Especially one who was likely to relay the whole conversation to his disapproving estate manager and his wife.

While he didn't really care if his employees thought he had the ethics of an alley cat when it came to women, he did not appreciate being gossiped about in his own home. Or judged.

Especially because he had been struggling not to judge himself, and the intensity of his desire for this woman, on the sail back.

There was something about Milly—about her eagerness and openness and her livewire response to him as well as that kickass attitude—that made this liaison different from the many, many others he'd had.

Not only had he never been quite this eager to bed anyone, quite this captivated or enchanted by watching a woman succumb to her own pleasure, but she was younger and a lot less jaded than the women he usually dated— and there was still that niggling thought he had brought her here against her will last night. All of which made him feel responsible in a way he didn't like.

He had no plans to demand anything of her she did not wish to give him, but he couldn't quite get past the look in her eyes—dazed and wary and even a little shocked, after she'd climaxed earlier, while holding nothing back.

She'd looked as if she'd never experienced anything so intense before. Which had made her seem oddly vulnerable—almost as if she was the virgin he'd teased her about being.

Which wasn't possible. While he had no experience of virgins, he very much doubted they responded with such captivating abandon.

Captivating? Seriously?

And that was another thing… Since when had he found inexperience—or even the hint of it—a turn-on?

'Roman, for goodness' sake, slow down,' she protested, tugging against his hold and trying to dig in her heels.

They had reached the pool terrace before he had calmed down enough to realise he was behaving like a caveman. Also not like him… He prided himself on being smooth and sophisticated with women. Especially women he wanted to bed.

He let her go, abruptly. She stumbled to a stop and huffed. Looking indignant and annoyed, but also confused.

That made two of them.

'If you've changed your mind about sleeping with me, that's perfectly okay. But you need to say so,' he managed, annoyed now, not just by her conversation with Marco, and what it had revealed—that she saw this liaison as a one-off booty call that she got to call the shots on—but also his ridiculous overreaction to it.

After all, he was hardly a stranger to one-off booty calls. So why did he suddenly feel used? It wasn't as if either one of them were looking for anything more than a chance to explore this explosive chemistry. Although, he was also wondering now why he was still so desperate to sleep with her, and why he was so sure this chemistry would take more than an hour to satisfy, when this was not the first time she had driven him crazy… And they'd known each other for less than twenty-four hours.

Her lips flattened into a line of displeasure, but the wariness and confusion in her expression remained.

'I… I didn't change my mind,' she said so cautiously, he felt like a bully. 'I just… I have to catch a bus back to Genoa from Sorrento today. It's an eleven-hour journey and I'm scheduled to be running a tour group at seven tomorrow in the marina and then I have a waitressing shift at three.'

He stared, momentarily nonplussed by the prosaic answer. For a split second, he wondered if she was lying to him, to gain his sympathy or something, because he was just that cynical. But he dismissed the idea quickly, because it was clear from her expression she thought what she had just confided was perfectly reasonable, when he knew it was anything but.

Her sister was married to a billionaire. She was part of said billionaire's family. Which made her Cade's responsibility. And yet it seemed the man had abandoned that responsibility with the same carelessness he had once rejected Roman, and his own child.

He blinked as the last of his indignation died. But his temper remained, although this time it was not directed at the young woman in front of him.

'Why are you working two menial jobs in Genoa?' he asked, keeping the disgust out of his voice with an effort.

He'd always known Cade and Cade's father were greedy, entitled, self-serving, irresponsible bastards—and he'd got over wanting things to be different a long time ago, even if the day he'd managed to arrange a meeting with the heir to the Cade empire, and beg him for a job, as a foolishly misguided sixteen-year-old, still smarted. But apparently even *he* had begun to buy into the media reports of Brandon Cade's blissful new marriage—and his enthusiastic embrace of family life and domestic responsibility. Because Roman was actually surprised by the extent of the man's callousness towards his own sister-in-law.

Who let their wife's sister work two menial jobs when they were loaded? And had been their whole life?

Milly, though, seemed even more surprised by his question, when her brows shot up, then snapped together.

'They're not menial jobs,' she said. 'They're the best jobs I could get. And they pay the bills…' She sighed. 'Until I can find the time to do more of what I actually want to do,' she added, and he found himself wondering what it was that she wanted to do. But then she propped her fists on her hips, drawing his attention to the way the worn cotton stretched over the visible outline of her nipples. 'Not everyone can be a media mogul, you know.'

'And yet your sister happens to be married to one,' he countered, dragging his gaze away from her breasts before his erection became unmanageable again.

Her expressive eyebrows launched back up. 'What exactly has what *I* choose to do for a living got to do with Brandon?'

No one *chose* to work shifts as a waitress, or ferrying tourists around, if they had other options, and from the wistful expression when she had mentioned having time to 'do what she wanted to do' it was obvious Milly Devlin *had* other ambitions. But he had no desire to clue her in to his personal animosity towards Brandon Cade, because that was way too much information for a casual fling— even if this fling already didn't feel all that casual.

So, he stopped himself from stating the obvious—that Brandon Cade had the money and the connections to nurture Milly and support her in whatever ambitions she had.

That Cade had chosen not to help her said more about him than about Milly.

But all that was beside the point. And haranguing her about what a bastard her brother-in-law was was not going to solve the problem at hand. Which was the one-hour time limit she had just put on their sex-fest—so she could spend eleven hours on a bus!

Seriously? Was she a masochist or something?

'How about I get my helicopter to escort you back to Genoa first thing tomorrow morning?' he offered. 'So you can skip the long bus journey?'

He wanted one whole night with her, and her deliciously responsive nipples. They'd started something on the beach he intended to take his own sweet time finishing—and somehow he doubted once, or even twice would be enough to discover all this woman had to offer, and satisfy the need that had been provoking him all day and most of the night.

She was a distraction, nothing more than that. But she was a fascinating and exciting one, which he wanted to savour. After all, it had been a good six months since he'd had the time, or the inclination, to sleep with anyone. And a great deal longer than that since he'd experienced the endorphin rush she had inspired in the last twelve hours simply by breathing—and antagonising him. And surely no-holds-barred, hard, sweaty sex was just what the doctor had ordered to get his downtime on Estiva off to a flying start.

He'd been struggling in the last six months with an endless feeling of boredom. And exhaustion. It felt as if he'd achieved everything he'd ever wanted to achieve. He'd lost his hunger, for work, for his business, which had driven and energised him for so long. And he wanted it back. His doctor had suggested a two-week break on Estiva from the pressures of work and social commitments. He'd balked at first, but, after another couple of months of struggling to focus, he had finally given in to the inevitable, that his lack of energy was not going to disappear on its own. But the truth was, even totally burnt out, it was going to be hard for him to relax… He hadn't had a proper vacation since he had begun his quest to unseat Cade Inc as the top media brand over a decade ago.

He didn't want to examine the root causes of this odd feeling of disconnection too closely. He just wanted it to go away. But surely having Milly Devlin in his bed would help get that process started, at least.

Plus, he certainly didn't want any FOMO hanging over him when he sent her on her merry way tomorrow morning. Because he had enough damn FOMO already, from the thought that what he had achieved somehow hadn't satisfied him, that it wasn't enough. And he didn't know why.

She blinked, clearly surprised by his offer. 'You have a helicopter here?'

It was his turn to frown. Actually, he didn't, the Garner chopper was in London, because he'd taken the company jet to Naples to get here, then piloted his own launch to the party on Capri—thanks to the hare-brained desire to meet Cade face to face for the first time in sixteen years at the Italian launch. Which he realised now had been based on some vaguely humiliating desire to show the man who had rejected him all those years ago that he was bigger and better than him now—or soon would be.

That would be the celebration Cade had chosen not to attend—and had sent his wife and sister-in-law to instead, to represent the company.

He couldn't help being glad Cade had been a no-show now, though. Not only would Roman never have met Milly, but he might have made an idiot of himself at the ball, confronting the man out of some misguided desire to prove himself.

He didn't need to prove himself to anyone any more. And certainly not Cade, but perhaps that was exactly the problem. He had run out of challenges in his life... Until Milly Devlin had tried to steal his boat.

'Yes, I have a helicopter here,' he lied smoothly, because he was not about to get bogged down in any more insignificant details.

He cupped her cheek and glided his thumb across that tempting mouth. Her lips parted as she sucked in a breath and her eyes darkened. The giddy heat leapt up his torso, and plunged into his trunks.

'So, is it a deal? You stay the night, and I'll get you back to Genoa in the morning?'

'Well, I'm not sure using a helicopter for such a short trip is very good for the environment,' she murmured, because she was just that contrary, but the heat flared regardless. Apparently, he found her contrariness as exciting as the rest of her.

What else was new?

'Stop prevaricating,' he said. 'Are we having this booty call, or are we not?' he demanded, letting his impatience show, and going full-on Captain of the Universe again. 'Because if you don't want to give me the whole night, you might as well go back to Genoa now. I have lots of plans to make you beg again—because you do it so well… But executing them is going to take considerably longer than one hour—and I do not like to be rushed.'

Indignant colour flooded into her cheeks on cue, but he could see the need in her eyes too and he had to bite back a laugh. And a groan.

The woman was so deliciously transparent—and easy to tease—it was practically a superpower. One he aimed to take full advantage of all through the night.

'You really are the pushiest man on the planet,' she announced, apropos of nothing. 'Do you always have to have everything your own way?'

'Of course,' he replied, clasping her wrist and tugging her towards him. 'But however pushy I am, I don't want you in my bed unless you want to be there. So, yes or no, Milly? It's a simple question.'

She huffed and tucked her bottom lip under her teeth to chew over the problem, then glanced at the villa. Something streaked across her face, which looked like the tantalising innocence again he had already decided was not real. But it had the same unpredictable effect, making the pulse of heat become a painful ache.

She nodded. *Finally.*

'I'm in,' she said.

Then shrieked, right in his ear, when he bent down, scooped her up and slung her over his shoulder.

'About damn time,' he said as he hefted her—laughing and kicking and gesticulating all at the same time—across the terrace and up the stairs to his suite.

Giddy desire warred with low-grade panic as Milly rode Roman's broad shoulder up to a white stone terrace overlooking the sea and pounded on his back with her fists, to no effect whatsoever.

'Put me down, you egomaniac!' she shouted, but her breathless laugh at his outrageous behaviour ruined the effect somewhat.

'Keep that up and I'll drop you,' he shouted back, then gave her bottom a stinging slap, which sent sensation skittering through her system and turbo-charged the endorphin rush that had begun to build as soon as he had interrupted her conversation with Marco.

'The signorina is not leaving tonight. And certainly not with you.'

The memory of the possessive frown on his face and the demanding tone sent another giddy rush through her already over-eager body.

Of course, Roman's terse comment had been unbelievably arrogant. But it had also been beyond exciting to realise he was as keen to explore their chemistry as she was—and he wasn't shy about staking a claim.

To be fair, her protests at his outrageous declaration had all been for show really after that.

She'd been unsure of herself when they'd arrived at the dock. Unsure of what she had committed to, and whether she was being too eager, too obvious. Which was why she'd had the conversation with Marco in the first place.

She'd got it into her head she needed to make it *very* clear—to herself as well as Roman—she had no preconceived notions about their hook-up. That she was as smart and jaded and sophisticated about sharing his bed as all the other women he had probably invited into it over the years.

She would have died of embarrassment if Roman had known exactly how much the epic orgasm he'd treated her to on the beach had meant to her. Or figured out it was the first one she'd ever had that she hadn't had to supply herself.

The delirious journey back to the villa in the boat, with his strong arms cradling her and his breath hot on her neck while he handled the sail with such skill, had been exhilarating, the afterglow still shimmering through her even more so, but it had also given her too much time to overthink what came next.

And how exactly she was going to pull off the flirty femme fatale act she was playing, given she was actually a clueless virgin, when they got to the main event.

Had she bitten off way more than she could chew with this man? Because what had seemed like a brilliant idea on the beach—to have her first sexual experience with someone as hot and gorgeous and cynical as Roman Garner—had started to feel more than a little overwhelming as the dock had come into view.

It had seemed smart and practical—because she really did have to hit the ground running and kickstart Operation Turn Milly into a Successful Artist in a Fortnight first thing tomorrow morning—to deal with how she was going to get back to Genoa, not to mention apologise to Marco for leaving his bike on the other side of the island.

But while Roman's intervention had surprised her, it had also reconfirmed that, however scared she was of making a complete tit of herself in his bed… She also still really, *really* wanted to give it her best shot.

Of course, the conversation had taken a weird turn—when he'd mentioned Brandon—but it had also been kind of sweet to have him offer to escort her to Genoa on his private helicopter just to extend their booty call. Knowing he wanted her *that* much had been beyond flattering and had boosted her flagging confidence.

Also, good to know she wasn't the only over-eager one here.

As he carted her across the terrace, she forced herself to let go of the last of her panic and concentrate on enjoying the fun and frolics Roman's outrageous behaviour promised. Time to satisfy the sexual tension that had been ramped up to fever-pitch on the beach and ignore the familiar brick of inadequacy in her gut.

So what if Roman Garner was much sexier and more demanding than any man she'd ever met before—and also a much better kisser? She would never see him again after tonight. This was not a lifetime commitment, because they had already established it was just for one night. And no one was going to be grading her on her performance.

Keep it fun. Keep it light. This is sex pure and simple.

You have nothing to prove. Not to him. All you have to do is enjoy yourself.

They were all good, she decided as he marched through the terrace doors and into a palatial, airy bedroom.

Upside down, she couldn't make out much more than an enormous four-poster bed, the luxury linen draped over its minimalist frame ruffling in the sea breeze from the open doors. The sight had her panic notching back up, but she didn't have long to think about it before she found herself bouncing off the mattress as he dumped her into the middle of the huge bed.

She laughed as he towered over her wearing a wicked grin—and looking like the master of all he surveyed. Including her.

She propped herself on her elbows and let her gaze glide over him—determined to be the mistress of all she surveyed in return.

Which was, it transpired, rather a lot.

Dressed only in the damp swimming trunks—which clung to his muscular thighs and that impressive bulge—he really was magnificent. His broad chest was roped with muscles, the sprinkle of hair on his pecs trailing into a thin line through ridged abs. She forced her gaze up, before she could get fixated on the bulge in his trunks again, but as moisture flooded her panties, the trickle of panic returned.

Because, seriously, how exactly was *that* going to fit?

But then she spotted the crossed cutlasses etched over his left pec again, which had intrigued her before. 'What's with all the pirate tattoos?' she asked.

His lips quirked in rueful amusement. 'My company was originally called Blackbeard Media.' Which wasn't really an answer. But then he pressed a hand to his chest, the wry smile mocking. 'I'm actually quite wounded you didn't know that already.'

'Sorry,' she said, not at all convincingly. Because she really had no interest in his business. Only in him.

'Oh, really?' he said, then snagged her ankle and dragged her down the bed. 'I'm not sure you're nearly sorry enough, actually.'

She let out a high-pitched squeal, which sounded perilously close to a giggle. He grabbed hold of her other ankle, then tugged off the shoes she had borrowed from Giuliana's daughter and flung them over his shoulder, while she attempted to kick his hands away, unsuccessfully.

He pulled down her shorts next, leaving her in nothing but her panties and the worn vest, her nipples already painfully swollen, and sticking out like bullets.

So much for playing hard to get.

'Now, where were we?' he said as she lay on the bed, panting, having comprehensively lost the first round. Standing, he rubbed his chin, that fierce gaze searing her sun-warmed skin, pretending to consider the situation. 'Ah, yes, I was about to make you beg again.'

'*Again?* What do you mean, again?' she scoffed playfully, enjoying the game, and knowing her part in it. Roman Garner enjoyed a challenge when it came to sex, and apparently so did she. 'You didn't make me beg the first time! That was just your enormous ego talking...'

But the rest of her protests got stuck in her throat when he kicked off his trunks and slung the damp fabric after her shoes.

Heat rushed into her cheeks, and several other important parts of her anatomy, as she got her first proper eyeful of that magnificent erection. Long and hard, the thick column of flesh bowed up from the nest of dark curls at his groin, the bulbous head shiny with precum.

She swallowed heavily as her mouth went bone dry… And the slick heat flooded between her thighs.

Apparently, his ego is not the only enormous thing about him.

'Hey, Milly. Up here.'

She heard clicking, but it took her a moment to realise he was snapping his fingers. Because… *Oh, my!*

Her gaze jerked to his face. The blush suffused her whole body as the visceral yearning increased.

He smiled. 'Have you entered a fugue state?' he teased, clearly enjoying her overawed reaction. 'I'm flattered. Assuming, of course, you like what you see.'

'Yes… I… I do…' she stuttered, trying desperately to regain her composure and her playful femme fatale persona. And not succeeding, from the wry amusement on his face.

Clearly shock and awe were not the usual reaction he got, but she was finding it hard to breathe.

She'd seen an erect penis before, of course she had. Like every self-respecting teenage girl she'd searched for pictures of naked men on the Internet as soon as she had saved up enough to buy her own laptop. But something about seeing Roman Garner in all his naked glory was so much better and hotter. And, well… Electrifying.

The heat swelled and eddied as she continued to stare at him.

'I feel like I'm at a distinct disadvantage here,' he said, climbing onto the bed. The husky chuckle managed to finally snap her out of her trance.

His big body made the mattress dip, along with her heartbeat. The erection brushed her thigh as he settled beside her. But the look in his eyes was curious as well as aroused when his hand landed on her midriff.

'How about you get naked, too?' he murmured, skimming under her vest to cup one aching breast.

She nodded, not quite able to speak.

The breath she'd been holding released in a rush as he kissed her neck. The mood had turned from playful to something else as he took matters into his own hands and paused to work her vest over her head.

She didn't object as he flung it away, too.

'That's much better...' he murmured.

He lifted one breast then captured the aching flesh in his teeth.

She drew in a sharp breath, impossibly aroused by the sharp nip, and the arrogant way he took control of the seduction. She would not normally succumb so easily to someone else's control... But as she began to pant and gasp, she couldn't find a single reason to object to his take-charge attitude—because he clearly knew exactly what he was doing.

He tongued one turgid nipple, then the other. Then captured each swollen peak in his mouth to suck them gently until she was writhing, desperate, the brutal darts of sensation arrowing down to her core.

How did he know just how to touch her to drive her wild?

The assault on her senses kicked up another crucial notch when his fingers trailed across her quivering belly and slipped into her panties.

She gasped as his thumb circled the sweet secret spot between her thighs, which she had discovered as a teenager, but now seemed to belong to him. Still tender from her beach orgasm, the slick nub throbbed as his finger swept over it with unerring accuracy.

She bucked, groaning when that teasing thumb drew away again as he pulled her panties off.

'Easy, Milly. We've got all night, remember,' he murmured, his husky chuckle so rich with appreciation she couldn't find the will—or the composure—to object to his smug tone.

Then he skimmed his thumb over the perfect spot again. And she launched off the bed, groaning. 'Oh... Oh. God. You bastard.'

'Better, Milly,' he said darkly, retreating again. 'But I want you to beg.'

'No!' She clung to his arm, wanting to stop him and yet... Not. But the sensations quickly became too powerful, too overwhelming as he caressed her clitoris—touching and retreating in a tantalising, tortuous rhythm that was driving her closer and closer to the point of no return... But not close enough.

She widened her knees and rode his hand. A part of her knew she must look desperate and unsophisticated, but as she continued to writhe, against that perfect-but-not-perfect-enough touch, she couldn't measure her breathing. She couldn't bear it much longer, as he held her on the brink, knowing just when to touch and when to tease, to drive her totally insane.

'Beg me, Milly,' he demanded, still working her into a frenzy. 'For what you need.'

'Please... Please,' she begged. 'I need you right... *There!*'

He centred on the perfect spot, at last, and rubbed. She stiffened, the brutal orgasm charging towards her. The pleasure slammed into her and the harsh coil released in a rush as sensation exploded.

She was panting, limp, steeped in afterglow—floating on the high bright cloud of endorphins—when he kissed her nose and murmured, 'Good girl. I knew you could do it.'

Her eyes opened, but she was too blissed out to find the words to argue with him… Especially as she had no ammunition whatsoever. She *had* begged. No question about it, but the reward had been worth it.

And anyway, as she watched him scramble to locate a condom and roll it on the thick erection with considerable haste, she decided he wasn't in total control any more.

She stretched, feeling languid and smug now, too. 'You're a bastard for teasing me like that,' she murmured. 'Perhaps I should make you beg now, too.'

His gaze locked on hers—the look in his eyes fierce with undisguised need and approval. 'You could,' he said as he grasped her hips and tugged her down until he could settle between her thighs. 'But I think we both know that would be entirely counterproductive,' he said, 'because you've already brought me to my knees.'

He smiled as he said it, to make it seem as if he were joking, but the low husky voice and the intense desire in his gaze told her he was as desperate as she was to finally feel him inside her.

Her heart battered her ribs and got stuck in her throat. The thought that she had made him want her, this much, both impossibly exciting and undeniably empowering.

'You ready?' he said.

She nodded, overwhelmed.

Why did this moment feel so significant? Was it because of the approval in his eyes, the thought that he didn't just want her, he needed her, too?

The foolishly romantic thought faded, to be replaced by shocking desire as he dragged his thick length through her folds, angling her hips to caress the too-sensitive nub.

Then he pushed against her entrance, his hips surging forward to impale her in one all-consuming thrust.

She bit into her bottom lip, the pinch of pain nothing compared to the visceral shock of having him buried so deep inside her. He felt huge, stretching her body to its limits.

He grunted and swore against her cheek, burying his face in her hair.

'Damn, you're so tight,' he hissed, his pained tone a vindication.

She wasn't the only one struggling to adjust to the exquisite torture.

He lifted up to stare into her face, and she let out a broken sob, the movement making her even more aware of how comprehensively he had claimed her. And stroking a spot deep inside that had the intense pleasure sparking along her nerve-endings again.

'Are you okay?' he said, surprise sprinting across his lust-blown pupils.

She nodded. It felt both raw and overwhelming to have him lodged to the hilt, but also so real and right... And unbelievably erotic.

He held still, a bead of sweat forming on his brow, making her aware of the effort it took him not to move as he gave her time to adjust.

He shifted, caressing the raw spot again, and she jolted, brutally aware of the pleasure flooding back now, to pulse and pound at her core.

He clasped her hips, and adjusted her pelvis, to get deeper still.

She groaned, clinging to his shoulders, trying desperately to anchor herself, to hold on.

'Tell me what you want,' he said, the teasing tone gone, to be replaced with urgency. 'Tell me what works for you.'

Emotion swelled and burned alongside the rush of returning pleasure—at the expression on his face, both concerned and determined.

She blinked furiously, far too aware of the burn in her throat, and the unexpected rush—both physical and emotional—at the thought that, in this moment, she mattered to him.

'Can you…can you move?' she asked. 'It feels good when you move.'

He laughed, the sound deep and rough. Then he pulled out and thrust back, slowly, carefully, the thick intrusion even more overwhelming.

'How about another please?' he said, the teasing tone back, but the look in his eyes still intense, and so focussed on her.

A strange euphoria—swift and strong—rose, to hammer against her chest and throb at her core. She laughed to ease the intensity.

'Please, Mr Garner, I want some more,' she murmured, threading her fingernails into the short hair at his nape and then tugging hard as her body devoured the delicious shiver of his response.

'You demon,' he said, but began to establish a rhythm.

The slow, powerful, undulating thrusts stroked the secret spot inside her and sent her senses soaring again, giving her exactly what she had pleaded for.

The coil tightened as she clung to his shoulders, trying to match his devastating moves. Her own were clumsy and frantic at first, and nowhere near as good as his, but before long she had got the gist of it.

Who knew she was such a fast learner?

They rode towards that high, wide plain together, the scent of sex and sea, the sound of skin slapping skin, filling the room, his grunts matching her sobs. A new pinnacle of pleasure beckoned—before she careered again into that sweet, shocking euphoria.

Well... Hell.

Roman shuddered on top of Milly, her sex massaging him through the final waves of the mind-blowing orgasm.

He breathed, inhaling her subtle, refreshing and unbearably erotic scent as he collapsed, face-planting in her hair, and let his mind and body drift... On the glittering cloud of afterglow, and the devastating feeling of connection.

What had she just done to him? Because that had been extraordinary. As if the bone-numbing climax had been wrenched from the depths of his soul.

Her hands swept over his spine and then she wriggled, making his erection—which was still lodged inside her—perk right up again... He frowned. Astonished, as well as impossibly aroused... *Still.*

How could he want to do it again, so soon after she'd just destroyed him? And frankly how could she? Because as they'd shattered together moments ago, he had seen the shock and awe in those whisky-coloured eyes too.

'Could you get off me,' she hissed, '*please.*'

He choked out a gruff laugh, the edge in her tone going some way to break the spell she had weaved around him. *Thank God.*

He braced his hands on either side of her, and pulled out of her as gently as he could. Because she had been a lot tighter than he'd expected. And he'd been concerned he'd hurt her when he'd first plunged into her.

Which didn't make a whole lot of sense. He was a big

guy, but he had never had any complaints before. And she had been more than ready for him. He'd made sure of it. In fact, he'd taken a great deal of pleasure in getting her stoked to fever pitch—because she was so responsive, and her no-holds-barred enthusiasm for his touch had driven him to desperation too.

But as he disengaged, she flinched again. He ran his thumb down her cheek to bring her gaze to his. Was it his imagination, or was she avoiding eye contact.

The sheen in those wide eyes had the concern returning full force. Alongside the pulse of arousal.

'Did I hurt you?' he asked, shocked to realise how much her answer mattered to him.

He prided himself on always pleasing the women he slept with, because the more equal the pleasure, the more it enhanced the experience for them both. But why did his desire to prove himself a good lover feel like something more this time? And why was he even worrying about it, when he knew she'd had several orgasms?

Perhaps it was just because it had been so long for him. And he'd enjoyed her responses so much. This wasn't new or different, it was just a bit more intense. That was all.

'No... I liked it,' she said. 'A lot. You're really good at...'

The surge of pride and the strength of his satisfaction surprised him. But not as much as the desire pounding back into his groin, and making him hard again.

'I've never had...' she continued, but then stopped abruptly, her gaze darting away as vivid colour scalded her cheeks.

'You've never had... What?' he asked, curious. Which was also odd. He wasn't usually a fan of pillow talk after sex. But then again, everything about this encounter had been a little skewered so far, so why not this too?

Had to be the long dry spell, he reasoned with himself.

'Nothing,' she mumbled, still staring out of the French doors towards the sea.

It was a breathtaking view from this side of the villa. The cliffs, covered with wild flowers this time of year, led down to a sandy cove, the glimmering blue water spotlighting the glowering presence of Vesuvius on the horizon.

But something about her stillness, and that telltale blush, made him sure it wasn't the spectacular view of the ancient still-active volcano that had all her attention. She still seemed dazed. And wistful.

He hooked one unruly curl behind her ear, then cradled her cheek, to angle her head away from the view, and back towards him, charmed.

'You've never had an orgasm that intense before?' he offered.

Her breath hitched, her eyebrows shooting up her forehead. 'How did you know that?'

He chuckled, finding her astonishment and the hint of irritation at his perceptiveness even more captivating. Her transparency was addictive, but not as addictive as the realisation she had no idea how easy she was to read.

'Because it was intense for me too,' he said. 'That was the best orgasm I've had in…' *For ever*, he thought, but stopped himself from saying, just in time. 'In a while.'

Get a grip. Talk about cheesy.

He'd had a lot of spectacular orgasms in his life with a lot of captivating women, all of them a great deal more sophisticated and amenable than this woman. Just because he couldn't recall a single one of those orgasms at the moment, or the women he'd had them with, wasn't anything to do with Milly Devlin.

Specifically.

She was captivating and adorably responsive, for sure.

But he'd also been suffering from burn-out for months now and not forgetting their unconventional meet cute and the head injury, the virtually sleepless night that had followed, the death swim this morning, and the long wait to finally consummate their chemistry after they'd hit on each other at the cove. He'd never been a big fan of deferred gratification, and this was why. Because if the events of the last twenty-four hours weren't a recipe for temporary amnesia and overkill, he did not know what was.

But even so, he couldn't bring himself to qualify the foolish admission any more when her eyes shone. And he could see how pleased she was by his approval.

'Well, it was very good for me, too,' she said, the tremble in her bottom lip captivating him all over again. And disturbing him.

How could he read her so easily? And why did it excite him so much? When the only time he'd enjoyed reading people before her was if he was trying to beat down their price, or print their secrets.

He shook off the disturbing thought, and pressed a kiss to her lips.

She opened for him, but he forced himself to drag his mouth away when the rush of need swelled in his groin again.

Time to start managing her expectations. And your own.

This had got way too intense, way too quickly—which was all down to their spectacular chemistry. It had to be. But if they were going to explore this connection for the rest of the night, and be ready to part in the morning, which was certainly his intention, he needed to cool things down.

He placed a hand on her belly, felt her delicious shiver.

'I say we grab a shower, then get Giuliana to cook us one

of her famous fried pizzas. She's from Napoli so it's one of her specialities. Plus, we need to keep our stamina up.'

A quick grin spread across her features, dazzling him. 'Okay... I'll race you to the bathroom...'

She had scrambled off the bed before he'd even managed to draw a breath. He swore, the adrenaline hit surging, as she shot across the room, her glorious bottom and those gorgeous breasts jiggling enticingly—and giving him all sorts of ideas about what to have for dessert. But as he flung off the sheet to head after her, something on the white linen caught his eye.

He hesitated. It took him a moment to process the small red stain.

Blood.

Was she on her period? Why was she bleeding?

But as he stared, another thought occurred to him. A reason for the bloodstain so far out in left field he couldn't quite compute it... But then he couldn't seem to shift it, or the strange way it made him feel. Weirdly flattered, and kind of possessive. As well as stunned. And confused. And wary. And deeply ashamed.

Not a good combination at the best of times. And certainly not when he was already hard for her again.

'Is something wrong?'

He raised his head. Milly's face peeked around the bathroom door. Guilty knowledge flashed across her expression when she spotted what he was staring at. And suddenly he knew what had made her so captivating from the start—the intoxicating mix of innocence and bravado, provocation and passion, which it now transpired had been entirely genuine.

'Are you a virgin, Milly?' he asked, even though he suspected he already knew the answer. And had no clue how to feel about it.

She blinked. 'Um…well…' she said, her uncertainty in contrast to her ballsy behaviour so far. Her gaze darted away from his. 'That's…'

'Don't lie,' he said, annoyed now and not even entirely sure why. Why did it bother him so much?

Her gaze met his at last, and her expression filled with that captivating mix of innocence, boldness and sass.

'No, I'm not a virgin,' she said, but before he could quiz her on the assertion—because he didn't believe her for a second—she added, 'Not any more, anyway.'

'What the…?' He swore softly, blindsided by the admission. And even more aroused by the way she announced it. As if it were no big deal.

Except it was, to him. Because he'd never been anyone's first before.

Why him? Why now? And why hadn't she said anything sooner? When he'd been pushing her to sleep with him? To spend the night? Had he taken advantage of her innocence without realising it?

Damn, was that why she'd flinched? Why she'd looked so shocked when he'd first entered her? Not because it felt good but because he'd hurt her, and made her bleed?

'Why didn't you tell me?' he managed, ashamed now of how eager and pushy he'd been with her. Because it made him feel like his father. A man he'd always hated, and never even met.

She shrugged. 'Why would I tell you?'

'Because…' He choked to a stop, both outraged and annoyed… And still aroused, which only outraged him more.

How did that even work? She'd set him up, made him feel like the reckless, womanising bastard who had sired him. And he hated to even think about that son of a bitch.

But worse, how could he still want her so much when she'd lied to him?

'I mean, I don't see how it's any of your business really,' she added.

'Of course, it's my business,' he shot back, losing what was left of his cool.

'Why is it?' she asked. Was she being deliberately disingenuous now, just to annoy him?

'Because I'm not in the business of deflowering virgins if I can help it,' he said flatly—then felt like a jerk.

He'd always been relaxed about sex, had certainly never taken it seriously, because as far as he was concerned it was a basic physical urge, to be enjoyed and then forgotten about. But somehow, she'd made him sound like a pompous seventeenth-century Lothario. *Deflowering virgins...* Who even said that?

'Okay,' she said, staring at him as if he'd lost his mind. But then her gaze drifted down to his lap.

He grabbed the sheet to cover the aching erection, but it was already too late, the colour in her cheeks had taken on a rich, redolent glow, the fierce sparkle in her eyes making the need swell alongside the indignation.

'Well, if it's any consolation,' she began carefully, her full lips quirking in a mischievous smile, 'for someone with no experience of deflowering virgins, you're remarkably good at it.'

'You little...' he shouted, flinging back the sheet.

He leapt out of bed, furious with her now, but also still furiously aroused. What the hell!

She slammed the bathroom door as he charged across the room, ready to... Well, he wasn't even sure *what* he was ready to do... But first he had to get his hands on her.

This was no laughing matter. He felt responsible for her

now, and weirdly ashamed. Somehow, she'd made this so much more than a one-night booty call.

And he was pretty sure it was deliberate.

One thing was for certain, she really was different from every other woman he had ever met. Because no other woman had ever wound him up to this extent. Not even his mother.

Alicia Rocco had never intended to drive him nuts, she had just been needy and fragile and pathetically desperate for any kind of male attention...

Milly Devlin, on the other hand, was a little ball-buster—who had deliberately tied him in knots as soon as he'd set eyes on her.

Good, hard, sweaty sex, on his terms, and at his convenience, had been supposed to remedy his Milly Devlin problem. Instead, she had just made it a hundred times worse.

He reached the door and slapped a palm against the wood while grabbing the handle with the other. But just as he twisted the knob, to yank the door open, he heard the lock snap shut.

He bellowed his frustration... The swear word bounced off the walls, making him even more aware of how comprehensively she had shot his usual charm and sophistication with women completely to smithereens.

Damn her!

'Open the door this instant, Milly.'

'No,' Milly shouted back through the wood, as she sank down against it, naked.

'I'm warning you, if you don't open it right now, there will be consequences.'

'I don't care,' she yelled back.

'Stop behaving like a two-year-old having a temper tantrum.' The door reverberated against her back as he tried to open it. 'We need to talk about this!'

'No, we don't,' she shouted. 'And FYI, I'm not the one punching a door naked, so if anyone's behaving like a toddler having a meltdown, it's you!'

The door stopped rattling. But she could hear him swearing in the room outside.

She frowned. What exactly was he so worked up about anyway? The history of her sex life—or rather the lack of it—really *was* none of his business.

'Fine! Stay in there and sulk,' he said. 'I'm going to the other suite to have a shower. But when I get back here you better be ready to talk to me about this. Or there *will* be consequences.'

'What consequences, exactly?' she goaded him. Getting annoyed now herself. She hadn't deceived him, deliberately. And anyway, how did any of this make him the injured party? She was the one who was sore, not him.

'Serious consequences,' he announced, ominously. 'Which have yet to be determined.'

'Maybe you could kidnap me…' she offered, suddenly desperate to humiliate him, too. 'Then have your wicked way with me.'

'That's not funny,' he declared.

The door began rattling again. Standing, she crossed the room and switched on the shower. The sound of the water jets pounding against the quartz almost covered the noise from outside.

'I'm in the shower, go away!' she announced, then stepped under the jets, ignoring him.

The rattling finally stopped. He must have gone to get his own shower.

She released the breath that had been trapped in her lungs ever since she had spotted him spotting the spots of her blood on the sheet.

Well, that hadn't exactly gone according to plan. Not that she'd had a plan, precisely.

But she really hadn't expected Roman to figure out the truth. So quickly. And his reaction had been even more unexpected. Because she had seen the different emotions sweep across his features in that moment—and for once they hadn't been masked by his arrogance, or his charm or that industrial-strength cynicism. She'd seen surprise followed by shock and confusion and then shame. Why should he be ashamed of sleeping with her when she had been more than willing?

She reached for a bottle of pricey shower gel. As she washed away the evidence of their lovemaking, she became brutally aware of all the places that were tender and sore. And the knot of tension in her throat threatened to choke her.

Should she have told him? That she was a virgin? Why had it mattered to him so much? When it really hadn't mattered to her… Especially as he'd been so careful with her. So quick to slow down, so determined to ensure her pleasure first before he took his own.

She'd known he would be a magnificent lover. Which was precisely why she'd chosen him to be her first after their make-out session on the beach. But she hadn't really expected him to be so generous and intuitive, too. Or that he would get so freaked out by her virginity. Not that she'd really thought about his feelings, at all.

She stepped out of the shower and turned off the jets. After grabbing a fluffy bath sheet from the pile of freshly laundered ones on the vanity, she wrapped it tightly around herself. A tremor ran through her body, even though the room was warm.

Maybe she *did* owe him an apology, she thought miserably.

She hadn't thought her virginity would matter to him, but it obviously had. The fact she hadn't even considered his reaction was also selfish and short-sighted and, well, pretty entitled.

Finding a bathrobe, she slipped it on, then folded up the long sleeves.

She studied herself in the mirror, trying to find any noticeable differences. She touched the rough marks on her cheeks where he'd kissed her so thoroughly, he'd given her beard burn. And became aware of the beard burn she had in another, even more intimate spot. Or two intimate spots, to be precise.

The blush rose up her neck to join the colour in her cheeks. Without make-up on, her skin flushed from the hot shower, and her body sore in all sorts of unusual places, she felt new and different somehow.

But how different was she really?

Maybe she'd finally discovered the truth about sex—about how wonderful and exciting and liberating it could be. But had it really made her any more mature?

Because she'd discovered something else while she'd been exploring the joys of sex in Roman's arms. The act was also scarily intimate and intense.

Even though Roman was still a stranger, because she hadn't made any effort to get to know him before she'd fallen into bed with him. But maybe she should have.

The truth was, she *had* used him, to lose her virginity. And she hadn't given him a choice in the matter. She'd been reckless and impulsive and done what had felt right in the moment, just as she'd done when she'd made the decision to leave London with only a backpack and less than two hundred euros in her purse. Or when she'd argued with her sister on the palazzo terrace in Capri and then borrowed the wrong boat. And now, as Roman had so helpfully pointed out, she would once again have to face the consequences.

A rap on the door made her jump.

'Time's up, Milly.' Roman's voice was husky and tense, but at least not mad. 'You need to stop hiding in there now.'

She bristled slightly at the dictatorial tone, and tied the robe tighter.

If only she could stay in here for the foreseeable future. Because she did not want to have this conversation.

'Could you hand me my clothes?' she said, because she had no intention of having this conversation naked.

'Sure,' he said, being surprisingly helpful, for Roman. He must really be freaked out.

A minute later, he tapped on the door again. She clicked the lock, and grabbed the clothes in his outstretched hand, before shutting the door and locking it again.

'You've got five minutes,' he said.

She got dressed slowly, making sure she took at least ten, just because. But then felt like a spoilt brat again.

She sighed.

Stop making this harder than it needs to be.

She owed Roman an apology. And the sooner she got it over with, the sooner she could leave. Because she doubted he would want her to stay the night now... Which only made her feel like an even bigger failure.

Little Miss Screw-Up goes large again.

CHAPTER FIVE

ROMAN WAITED IMPATIENTLY on the terrazzo, aware of his housekeeper giving him the evil eye as she laid out the lavish lunch he'd ordered while waiting for Milly to put in an appearance.

'Do you want anything else, *signor*?' Giuliana asked in Italian, the question perfectly polite, the tone anything but. His housekeeper hadn't commented on the young woman still hiding in his bathroom, but it had been fairly obvious what she—and no doubt her husband and the rest of his staff—were already thinking.

That their boss was a vile seducer who had taken advantage of poor little Milly Devlin today, after kidnapping her last night. From the sharp, judgmental frown on the older woman's face, he was probably fortunate she hadn't already called the *polizia*.

'*No, grazie*, Giuliana,' he said, grateful when she gave a stiff nod and left.

If only he could dismiss Giuliana's judgment as easily. He knew full well Milly had enjoyed her time in his bed, she'd even begged him for release—more than once. Damn it.

But the niggling feeling of shame remained lodged in his solar plexus.

At least, he had managed to calm down enough in the shower to get things in perspective—and make some crucial observations while waiting for Giuliana to finish serving the lunch.

He'd overreacted. That much was obvious. Just because he'd taken a woman's virginity, it didn't make him anything like his old man. After all, he hadn't done it deliberately. Milly's innocence, and her hyper-responsiveness to him, had captivated him and made him want her, a lot, but who said the two were linked? And anyway, how could he have known her innocence was genuine, when she hadn't told him he was her first?

And if he hadn't *known* she was a virgin, how could he be accused of deliberately exploiting her innocence, like the man who had seduced his mother as a teenager, made her his mistress, got her pregnant and then dumped her without a backward glance.

Roman might be rich, but he'd given Milly a clear choice and she'd taken it. And unlike his mother, who had been barely eighteen and still at school when she'd had the bad luck to catch his father's roving eye, Milly could hardly be described as fragile or vulnerable. Not only was she more than capable of holding her own with him, she'd tried to steal his boat!

They were consenting adults, with a rare, visceral chemistry that they had both enjoyed. And most importantly of all, he'd worn a condom. He hadn't been careless or cavalier, he'd protected her. Plus, he'd been aware of her pleasure, every step of the way.

And the kidnap thing had never been serious. It had been a joke. *Mostly.*

The prickle of shame niggled, though, as his gaze swept across the breathtaking view from the bedroom's terrace. The large pool below sparkled in the sunlight, the blue water highlighting the Blackbeard logo he'd had installed in marble mosaic tiles on the pool's bottom. Then there were the formal gardens, which were kept pristine all year round by a team of gardeners, the pool house and two other guest villas, the lemon and olive groves that led down to his private dock, where he kept a sailing clipper, the motor launch Milly had tried to pinch and the dinghy they had used to return from the cove. Of course, he also had a luxury super-yacht, which was currently anchored in the bay and which he barely used. And the helicopter and private jet he owned to travel to his different homes—in Mayfair, the Hamptons, Rome and the Cayman Islands—and his business headquarters and penthouse apartments on Manhattan's Upper West Side and the City of London.

Okay, he wasn't just rich, he was phenomenally rich. Much richer now than the bastard who had broken his mother's heart had ever been. But he'd always believed his wealth—the luxuries he enjoyed, the homes and properties he had acquired—were the justifiable rewards for his success. He hadn't used them to exploit anyone.

He'd worked extremely hard to throw off the shackles of the poverty he'd grown up in. But as he stared at the view, surveying the riches he had accumulated over the past decade and a half, he found himself wondering how much of his drive and ambition had come from the desire to escape his miserable origins, and how much had been a need to prove he was better than the Cades. Better not just than Alfred Cade, but also his half-brother, Brandon. The man who had inherited everything, when he had inherited nothing.

He thrust his hand through his hair, hating the direction of his thoughts, and the feeling of shame he couldn't quite shake. Because it was forcing him to acknowledge his reasons for bringing Milly here hadn't been a joke. Not entirely. After all, he'd known who she was, who she was connected to, even if he had also wanted her, as soon as he'd caught her driving his boat.

It had never even occurred to him until now that his pursuit of wealth might not all have been about lifting him and his mother out of poverty. Might it also have been the low-burning anger and sense of injustice that had marred so much of his childhood? Because if that was true, it was beyond pathetic.

He frowned.

Okay, get over yourself.

Where was all this existential angst coming from?

Was this a symptom of the burn-out too? Because he was basically re-examining his whole life and career trajectory based on one booty call, just because he'd discovered Milly Devlin was a virgin.

He heard a polite cough and swung round.

At last.

Milly stood on the terrace behind him, looking sheepish and way too cute in her borrowed cut-offs and the worn vest, her cheeks reddened from his kisses.

The shaft of longing surged through him again. Rich and fierce and fluid.

Apparently, their chemistry was even stronger now he knew what it was like to see her expressive face contort with pleasure and feel her massaging him to orgasm.

Terrific.

He straightened away from the terrace railing and shoved his fists into the pockets of his sweatpants. Because he wanted to touch her again. And that wasn't going to happen until they got a few things straight.

But something about his visceral reaction also felt like a vindication. One thing was for damn sure, his motivations for sleeping with Milly Devlin hadn't had anything to do with her connection to Brandon Cade, and everything to do with the kinetic chemistry they shared.

The last of his shame and confusion began to release its stranglehold on his throat when her eyes met his and what he saw in her expression was guarded determination. Not fear or vulnerability. Yet more evidence he had totally overreacted.

Time to defuse the situation, before it got more awkward.

'How about we start over, Milly?' he said.

At exactly the same time as she said, 'I'm sorry I didn't tell you I was a virgin.'

'Okay,' he managed, the earnest apology starting to make him feel like a bully again. He shouldn't have browbeaten her about her inexperience.

Her virginity had only freaked him out because of stuff in his past that had nothing to do with her... Or what they'd shared in his bed—which had been great. And not a lot to do with him either. He hadn't chosen to be fathered by a man who took pleasure in exploiting and hurting virgins. So why had he framed their lovemaking according to that man's sins?

But before he could say any of that, she launched into a heartfelt little speech.

'Honestly, it didn't even occur to me to tell you,' she rushed on. 'I didn't think you'd care. It wasn't that big a deal to me, so I didn't think it would be that big a deal to you. And the only reason I'm still a virgin at twenty-two is because my family life was pretty complicated for a while and I just didn't have the time to date like the other girls in school.'

'Complicated how?' he asked before he could stop himself.

This was just a booty call. But he'd already taken it to the next level with his freak-out… And he was desperately curious to know, why hadn't she slept with anyone before him? When she was such an eager, artless and enthusiastic lover?

She shrugged. 'It's kind of a boring story…'

'We've got time,' he prompted.

'Okay, if you really want to know.' She sighed. 'Basically, when my mum died, I was only fifteen and Lacey was just eighteen, and our father—who had a new family by then—wasn't interested in being a dad to us, too. Luckily, social services gave Lacey custody of me, but it was really important to me not to be too much of a burden, which meant I didn't have time to party and do all those normal teenage things. Then Lacey got pregnant the year after and we had Ruby to look after.'

Anger twisted in Roman's gut. That would be Brandon Cade's daughter—who the bastard hadn't acknowledged for four years.

'I did the bulk of the childcare, after school, because Lacey had to work.' She glanced at him and her expression brightened. 'Don't get me wrong, we both adored Ruby from the moment she was born. She was never a burden or anything.'

Like hell she wasn't, Roman thought resentfully. The child had been Cade's responsibility, but he'd shirked it. It just made him despise the man more.

'But Lacey was the one with the career as a journalist, so it made sense for me to look after Rubes…pick her up from the childminder and then the nursery after I finished school, stuff like that.' Milly was still talking, but Cade's failure to live up to his responsibilities only annoyed Roman more. Why had Lacey and Milly accepted the man's behaviour so easily? And how could Milly like the man now, when he had effectively stolen so much of her adolescence?

'I loved watching Ruby grow and…'

'Okay, hold up,' he said, raising his palm to stop Milly from waxing lyrical about being made responsible for the care of a child that wasn't even hers.

He also didn't want to hear another word about how that bastard had robbed Milly of her teenage years. Because it would just make him more involved, and he was already involved enough.

But her forthright explanation also made it even more obvious he'd overreacted about her virginity. And turned a hook-up that should have been fun and exhilarating into something awkward and emotional.

The window she had given him into her past—and the news she had also been abandoned by her father—bothered him, too. Because it seemed they shared more than he had realised. After all, he knew what it felt like to have your father not give a damn about you. But he didn't like how much he was starting to admire and sympathise with Milly.

Because these feelings were way too intense for a casual hook-up.

'You don't owe me an apology, or an explanation,' he managed, round the thickness in his throat. 'In fact, I probably owe you one. I overreacted about the virginity thing. And you were right, it was none of my business.'

She nodded, then sighed, her face softening with relief. 'Okay. Thank you. Apology accepted. Does that mean we don't have to talk about it anymore?' she asked, her hopeful expression nothing short of adorable.

'Absolutely,' he said, as relieved as she was to end the conversation.

'Oh, thank goodness,' she said with such enthusiasm, he laughed. 'Because that was excruciating.'

Adrenaline shot into his bloodstream. And then straight beneath his belt.

'Agreed,' he said as the last of the shame finally took a hike.

Milly Devlin was captivating and fascinating. And he'd always found her transparency extremely hot. He was glad that hadn't changed.

Now they'd got the awkward out of the way, and he'd got being her first lover into perspective, he couldn't help thinking her lack of experience, while problematic, was also a turn-on.

She'd never made love to another man. Which meant no other man had experienced her exquisite responsiveness, or her forthright pursuit of pleasure. While he was not a possessive guy, why shouldn't he make the most of the chance to explore that more?

Milly Devlin was a woman who enjoyed sex, and she wasn't afraid to show it. She didn't seem to have a cautious or coy bone in her body. She was reckless and impulsive and held nothing back—even though she had no clue what she was doing—and there was something unbearably erotic about that.

Not to mention the fact she had given him one of the best orgasms of his life already. So why not press for more while she was here? After all, he had nothing else to do.

He'd never seen himself in the role of a sexual Svengali before, had always preferred when women told him exactly what they wanted. But the thought of giving Milly the benefit of his expertise and watching her indulge a part of herself she'd been forced to deny was something he could get behind one hundred per cent.

He was more than ready to devote himself to the cause.

'How about we eat...?' he offered, by way of changing the subject completely.

But as he placed his hand on her lower back, and felt her tremble, the need and longing shot through him. As she let him seat her at the terrace table, he couldn't help thinking that one night would not be enough to enjoy all this intoxicating woman had to offer... And he had to offer her in return, sexual Svengali-wise.

And having her here had the potential to make the next two weeks—which, when the doctor had recommended this break, had stretched before him like a smorgasbord of boredom—a whole lot more exciting.

Milly sipped the delicate wine from a local vineyard that Roman apparently owned—if the Azienda Agricola Blackbeard mentioned on the label was anything to go by—and watched Roman finish off another helping of Giuliana's delicious antipasti.

She was stuffed, having dug into the food with more enthusiasm than necessary, probably because she was starving after all the physical activity of earlier, and beyond grateful the 'virginity' conversation had been blessedly short and hadn't had any of the consequences she'd been expecting.

Most important of which was, he hadn't asked her to leave.

He had been tense when she'd explained exactly why she had still been a virgin at twenty-two. And she wasn't entirely sure why. She also couldn't help wondering why he had overreacted so spectacularly earlier, especially as he seemed to be totally over it now.

But as he polished off the last of Giuliana's delicately spiced carpaccio—his appetite even more voracious than her own—she knew she wasn't going to ask him. Because that would just bring back the awkward, and ruin the rest of the hours they had left together, which were already going by too fast.

She studied the stunning view of Roman with Vesuvius on the horizon, and imagined the imposing composition in pen and ink. The man juxtaposed with the volcano was such a fundamental yet vivid expression of power and danger and volatility.

She attempted to imprint the image in her memory to draw later, if she ever found the time, when she got back to Genoa.

He glanced up from his plate. And his intense gaze locked on her face—making her skin prickle with awareness. And her heart hitch in her chest. Why did she get the impression he could read every one of her thoughts? All the time? And why was it both disturbing, and incredibly hot?

'Problem?' he asked.

'Not at all,' she said, and sent him her best *I'm sophisticated* smile.

He put down his fork and studied her some more, sending the prickle of awareness to some even more disturbing places.

'Are you sure there's nothing, because you looked as if you wanted to ask me something,' he said, the husky tone and the twinkle in his eye suggesting he was aware of the prickle.

'I don't suppose you'd let me sketch you?' she blurted out, because she did not want to give in to the prickle, yet.

She was still tender from their lovemaking earlier. And getting Roman back into bed too soon would make the rest of their day together go even faster. Plus, she enjoyed spending time with him out of bed, too. He intrigued her.

The man was a puzzle in so many ways. And it was kind of thrilling to be this man's lover, however temporarily.

He looked momentarily dumbfounded by her request. But then his lips quirked in a wicked smile. 'What? Naked?'

'No, not naked, Mr One-Track Mind!' she replied, wanting to be outraged at the suggestion, but knowing she wasn't, because she was far too turned on instead.

A life drawing of Roman Garner would be quite something. She swallowed down the ball of lust forming in her throat, determined not to get sidetracked. Again.

'Actually, I'd like to sketch you here, with the volcano in the background. It's an arresting image. And then I could finish the work later...' She huffed. 'If I can find the time.'

'How would you envision using my image, exactly?' he asked, confusion turning to scepticism. She recognised that look from yesterday night, when he'd caught her 'borrowing' his boat—and accused her of stealing it. The man was nothing if not suspicious. But this time, she was not going to let his trust issues get to her.

'I usually do a pencil drawing, then I build on that using ink and watercolours or acrylics, depending on what works best,' she began, giving him way more information than he needed, but wanting him to know her art was one thing she took very seriously. 'But I don't do faces,' she continued because he hadn't said anything. 'You're in silhouette at the moment because the sun is starting to set and those shapes are what I'd want to work with. Anonymity preserves the image's power and the exquisite quality of the light suits what I want to do with the composition. But, if I ever get a chance to show the work, which is highly debatable given my track record so far,' she muttered, in the interests of full disclosure, even though it made her heart sink to admit to him what a failure she was, 'no one will be able to tell it's you, I promise.'

She picked up her wine glass and drained it, much more nervous now about his reaction than she'd been when she'd agreed to sleep with him. Or when he'd figured out she was a virgin, even though his reaction then had been a lot more volatile.

She waited for him to say something, anything really, getting more anxious by the second when he just continued to stare at her. His brows flattened and he tilted his head to one side, the quizzical expression intense, as if he were trying to figure out something really complicated.

Then his eyes sparkled with understanding, and he smiled. 'You're an artist!'

'Well, yes, I'm trying to be one,' she said, not sure why he seemed so pleased with himself.

'That's what you really want to do,' he said. 'Instead of being a waitress or a tour guide. You want to create art and show your work.'

'Eventually, yes,' she said, although it hadn't really been a question. Why did he look as if he'd just discovered the meaning of life? 'That's the plan anyway, but first I have to get a decent portfolio together.'

'So why haven't you done it?' he asked. 'Instead of doing menial jobs which take up all your free time?'

'Um…maybe because I have to do this really annoying thing called eating,' she snapped, irritated they seemed to have returned to the *Why-is-Milly-a-pauper?* conversation. 'And paying rent. Plus, they're *not* menial jobs.'

Of course, Roman Garner didn't understand why she had to work for a living, the man owned a private island, but did he *really* have to be quite this blunt?

'Listen, if you don't want me to sketch you that's perfectly fine,' she continued as her stomach clutched with disappointment. 'Just say so,' she finished, even though it hurt to know she would never get to realise the spellbinding image of Roman and the Volcano.

'What if I told you I have a better idea?' he replied, then picked up the fist she had clenched on the table, by her empty glass, and lifted it to his lips.

She shuddered, aware of the hunger in his eyes—and the answering hunger in her abdomen—when he eased open her fingers and pressed his lips to her palm.

'What idea?' she asked, getting sidetracked by those nibbling kisses, and the prickle that had morphed into a buzz now and was doing interesting things to the hot spot between her thighs, despite her best intentions.

'How about,' he said, still playing fast and loose with her hand, 'instead of going back to Genoa to work your two not-menial jobs—you stay here as my guest for the next two weeks and work on your portfolio?'

'You're not… You're not serious? Why would you do that? You hardly know me.'

Roman grinned at the flicker of astonishment in Milly's eyes—and the glitter of hope.

'I know enough…' he said, stroking his thumb across the pulse point battering her wrist. 'And I like having you here.'

Awareness darkened her eyes, and the spark of attraction fired the air, but then she tugged her hand out of his grasp.

'I can't accept,' she said, although he could see the bone-deep disappointment.

'Why not?' he asked, genuinely stumped by her refusal. This solution was perfect. She needed someone who would give her time away from working menial jobs so she could dedicate herself to the work she clearly loved. And he wanted company for the next two weeks, so he could get the downtime his doctor had ordered without dying of boredom. He wasn't an art expert, and he had no idea if she was any good, but he'd seen the passion in her face, heard the purpose in her voice when she'd described the work she wanted to create. He knew what it was like to have a vision. So why shouldn't he help her facilitate this one?

'You know why,' she said, her gaze locking on his, the embarrassed flush making her cheeks glow.

'Actually, no, I don't. You just said you want to sketch me, and…' He cleared his throat, a bit uncomfortable at the thought of having anyone paint him. 'Although I'm not one hundred per cent on board with that, because I'm not great at sitting still for long periods of time, I'm up for it. If that's what you need.'

She sent him a level look. 'Yes, but that's not all you're up for, is it?' she said as her gaze flicked to his crotch, to emphasise her point.

'True.' He laughed. 'Are you saying you're not up for that too, then?' he countered.

The flush on her cheeks heated, but the awareness flared.

Gotcha.

'Well, no,' she stuttered, comprehensively hoist by her own petard.

He lifted his palms off the table, in a gesture of surrender—even though it was anything but.

'Hey, there's no need to get your panties in a wad, Milly,' he added, tickled by the combination of heat and indignation in her expression. 'My offer comes with no strings attached. I can ask Giuliana to source you all the art supplies you need from Naples. As my guest you can stay in any room you want and paint for two weeks straight without even having to talk to me. If you don't wish to work on your booty-call portfolio too—even though it has been sadly neglected up to now,' he added, attempting an expression of regret. Not easy when the thought of inducting Milly into the Booty Call Hall of Fame was making the adrenaline rush sink into his shorts. 'With a guy who knows how to make you beg and is more than willing to dedicate himself to your "sex education",' he teased, doing finger quotes. 'But if the answer is no, just say so. No pressure, whatsoever.'

Her eyebrows rose towards her hairline, but she couldn't keep a straight face. 'My sex education...?' Her husky chuckle was a delightful mix of disbelief and desire. 'That's very altruistic of you, to offer to be my teacher in all things bootylicious.'

'I thought so,' he said magnanimously. Making her laugh more.

Standing, he grasped her wrist and tugged her out of her chair until he had her back in his arms. He leaned against the railing, banding his arms around her waist. Funny that she felt so right standing with him in the sunlight. The warmth in her golden eyes wrapped around his chest, another new experience for him. Sex—or the promise of sex—had never made him feel this good before. But he decided not to question it as he cradled her cheek and absorbed the rush of anticipation. 'What do you say? Wanna stay here and paint, while also getting a diploma from a master sexologist in Mind-Blowing Orgasms for Beginners?'

She grinned. 'Your ego is actually out of control right now, you do know that?'

'And your point would be...?' he teased.

His ego had always been robust, and he'd never been ashamed of that, but the vivid approval in her eyes had brought some of the fizzing excitement back he'd always taken for granted...

The next two weeks held so many more possibilities now... He could beat this burn-out, get his mojo back and figure out where he wanted to take his business next, while she took a shot at her dreams.

And he actually couldn't wait to take his own sweet time exploring their chemistry.

'Yes or no, Milly, it's a simple question,' he said, then dragged her flush against him, so she could feel how much he wanted her. And he could kiss the pulse point in her neck, which he knew would drive her wild.

She huffed out a laugh, then plunged her fingers into his hair, to draw his head up.

'No fair kissing me while I'm trying to decide,' she said, but he could see the acceptance in her eyes already. And the fizz of excitement went nuts.

It was actually an effort not to push, not to press, to keep his cool when he murmured, 'Well, then, hurry up. Because if I get any more invested and the answer's no I'm looking at another two-mile swim to the cove to cool off again.'

It was precisely the right thing to say, he realised, when her expression became joyful and her breathing became a little ragged.

So, Milly Devlin was a praise junkie. He filed the thought away, to use to his advantage at a later date.

'Okay, I'll stay, but you've got to make me a promise...' she said, the teasing light in her eyes taking on a wistful glow. 'Several promises actually.'

He didn't usually negotiate over sex, or make promises, of any kind, to the women he slept with. Because he would inevitably have to break them. But he was willing to make an exception in Milly's case, because she was different from his previous dates. She was innocent while also having been forced to mature way too soon, and if she had any unrealistic expectations about his offer, he owed it to them both to debunk them now.

'Fire away,' he said, willing to be flexible about his usual rules, up to a point.

But then she surprised him. 'You mustn't fall in love with me. I don't want to get over-invested, so neither should you.'

His lips quirked at the serious expression on her face, which was a fascinating mix of guilelessness and pragmatism. 'Not a problem,' he replied. 'I'm a master at not getting over-invested. And love's not something I need.'

There was no chance he would fall in love with her, however captivating she was, because he simply didn't do that level of emotional engagement with anyone.

'My ego's way too big for that,' he offered, then added, 'So you better make sure you don't fall in love with me either.' Although, he decided, she was way too smart to make that mistake—which made the next two weeks even more perfect. He wouldn't have to hold back, wouldn't have to pretend he felt something for her he didn't, because, on some level, he knew she understood he had nothing but sexy times to offer her.

She nodded. 'I won't.'

'Anything else?'

'You agree to pose for me naked, if I promise not to show the work.'

He laughed but the sound was raw and husky, and the

ridge in his pants shot straight to critical mass. 'You drive a hard bargain.'

She swivelled her hips against his, trapping his erection and making him groan. 'It seems I'm not the only one,' she said, the challenging tone making his excitement hit fever pitch. 'Yes or no, Garner, do we have a deal?' she mocked. 'It's a simple question.'

'Yes, damn it,' he said, then boosted her into his arms.

As she laughed and wrapped her legs around his waist, he wondered who was seducing whom, here. With his hands massaging her butt, he marched across the terrace towards the bedroom. She laughed breathlessly as he threw her onto the bed, then climbed on top of her.

Grabbing her wrists, he lifted her arms above her head and anchored them there with one hand, while using the other to tug up her vest and expose her beautiful breasts to his gaze.

'Here begins lesson one,' he declared, before dragging his tongue across one tight peak. He captured the swollen flesh between his teeth and gave it a gentle tug.

She bucked against his hold, her incoherent sob like music to his ears.

'Pay attention, Milly,' he said as he worked his free hand into her cut-offs and found her wet and ready. 'Because you're going to be tested later…'

She undulated her hips to increase the friction, while he teased her with his fingers. 'Yes, sir,' she groaned. 'Now please get on with it…*sir.*'

He chuckled at her impatient demand, before concentrating on teaching his first formal class in Mind-Blowing Orgasms for Beginners.

CHAPTER SIX

'RELAX, ROMAN, YOU don't have to stay completely still, I can work around movement,' Milly said, busy fleshing out the line drawing, adding shading and emphasis to the sketch. A smile curved her lips as her subject frowned at her.

The man was as stiff as a board, and not in the usual way. She had never expected him to be self-conscious about posing for her when he didn't seem to be self-conscious about anything else. But when she'd suggested they do the life drawing this morning, after a particularly energetic bout of lovemaking, he'd found about a million and one reasons why that was a really bad idea. After over three hours of prevarication—during a morning hike, then brunch, then more lovemaking, then a snorkel safari in the private cove below the villa, she had finally had to put her foot down and remind him of the promise he had made to her a week ago.

Gosh, is it already a whole week? Since we made our Devil's Bargain?

She paused for a second, to let the ripple of disappointment at how fast their time together was slipping away wash over her, then started sketching again with renewed vigour.

The last week had been so much fun. That was all. She was not getting emotionally invested in her spectacular fling with Roman Garner, she was just appreciating how much she had enjoyed it so far. And how much she intended to enjoy the time they had left.

The last seven days had flown past in a haze of incredible sex, delicious meals—provided by Giuliana, who was a fabulous cook—and all the other vigorous activities Roman enjoyed so much. The man was a natural athlete with energy to spare. But in between the sex, and the swimming and hiking and sailing, Milly had also managed to fit in some invigorating bursts of creativity putting together a portfolio she was already excited about—while Roman slept, something he also did with a kind of all-or-nothing determination.

The island and Roman as subjects for her work had become intertwined in her imagination, both rugged and restless with their own powerful purpose, providing her with a wealth of inspiration.

This was the first time she had managed to get him to pose for her properly. She'd loved the drawings she had done of him already, which she had worked on during the rare occasions when he was still—either while he was sleeping or eating. But she wanted something more detailed this time. As she had promised him originally, this particular composition wouldn't be for public consumption, because he would be identifiable—and gloriously naked—but she wanted to get the details of who he was on paper, to remember these two seminal weeks of her life, with her first lover, when they parted ways.

She swallowed down the new ripple of regret, ruthlessly.

'When I agreed to do this, I thought it would be a lot sexier,' he murmured grumpily, from the bed, adjusting for about the two thousandth time in the last fifteen minutes the sheet Milly had draped over his lap.

A chuckle popped out as Milly focussed on the sketch, already realising the amount of time she was going to be able to get him to sit for her would be limited.

'Why do you find it so hard to sit still? Do you know?' she asked, deciding that maybe if she could distract him, and get him talking about himself, she could help take his mind off his discomfort. Also, she was curious about him—and his refusal to talk about anything remotely personal.

'Does anyone find it easy?' he asked, with the deflection she had become used to.

'I suppose not,' she said, concentrating on the line of his torso, and adding shading to the defined musculature of his chest.

She'd done life drawings before during the evening classes she'd taken while working as a teaching assistant—before Brandon Cade had come into her and Lacey's and Ruby's lives and blown their normal everyday activities to smithereens. But the models had always been professional. She supposed it made sense this wasn't easy for Roman—because he was such an active man—but it was his self-consciousness that really surprised her.

'Although, you usually enjoy being naked,' she added. They had been skinny dipping only yesterday, in La Baia Azzurra, away from the prying eyes of the staff, and Roman was the one who had suggested it.

'It's a lot more fun being naked when you are too,' he offered. 'Perhaps that would work,' he added, his voice taking on the husky tone that could mean only one thing. 'Why don't you strip off while you sketch? That would totally help me to relax.'

She laughed, still sketching. 'I don't think so! Mr One-

Track Mind. If I got naked we would *definitely* get side-tracked and this would never be finished.'

'And that would be bad because…?' he murmured.

She added detailing to the hair on his pecs, then concentrated on the design of the tattoo over his heart.

'Why did you originally call your company after a pirate,' she asked, changing the subject before she got pulled under again—into that bottomless pool of desire that they hadn't come close to tapping, even after seven days of virtually non-stop sex.

She swallowed, attempting to ignore the liquid pull in her abdomen as she worked on drawing his torso. Not easy.

'Why do you want to know?' he countered.

She stopped sketching. 'That's not an answer.' It wasn't the first time she'd asked him about his tattoos. And the pirate theme. It also wasn't the first time he'd avoided giving her a straight answer… Or any answer at all really.

He shrugged. 'Pirates are thieves but they're also romantic, mythical figures. At the time I had convinced myself I was stealing my legacy back, so it fitted.'

'Who were you stealing your legacy back from?' she asked, intrigued by the hint of bitterness in his tone. Was she finally getting a glimpse of the man behind the devil-may-care charm?

Roman went out of his way to seem reckless and unserious about everything. But she knew beneath that casual, careless, carefree persona was a man of strong passions—because that was the way he made love. Even when sex between them started out flirty and fun, it never stayed that way. He seemed to want to make her desperate for release, by tempting and torturing her until she begged. And when he finally found his own release, his focus was so intense she often felt burned by the passion they shared.

'It's just a figure of speech,' he said, evasively.

He was a difficult man to read, but when his gaze dropped away from hers, she knew he was lying. And she wondered why. Who had stolen his legacy? Was that where his phenomenal drive and ambition had come from? A sense of injustice? Because he had become remarkably wealthy and successful for a man only in his early thirties.

'But you didn't come from wealth, did you?' she probed, sure she'd heard something about him being self-made. 'Not like Brandon?'

She knew her brother-in-law had inherited the Cade empire while still in his teens, from his father, who had been an autocratic and unloving man, according to what Lacey had confided in her. In the years since his father had died, Brandon had modernised and expanded the Cade businesses—turning Cade Inc into a global media brand. But from the things Giuliana had told Milly about her boss, while the two of them chatted over breakfast each morning because Roman rarely woke before noon, Roman was almost as wealthy. And Garner Media had a similar reach. Which, now she thought about it, really was an incredible feat. To have built so much, so quickly, from what sounded like very little.

Roman straightened, the quirk on his lips flattening out. 'What has your brother-in-law got to do with anything?'

She blinked, taken aback by the edge in his voice. He'd mentioned in passing he and Brandon knew of each other because they had some rival business interests, but what she saw in his expression seemed remarkably personal.

'Just that you're a similar age,' she explained slowly. 'And run similar companies, but I know Brandon inherited his from his dad. And I'm assuming you didn't inherit anything, from what you just said about legacies. That's all.'

The silence seemed to stretch out between them as he studied her. What was he looking for, with that suspicious frown on his face? And how had a fairly innocuous conversation suddenly become so tense?

She hadn't asked him about his business before now, partly because she knew nothing about it, but also because she had discovered from Giuliana he was on the island to relax and get away from the stress of being, by all accounts, a workaholic. She and Roman had made a pact, to share their downtime here, so he could enjoy his break and she could focus on building a portfolio. All the extra-curricular sex had been hard not to binge on, because it made her feel so good, and so liberated. As if she'd discovered a side of herself she had never known existed—the insatiable sex goddess side, which she had spent so long denying.

What he'd given her with this break already felt like an enormous gift. But she was trying hard not to get it out of proportion. To give it more emphasis than it deserved. Or become too invested in this holiday from her real life.

But as he stared at her, his expression tightening as he continued to look for something she didn't understand, it felt as if she had stepped over a crucial line by mentioning Brandon, of all people.

'You said you and Brandon have similar business interests,' she continued, because he still hadn't said anything. 'There's not more to it than that, is there?'

He let out a rough laugh, but the sound was forced. And his gaze was still probing. He shifted, and sat up, throwing his legs over the side of the bed, the sheet pooling in his lap.

'Are you finished with the sketch?' he asked, not answering her question. *Again.*

Her fingers jerked on the charcoal. She stared down at the work she'd done. The line drawing was finished—

ready for her to figure out what she wanted to do with it next. But she took a moment to gather herself and wait for her heartbeat to slow down. The sudden fear she might have ruined everything gripped her, and she found herself searching for a way to step back over that line. To return them both to where they had been before she'd somehow wandered into no-man's-land.

When she looked back at him again, he was still watching her. But the spark of arousal had darkened his gaze. The visceral tug of longing—which never seemed to be far away—bloomed in her abdomen.

'Yes, I guess so,' she managed.

'Good.' He beckoned her with one finger, the seductive intent in his eyes turning the deep green to a sparkling emerald. 'Time for you to get naked, too, then.'

The request was edged with demand. She could have refused him. But she found she didn't want to. Sex was simple, and distracting. And it didn't require an emotional commitment from either one of them.

But as she placed her sketchbook on the dresser, then stripped in front of him and watched his gaze darken, the lust eddying through her didn't feel quite so fun and flighty and simple any more. It felt edgy and deep and compelling, and more than a little out of control.

Once she discarded the last of her clothing, he rose from the bed, throwing off the sheet to reveal the thick erection. Her throat went dry, her bones liquid, the heat at her core all but unbearable.

Placing his hands on her hips, he kissed her, his mouth ravaging hers, his need suddenly so intense she felt branded. Where was this coming from? And why couldn't she seem to stop herself from thrusting her fingers into his hair and dragging him closer still to take more?

As they finally came up for air, her breath squeezed in her lungs, the furious hunger on his face echoing in her soul.

He turned her away from him. Then pressed a hand to her back, to bend her over the dresser. 'Why can't I stop wanting you, Milly?' he murmured, his voice thick with lust, the question one she couldn't answer, because she felt it too. This incessant desire, which seemed to have imprisoned them both.

She quivered, placing her palms on the dresser, then bucked against his touch as he dragged a finger through her folds, testing her, spreading her.

'Tell me you want me,' he said. Or rather demanded.

'You know I do,' she replied.

He entered her with one powerful thrust, impaling her to the hilt and caressing the spot deep inside only he had ever found.

She sobbed, the pleasure immense, the emotion she didn't want to acknowledge all but choking her as he began to move, in a fast, furious rhythm that he knew would force her swiftly to peak.

She shattered, but the pleasure built again instantly as he continued to plunge into her, the brutal waves thrusting her back into the storm. He gripped her hips, his grunts of fulfilment joining her cries as the tempest battered them both. But when she peaked again, and crashed over, she didn't just feel different any more, she felt fundamentally changed, in a way she wasn't sure she would ever be able to un-change.

And he was the cause.

She had glimpsed the ruthlessly guarded man who lurked behind Roman Garner's billionaire playboy exterior and she felt connected to him. Connected enough to want to know more about that man. To be fascinated by his secrets. Even though she already suspected he would never reveal them to anyone, including her.

'Hey, can I see the sketch?' Roman asked, dragging the sweaty hair back from Milly's brow as they lay sprawled on the bed.

She glanced up at him, and sent him an easy smile, but he could see the wariness in her eyes. And felt the tension he'd caused snapping in the air.

He'd messed up, nearly blurting out the truth about him and Brandon Cade, after she'd asked an innocent question. Why had he told her so much? He needed to be careful now, or this fling would get more complicated... And it already felt complicated enough. Because in the last week, things hadn't gone according to plan. This was never meant to be more than a casual hook-up, diverting and fun for them both...

But he had started to enjoy her company, too much. And not just in bed.

Showing Milly Devlin her passion and then exploiting it had been intoxicating. But more than that, her smile, her laugh, her challenging provocative nature and her passion for her work had begun to captivate him, too... So much so, he'd almost told her something virtually no one else knew. Only his mother and his father, and they were both long dead. And Brandon Cade.

Eventually, she'd find out his business rivalry with her brother-in-law was acrimonious, and he was okay with that. But where the hell had that irrational reaction come from when she'd mentioned his half-brother's name? The man was married to her sister, and this was the first time in nearly a week Cade's name had even been mentioned.

But even so, the fierce sense of something that had felt a lot like jealousy had made him want to brand her as his. In the only way he knew how.

And as a result, he'd let her see a part of himself—a desperate, wild, possessive part of himself—he'd never shown to any other woman. Never even felt for any other woman, which could not be good.

'Yes, of course, you can see the sketch,' she said. But as she lifted herself off him, to get the pad she'd left on the other side of the room, uneasiness engulfed him and he grasped her wrist.

'Hey, I'm sorry,' he said, watching her like a hawk. He hadn't intended for things to get heavy, had promised her from the outset that neither one of them would get over-invested. So why did it feel as if he'd slipped into something deeper than he had intended with her? That this wasn't just about sex any more?

'What for?' she asked, with a puzzled frown.

Her artlessness had captivated him right from the start, because it was juxtaposed with that feisty independence... But now it just made the uneasiness settle like a lead weight in his gut. However smart and provocative she was, however ready to stand her ground, however unfazed by his demands, she was vulnerable, and innocent. Because he was the first man who had ever discovered her passion— and exploited it.

But where had the desire come from to be the *only* man ever to exploit it...?

He cut off the thought before it could take root. And forced himself to say what needed to be said. 'I was kind of rough.'

Her smile became quizzical.

'Were you?' she said. She settled back onto the bed, and

folded her arms across his chest, then sent him a saucy grin. 'Well, it was super-hot, so no apology required.'

He let out a strained laugh, trying to see the funny side of it, too. But he couldn't, quite. Hell, she had no idea who he really was.

Not only did she not know how much he despised her sister's husband—a man who, for some unknown reason, she appeared to admire—she also didn't know how easy it had been for him to consider using her when he'd first found out about her connection to Brandon Cade.

He had jettisoned that plan before they'd slept together, but why then did the thought of having to let her go in a week—and return to his business—feel so hard? He'd enjoyed her company, sure, and the incredible chemistry they shared, and her livewire response to all his caresses. He had even loved watching her draw, because of the enthusiasm she threw into her work and the little frown of concentration on her forehead, which was so damn sexy. He'd hated posing for her—especially once he'd got it into his head, as she studied him so intently, she might be able to see more than he wanted her to see—but he'd even been conflicted about that. Because having her focus on him had also made him feel weirdly vindicated.

It was all so confusing. Especially as now he didn't even have the excuse of being burnt out—because over the past week he'd slept more deeply than he had in years, because she was curled up beside him, so trusting, so content, fitting so perfectly into his arms.

He'd definitely got his mojo back. But he wasn't looking forward to leaving the island, because it would mean leaving her.

He tried to shake off the melancholy thought, which had started to bother him more and more as the days had gone by. He'd always been a loner, so it made no sense. Especially as he'd gone out of his way not to deepen this relationship, not to let her see more of him.

Until that moment, twenty minutes ago, when she'd looked at him with that captivating combination of innocence and curiosity in her eyes, and questioned him about Cade...

He patted her bottom, desperately trying to make things light, and shallow, again. And get back to the sexy sparring of before, despite the weight pushing on his chest.

'Okay, go get the sketch, then,' he said.

She bounced off the bed, gloriously unselfconscious as she retrieved the sketch. She handed him the pad. And snuggled back against his side.

But his fingers tensed as he got his first glimpse of her work. He stared, the weight dropping into his stomach like a stone.

How had she captured him so perfectly? He could see the tension in his muscles, the struggle to remain aloof and indifferent in the stiff lines of his body. But what stunned him even more was how she had captured the wariness in his eyes. Because in that expression, he didn't see the man he had worked so hard to become. The confident, arrogant, cynical playboy... Instead, he saw the guarded, needy, resentful boy he'd left behind long ago. The little bastard who had changed his name and worked his backside off for years, taking insane risks to make his mark—and best the half-brother who had made it clear, the one time he'd met him, he didn't even care he existed.

The blip in his heart rate soared.

'What do you think?' she asked softly.

She was watching him intently, but the caution in her

eyes told him his opinion mattered, and, strangely, he couldn't find the strength to lie.

'It's good, but it's not what I expected,' he murmured.

'How so?' she asked, the compassionate expression disturbing him even more.

How could she see that kid? When he'd kept him hidden so successfully, for so long?

He flipped the cover over the sketchbook, dropped it on the bed. 'It's just… It's weird, it's like you can see who I was, not who I am now. I'm not sure I like it. Because that kid is long gone.' He'd made sure of it. 'And good riddance.'

What was he so afraid of? Even if she had seen who he was, she couldn't make him go back there, couldn't resurrect that angry boy.

He rolled over, trapping her beneath him, letting her feel the hard length. Wanting her to know this could never be about anything other than sex. Because she wouldn't want that boy, no one had.

But her curious, compassionate smile didn't falter.

'Who were you?' she asked. 'And why do you dislike that boy so much?'

He could have deflected the question, could have simply refused to answer it. After all, he'd never had a problem avoiding questions he didn't want to answer before. But something she'd said about her own childhood had niggled at him all week. And he couldn't shake the strange conviction she would understand that boy. And forgive him, in a way Roman had never been able to.

'Because that kid was a nobody, and a born loser,' he said, flatly.

'Oh, Roman.' She cupped his cheek, traced the line of his lips. He bit into her thumb, suddenly needing the sexual heat to ease the tension in his gut. But while her expression darkened, the sympathy didn't budge.

'Why would you think that?' she asked. 'No one's born a loser. And certainly not you.'

'You think?' he said, then rolled off her and flopped onto his back. He stared at the ceiling fan, of the villa he'd rebuilt, felt the warm breeze from the cove he owned, and the whisper of afterglow still lodged in his gut from the best sex of his life, which he'd indulged in to his heart's content for seven days straight...

'You really wanna know? I'll tell you exactly why that kid was such a loser...' he said as the resentment surged all over again.

Because he couldn't destroy the feeling that there was something he needed, something he wanted, but something he could never have.

'My old man didn't want me,' he confessed, the old bitterness curdling in his stomach.

Of course, his half-brother hadn't wanted him either, but he had no intention of cluing her in to the identity of the legacy he'd fought so hard for, or she would know exactly how pathetic he had once been—because begging Brandon Cade for a job as a clueless kid had definitely been his lowest point.

'How do you know that?' Milly asked, her incredulous voice tempting him away from the bitterest memory of his adolescence.

He glanced her way, and the weight in his gut twisted. Damn, she really was clueless about how the world worked. Even if her own father had rejected her, too. Perhaps it was time to set her straight, and tell her the whole sordid story, so he could lift this weight once and for all.

'My mum became his mistress when she was still a

teenager.' He shrugged. 'Eventually, he got her pregnant. He was furious and gave her the money to get rid of the problem.' If he told her the shame he had lived with for so long, the truth would have no power over him any more. 'But she wouldn't have a termination—because she had some stupid idea she loved him and if she had his child, he would marry her. She was pretty naïve about men. So, of course, he dumped her and she was left destitute, with a kid she couldn't afford, and eventually couldn't cope with.' Because he'd taken so much of his anger and resentment out on her. 'If that's not being born a loser. I don't know what is.'

'It sounds to me like your father was the loser. Not you,' Milly said softly, feeling sick at what Roman had told her. And the way in which he'd said it, as if he were talking about another person. In another life. She supposed, in some ways, he was.

She understood now, where his drive and ambition came from.

He turned to stare at her, but then his lips curved in the cynical smile she remembered from when they had first met, but she hadn't seen in a while.

'He wasn't my father…he was just a sperm donor. I never even met the guy.'

'How can you be sure, then, that he wanted your mother to get an abortion?' she asked, her heart breaking for the child who had been led to believe he didn't matter.

'Because my mum told me,' he said simply, as if it weren't a big deal.

Milly stared at him, horrified. 'But that's… That's dreadful. She shouldn't have done that.'

The cynical smile spread, becoming almost pitying.

And her heart broke even more, not just for the boy he'd been, but also for the man. She already knew he didn't believe in love. Because he'd said as much when they'd embarked on this two-week fling. But it seemed his cynicism was more ingrained than she'd realised.

'Why shouldn't she have, when it was the truth?' he asked.

'Because no child should be told something like that,' she said, disturbed by how easily he had accepted his mother's actions—and she suspected internalised that hurt. Or how could he seem so blasé about it now?

'You don't know what a pain in the backside I was as a kid,' he said ruefully. 'I resented how we had to live, the guys she would bring home to keep her company. I bunked off school, got into trouble with the law when I was still barely a teenager... I made her life hell. And she was sick of it. I guess she wanted me to know what she had given up to have me...'

'That's beside the point,' she cut in, imagining him as a child, and how the rough upbringing he had described must have limited his opportunities. How had he triumphed over that?

'My dad left us when Lacey and I were still little,' she said. 'And he never wanted visitation rights. Because he was only interested in his new family. But my mother went out of her way to let us know that his actions had no bearing on who we were, or what we did. I think it's a shame your mother made you think that circumstances that occurred before you were even born were somehow your fault.'

He tucked a knuckle under her chin, drew her face up to his. 'That's cute,' he murmured, the mocking tone deliberate, but the cynicism had lost that hard edge when he added, 'But you don't have to defend that little bastard. Because he doesn't exist any more.'

Except he does, she thought as he pressed his lips to hers. The kiss went from casual to carnal in a heartbeat, as the passion flared anew. But as he caressed her in ways he knew would drive her wild, and the intoxicating sensation spread, emotion wrapped around her ribs and squeezed.

She cradled his cheeks, drew his face to hers. But in those deep green eyes she could still see the wary tension alongside the fierce desire.

The boy was still there, inside the man. Scared to love, scared to be vulnerable, because he had once been told he didn't matter, by someone who should have protected him—the way her mother had always protected her.

She clung onto that thought as they made love again. And afterwards, as Roman slept beside her, his face relaxed in sleep, she knew she would be wrong to believe she could change him. She couldn't undo his past, nor could she make this relationship last, but at the same time she wanted him to know he mattered to her. And he always would.

He'd given her the opportunity to find herself and her passion—not just for her art, but also for her future—in this brief interlude… She was so much more optimistic now about her goals, and her ability to achieve them, but she was also so much more confident now about who she was as a woman. And he'd given her all that.

It seemed only fair for her to find a way to return the favour.

CHAPTER SEVEN

'MILLY, WHY DON'T you come to New York with me this weekend instead of heading back to Genoa?'

Milly glanced up from the delicious *pansoti* pasta in nut sauce Giuliana had made for their evening meal, which she'd been playing with for the last twenty minutes. To-morrow they were leaving the island, so this was their last night together, and she'd had a hard time eating anything. The regret that she had kept so carefully in check for days starting to strangle her.

But had she just heard him correctly? That he didn't want this to end?

'I've got a place on the Upper West Side and I have to be there for a board meeting on Monday,' Roman added, the easy smile making hope surge in her heart. 'Plus, there's a ton of great art galleries in Manhattan that you could show your work to.'

'Really?' she asked, a little breathlessly, the hope all but choking her. 'You want me to come to New York with you?'

The last week had shot by even faster than their first. But ever since Roman had told her a little about his child-hood, and they'd shared that rare moment of connection, things had changed between them. Even their lovemak-ing had become more intense, something she wouldn't have believed possible. Her feelings had been so crisp, so clear, but also so close to the surface. Her passion for her work and the time she got to spend with Roman had made her feel more alive and seen than she had ever felt before in her life.

But the growing feeling of intimacy between them— every time they made love, every time he looked at her as if he wanted to say more, every time he challenged her and provoked her and seemed to revel in her reaction— had begun to torture her, too. Because she'd been forced to hold back, to swallow her needs and desires, determined not to ask for more, when she had already been given so much. Determined not even to acknowledge to herself she *wanted* more, because it would devastate her if he said no. And always aware she had begun to invest much more in this relationship than she should have already.

They had never spoken about anything to do with his childhood—or hers—again.

She suspected he had instantly regretted revealing so much. Because when she'd probed again, she had been met with a brick wall.

She had forced herself not to let it upset her. Had even convinced herself it was for the best. She needed to protect herself now. Because it would be far too easy to fall in love with this hot, taciturn, charming and devastatingly fascinating man. And she already knew that would be bad.

But now he was offering her a lifeline and it was hard not to feel elated. *Could* there be more? If they had the time to develop it?

'Sure,' he said. 'I still like having you around.'

She made herself breathe. And crush the bubble of hope. His easy answer and casual expression made her feel embarrassed about the surge of excitement.

Roman wasn't offering anything more than he already had... And while it would be so easy to say yes to him, unlike him, she had become a lot more emotionally invested. She needed to be cautious. She mustn't allow any romantic notions—which had been given far too much oxygen already in the past fortnight of great sex and even better companionship—to blind her to what was. Or what could be.

'How long are you going to be in New York?' she asked, to give herself a chance to calm down and get what he was saying into perspective.

'Couple of weeks,' he said, then reached out to thread his fingers through hers. 'I could show you the sights, in between bouts of enthusiastic sex—because we do that so well,' he added, with that seductive grin that always turned her insides to mush. 'And you could paint in my apartment, while I'm getting back into the swing of stuff at Garner's New York offices. It's a great space, full of light. You'll love it.'

She tugged her fingers out of his. Hopelessly tempted. But also stupidly disappointed. It sounded as if he'd thought about his offer quite a lot. But why had he sprung it on her on their last night together? When she'd been looking for something—*anything*—from him for over a week?

The obvious answer was staring her in the face. He'd made his offer at the last possible moment because he wanted to keep it casual. To keep it light. To make sure she didn't think he was offering more than an extension of their fling.

Roman wasn't offering her a commitment here. And while she would love to spend more time with him, she needed a bit more than 'I still like having you around' to uproot her life in Italy—completely. Her two shift managers in Genoa—at the restaurant by the quay and on the tour boat—had been okay with her taking a couple of weeks out of the rota, but she would risk losing both jobs if she asked for more time off.

She also had a commitment in Wiltshire this weekend that she couldn't shake. Plus she only had enough money saved to get there and back before she would have to throw herself into her two 'not-menial' jobs again to make ends meet.

'I—I can't,' she said. She hated that this would have to be the end. But she would be setting Future Milly up for heartache if she allowed Present Increasingly Deluded Milly to believe Roman was offering her more than he actually was.

'Why not?' he asked, still with that easy smile on his face.

There were so many things she could say to that… But every one of them would expose how over-invested she had already become—and she didn't want to make this emotionally messy, for either one of them. So she fell back on a practical answer he would understand.

'I have to go to my nephew Artie's christening in Wiltshire on Saturday. Lacey and Brandon are expecting me. And my niece, Ruby, will be devastated if I don't show up. She's not adjusting all that well to having a baby brother, by all accounts.'

Something flickered in his eyes that she'd seen before and still didn't understand at the mention of Brandon's name. Something hard and flat and remote. But then his lips curved again. And something sparked in the deep green depths. Something exciting.

'I know, how about I come with you? As your date. Then we could take the jet to New York from the UK on

Sunday. It's in London at the moment anyway, so I would have had to stop over there.'

'You... You want to come with me to the christening?' Her heart leapt in her chest. The suggestion still seemed casual, but how could it be?

Roman wanted them to go to her family event as a couple? This felt huge, and significant somehow... A step towards something more than just a casual fling. And she would love to have him there. She hadn't said anything to Lacey about where she had been and who she had been with for the past fortnight—mostly to cover for the white lie she'd told her sister when she'd first arrived on Roman's island. But she would love Lacey to meet him. Her big sister would probably have a cow, on one level, because she had always been far too overprotective. But once she met Roman and discovered how happy he made her, Milly knew her sister would be supportive, especially when Milly told her how Roman had encouraged her work.

The bubble of hope expanded.

'Are you sure?' she asked again. 'It won't feel awkward? Given that you said yourself you and Brandon are business rivals?'

She had no idea what that actually meant, seeing as she'd never taken any interest in her brother-in-law's business, but she didn't want to put Roman on the spot—or Brandon, for that matter. And she'd got the distinct impression from the way he'd reacted to the mention of her brother-in-law's name last week there might be more to their rivalry than she knew about. What if they had gone after the same media property, and had some kind of billionaire face-off over it? Perhaps the fact Roman's company had offered Lacey a job when Brandon and Lacey had first married had rankled, although that seemed a bit far-fetched. Would that be enough to make things difficult if he came to the christening?

Roman's cheek tensed, but he barely blinked before saying, 'I've never actually met your brother-in-law face to face. There's not a lot of cross-over between our two organisations—Cade Inc specialises in hard news, while Garner Media is all about entertainment and celebrity journalism. We're only really business rivals insofar as we run in the same general field.' He grasped her hand, threaded his fingers through hers again and lifted them to his lips. 'But if you think they might object to me attending, I can always just come get you when you're ready to leave.'

She smiled, flattered—and hopelessly encouraged—by the tension in his jaw as he waited for her answer.

He wanted to meet her relatives, but he was also being sensitive to her needs. How wonderful was that?

'No, don't be silly.' This answer was at least easy. While Brandon and Lacey would no doubt be astonished when she turned up with Roman Garner, no way would they make things uncomfortable for her or him. Because they loved her. 'Brandon is always adamant about making sure his business interests don't interfere with his family time. And I'm sure Lacey will want to meet you, once I tell her what I've been doing for the last fortnight!' she continued, her confidence building.

She wasn't getting ahead of herself. This was still just an exciting fling. Neither of them had committed to more than that, and she was good with that. But getting to spend two more weeks enjoying their time together—in New York, no less—and getting more time to paint, and discover more about this fascinating man, this time with her family's approval, was surely worth the risk? Plus, one thing her time with Roman had also proved was that she needed to make the leap now and start investing more in her career goals. She could take him up on his suggestion of approaching the galleries in New York with her portfolio to see if she could get a showing. And then she wouldn't need to return to her jobs in Genoa, when this ended... *If* it ended, her heart whispered.

'Great, so it's a date,' Roman said as he stood and dragged her out of her chair.

He wrapped his arms around her waist and pulled her against him, so she could feel how much he wanted her.

Her exhilaration surged as she wriggled her hips against the ridge in his pants—to tease and tempt and make him want her more.

'If you don't stop that... I may have to make you beg again, all night,' he murmured, dropping his forehead to hers and sinking his hands beneath the waistband of her shorts, to caress her bottom. 'And then you'll be walking funny when I meet your sister.'

Laughing, she grasped his shoulders and jumped into his arms.

He caught her instinctively—the provocative look in his eyes as captivating as the confidence swelling in her chest.

'Give it your best shot,' she said, nibbling kisses across his chin, his cheek, his jaw, and settling on the pulse point under his earlobe she knew was particularly sensitive. 'But by Saturday, I'm betting you'll be the one walking funny, not me.'

He marched with her into their bedroom, chuckling now too.

'Challenge accepted!' he declared, tossing her onto the bed.

CHAPTER EIGHT

WHAT WERE YOU THINKING, coming here?

Roman's insides clenched, the sick feeling in his gut threatening to push into his throat, as the Garner helicopter approached the sprawling Wiltshire estate that had once belonged to Alfred Cade, aka the sperm donor. And now belonged to Brandon Cade, the half-brother who had disowned him.

The Palladian mansion where the Cade family had lived for five generations came into view over the rolling downs, its formal gardens like a canvas framing the imposing sixty-room building of pale stone and antique glass.

'We have permission to land, Mr Garner,' the pilot's voice barked over the headset.

'Thanks, Brian,' he answered.

Milly grinned opposite him, wearing the same borrowed designer gown he remembered from their first night on his boat.

'I told you Lacey would arrange it,' she shouted over the sound of the bird's blades.

The glittery fabric clung to her perfect breasts. And the hunger, which was never sated, went some way to obliterating the needy, angry tension that had been cramping his stomach muscles ever since he'd overheard her on the phone to her sister that morning in his London penthouse.

He'd heard the excitement in her voice, seen the anticipation in her eyes, when she'd been updating Lacey Cade on the 'date' she was bringing to Arthur Cade's christening this afternoon—which was threatening to be the biggest social event of the season—and Roman had felt like a total fraud.

Because she didn't know why he'd really wanted to come here. With her.

But as the chopper settled on the large H cut into the lawn on the far side of the mansion, the truth was he wasn't even sure himself why he'd suggested it two days ago on Estiva any more.

Part of it had been panic, because he'd known for at least a week he wasn't ready to let Milly go, had already envisioned all the things he wanted to do with her in New York. When she'd mentioned the event, it had given him pause for a moment. Brandon Cade was a part of his past he did not want to dwell on any more. And was certainly a complication when it came to his liaison with Milly. But he'd never been good at subterfuge, and as soon as he'd thought of inviting himself to the event, it had seemed like a good solution.

Why not present him and Milly to Cade as a *fait accompli*? What could the guy say anyway? Seeing as Cade had never acknowledged their connection, he could hardly make an issue of it now. And he was unlikely to do it in front of his wife and family, because Roman was, and had always been, the Cade family's dirty secret. And these days he was more than happy for it to stay that way. Although Cade didn't need to know that. The thought of having the opportunity to shove his success and influence in the man's face, to let him know he was dating his sister-in-law and there wasn't one damn thing he could do about it, had felt cathartic and right in that moment. And afterwards, he'd made love to Milly and believed he was staking a claim, not just to her body, but her affection, too.

He knew she'd started to have feelings for him. He could see it in those expressive eyes, every time she challenged him, and every time she fell apart in his arms.

Hell, he'd started to have feelings for her, too. Why deny it? She was beautiful and talented and more captivating and challenging than any woman he'd ever met.

But as Milly tore off her headset, and hopped out of her seat, and he watched the Cade family—Milly's sister and his brother, with two young kids in tow—head across the lawn in their finery to greet them, he couldn't seem to shift the tension in his gut. And the shame and anger that came with it.

He'd never been here before. But he'd seen pictures of the ancestral home, and made himself ill with both longing and envy as a kid, because Brandon Cade had everything—while he and his mother had nothing.

He'd met Brandon Cade only once, when he'd managed to blag his way into Cade Tower on the Thames and begged the guy for a job, *any* job, age sixteen, full of misplaced pride and ambition. And been summarily dismissed before being manhandled out of the building and literally thrown onto the street outside.

He'd thought he'd got over that rejection a long time ago. But now, as he watched Cade approach—with a little girl in his arms, who clung to his neck with thrusting affection—the tension in his stomach lodged in his throat.

His half-brother had filled out some since that day sixteen years ago. He hadn't actually been much older than Roman at the time, having inherited Cade Inc as a teenager. They were the same height now, virtually the same build, and he already knew they had the same colour eyes.

This moment was supposed to be good for him. A chance to finally throw off the shackles of his past, and get over the crappy hand he'd been dealt by Alfred and Brandon Cade. By making the guy eat the decision he'd made all those years ago, not to give Roman a chance. By showing him once and for all he didn't care about what he'd been denied.

So why did his stomach feel as if it were being tied into tight, greasy knots? And where was the hot flush of guilt coming from? It was making him feel like an interloper, like the feral kid he remembered, always on the outside looking in.

But he knew why, as Milly grasped his hand and tugged him down the helicopter's steps. As always, she had been completely transparent in the past two days, her excitement like that of an eager puppy who had no idea she could be kicked in the teeth at any moment.

'Come on, Roman,' she called above the whir of the slowing blades. 'We're going to meet my family and there will be no shop talk, promise.'

'Sure,' he murmured, doubting very much Cade would wish to speak to him at all.

Letting go of his hand once they reached the grass, Milly rushed to her sister and hugged her, around the baby she held, then she scooped the small bundle out of her sister's arms and cuddled it. Her niece bounced in her father's arms. So Milly gave the baby back and greeted the little girl next. Brandon Cade was frowning at him, and watching him, but Roman couldn't seem to concentrate on the man, or his reaction to him, because all he could see was Milly with the child. Cade's child. And everything inside him clutched tighter.

Envy, sharp and strong, twisted in his gut, right alongside the shame and guilt and anger. Because as they all stood there together, they were a family.

A family he should want no part of... But apparently some of that needy boy still lingered inside him. Because as Milly walked towards him across the grass, the little girl holding her hand and staring at him with wide green eyes, not unlike his own, the sick feeling morphed into an intense sense of longing he didn't understand.

'Roman, I want you to meet my niece, Ruby.' Milly grinned at the child, the smile on Milly's face full of the beauty he had gorged on for days. But never seemed to get enough of. 'Ruby, meet Roman, my...umm.' A beguiling blush lit Milly's cheeks as she hesitated over how to refer to him, her eyes full of that intoxicating combination of awareness and innocence. 'My new friend.'

Nice catch, he thought, at exactly the same time as he found himself wanting her to claim him as much more than just a friend.

'Hello, Row-mam,' the little girl said, mangling his name and forcing his attention back to her. Then she dropped her head to one side, studying him with a focus that stunned him.

He knew nothing about kids, had barely ever been one himself. But something about the perceptive way she was staring at him made him feel supremely uncomfortable. As if she could see all his lies.

'Hey, Ruby,' he managed, not sure how you addressed a child.

'I like you,' she said, sending him a gap-toothed grin. 'You look like my daddy.'

He blinked, and stiffened, so shocked by the child's bold statement, and the way it made him feel—angry and bitter, but also ashamed, for inviting himself into this family without ever belonging here.

'Actually, now you mention it, they do look a bit alike, don't they?' Milly said, still smiling, still happy, still unaware of the house of cards she'd built around the man she thought he was.

But just as he was coming to terms with how not good he felt about being here, Cade stepped forward.

Roman braced himself for Cade to destroy his relationship with his sister-in-law—because Roman had been fool enough to give him all the power, again—but instead, he offered Roman his hand.

Roman stared at it, dumbly, not sure what was happening now.

'Hello, Garner,' Cade said, with an edge in his voice. He wasn't happy to have Roman here, clearly, but he was going to play nice in front of his family.

Which was good. Wasn't it?

Roman shook his hand, surprised to find his brother's grip firm, but completely astonished when Cade added, 'You're welcome in our home. My wife tells me we are not to come to blows over the Drystar acquisition,' he said dryly, mentioning the takeover Roman had deliberately engineered eighteen months ago—when the chance to frustrate Cade Inc's business plans and expose him as a deadbeat dad had been irresistible. But then Cade added: 'Although all bets are off regarding my sister-in-law...' The warning in his tone was unmistakeable. 'Because Milly is very precious to us.'

Roman gave a curt nod—the anger rising up his throat again, to dispel at least some of his confusion.

Where did the son of Alfred Cade get off, portraying himself as a protector of women?

'She's precious to me, too,' he murmured as he disengaged his hand from Cade's intimidating grip.

But it was only as he followed the Cades and Milly into the ornate chapel on the grounds and the lavish christening ceremony began, with Milly beaming at him while she fulfilled her role of godmother, that it occurred to him he'd told Cade the truth about his feelings for Milly.

And the fear and shame and confusion threatened to gag him all over again.

'She's precious to me, too.'

Milly could feel her heart floating as she ran the words Roman had uttered over two hours ago through her head again, while trying to spot her date amid the cluster of three hundred carefully selected guests at the 'intimate' garden party Lacey had arranged to follow Artie's christening.

Roman had sounded almost grudging when he'd said it—and there was definitely tension between him and Brandon, which she had decided was basically a mutual respect kind of a thing—but somehow the tight look on his face had only made the comment more meaningful. And more perfect.

Roman was not a man who flaunted his emotions. In fact, she was fairly sure he'd convinced himself a long time ago he didn't have emotions. So, hearing him say she mattered, especially to Brandon, who had set himself up as her father figure ever since he'd rescued her and Lacey and Ruby from the press intrusion that had dogged the early part of her sister's marriage, felt so much more significant.

As with all the Cades' social events, the eclectic crowd ranged from the families of Ruby's schoolfriends at the local primary she attended in Hackney, to valued members of the estate staff, and A-list film stars, politicians

and assorted movers and shakers that Brandon did business with on a regular basis.

She grinned as she finally located Roman across the
gardens, talking to a junior government minister, who he
probably knew too, she thought proudly. His head lifted,
his gaze locking on hers, as if he had sensed her watching
him. The frission of sexual energy ricocheted through her
body, the desire to be near him drawing her like a physical force.

'It's lovely to see you again, Mrs Ettock, don't forget to
try the rhubarb fool, it's delicious,' Milly said, forcing her
gaze back to the elderly retired lady she had been chat-
ting to, who had been one of Brandon's many governesses,
apparently. The woman was a font of knowledge about
childcare, but Milly just wanted to say her goodbyes now
to everyone, and leave with Roman—so she could bask
in the words he had said to Brandon earlier while also indulging that hot look in his eyes.

He'd seemed uncomfortable ever since they'd arrived,
maybe even before they'd landed. From what he'd told
her about his past, she suspected he wasn't used to family
gatherings of any sort, even big social occasions like this
one. Plus, they'd barely been able to talk, let alone touch,
because of her chapel duties as Arthur's godmother during the afternoon, and then her hosting responsibilities as
Lacey's sister as evening approached.

There had also been that strange moment when Ruby
had noticed his resemblance to Brandon. Odd that Milly
hadn't noticed that herself—clearly the unusual green
shade of Brandon's irises, which he shared with his daughter, was more common than Milly thought, but the fact they
were virtually the same height and similar builds wasn't
that surprising… Then again, how weird was it *really* she

hadn't noticed the vague similarities between the two men, which could only be a freaky coincidence? After all, she'd never been remotely attracted to her sister's husband, probably because nowadays he was like a big brother to her—and at first, he'd been distant and intimidating, which had reminded her rather uncomfortably of her father.

'Do enjoy the rest of the party,' she added to the older woman, before turning her attention back to Roman, who was still watching her, ignoring the junior cabinet minister and sending her 'let's get out of here, right now' vibes strong enough to melt her brain cells—and her panties—from thirty feet.

'I will. And you enjoy your young man, Milly,' Mrs Ettock said, but as Milly lifted the hem of her gown, planning to dart through the crowd and do exactly that, the older woman touched her arm to stay her getaway. 'You know, he reminds me of Alfred.'

'Really? How nice,' Milly said as politely as she could, while trying to stifle her impatience. The old woman was probably talking about her dead husband, whose name Milly could not remember for the life of her.

'Not really, dear,' Mrs Ettock replied, her voice hardening. 'Alfred Cade was a tyrant and a bastard. But Brandon's father was also a handsome devil. And he certainly knew how to make women fall in love with him, the poor things. Although they always lived to regret it, I fear.' The old lady's gaze became clouded with pity, before she headed towards the dessert table.

Leaving Milly stranded in the centre of the crowd, alone and dumbstruck.

Alfred Cade? How was that possible? That Roman looked like Brandon's father?

She'd never seen any photos or pictures of the man,

because by all accounts Brandon did not have any fond memories of him.

Even so, her heartbeat stumbled, a strange void opening in her stomach, which she recognised from over a week ago, when her conversation with Roman had taken that uncomfortable turn when she'd mentioned Brandon.

She was still standing in the middle of the crowd, trying to stifle the uneasy feeling, the sense that something was going on that was definitely not good, when Lacey appeared beside her.

'Milly, I'm so glad I caught you.' Her sister smiled, but there was something concerned and apologetic in her expression, which only increased the weightless, unpleasant sensation in Milly's stomach. 'Brandon and I would like to have a quick word with you, in private. In his study.'

'What about?' she asked. She knew that look. It was her sister's *I-don't-want-you-to-get-hurt* look. Milly had seen that look before, when she had been forced to give up her job at the preschool and decided to run off to Europe and become an artist. And way back, when Milly had gone through a bit of a crisis after their mother's death, and the hideous meeting with their father at the funeral—when he had rejected them both.

The look had the same result now as it had then. It made Milly feel defensive and rebellious. Especially when Lacey said, oh-so-cautiously, 'It's about Mr Garner.'

'He's not Mr Garner, Lacey. He's Roman. And I like him. A lot,' she said. And knew it was the truth. No matter what anyone else thought or said.

Mrs Ettock had seemed lucid, but she was old, and could easily be mistaken. Roman probably looked nothing like Brandon's bastard of a father. Why was she getting worked up about any of this?

'So, it would have been helpful if you and Brandon hadn't been quite so stand-offish with him earlier,' she added.

But even as she said it, she knew she wasn't being entirely fair. If anything, Brandon had made a considerable effort not to show Roman any animosity—despite their business rivalry, which she had gathered from the various surprised reactions of the other guests at seeing him here, was more involved than Roman had let on. But when Roman and Brandon had met briefly earlier, there had definitely been an edge to Brandon's welcome, and Roman had picked up on it. Because so had she. Which was probably why Roman wanted to leave early.

'I'm sorry, we were trying not to judge,' Lacey said, her concerned look intensifying—which only upset Milly more. 'But there are things about Roman Garner Brandon wants to make sure you're aware of,' Lacey added. 'Just in case it has a bearing on...' Her sister paused, her expression becoming strained. 'On his decision to date you.'

The surge of defensiveness and anger became a tidal wave. *What the actual...?*

Could Lacey and her brother-in-law actually *be* any more insulting? What were they implying, exactly? That Roman had some ulterior motive for sleeping with her?

'Fine. Terrific,' Milly said through gritted teeth. 'Let's get it over with, then.' She marched past Lacey, striding towards the house, and Brandon's study.

But even as she forced her irritation with her sister and Brandon to the fore, determined not to let them derail her happy glow, she couldn't seem to dispel the sinking feeling in her stomach, and the hideous sense of uncertainty and confusion that she remembered from being that broken teenager, standing in the Golders Green crematorium, convinced she was somehow responsible for her father's indifference.

* * *

Roman stared at the spot where Milly had been standing, sending him hot looks, only moments before, and tuned out the conversation from the government underling who had been boring him senseless for ten minutes. Right now, all he cared about was what Lacey Cade had just said to Milly. Not to mention the old lady she'd been talking to before that.

She'd gone so still. Her body rigid with shock.

Then, when her sister had approached her, she'd glanced his way. He couldn't read her expression from this distance. But the sense of foreboding, ever since they'd boarded the helicopter this morning, had hit critical mass as the sisters had left the garden together.

So what are you doing standing here?

'Take this up with my PA, Geoff,' he murmured, dismissing the underling, before heading through the crowd after them.

He dumped his full glass of champagne on a passing tray as he left the party and entered the estate's impressive gardens. As he strode through the ornate flower beds, the sculpted hedgerows, the late summer twilight starting to fade into night, he paused for a moment, disorientated. He couldn't see Milly. Panic pressed on his chest. But then he spotted the two women, walking past the arched windows of a summer gallery.

He forced himself to follow them through stained-glass doors into the mansion itself.

The place smelled of the fresh flowers artfully arranged in large vases, and new paint. But even so, as he made his way down the long corridor past portraits of people who might well be blood relations, the atmosphere felt oppressive and made the panic and the anger crush his ribs. The priceless antique furnishings and elaborate art made a dire contrast to the places he'd grown up in. The two-room bungalow in Hampstead he barely remembered, which Alfred Cade had rented for his mother before he got bored with her; the damp walls of the council flat where they'd ended up and the increasingly dilapidated homes in between; right up to the tiny bedsit he'd lived in as a teenager after her death. Each home had been more soulless and squalid than the last, until his hard work had begun to pay off.

The centuries-old splendour surrounding him now only reminded him of all the Cades possessed. And the old resentments he'd finally buried eighteen months ago, after making his first billion-dollar deal and acquiring Drystar ahead of Cade Inc to break the story of Brandon Cade's illegitimate kid, rose up his throat again.

He'd had no qualms about breaking that story at the time. And he had no qualms about it now, he thought, even though his stomach churned at the memory of that little girl beside Milly staring at him so guilelessly and stating something her father had always denied.

Finally, he reached a lobby area with a vaulted ceiling. A large winding staircase led to a balcony above, which no doubt led to the other wings of this palace. He forced himself to refocus, and rebuild his anger, to alleviate the crushing pain in his chest.

He caught the sound of voices coming from an open door on the opposite side of the space and walked towards it.

'Please, Milly, don't get upset, okay.' It was her sister's voice. Pleading, conciliatory. 'We're not trying to turn you against Mr Garner, we're just telling you about the source of the stories that came out about Ruby, and me and Brandon.'

'Roman's not responsible for everything the magazines he owns print. That's ridiculous!'

Milly was defending him. Her voice sure, and unwavering. But it only made the tension in his stomach add to the weight in his chest.

How could she be so sure? So certain? Especially as she was wrong about his involvement in that story. And why did he now feel more ashamed of how vociferously he'd had his columnists pursue Cade and his wife and child at the time? He'd had every right to expose the Cades' generational hypocrisy. After all, Brandon Cade had done to that little girl exactly what their father had done to him—denied her existence.

But then came another voice. His brother's voice. Measured and direct, and firm, determined to destroy Roman all over again.

'Milly, you're young. And you're obviously falling for him. He's a charismatic man. Which he uses to his advantage. But believe me when I tell you, from the dealings we've had with Garner Media, Roman Garner is also extremely ruthless. How can you be sure he didn't date you and offer to support your work to get a tactical advantage for his business because of your connection to me?'

Roman felt something snap inside him, making the visceral rage he had made himself bottle geyser up. And he was thrown back to that day when he'd begged that bastard to give him a chance. He'd been too cowed and desperate at the time to use their relationship, but he was damned if he wouldn't use it now—to stop Brandon Cade from trying to prevent him getting what he wanted all over again.

Milly's voice, calm and still so sure of him, poured fuel on the fire of injustice that had burned inside him then too.

'Because I know Roman,' she said. 'He wouldn't do that. He would have told me...'

He marched into the room. Milly turned, her face lighting up when she saw him. He basked in it for one bitter-sweet moment, but then his gaze connected with Cade.

'Well, well, well, isn't this cute?' he said. 'How very bourgeois and entitled of you to assassinate my character without even giving me a right of reply.'

Instead of looking astonished though, or even guilty at the nasty trick he'd tried to pull, Cade tensed his shoulders and the self-righteous glare—which he had no right to whatsoever—intensified.

'Garner. Why am I not surprised to find you sneaking around my house like a bad smell?'

The derogatory statement made the final straw snap on Roman's control.

'Roman, I'm so sorry you heard that,' Milly began. But he couldn't look at her, couldn't let himself be swayed by feelings that didn't make sense and never had.

'Don't be, it's exactly what I expected,' he said, his tone surprisingly measured considering he could feel his rage burning. He was Cade's equal now in every respect and he'd worked like a dog for sixteen years to prove it. But Cade would never accept that. Maybe it was time he made him.

'If you don't want me dating Milly, why don't you at least have the guts to admit the real reason?' he barked, making both women flinch.

But he couldn't see Cade's wife any more, he couldn't even really see Milly—her open, honest, beautiful face something he had come to rely on in the last weeks, to soothe him and excite him and make him ache. All he could see was the man in front of him, who had once stood in the way of everything he wanted, everything he needed, and was doing it again now. With her.

'What the hell is that supposed to mean?' Cade yelled

back, still maintaining the lie this wasn't personal. 'You think I'm not entitled to protect a woman I think of as a sister from the likes of you?'

'You may think of her as a sister, but it's a good thing she's not your actual sister...' The bitterness flowed through his veins on the tsunami of rage, spewing out of his mouth on a wave of righteous fury. 'Because then, me sleeping with her would be kind of incestuous, now, wouldn't it?'

But Cade's reaction was not what he expected. Instead of looking guilty or humiliated the way he was supposed to, his face went blank with shock and confusion. *'What...?'*

'You really don't recognise me, do you?' he said, the bitterness scalding his throat.

The fact Cade hadn't ever figured out who he was only made the man's self-serving destruction of Roman's character in front of Milly that much worse.

'I'm the kid who begged you for a job, sixteen years ago in Cade Tower,' he said, determined to jog the bastard's memory. 'The kid you had thrown out in the gutter by your security guards. The kid who was dumb enough to give you his real name at the time... Dante Rocco. The son of Alicia Rocco, your old man's mistress. The kid you pretended not to know was your old man's bastard. And your half-brother.'

Cade didn't look shocked any more, he looked... What even was that?

But before Roman could gauge the man's reaction, he heard a gasp. And swung round, to find himself staring into Milly's pale face. The rage curdled, and the fog of anger and aggression caused by hurts from long ago cleared, to be replaced by a slice of agonising pain that plunged into his chest as he noticed the glitter of tears in her eyes.

'Roman, I'm… Why didn't you tell me?' she whispered, but there was no accusation in her voice, only sadness and sympathy and regret… And acceptance.

The fear slammed into him again, so much bigger than before. Because nothing mattered now, except her and what she thought of him. And that couldn't be right, because he didn't care what anyone thought of him. *Ever.*

But even as he tried to tell himself that, the guilt and remorse continued to sideswipe him. He turned back to Cade and his wife, who were still staring at him, speechless.

Everything was wrong. This wasn't how this was supposed to go. He'd envisioned this showdown in his mind a thousand times and he was supposed to feel vindicated, assured. Instead, his stomach was in freefall. And he knew he had screwed up. Badly. But he didn't even know how, or why.

As the devastating feeling of being exposed, of being raw, of never being enough closed in around him, he said the only thing he could think of to protect himself. And his pride.

'You'll be glad to know, I'm leaving as soon as my helicopter arrives,' he said to the Cades. Then he forced himself to turn to Milly. 'Come with me or stay here. I don't care that much either way.'

But as he strode out of the room, the heavy silence behind him like a weight bearing down on his soul, and tugged his phone out of his pocket with shaking fingers to text his pilot, he knew he did care. Far too much.

CHAPTER NINE

MILLY STOOD IN the middle of Brandon's study, but felt as if she were floating outside herself. She trembled, trapped in the strange limbo—between sadness and shock and confusion—as the voices of her sister and her brother-in-law drifted around her.

'Do you remember him, Brandon?' Lacey's voice whispered through the numbness.

'Yeah, weirdly, I do remember that kid.' Brandon had collapsed into an armchair, and was running his fingers through his hair, looking more agitated than Milly had ever seen him. 'He made quite an impression. How the hell he had managed to get into the executive suites at Cade Inc, I'll never know as there were three levels of security. But I don't remember asking to have him kicked out.'

'Could what he's saying be true?' Lacey said, sitting beside her husband and pressing her hand to his knee. 'That he's your brother?'

Brandon gripped Lacey's hand, then let out a heavy sigh, the ghosts of a childhood Milly knew he'd spent years dealing with flickering through his expression. 'I never knew the names of any of my father's mistresses, so I never made the connection. But I wouldn't put it past the bastard to deny his own flesh and blood.' He sank his head into his hands. 'No wonder Garner has aways hated me.'

Milly felt the murmured conversation—and what it revealed—like a physical blow.

Roman was Brandon's half-brother. And Alfred Cade was the man who had tried to force his mother to have an abortion. To ensure he didn't exist.

The agony in his face, when he'd turned to her in that moment, made total sense now.

She scrubbed the tears off her cheeks. She had to go to him. She could help him, soothe him, tell him how much he meant to her.

But as she lurched out of her shocked stupor, ready to run after him, Lacey leapt up and grabbed her. 'Milly, where are you going?'

'I'm going after Roman…he's hurting and he needs me.'

But instead of letting her go, her sister grasped her other arm and gave her a subtle shake, the expression on her face full of sadness and sympathy.

'Yes, he is hurting. And what he revealed explains a lot. But you need to stop and think now, Milly. *Think* about why he came here. Why he was dating you. If anything, what we've just discovered about his past makes his motivations for being with you even more suspect.'

Milly shook her head, rejecting her sister's assessment in every aspect of her being. Lacey didn't know what they had shared over the last two and a half weeks, the sweetness, the wicked fun, the laughs, the excitement, the intensity not just of their lovemaking, but the companionship and the confidences they'd shared. She knew now why Roman had seemed so off as soon as they'd arrived. Knew why he had struggled with her close relationship to Brandon.

'You're wrong,' she said simply. 'About him, about us, about everything. You don't know him like I do.'

'Please, Milly, don't do this. He used you, for whatever reason, surely you can see that now?'

'No, he didn't. He wouldn't.' She yanked herself free of Lacey's hold, rejecting the statement categorically. 'I'm a grown woman, and I'm going with him, Lacey. And you can't stop me.'

She rushed out of the room and ran down the corridor towards the gardens and the heliport—her sister's protests fading behind her. Until all she could hear was her heart punching her ribs and her heels landing on the marble floor of the summer gallery.

She would tell Roman she loved him. Everything he was and everything he had been. Right back to that neglected boy, he had taught himself to hate because the people who should have loved and protected him had rejected him.

And everything would be okay.

She finally located him ten minutes later, standing in a gazebo near the exit to the heliport, alone. And waiting... For her.

The buzz of conversation from the party on the other side of the garden walls helped to calm the pulse still thundering in her ears as she tried to calm her breathing.

He stood in the shadows, his body tense, his face lit by the last of the sunlight and the torches that dotted the gardens. His tortured expression made her heart swell.

'Roman,' she called to him, stepping into the gazebo.

His head jerked up, and her heartbeat skipped into overdrive. Joy swept across his harsh handsome features, but it disappeared so swiftly, she wasn't sure if she had imagined it.

'Milly?' He frowned, his expression becoming wary and guarded. 'What are you doing here?'

'Coming with you, of course.'

She wrapped her arms around his waist and tried to smile at him. So sure of her feelings as she hugged him tight, she was surprised her heart didn't burst right out of her chest and land at his feet. She breathed in the delicious scent of salt and sandalwood and man, mixed with the fragrant aroma of jasmine and vanilla from the honeysuckle and clematis climbing the trellis.

But instead of smiling back at her, instead of looking pleased to see she had chosen him, he tensed, then lifted his arms, to dislodge her, and stepped out of her embrace.

'Why?' he said, his hard expression as closed off as the sharp edge in his voice.

She refused to be thwarted though. Or denied. She had to tell him now, how she really felt. No holding back. So he would know. She trusted him. Always. And completely.

'Why? Because I'm falling in love with you, Roman, and I know you would never use me, like they said,' she declared, putting every ounce of her new-found confidence into the words. 'Although there's no pressure,' she added hastily, when his expression barely changed.

Had her declaration been a bit premature? Perhaps she should have kept that to herself? After all, he was hurting. She wanted to be supportive now, not needy.

'I thought you should know, my feelings for you are pretty strong. And I… I still want to come to New York. I'm a little hurt you didn't feel you could tell me about your connection to Brandon. But I want you to know now, you can trust me too. I want us to have fun again. And enjoy each other's company.' She wiggled her eyebrows, desperate all of a sudden to lighten the mood and take that blank look off his face. 'In all our favourite positions.'

But instead of his giving her the hot look she had come

to love, his frown became a scowl, the sceptical expression making the words dry in her throat. Why had his expression tightened even more?

'*Really?* Just like that? You think you love me? And you want me to trust you?' The harsh tone didn't register at first. But the hope died inside her at the irritation in his voice when he spoke again… 'You're pretty naïve, aren't you?'

The cruel words found the insecure and unhappy teenager she'd once been, standing beside her mother's casket as she listened to a man she didn't recognise inform her sister he really didn't have time to be a father to them.

'I'm not naïve, what do you mean?' she managed, around the blockage forming in her throat. The memory of that hideous, humiliating moment as raw and painful now as it had been on that rain-slicked November afternoon.

'You've just told a man you've known for a little over two weeks you love him,' he said. 'I'd call that naïve, sweetheart.'

Sweetheart? Why was he calling her that? When he had never used that generic term before, which now sounded vaguely insulting. And why did she suddenly feel invisible? The way she had the day of her mother's funeral.

She shivered, the summer air chilling.

'Roman, why are you behaving like this?' she asked. Unsure now. And a little scared.

'You want to know what you really love?' The question sounded cynical, but then he cupped her cheek. She leaned instinctively into the caress, his touch possessive and addictive as his thumb stroked her lips. He pressed her back against the trellis, until she sank into the flowers, her body softening for him, yearning for his touch.

'This is what you love, Milly,' he murmured, the tone still harsh, but his touch, so right, so seductive, so perfect.

Cradling her head with one hand, he tilted her face up to suckle the sensitive pulse in her neck. The tsunami of sensation built instantly, uncontrollably, as he dragged up her dress with the other hand, then pressed his palm to her panties, and slipped clever fingers under the waistband.

'So wet for me, aren't you, Milly?' he murmured, still kissing and caressing her, knowing just how to touch her to provoke her response, and make her desperate for more.

Moisture flooded his hand as she bucked against his hold, and he worked the slick, swollen nub with ruthless efficiency.

'Why don't you show me how much you love me, Milly?' he whispered, his voice demanding, and unforgiving.

She rode his hand, panting, sobbing, unable to hold back, even if she'd wanted to. But she didn't want to. This was who they were. This was what they did best. And she loved him for this, too.

'Come for me. Like always,' he demanded.

The climax slammed into her. But as she shuddered through the last of the pleasure he eased his hand out of her panties and let her go.

She stood shaking, her knees trembling and her mind in disarray, the sound of his helicopter approaching becoming as loud as the punch of her heartbeat.

He sucked his fingers. 'Sweet, as always,' he said, the strain in his voice unmistakeable.

But as she reached for him, to cradle the thick ridge she could see in his suit trousers, to make him shatter too, he grasped her wrist and dragged her hand away. 'Don't.'

'Why…? Wh-why not?' she asked, feeling exposed and raw again—and scared, the fear so huge it was choking her.

'Don't you get it? That's all we ever had, Milly. You

don't love me…you just love the sex.' She thought she heard regret in his voice, but even as she tried to hold onto it his expression became distant and intractable.

She felt the chill right down to her bones when he shouted over the deafening hum of the helicopter landing. 'It was nice while it lasted, sweetheart. But all good things come to an end.'

He marched past her, heading through the garden exit towards the heliport. And she let him go. The desire to be seen, to be loved in return, morphed into the hideous kiss of pain. And humiliation, his intoxicating touch still reverberating in her sex.

She steeled herself against the brutal yearning, and wrapped her arms around her waist, to hold back the agony of loss as he disappeared through the gate.

But the tears streaked down her face regardless because, this time, the rejection hurt so much more.

As she watched the big bird lift into the sunset with a deafening roar, flattening the dress against her too sensitive skin, the sadness and emptiness swept through her on another wave of pain. And the questions that had battered her as a rebellious teenager shattered her all over again.

Why was she not enough? Why was she *never* enough?

She had opened her heart to Roman Garner. And he was wrong, she *had* fallen in love with him. This wasn't just about sex, not for her. But he'd thrown her love back in her face.

Silent sobs wracked her body as she finally acknowledged the brutal reality.

Lacey had been right all along. Roman *had* been using her.

She had thrown herself at him, like a fool. But he hadn't wanted her love, hadn't really respected or cared for her.

The connection she'd convinced herself they shared had all been in her head. All he'd wanted was the sex, and the chance to confront Brandon in his own home.

He was a ruthless, cynical man. Probably because he'd had to be, from a very young age. But while she felt so much compassion for the boy, she had to cauterise her feelings for the man.

Because she knew now, he would never have been able to love her back. Nor did he want to. Not at all.

CHAPTER TEN

One week later

ROMAN GARNER STOOD at the floor-to-ceiling window of his executive office in the Garner Building and stared down at the River Thames as it wound through the City of London thirty-two floors below. A light summer rain was falling, obscuring the stunning view he'd worked his ass off to earn. But it didn't really matter, because nothing seemed to matter any more.

He felt like crap.

He'd cancelled the trip to New York he'd planned to take with Milly, not able to face the loft apartment—or dealing with the thousand and one things he'd left hanging in the US for over a month—without having Milly there with him, the way he'd imagined.

Without her vibrant personality brightening up the soulless concrete and steel design, and the empty spaces in his heart—which he hadn't even known were there until he'd met her.

He raked his hand through his hair. And cursed under his breath.

How come he could still smell her? That intoxicating aroma of sex and flowers with the slight hint of turpentine from her art that had driven him wild on Estiva and made him want her, always. And how come he could still see the devastation on her face, when he'd walked away from her that evening in Wiltshire, after shooting everything to hell, deliberately?

He'd done her a favour, damn it. Done them *both* a favour. He had nothing to offer her. Or any woman. He never had. Never would.

He'd always been broken. He could see it with such clarity now. He'd always shied away from commitment, from intimacy, for a very good reason. It was way too much trouble. And offered way too much opportunity to get hurt the way he'd been hurt as a boy. And he was right about the romantic declaration of love she'd thrown at him out of nowhere. She didn't love him, she didn't even know him, not really. They'd had two glorious weeks of sex and sparring, shared a few half-hearted home truths. That was all. And however jaded and tough and independent she thought she was, she had no idea how the real world worked. Or she wouldn't have fallen for a man like him, decided to trust him, so easily.

But even if all the rational arguments, the qualifications and explanations for the way he'd deliberately used and humiliated her made total sense in his head—because he'd done it for her own good—he couldn't seem to come to terms with the thought of never seeing her again. Never touching her or having her wake up warm and willing in his arms. Never being able to tease or tempt her, or watch her paint as if her life depended on it… And he couldn't lose the scent of her in his nostrils. Like a phantom, torturing him, making him hard and ready when he woke up sweaty and yearning for her in the night.

He couldn't sleep now, couldn't eat, couldn't even throw himself into work because he didn't care about any of it any more. He felt more exhausted now than he had while he was struggling with the burn-out.

And worst of all, he couldn't forget her—not her forthright, snarky, endlessly funny and challenging personality, not her succulent, seductive, responsive body, or her open, generous and honest heart.

He missed her, so much. And he was scared that would never change.

Not so much because of the stupendous chemistry they shared, or all the ways she had lit up his life—energising and invigorating him and making every single day seem richer and better and more exciting than the last—but also the way she had stuck by him.

Because no one had ever done that before. Not unless he was paying them.

She'd stood up to her family on his behalf, and made him want more. In the end, it had terrified him enough to make him determined to push her away as soon as he'd left Cade's study.

Why, then, did he keep reliving the moment she'd told him she loved him? The way she'd hugged him and held him, when he'd needed it the most. In those raw, visceral, terrifying moments after he'd finally slammed Cade with the truth... And realised the guy had *never* known who he was.

And why did some daft part of his heart want to believe that declaration still?

Because thinking about it incessantly was starting to drive him insane.

The intercom on his desk clicked on, and his PA's voice echoed round the office.

'There's a Mr Brandon Cade here demanding to see you, Mr Garner. He has two solicitors with him.'

The name got his attention. And sparked his fury.

He swore again. But the fury died as he strode across the room, feeling weary right down to his bones.

He was too tired to deal with this nonsense now. But he supposed he was going to have to. After all, he'd been waiting for some kind of response to his accusations ever since he'd made them. He hadn't expected Cade to turn up in person. But the legal team didn't surprise him. He was probably going to get served with a lawsuit, now, for having the gall to suggest the Cades' precious blood flowed in his veins.

'He doesn't have an appointment. Shall I insist that he make one?' his PA asked, knowing Roman was not in the mood to see anyone, and hadn't been ever since he'd returned to the office a week ago.

He toyed with the idea of sending Cade packing. It would serve him right for showing up unannounced. But he couldn't even find the energy to despise Brandon Cade any more. Which just went to show how low Milly Devlin had brought him.

He snapped on the intercom. 'No. Send him and his vultures in and hold my calls.'

He might as well get this confrontation over with. After all, everything else had been shot to hell, why not let his half-brother join the feeding frenzy?

Cade entered the office first, wearing a dark, double-breasted designer suit. His gaze was flat and direct, but seemed surprising neutral. Then again, he got the impression Cade wasn't a man of strong emotions, unless his family was involved.

Unlike Roman, apparently.

Roman held out an arm to indicate the sunken seating area in the far corner of the room. 'Take a seat. If you want a drink you'll have to help yourself,' he all but snarled, as a young man and an older woman, also sharply dressed in business attire, followed their boss into the open-plan space, both carrying briefcases.

All the better to screw him over with.

He turned back to the rain-fogged view, the prickle of resentment going some way to cover the cramping emptiness in his stomach.

'I'd prefer to stand, thanks,' Cade said.

'Suit yourself.' Roman threw the remark over his shoulder. 'Say whatever you've come to say, then get out. I've got work to do.'

Which would be true, if he could conjure up the energy to do any of it, but Cade didn't need to know that.

Cade cleared his throat. 'Okay, Roman,' he said. 'I don't blame you for making this difficult. I deserve that.'

The prickle of resentment became a flood at the use of his given name. The condescending bastard.

But then Cade continued. 'I'd like to start by apologising for my father and Cade Inc's appalling behaviour towards you and your mother over the last thirty-two years.'

The words—delivered in a low voice, grave with purpose—didn't register at first, the buzzing in Roman's ears becoming loud and discordant. He swung round, forced to look at the man.

Terrific. Was he having audible delusions now, too?

'What did you say?' he asked. Surely, he hadn't heard *that* correctly. Was this some kind of a trick? To get him to drop his guard?

But Cade's expression didn't look cagey, or surly or combative. It looked one hundred per cent genuine. Reminding him for one agonising moment of Milly again— as if he needed any reminders of her.

'I'm here with the head of my legal team, Marisa Jones,'

Cade continued, indicating the woman with him, who gave Roman a brief nod.

'Hello, Mr Garner, nice to meet you,' she said, as if they were all at a tea party in Buckingham Palace. What the hell?

'I want to make some kind of restitution in the only way I know how.' Cade swallowed, but his gaze remained locked on Roman's. 'It's taken me a week to work out all the details. But I'd like to offer you fifty per cent of the Cade Inc shares and the real estate portfolio I inherited from my father. The property in the will included an island in the Bahamas, estates in New York, Paris and Melbourne and, of course, the ancestral estate in Wiltshire. Take your pick. Although I should probably warn you, our ancestral estate is a total money pit.'

Our?

Roman jolted, certain he was having some kind of massive delusion now brought on by stress and exhaustion... And heartache.

'Is this some kind of a joke, Cade?' he bit out. 'Because I'm not laughing.'

Why was the guy trying to mess with him? Hadn't they already messed with him enough? He and his wife and his cute little daughter, and most of all his sweet, headstrong and unbearably hot and intoxicating sister-in-law?

'Call me Brandon,' the man said, which wasn't a reply. 'After all, you're the only brother I've got.'

Roman swore a blue streak and collapsed into a chair to hold his head, which felt as if it were about to explode. Because now nothing—not one thing in his life—made any sense any more.

Cade took charge, because of course he did, the domineering bastard, ushering out the legal team and pouring Roman a glass of water from the room's bar.

But Roman was only dimly aware of it. His mind reeling, and his emotions—which had always been so steady and predictable up to about three weeks ago, before a certain someone had tried to steal his boat—all over the place again.

He finally ran out of curse words. A glass of chilled water appeared at his elbow.

'I think you'd better drink this,' Cade said. 'You look like you need it.'

'What I need is a double shot of vodka and a Valium,' Roman said, but took the glass and downed the contents in several quick gulps.

It didn't do much for his cartwheeling emotions, or the cramping pain that had now tied his stomach into a knot, but at least it stopped him going for a gold medal in the profanity awards.

'I can see I've shocked you,' Cade began. 'That wasn't my intention. Maybe I shouldn't have come here, but I felt I should speak to you in—'

'Why?' Roman interrupted him. He didn't want excuses or clarifications, or carefully worded apologies three decades after the fact. Nor did he want any part of the Cade legacy, or the Cade money, not any more, because he had his own. But he did want to know what the hell was going on.

'Why would you do this? When you hate my guts?' he added, when Cade seemed nonplussed by the question.

The man blinked, clearly taken aback. 'I never hated you, Roman, even when I just thought you were a business rival. The truth is, I admired you, your bravery and tenacity, even if I did not agree with your methods most of the time, or some of the stories you chose to print.'

He heard the edge he'd noticed before. But it was blunter now, and held no bitterness.

'Just to clarify something,' Cade continued, the edge

softening even more. 'Was that why you were so focussed on outing me as a deadbeat dad? Because you believed I had chosen not to acknowledge Ruby, you thought I was just like him?'

Roman shrugged, but the movement felt stiff and surly as he ran his thumb down the frosted glass, not quite able to look the man in the eyes. 'Yes,' he forced himself to admit, even though it felt too revealing.

'I see. Well, just so you know, I had no idea I had a daughter until Ruby was four years old. Which, to be fair, was mostly my own fault, so I don't blame you for coming to that conclusion. But I should also make you aware, I would rather cut off my left nut than be anything like the bastard who fathered us both.'

Roman swung his head around to stare at Cade, but the fierce frown made it clear the man meant what he said.

'You didn't like your father?' he asked, stunned by the revelation. And the disjointed way it made him feel. As if his whole life had just been broken apart like a jigsaw puzzle and fitted back together to create an entirely different image.

'*Our* father, you mean,' Cade corrected him, gently. 'But to answer your question… No. I didn't like him. For most of my childhood and adolescence, I was terrified of him. My mother died when I was a baby. She killed herself, probably to get away from him,' he added with a wry sadness that stunned Roman even more. 'After that, I was brought up by a string of governesses who he would fire if I got too attached to them. When I was five, he decided to ship me off to a succession of increasingly austere and disciplinary boarding schools to show me how to be a man. The only times I ever saw him was when he wanted to punish me, usually with random acts of cruelty, which…' he paused, his expression becoming rueful as he sighed

'...after over a year of therapy at my wife's insistence, I have finally come to realise he took great pleasure in administering because he was a sadist. But were never, *ever* my fault.'

Roman straightened, horrified but also strangely moved by Brandon Cade's forthright and unsentimental recollections. His father—*their* father—had been a monster. Why had he never considered that Alfred Cade's crimes might have extended far beyond the man's callous treatment of his mother and himself?

'Sounds like I dodged a bullet never having to meet him,' he muttered.

'You have no idea,' Brandon murmured vehemently. 'Our father was a sociopath and a narcissist, who was never capable of loving anyone but himself. So it doesn't surprise me he didn't acknowledge you as his son. But you have to believe me when I tell you, I had no idea we were related that day in Cade Tower.'

Roman nodded. Surprised to realise he believed him. And it made a difference. A *big* difference, to how he remembered that day. Why wouldn't Brandon Cade have had him kicked out of his offices, when all he'd seen was a mouthy little upstart with no prospects? After all, that was exactly what he had been. He might well have kicked himself out, under the same circumstances.

But then Brandon surprised him even more when he added, 'Unfortunately, though, the personnel manager with me when you confronted me did know who you were.' He took a deep breath, let it out again, his expression pained. 'I'd inherited John Walters from my father. He seemed competent. But what I didn't know was part of his job during my father's tenure was also to manage his "indiscretions". I asked Walters to find room for you on our apprenticeship programme that day, because it was clear to me you had potential as a journalist. You were smart and articulate and tenacious, and I was impressed with your gall. But when you said your name, Walters recognised you as my father's illegitimate child. And had you kicked out of the building. I should have checked up on you, though, made sure Walters had followed through on my request, and I didn't. So you're going to have to accept my apology for that, too.'

'Okay,' Roman said carefully, stunned again by Brandon Cade's honesty and integrity. And his willingness to take the blame for crimes that had never been his.

'Good.' Brandon stood, then glanced towards the door. 'How about we call Marisa and her assistant back in and I can give you the documents we've been working on relating to your inheritance? Nothing has to be decided today, obviously, but I—'

'No.' Roman interrupted him. 'Thanks,' he added, when Brandon's expression became mulish. 'I don't need any part of your inheritance,' he continued. 'It sounds like you earned the Cade legacy the hard way by having to deal with that bastard. So I'd say we're even on that score.'

'That's not why I told you about our father,' Brandon said, the edge right back again.

'I know, but it's the truth, though, isn't it?' Roman sighed and stood up, so he could stand toe to toe with his brother.

Weird, but, even though he'd always known their blood connection, he'd never really thought of them as being related until this moment. But when Brandon glared at him—the stubborn glint in his eye making it clear this was not the end of the inheritance discussion—Roman recognised the expression, because he'd seen it in the mirror often enough.

He didn't know if they could ever be brothers. There was a lot more baggage to unpack before that could happen. But right now, it didn't really matter to him. Because the only thing that actually mattered was what he had learned this afternoon.

His father had been a pig and now he was really glad the man had never wanted him.

Brandon Cade was a better man than Roman had ever given him credit for.

And, most importantly of all, he'd thrown something away that he shouldn't have thrown away, over something that had never really mattered in the first place!

He'd spent the first thirty-two years of his life believing the wrong thing about himself, about his past, about every damn thing really. And because of that, he'd been beyond terrified when Milly had looked at him with love and understanding in her eyes, and told him she trusted him, because a part of him was still that boy—scared of needing more, in case he didn't get it.

Well, to hell with that.

He'd been utterly miserable in the past week, because he'd believed he was doing the right thing by pushing her away. But life was too short to make that kind of stupid, self-defeating sacrifice.

If Brandon Cade could come to him, swallow his pride and try to make amends for something he hadn't even done, then Roman Garner—aka that mouthy little upstart Dante Rocco—could fly to Genoa and tell Milly Devlin he had made a terrible mistake. And beg her to give him another chance.

After the way he'd treated her, she might not want him back, she might well decide she never wanted to see him again. And he wouldn't blame her. But one thing he was not prepared to do was not give it his best shot. And if that meant kidnapping her and seducing her into a puddle of need until she agreed to give him that chance... So be it.

But for any of that to happen, he needed to find out where she was living first.

'There is one favour I want, Brandon,' he said, laying on the reckless charm he'd once taken for granted. 'And then we'll be all square.'

'Consider it done. What is it?' Brandon said, falling neatly into his trap.

'I need contact details for your sister-in-law in Genoa.'

Brandon frowned, the stubborn expression back with a vengeance. 'I'm not about to tell you that. Milly is vulnerable, and you hurt her. A lot.'

Roman struggled not to wince. *Fair.*

'She doesn't need you to drop back into her life and sweep her—' Brandon continued.

'Save it, bro.' Roman cut off the lecture. 'I'm not asking for your permission to date her. That's her decision. But, FYI, she's perfectly capable of telling me to take a hike herself.'

Or at least he hoped she was, because if he'd hurt her to that extent, he'd never forgive himself.

'Why, *exactly*, do you want to contact her?' Brandon asked, driving a hard bargain. But it only made Roman admire the man more. His family was important to him. And while Roman knew nothing about that kind of loyalty, the fierce need to protect Milly was something he understood. Even if it was him she needed protecting from.

'Because I need to grovel. A lot,' he said, forced to come clean about his intentions, but debasing himself in front of Brandon seemed like good practice for what he might have to do when he found Milly. 'And the sooner I get started with that,' he added, 'the sooner I can get round to begging her to take me back.'

Brandon still didn't look convinced, though. 'It's nice that you care about her, but I'm not giving you her address.'

'Why the—?'

'Because we need to ask my wife first,' Brandon interrupted, neatly cutting off Roman's temper tantrum.

'Do you have to get your wife's permission for everything?' Roman goaded, realising the grovel quotient was about to go up exponentially if he had to prostrate himself in front of Lacey Cade now, too.

He didn't have time for this. He wanted to get to Milly before she let what he'd done to her in that gazebo—intentionally humiliating her with her own quickfire response to his touch—fester any more than it had already.

'Have you ever had a long-term committed relationship, Roman, with a woman you love and respect?' Brandon replied, doing that really aggravating thing of answering a question with another question.

'No, but I'd like to try for one… With Milly,' he muttered, surprised the fear didn't kick him in the gut all over again when he admitted the truth out loud.

'Good answer.' Brandon smiled, surprising him even more. Then he clapped a hand on Roman's shoulder. 'Consider this your first valuable lesson, then, in long-term-relationship etiquette. If you want to get Milly back, the very best way to convince her you care about her is to persuade her sister you do.'

'But that doesn't even make sense,' Roman said, his head starting to explode again.

Brandon's smile only widened. 'Which brings me to valuable lesson number two. Which is that sense has sodall to do with love, little bro.'

CHAPTER ELEVEN

Another week later...

'*PERFETTO*, MASSIMO.' MILLY managed a smile for the young assistant who had helped her hang the last of her art.

Her first ever showing was tonight, in two hours' time. The historic building that housed the small but exclusive gallery near Genoa's port was the perfect venue—full of light from the floor-to-ceiling windows—plus the curator had loved her work from Estiva and had a reputation for breaking new talent and championing artists who liked to work in a variety of mediums...

Milly should be ecstatic—this opportunity was something she'd dreamed of ever since she'd picked up her first piece of charcoal in her school art class, age fourteen. But as she walked through the gallery, checking each work to ensure the light hit each piece just right, she couldn't seem to conjure up any excitement at all.

Had Roman robbed her of this, too? Not just her self-respect and her confidence in herself as a woman, but also her enthusiasm for her work?

The truth was, she'd struggled to even look at the compositions she had done on Estiva since returning to Genoa—and it was even harder to look at them now, so beautifully displayed in the cavernous, elegant space.

Because Roman, or the essence of him and how she felt about him, suffused every one of them. The joy and drama and excitement of her first love were vivid in every line, every brush stroke, every element of the work.

She finally stood in front of the acrylic and line drawing she had done of Roman and the Volcano, remembering that day full of promise and possibility as they sat on the terrazzo discussing the parameters of their booty call... Except it had never been just that for her, she could see it so clearly now.

She rubbed her hand against her breastbone, to disperse the familiar ache, and blinked furiously to dispel the sting of yet more tears scalding the backs of her eyeballs.

You are not going to cry again, Mills. It's not allowed. This is the best day of your life and you are not going to let him ruin this, too!

He hadn't wanted her. Or her love. And she just needed to get over it now. It had been two whole weeks, for Pete's sake. She'd been without him almost as long as she'd known him. And she was never going to see him again.

Thank goodness.

And sure, maybe the pain and humiliation of their final parting would always be there in some hidden corner of her memory. But that just meant she would never be that naïve and gullible again. To assume, just because she had fallen hopelessly, irrevocably in love with someone, the other person felt the same way. Or was even capable of feeling the same way.

Lesson learned.

Roman had been a complex, unknowable and extremely guarded man. Exciting and charismatic on the surface but carrying unseen scars from his childhood, which would probably never heal. It had been beyond reckless of her to think she could break through the protective wall he kept around his emotions in the space of a few weeks just because they shared an incendiary chemistry and the same impulsive personalities.

'Signorina Devlin, the new gallery owner has arrived and wishes to meet you.'

Milly swung round to find Massimo standing behind her, looking anxious.

The gallery had a new owner? This was news to her. She'd met Signora Spinola just two days ago and the woman hadn't said anything about selling.

'Umm, okay. Do you know why?' she asked, but Massimo simply shook his head.

'He did not say. He waits for you in the curator's office upstairs.'

She swallowed the lump of melancholy in her throat, and tried not to let her new-found pessimism derail her Best Day Ever again.

This didn't have to be a bad thing. The guy was probably just here to say hello and find out about the new show.

Even so, the dead weight of anxiety slowed her steps as she took the stairs to the beautifully appointed office on the top floor of the building. But when she walked into the luxurious space, the room was empty.

'Ciao? Signor?' she called, then noticed a man standing on the balcony outside, silhouetted against the early evening sunshine.

His tall, muscular frame was instantly familiar as he walked into the room. But she couldn't process her reaction, couldn't even catch her breath, all she could do was stare, the sting in her eyes and the twisting pain in her stomach becoming excruciating.

Was this some kind of cruel hallucination? Sent to punish her for being foolish enough to fall in love with the wrong man?

'Roman?' she murmured.

She had to wrap her arms around her midriff to hold herself together, to keep herself upright, when he stopped in front of her. The smell, of sandalwood and soap, the sound of his breathing, so loud, so real, in the empty room.

But surely she had to be dreaming?

'Are you...? Are you really here?' she asked, her voice a whisper of distress and yearning—which she would have been ashamed of, if she could make her brain work.

He nodded, and his lips twitched, but the seductive smile was comprehensively contradicted by the wary light in his eyes, and the intense concentration on his too-handsome face.

'But... Why?' she asked, still convinced she'd entered some weird alternative reality in which all her dreams and nightmares had combined to taunt and torment her.

He sucked in a hefty breath. The small smile disappeared as he let the breath out slowly.

'I came to apologise to you, Milly. For everything. And to ask you to come back to me,' he said.

The words simply wouldn't compute.

She shook her head, trying to shake loose the unsettling dream, the potent mix of need and desperation in his gaze triggering the languid heat in her abdomen, right alongside the pain and yearning.

But then he tucked a knuckle under her chin, to lift her face to his and brush his lips across hers.

She jerked back, the shock of his kiss—potent, proprietorial, possessive—almost as devastating as the rush of longing that accompanied it.

'Don't...' She slammed her palms against his chest, shoved him back.

This was not a dream.

Roman Garner was actually here. In Genoa. Standing in front of her. Two weeks after dumping her in the most humiliating way imaginable. He'd even bought the gallery where she was about to have her first show? Why? To take that away from her too?

But she could not begin to figure out the logic of that development, because she couldn't get past the outrage of what he had just said to her.

That he wanted her back?

'How dare you...?' she murmured as fury rushed in to fill the vicious vacuum that had opened up inside her the night he had discarded her so callously.

She welcomed the anger in, to chase away the humiliation that still lingered, and the brutal pain.

She fisted her fingers, the urge to slap his handsome face—when she'd never hit anyone before in her entire life—so strong she had to stuff her fists into her pockets to contain it.

He shoved his own hands into his suit trousers. And seemed to brace, before sending her a pained look.

'How dare I what, Milly?' he asked gravely, but the strain on his face didn't fool her for a second. 'Perhaps you should get it all off your chest.'

'Get it off my...!' she snapped, incredulous.

Was he actually serious, right now? Did he really need to have the crummy way he'd treated her spelled out to him?

She spun around, paced to the end of the office and back again, so furious with him, and herself, she couldn't even speak. How could she still want him, how could she still hurt this much, after the way he had treated her? It was beyond pathetic.

But when she walked back to him, and he still stood there, patiently waiting, she let it rip, the words spewing out on a tidal wave of rage and pain and heartache.

'How *dare* you think you can kiss me again? How *dare* you think you can ask me to come back to you? To do *what* exactly? Break my heart a second time?'

He flinched at that, but didn't look away. Which was something. But not enough. Not nearly enough.

'You made me feel so small, so insignificant that night. I understood you were hurting, and maybe I shouldn't have burdened you with my feelings when you were dealing with so much else, but there was no need for you to be so cruel. When a simple "I don't love you back, Milly," would have sufficed.'

'But I…' he began.

Her palm shot up, to cut him off.

'Shut up. I'm talking now.' She gathered in another ragged breath and charged on. 'I told you I loved you, that I trusted you, even though you lied to me about your connection to Brandon, and you accused me of being some naïve little girl who couldn't possibly know her own mind. And then you added insult to injury by making me climax for you… You… You used our…our…' She paused, the brutal tears overwhelming her again.

She scrubbed her cheeks dry, ignoring the choking sensation in her throat, determined to get every single miserable thing she'd dwelled on and cried over for a fortnight right off her chest and shove it onto his.

'You made our chemistry, and my body's reaction to you, into a bad thing. Like that proved what a romantic fool I was. You made me doubt myself. And you tried to destroy my confidence.' She lifted her fists out of her pockets and slammed them onto her hips. The power returned to fill up the huge holes in her heart, at least some of the way.

A part of her knew she would never be over him. He'd been her first lover, and she would never be able to replicate the adrenaline rush of those two magical weeks. But at least now he knew she wasn't a complete pushover, and that felt important.

'But you know what?' she said. 'It didn't work. I know who I am. I'm not naïve. I do love you. But I am also worthy of love in return. So, if you think you can just snap your fingers and I'll be willing to jump back into your bed for more of the same… The answer is no!'

She stood shaking, and exhausted. And still sad. But somehow she knew… Even if she never stopped loving him, she would be okay.

But then he ruined it all, when the heat and longing she adored flared in his eyes, and he murmured: 'Damn it, Milly, you are absolutely magnificent. No wonder I love you so much.'

'Wh-what…?' she gasped, her tired body reverberating with shock. And hope. Which was the cruellest trick of all.

But then he made things even worse, by sinking onto his knees, banding strong arms around her hips, burying his cheek against her midriff.

'I'm sorry,' he said, his voice rough with regret. 'For all the crap I threw at you that night.' He looked up at her, the sheen of emotion in his eyes stunning her even more. And making the bubble expand against her ribs. 'But I can do better.'

He hugged her tighter, as if he would never let her go.

'Whatever you need me to do, I'll do it…' He groaned. 'I've already grovelled to Cade and Lacey so I'm pretty sure nothing you can make me do could be worse than that.' The rueful, self-deprecating smile was impossibly appealing. 'But you said you still loved me, right?' he continued, the hope in his expression matching the cruel bubble still wedged against her heart. 'So, please will you give me a chance to make this right?'

She lifted her arms, her whole body trembling.

She wanted to believe him, wanted to sink her fingers into his hair and drag him to his feet so he could hold her properly. But how could she know that this was real? That this was really what she needed?

'What made you change your mind?' she asked, hating the quiver of uncertainty in her voice. 'About us?'

He let out a huff of breath. Then released his hold on her, so he could stand. Cradling her face in his palms, he dropped his forehead to hers, then let his arms fall, to band them back around her body, and hold her close as he spoke.

'I didn't change my mind, Milly. I think I always knew this was different. That you were different. Right from the moment I came out of that cabin and you were steering my boat.'

Her heart jolted and filled. But she made herself step out of his arms—which was the hardest thing she had ever done in her entire life. 'But if that's true… Why did you push me away?'

He dropped his head back to stare at the ceiling for a moment. When his gaze met hers again though, she could see the emotion swirling in his eyes.

'Honestly? Because as soon as I figured out how much I felt for you, I was absolutely terrified. I've never loved anyone before. And I've never admitted I needed anything from anyone since I was sixteen and I got kicked out of Cade Tower…' He sighed. 'By mistake, as it turns out. The truth is, I don't know how to do this… At all. Brandon's already given me a few lessons. But fair warning, you're going to have to teach me how to handle this feeling...' He thumped a fist to his chest, his gaze still locked on hers. 'Because it still scares me... A lot.'

'Okay.' She nodded, biting into her lip as her eyes misted up again.

He'd had no one, not really, for most of his life. And he'd learned to survive, to prosper on his own. Of course, he was scared. But then, so was she.

'Hey! Don't.' He cupped her cheek, dragged her back into his arms and held her close. 'Please don't cry. I swear, I won't ever treat you like that again.'

She choked out a sob, but when she pulled her head back to look up, she could feel the smile spreading across her lips, and into her heart. 'It's okay, Roman, these are happy tears.'

His brows lifted but then he smiled back at her, the quick, reckless grin as triumphant as it was seductive. 'Does that mean you'll come back?'

She nodded, and then let out a giddy laugh when he whooped and boosted her into his arms.

She clung to him as he spun her round. Then clasped his head and settled her lips on his, kissing him with all the joy and hunger in her heart.

This was still new and raw and there was bound to be a ton more twists and turns along the way. But as he dropped her onto the office couch, and they tore off each other's clothes with a haste that would be shocking, if it weren't so delicious, Milly knew every road bump would be worth the ride.

Twenty minutes later, as she lay in his arms, still naked, still seeped in afterglow, she glanced at the clock on the wall. And shot off the couch so fast she heard him grunt.

'The show!' she yelped. 'Roman, get up. We can't be late. And I don't want the curator to find us naked in here.'

'Who cares? I own the place,' he said.

She gathered up her clothes in a rush as he chuckled. 'This is not funny. It's my big break and I'm going to be late.'

He lay gloriously naked, his head propped on his arm, watching her. 'Don't get your knickers in a twist,' he said provocatively as she scrambled to get them on while hopping on one leg. 'I can always postpone the show, or, better yet…' his eyebrows lifted lasciviously '…you could host it naked.'

'Also not funny…' She glared while struggling into her bra. But once she'd snapped the clasp closed, she stopped dead, an awful thought occurring to her. 'Wait a minute. When did you buy the gallery? You're not the reason I got the offer of a showing, are you?'

While she was stupidly flattered he might have gone to those lengths to please her, at the same time it would diminish the happy glow still coursing through her body… Just a little.

What if she hadn't really earned this chance on her own?

He got off the couch, and strolled towards her, still gloriously naked. And distractingly gorgeous.

'Oh, ye of little faith,' he said, then cradled her neck and pressed a kiss to her forehead. 'I bought this gallery yesterday, after I found out you were doing a showing here. Because it was the only way to see you alone.' He scooped his boxers off the curator's desk and tugged them on. 'You can thank your sister, who would not give me your address in Genoa or any contact details. Even though I begged for close to a week.'

'But… *Really?*' she said, trying to look contrite when

she was overjoyed at the news… He'd wanted to see her *that* much? 'You begged?'

He laughed. 'Yeah, I begged.' He gave her bottom a pat, then grabbed his shirt from the light it was hooked over. 'But, be warned,' he continued as he buttoned it up, covering up that mouth-watering chest, sadly, 'I intend to get payback later tonight.' The teasing threat was as delicious as the giddy skip in her heartbeat. 'Much, much later, after you take the Genoa art world by storm. And make me a terrific return on my investment.'

'I'm not so sure about that,' she said wryly.

'You don't have to be sure,' he said, the love and approval in his gaze making her heart press into her throat. 'Because I am.'

As they finished getting dressed, then made their way down to the gallery—together—her heart continued to pound against her ribs in that giddy tattoo.

By the time the gallery doors closed that evening, and every one of her pieces had been sold—and not all of them to Roman—she knew they were both going to get a terrific return on this investment. Because her new career as an artist promised to be as much of a stupendous success as her love life.

Almost.

EPILOGUE

One year later

ROMAN LET GO of the breath that had been trapped in his lungs for what felt like weeks as he glanced over his shoulder and spotted Milly at the end of the aisle, heading towards him, at last. Her sister walked beside her, their arms linked. But all Roman could see was his bride in a luminous concoction of cream and white silk, accentuating every one of the curves he adored—and worshipped regularly. A light blush added lustre to her skin as her gaze connected with his, full of heat and longing and love.

'The Devlin women are quite something, aren't they?' his brother murmured next to him, his voice barely audible above the swell of music and the whispered approval of the small crowd they'd invited to witness their marriage.

Roman nodded, because he couldn't speak. The answering heat and longing and love were lodged in his solar plexus, the way they had been ever since the day he'd proposed on Estiva four months ago, while they were hosting Milly's family—or rather *their* family—for a week-long vacation.

He hadn't wanted to wait four minutes, to actually seal the deal, but Milly had insisted they had to do it 'right'—which meant in the Cade Chapel in front of all the people who mattered to them. So instead of politicians or celebrities, they had Giovanni and Giuliana in the front row, Milly's friends from Genoa and her previous job as a teaching assistant, the work colleagues he socialised with, and of course Brandon and Lacey—as best man and maid of honour/mother of the bride. As Milly finally reached him and Brandon, he spotted Ruby behind the two sisters, busy trying to rein in her dog, Tinkerbell, who, Roman had been reliably informed, was already a professional when it came to wedding parties.

It didn't look like it to him, from the way the dog was sniffing the back of Milly's gown, but when Ruby sent him a proud grin, he winked at her and grinned back. Because he'd learned to embrace the chaos in the past year.

He directed his attention back to Milly, and his smile spread through his heart. Unable to keep his hands off her, he cradled her cheeks and pulled her in for a kiss. As soon as his lips touched hers though, and he heard her familiar sob of surrender, he began to devour her.

Brandon cleared his throat loudly behind him, forcing Roman to draw back. There would be more than enough time to devour his almost-wife later. He grasped Milly's hand and held on tight while they turned to face the vicar together.

The words swept through him, on a tidal wave of pride and excitement, while he tried to concentrate on the vicar's words, so he didn't miss his cue.

When they finally got to say their 'I dos', he gripped her fingers a little tighter. And felt her squeeze his hand in return.

My wife.

They had this, he thought, as the vicar finally stopped talking and he got to kiss Milly for real. The swell of applause from the crowd and the sound of their canine bridesmaid going berserk were nothing compared to the cacophony of joy in his heart.

Finally, they could start the rest of their life together.

Three hours later

'Come here,' Roman demanded. 'You're too slow,' he added as he dipped and hefted Milly onto his shoulder.

'For goodness' sake, Roman, put me down, someone will see us,' she said, but she couldn't stop laughing as he marched with singular purpose down the darkened corridor towards the huge guest suite Brandon and Lacey had arranged for them at the Cade estate for their wedding night. And away from the reception in the ballroom below— which they had finally managed to sneak away from...

He ignored her protests—because, of course, he did— but when they finally reached the suite and he deposited her back on her feet, the wicked glint in his eyes faded abruptly.

'Hey, are you okay?' He cupped her cheek. 'I totally forgot about your tummy. You still good?' he asked, recalling the time, well over a week ago now, when she'd been violently ill one morning in his New York penthouse.

She smiled, and clasped his fingers.

'No, I'm all better. And I secretly love it when you go all caveman on me,' she added, but the thickness in her throat made the words come out without the teasing lilt she had intended.

'Hey...' He cupped her cheek again, his eyes narrowing, the serious expression making her heartbeat tick into her throat. 'What is it? Is there something you're not telling me?'

Her heart swelled against her throat at the concern in

his voice, and the intuition in his gaze. Apparently her new husband could still read her far too easily.

He'd been adorably solicitous while she was puking her guts up. But he'd also been worried about her. She'd passed off the sickness with some white lie about wedding jitters. But she knew she needed to tell him now what was really going on, when he added, 'You don't regret marrying me, do you, Milly?'

'Roman, today was the happiest day of my life. Bar none,' she continued, glad when the ticcing muscle in his jaw relaxed. 'Except maybe that day you seduced me on the beach in Estiva,' she added cheekily, impossibly glad when he choked out a laugh.

'Thank God,' he murmured, then drew her back into his arms. 'That goes for both of us,' he said, his voice becoming a husky purr. 'But I intend to make this day the best yet right now.'

But when he reached for the zip on her dress, she clasped his fingers to halt his progress.

'But there is something I need to tell you…' She forced the words out, still a little shocked herself at what she and Lacey had discovered that morning. 'I… I took a pregnancy test before the wedding at Lacey's suggestion.'

'You… What?' His hand dropped away as his gaze dipped to her waist. He looked shocked, but not panicked. She took that as a good sign. Hopefully.

'I think the tummy bug must have messed with my contraception…' she added, still not quite able to get the words out. This wasn't planned. They hadn't discussed children. Not yet. Although Roman adored Ruby and Artie. Seeing him develop a relationship with his new niece and nephew in the past year had been one of the most amazing things.

But this was different. Roman had adjusted to a lot in

the last twelve months, not just their relationship, but also finding out what it was like to be a part of a family. Brandon and Lacey had been incredible, welcoming him in with open arms, and she thought he'd enjoyed the experience. He certainly seemed to have adapted to it. Even his relationship with Brandon had become a lot less prickly, watching their trust and friendship grow something Milly had also adored observing. But having their own child was huge. And they hadn't even talked about it. Let alone planned for it.

His gaze rose to hers again. But before she could choke the words out, past the ball of anxiety in her throat, he clasped her neck, tugged her forehead to his and said, 'If you tell me you're pregnant right now, I may actually explode with happiness, fair warning.'

She laughed. The trickle of happy tears reminding her of the day he'd come back to her in Genoa and declared his love.

'Really?' she said, a tiny part of the insecure girl still there, despite everything.

'Yeah, really...' He caressed her neck, making the ache in her core join the swell of happiness in her heart. Then he brushed the tears away with his thumbs. 'Now stop keeping me in suspense, or I may have to seduce the truth out of you.'

She huffed out a breath. And chuckled as the last remnant of that girl finally died inside her. 'We're going to have a baby, in about eight months' time.'

He roared his approval, then banded his arms around her waist and lifted her up to spin her around.

She clung to his shoulders, sinking into a deep, abiding and unbearably hot kiss when he finally let her down again.

As he scooped her into his arms, and marched towards

the bedroom, he added, 'I hope you know you've made me the happiest guy alive.'

She laughed as he placed her on the bed. 'I hope you're still saying that when Junior asks for a puppy.'

'Even then,' he replied, before he began to strip her naked in earnest, and made her forget everything…

Except how much she loved him.

* * * * *

MY ONE-NIGHT HEIR

NATALIE ANDERSON

MILLS & BOON

CHAPTER ONE

Talia

'OH, TALIA, thank heavens you're here!'

Despite my exhaustion I shoot Kiri a massive grin. 'Where do you need me?'

'Everywhere.' The chef looks near tears. 'The servers are so inexperienced they need *training* more than guidance but there isn't time. The fryer won't get to temperature and I can't—'

'Leave the servers with me,' I interrupt. It's clear Kiri's hit peak stressed chef and I need to move. Happily, sorting an imploding kitchen situation is something I've done more nights than I want to remember. If I quickly smooth front of house, Kiri can concentrate on her magical plates. She just needs confidence in me for calm to return.

'There aren't enough glasses for the affogatos.' Kiri continues listing the catastrophes.

'I'll find alternative ones.'

'Yeah, but the coffee machine is misfiring and the primary ordered espresso martinis ten minutes ago even though we're only through the third course and have another two—'

'Affogato *and* espresso martinis?' I interrupt again.

'She requested tiramisu as well.' Kiri growls.

I chuckle. She's a customer after my own heart. Coffee's my one true love and I'm going to need my own caffeine hit to get through the next few hours.

'The hired entertainment is late and has only just got onto the gondola.' Kiri tosses a pan into a sink with more force than necessary. 'Typical.'

It's just over a twenty-minute ride in the suspension car to the exclusive restaurant at the top of the mountain so, what with the diva espresso machine and delayed entertainer, there's a gap in proceedings. I can't entertain, but I can tame a coffee machine.

'I'll stall with the martinis,' I reassure Kiri as she whirls back to another pan, furiously stirring its bubbling contents into smooth submission.

'Did you see the forecast?' Kiri growls, stuck in her doom spiral. 'Some apocalyptic storm is due.'

'Yeah?' I bite back a laugh and resort to my fool-proof trick to distract Kiri. 'Well, it only needs to hold off for another couple of hours, then you'll be back down the mountain being massaged by your unreasonably hot husband.'

Kiri's eyes glaze over and her frantic stirring stops. She snaps out of it in time to catch my amusement. 'I know.' She finally cracks a smile. 'I'm losing it.'

'You're fine. Focus on your food. I'll take care of the extraneous. But not even I can change the weather.'

'You sure?' Kiri chuckles mid-sprint from counter to flaming grill. 'I think you're a goddess.'

I'm not. But I *am* used to working back-to-back shifts. I've been doing it since I was thirteen and got my first kitchen-hand job. When Romy—owner of the café I work a day shift at—phoned half an hour before closing saying the manager at the gondola restaurant was down with flu and they desperately needed a head waiter, I said yes. Sure I've already worked a twelve-hour day, plus I have a midnight-till-closing shift at a dive bar later tonight, but I need the money. And not just because of the cost of living here.

Queenstown is mega-expensive. The snowy mountain paradise in New Zealand's South Island is stunningly beautiful with incredible views and adventurous opportunities. It's super popular with the wealthy—there are vast numbers of stunning, luxury leisure homes everywhere. It feels as though every other café customer is a billionaire. They dress in sleek merino jumpers, rock-star jeans and mingle with the travellers who flit in to enjoy the slopes and adrenalin hits. They *all* have high expectations of service. Because I'm reliable I've got more work than I can manage. I hold down multiple food service jobs while building a social media side hustle because, not only do I need to make enough for my own survival, but I support my sister. Ava's four years younger than me and a genius but even with her scholarships she needs additional support, and I don't want our screwed-up family stopping her from succeeding.

So I quickly head out to scope the situation. Honestly, it's pretty wild. Primary guest Simone Boras is Australian, as are her mostly female guests, and for her seventy-seventh birthday she's booked out the entire restaurant. They're loud, they're laughing, they're definitely here to have a good time and we're going to need that entertainment soon to keep the energy up and divert attention from the delay on dessert.

'Simone, I'm Talia.' I smile at her. 'I'm here to make your martinis.'

Simone's polite and charming enough but I recognise the slight edge in her smile. She expects the best. If I deliver, she'll approve. So I move fast. It doesn't take me long to get to grips with the coffee machine and I make her martini. No one makes a meaner coffee than me.

And her delight is genuine. 'Thank you, Talia.'

I don't mind guests with high standards when they appreciate my work.

'Can we get two more of those?' one guest calls to me. 'They look amazing.'

'Of course.' I smile. 'I'll bring them right over.'

As I make more martinis I talk strategy with the servers

and send them out with the cocktails. The vibe of the room lifts. When I get a chance I check on Kiri. She's still sweating bullets but the kitchen feels less chaotic.

Pleased, I take a breath and roll my shoulders. While I'd managed a swift shower, put on a clean dress, redone my hair and minimal make-up, my freshen up was only superficial. I'd kill to put my feet up. Instead I head to the storeroom to find those extra glasses. Hopefully a few moments' respite from the noise will help. The view from the floor-to-ceiling windows on the way certainly does. The sun is just setting. Wild clouds skitter over the wide sky, threatening to cloak the mountains in a moody shroud. Below, the city lights twinkle obliviously and the lake stretches into the distance. Some time I'll actually have a day off. I'll not stand for hours, not wait on others. I'll curl in front of a cosy fire and a big window, drink something hot and sweet and do *nothing* but gaze at the view. I'll just *breathe*.

But right now breathing is the *only* thing on that list that I can accomplish. I go into the storeroom, lean back against the door to close it and—

Breathing stops. Jaw drops. Brain…brain…?

Tall. Muscular. Shoulders. Ruffled hair. Rippled abs. Blue eyes. Intense blue eyes. Very intense.

In a succession of still shots, details imprint on my mind one at a time. Matching the frantic beat of my heart.

I know about the abs because he's half naked. He's a chiselled, X-rated, total wow of a man. And he's half naked.

He has a crisp white shirt in his hand and apparently does not give a thought about his state of undress and my observation of it. As I stare he shakes out the shirt and shrugs it up over those broad shoulders. I realise my mouth's ajar but it's dry and I don't shut it. I can't. I can't do *anything* because my brain is completely incompetent. The visuals are more than it can handle. He leisurely begins buttoning the shirt, his abs and pecs and other muscles ripple. He's honestly like not from this earth. And that's when it dawns on me.

'*You're* the entertainment...' I slowly mutter. And yes, I'm marvelling.

Wow. Good for Simone. I really want to be her when I grow up.

His long fingers pause on the third button down. His eyes widen.

'You're late,' I add after an uncomfortable beat. 'It's okay though. They're not even onto dessert yet. They're too busy talking but you're going to stun them into silence.'

There's silence right here, right now. And it only grows.

He's frozen—the half-buttoned shirt still reveals a wide expanse of muscled body. I feel my face getting hotter.

'Is there a problem?' I blink and the smallest portion of brain comes back online. I'm used to sorting problems. 'Do you need help or something?'

'I had to sponge a mark off my shirt.'

'Where?' I squint. It looks perfect to me.

'Here.'

I have to step closer to spot the small smudge.

'Oh, they're never going to notice *that*,' I scoff. 'You should've made it more wet,' I joke. 'That would be...'

At his jerky movement I trail off and clear my throat awkwardly.

'Would be...?' He prompts me.

I glance up and am ensnared in his gaze. He's insanely good-looking. But of course he is. Simone is the type to have only the best money can buy. He must command squillions per performance.

'I thought you guys had like special tear-away shirts and things,' I mumble inanely, trying to turn away but only half succeeding. His isn't some cheap satin suit with easy-open Velcro sides or anything. It's high end. 'Those shirt buttons are stiff. Is it a deliberate thing? To prolong the tease?'

'The tease?' A strange tenor flecks his low echo as he re-sumes fastening the buttons.

I suppress the shiver skittering down my spine. 'That's what it's all about, right?' I can't stop myself babbling. 'Taking the time, building the anticipation…'

Shut up, Talia.

'Mmm…' He nods and reaches for a black jacket I hadn't even noticed slung on a nearby shelf and pulls a strip of black silk from the pocket. There's a gleam in his eyes that makes shivers ripple through me. 'Could you help me with my tie?'

I don't believe for a second that he can't tie his own bow tie. He'll be taking it off and on multiple times a night.

'I can't do it without a mirror,' he adds, apparently having just read my mind.

I summon self-control. Because I fix things. I oblige. It's what I do. 'Of course.'

I step closer and take the silk. He is much taller than me and I have to rise on tiptoe. Freshly shaven, his jaw is sharp and smooth and I smell a hint of cinnamon. His eyes are very blue and, honestly, I forget what I'm meant to be doing. I wobble. Instantly he puts a hand on my waist to steady me but the contact hits like an electrical current and it resets my heart. It beats faster. I breathe faster too. And my skin seems to have tripled in sensitivity because I *swear* I can feel the heat of him through my dress. Now my legs are wobblier still and suddenly it's not just his hand at my waist, but his arm curled around my back pulling me closer until I'm all but leaning against him. It's *super* embarrassing but there's a glint in his eye that makes me refuse to step back and admit my mortification.

I'm all thumbs. I make myself remember what I'm supposed to be doing. *Simone.* The birthday guest should have the best night of her life.

'They're pretty noisy but in good spirits,' I babble as I tie the silk. 'Mostly women. It's a birthday, you know?'

'I know.'

Yeah, of course he does. He's an absolute professional. He has a calm, confident deliberation about him, there's no rushing him. I can't resist breathing in again to appreciate that cinnamon. His hair has an ever so slightly damp look to it. He's a pillar of sensual heat and I've basically plastered myself all over him.

I'm jealous of Simone and her party. Would it be okay to loiter at the back of the room during his show?

A wave of lust washes over me. I almost choke. I don't behave like this. I don't gawp at men. I prefer to avoid them—I have other priorities. Besides, I don't want to risk discovering I've inherited my mother's appalling taste in men. But I can't stop staring—or *leaning* on him. I even pat his chest once I've finally finished the tie.

'You'll give her a good time, won't you?' I mumble. 'She's nice.'

He blinks. 'A good time?'

My fingers seem to be stuck to his chest. I can't lift them away from the heat of him. The hard strength is compelling. Instinctively I spread them wider. He tenses even more. We're so close and it's madness. I manage to lower my gaze from his but I only get as far as his mouth.

'Do I pass inspection?' he mutters.

'I guess…' I bite my lip.

'Aren't you in charge around here?'

I shake my head. I'm not in charge of anything right this second and that is so not like me. 'I'd better get back to…'

'To what?' He leans a little closer.

I manage to breathe but I get another hit of that soap and I'm brainless again. 'Making coffee. I make a lot of coffee. But that's okay. I actually love making coffee.'

He nods. 'I love my job too.'

Yeah. 'I bet you're really good at it.'

'So I've been told,' he says gravely.

I should step back but he hasn't released me and I'm completely immobilised. There's another long moment where we stand too still, too silent, too close. My heart is pounding so hard he must be able to feel it. His mouth moves and he actually smiles. Everything seems awfully intimate but at the same time it's shockingly *easy*. I don't know this feeling. It's as if I've stepped through a portal and now a swirling bubble of heat spreads from a secret source low in my belly. Warmth and light ripple through me, and something silkier—something forbidden. It snakes around me like a ribbon, drawing me closer. Binding me to him. I don't want it to end.

I hear something like a groan and with a small gasp I realise it came from *me*.

I'm too busy. I'm too alone. But I need to be. Ava is relying on me. Romy is relying on me. Kiri is relying on me. So is Simone. And *I'm* relying on me. There's no one else I *can* rely on.

'You really shouldn't be any later,' I say firmly.

'You really care about whether she has a good time?'

'Yes,' I growl. 'I really do. And not because she's paid for it. She's a nice person. How people like her treat people like me and you is very telling.'

'People like her?'

'Obscenely wealthy.' Aside from the whole book-the-whole-restaurant-out fact, Simone has the look—the silk clothes and gleaming jewels. Most of the ultra-wealthy people I've met are too used to getting whatever they want. At best they take people like me for granted and at worst, treat me like dirt. Either way I know very well I don't fit in their world. 'But she's a good one.'

His expression tightens. 'To people like you and me?'

'Service industry survivors.' I half smile. Bracketing myself with him feels good. 'She deserves a good night,' I say softly. 'Don't make her wait any longer.'

'Okay,' he agrees equally softly but he doesn't release me. 'I won't make her wait...'

I'm struck by the craziest thought that he's about to kiss me. The even crazier thing is that I'm about to let him.

'Talia?' Kiri's voice pierces through the door. 'Any luck?'

I flinch, returning to reality with a jump. He steps back. Cold air ripples over the space on my back where his arm rested. I brace to stop myself stumbling after him.

Kiri's question slowly sinks in. I've completely forgotten why I came in here and I have no idea how long I've been standing here just—

'Glasses,' I remember dazedly. 'I need to find glasses.'

'That's why you needed to get so close just now?' A low laugh escapes him. 'So you could see me properly?'

'See your tie. Yes.' But I can only stare at him again—his smile steals everything.

'Sorry, sweetness. No luck tonight.' He leans forward and kisses me on the cheekbone. It's such a soft, swift brush of his lips that I wonder if I imagine it.

I don't answer. I can't. My brain is mush.

CHAPTER TWO

Dain

I CAN'T REMEMBER who I am or why I'm here or what I'm supposed to be doing. All I know is a scrap of a waitress urged me to do a 'good job' and all I want is to please *her* in every carnal way imaginable. *That* urge was so overwhelming I just kissed her cheek and a bolt of electricity slammed into me. Fortunately my reason returned with the force of it. Even so I stare at her for a second longer. She has shockingly pretty, big brown eyes—like a deer. She's a bit of a Bambi all round with her slim, leggy build and her glossy black-coffee hair. Pretty thing materialised just as I'd sorted the ink stain on my shirt and helped me dress like some over-efficient boarding-house matron with nimble fingers and sweet concentration. Most women undress me. This one helped me do the opposite and it was one of the hottest moments of my life. Go figure.

Talia. It's a delicate name for a delicate creature and I've a craving to taste more than just her name. Sex is a private pleasure I don't take too seriously but I must admit that being mistaken for a stripper is a first. I'll strip if she wants—*her*, that is—out of that black dress. I want to do more than strip her. I want to hear her moan again. I want her to melt against me.

It's instant and it's *intense*.

But given I haven't indulged recently, maybe it's reasonable that desire bites so hard now. My work-life balance has been more out of whack than usual. But *she's* at work and I can't harass her. Plus she's even more confused as to who I am and why I'm here than I am. Right now I'm too amused and bemused to tell her. And, all right, yes, aroused. So I walk out of the room and down the corridor. There's a ripple as I walk into the restaurant. I glance behind me, stupidly vain enough to hope she sees the reaction to my arrival. But she hasn't followed me. Deflated, I stroll towards Simone, seated in the centre of the party. The woman beside her moves to make room for me.

'You were supposed to be here hours ago,' Simone admonishes as we hug. 'But I don't mind.'

Some people write Simone off as an airhead—a Sydney society eccentric. They're wrong. She has an astute business brain. She's also the only person from my past with whom I retain consistent contact outside the boardroom.

'I'm glad you made it,' she adds.

So am I, though not for any reason to do with my god-mother. I'm haunted by the sound of a sexy little inhale as I brushed that completely inappropriate kiss on Talia's cheek.

'What held you up?' Simone asks.

I'm not about to offer full disclosure. 'Meeting ran over-time. You forgive me, right?'

Simone smiles. 'If you invest in this project, you know I'll forgive you anything.'

My smile becomes a little fixed. Even though she's almost family, Simone still wants my money. Like everyone. 'You know I can't give you an answer on that without seeing the paperwork.'

She sighs dramatically. 'Must you be so vigilant, Dain?'

'Always.'

Business comes first but I do owe Simone and that's why I'm here.

My family's been in the residential property development business for decades. My great-great-grandfather founded the business and built it to a high level of success that was subsequently almost entirely destroyed by the viciousness of my parents' divorce. They tore the company apart as well as their marriage. As well as me.

But it was down to me to resurrect what I could from the wreckage of it all. Because of Simone I was able to fulfil the promise I'd made to my grandfather. And I've done it. Anzelotti is the largest luxury apartment building company in Australia. We build thousands of them each year and still can't satisfy the waiting list.

Expansion into New Zealand hasn't been a priority, but Simone's been making a case for my investment here for the past two years. Having her birthday party tonight was in part a deliberate act to entice me back to Queenstown. I was happy to indulge her but now I'm distracted because Talia appears in the room. Yeah, she *is* the one in charge. She's ultra-efficient—minimal actions, maximum impact—and happily she's aware of me. It's barely two beats before she spots me sitting next to Simone. Her face is a picture before she pulls on a professional mask. She approaches immediately. Not going to lie, I'm delighted.

'Is everything to your satisfaction, Simone?' she asks.

She doesn't look at me as Simone answers in the affirmative.

I can't resist teasing her. 'I heard something about the entertainment having arrived?' I cock my head. 'Or is it running late?'

A flush sweeps her cheeks and she flashes a baleful look my way. 'I'll find out and get back to you as soon as I can.'

I can't help but chuckle. Then I count the seconds until she returns.

'It'll be just another few minutes and then the singer will be here,' she says.

'Singer?' I clarify coolly. 'Not a dancer?'

'No.' Her teeth snap as she smiles sharply.

'I'm going to need more coffee to keep me awake for the performance,' Simone says, seemingly oblivious to the undercurrents between the waitress and me. 'Any chance of a latte?'

'Of course,' Talia says. 'I'll get that right away.'

I can't remain still for more than a few moments. 'Excuse me, Simone,' I mutter.

Talia stands by the coffee machine. As I approach I have to suppress the maddening urge to run my hand the length of her stiff spine and soften her curves against me again. I take a sharp breath instead. Public flirting is not my thing and I definitely don't touch a woman in view of anyone else—I don't even hold hands. Discretion is everything to me. My personal life is and always will be utterly private. So that I'm openly obvious with my attention is a first. Women are usually obvious with me. All I need do is discreetly nod and they approach. From there it's to my private suite. I know that sounds arrogant but it's just true. It's what happens when you're one of Australia's wealthiest bachelors. Only I'm not in Australia now and this woman avoids my gaze entirely. But I know she's aware of me. There's strong chemistry between us and we both know it.

'I'm really looking forward to the singer,' I say conversationally.

Her body goes tense.

'Or is there some problem?' I add. 'Perhaps you'll have to step in and fill the breach?'

She ducks her chin and her flush deepens. I actually feel a little bad for teasing her.

'You should have told me you were her date,' she mutters meekly.

I blink. She thinks I'm Simone's *date*? Good grief, I've gone from stripper to escort. She glances up and that's when I spot the gleaming tease in her eyes. It tugs deep in my gut—it makes me want to use some sort of *physical* correction with her.

'Simone Boras is my godmother,' I inform her as coolly as I can. 'She's the nearest thing to a grandmother I have.'

Talia's expression flickers with smug amusement before she smooths it. I narrow my gaze on her.

'So I'm not about to give her or any other woman here a lap dance.' I lean close. 'Though I'd make an exception for you.'

That colour deepens her skin but I'm struck by the molten emotion in her bottomless eyes. I shouldn't have said it. I'm like some lecherous party guest. But she provoked me and we had shared a moment in that storeroom. Now she presses her trembling lips together—not pursing them in disapproval, but suppressing her smile. That ache tugs deep inside me again and I want everyone in this room to vanish so we can be alone.

'Can I please get a coffee too?' I mutter. 'Black. No sugar.'

'Of course.' She swiftly operates the machine.

Even though I never do this—I never usually *have* to—I somehow end up telling her who I am. 'My name is Dain Anzelotti.'

Her expression is back to bland. 'Am I supposed to recognise your name?'

'Many people would.' My name is on a lot of contracts.

But I'm not surprised she didn't recognise my face. I avoid all kinds of media. I can get some stories scrubbed before they hit the mainstream press and I only attend social events where discretion is assured. I'm not on any social media platforms. I don't have a personal email address. When you're as wealthy as I am it's advisable to remain as unreachable as possible. So as far as I'm aware there are no social media pictures of me anywhere now and, yes, I'm too precious but I've had more than enough of those in my past when I was used as a pawn during my parents' drawn-out separation and brutally public divorce.

She looks down at the coffee cup she's filling. 'You're not local, right?'

'Right. But…' But most people recognise my name.

'Are you famous or something?'

'Or something.'

'By that you mean wealthy.' She shoots me a cutting glance. 'So what? In Queenstown every other customer is an arrogant billionaire. Which sort are you? Tech? Rural? Some sort of amazing eco-friendly attire?' Her gaze rakes over my suit. 'Snowboard champion?'

'Property development,' I mutter.

She doesn't look impressed. 'Hotels?'

'Apartments.' I don't know why I'm suddenly like a schoolboy struggling to impress the girl he fancies on the bus.

'Good for you.' She shrugs dismissively.

'You'd prefer I was an…entertainer?'

She pauses. 'Well…' Her voice drops. 'It does seem like a waste of your other assets.'

I'm so shocked I can only stare as that husky little sass repeats in my head. Desire paralyses me. The images in my head—how I could use the 'assets' she's thinking of—are shockingly inappropriate. I don't lose control of myself like this. Definitely not in public. I blink, needing to distract myself before this very crowded room sees the effect this woman has on me. My gaze drops and I see the latte she's made for Simone. I've seen fancy patterns on top of frothy milk before, but this one is particularly artistic with a highly detailed bird hovering over a flower.

'That's amazing,' I mutter hoarsely.

'Yes.' She glances up and looks me directly in the eyes. 'Tastes even better.'

I'm gone. Brain dead. Body slammed. Stunned into silence. I don't respond at all. Where did this vixen come from? I've been hit on more times than I can remember but this tiny attempt has me sizzling in a way I can't handle. I recall the moments in that storeroom where she was pressed against me. I want that again. I'm all but overpowered by the urge to toss her over my shoulder and carry her back there to finish what we started.

But I don't. I can't. I remain still and silent. Struggling to process, to regain control of myself. It takes too long. Belatedly I realise a flush has swept over her face. Before I can think to respond or am able to un-gum my mouth, she drops her gaze. Swiftly she sets the coffees on a small tray. Distractedly I notice other differences between my small, plain drink and Simone's.

'Don't I get a cookie too?' I ask feebly.

It's too late. She doesn't answer. She doesn't look me in the eyes. Since when was I so incompetent with a woman? I follow her like a redundant fool. She's mortified. Even the tips of her ears are scarlet. I slip back into my seat.

'Have you been giving her a hard time?' Simone asks quietly as I watch Talia march back across the room—stiff-backed, scarlet-cheeked.

Not the kind of hard time I want to give her, no.

'She's not your usual type,' Simone adds speculatively.

'Surely you don't think I have a singular type.' I sip my scalding coffee to hide the frustration overflowing within me but I can't lift my attention from Talia.

Simone's tone warms with exasperated amusement. 'Aren't you ever going to settle down?'

'Surely you don't need to ask that.'

Because it was Simone who pulled up to my boarding school and helped me escape one of the worst moments of my life—the media intrusion and the shock of secrets kept from me until it was too late. She knows how I was caught in the midst of an emotional massacre and that I'll never accept the blistering bonds of a committed relationship myself.

'No,' Simone acknowledges. 'But you're never obvious in public. This is intriguing.'

But I haven't felt temptation like this. Or such uncertainty. I don't usually have to work for it.

I tear my gaze from Talia to focus on Simone—she's the reason I'm here, after all, and Talia was right, Simone is one of the good ones. 'I'm sorry. It's your birthday.' I pull a small box from my pocket and put it on the table between us.

Simone all but shimmers. 'Is it a pen to sign the investment papers?'

I laugh at her persistence. 'You know any deal will be negotiated in the office.'

But I remind her gently because Simone tried to help me all those years ago. A close friend of my grandfather, she disapproved of him keeping secrets from me. And she was the only one to take action when the press found out he was terminal.

'I promise I'll look at it properly tomorrow,' I add with a smile. 'I'll be there at nine.'

I enjoy the coffee and the dessert and talk to Simone and several of her guests. I also enjoy watching Talia care for the guests. That she's determined not to look in my direction is actually reassuring. She's as aware of me as I am of her and I just need another moment with her. Alone.

A guy with a guitar arrives. The long-haired crooner sings hits of bygone years. Simone loves it. But partway through his fourth item I sense an emptiness in the room. It's only been a few moments but I'm acutely aware Talia's gone. I mutter something to Simone and move.

I catch up with a young waiter in the corridor. 'Where's Talia?'

The young man looks both startled and awkward. 'She's just finished for the evening.'

Disappointment floods me. 'She's not staying till closing?'

The youth fidgets. 'She was only helping out for a while before she had to—' He stops before saying anything truly useful. 'Is there something I can get for you, sir?'

'No, that's fine. Thank you.'

I message Simone to apologise for my sudden departure and confirm tomorrow's meeting time. I know she won't mind—I've stayed longer than she'd have expected me to anyway. Striding towards the gondola, I notice the sky has darkened. The wind's lifted, whistling around the outside of the building. There's only one way down from this place and this is one ride I refuse to miss.

CHAPTER THREE

Talia

IN THE SMALL crew room I scoop up my small backpack, shove my apron into it and hurry down the corridor. I can't get out of here quick enough. I've made a massive fool of myself trying to flirt with that guy. He's more than a guest of the primary, he's her *godson*—practically family. Of *course* he wasn't a stripper, not in a suit that beautifully made and fitted and from fabric that soft and flattering. Why did I leap to such an inappropriate conclusion?

Because he was half naked and is so stunningly sculpted it was the only possibility to hit me. Yes, I objectified the guy. And no, I don't usually do that. I've avoided guys my whole life. That's what happens when your 'charming' father's a serial cheater and your co-dependent mother's a serial sucker—falling for the same type over and over. That kind of example puts a girl off even trying.

But Dain Anzelotti could have corrected me sooner, instead he let me make a bigger and bigger fool of myself until at last he revealed his innate arrogance. He flipped from smoothly amused to steely and silent—shooting me down without uttering a word. I was incinerated on the spot. But *he* kissed *me*—the patronising jerk only wanted to hook me in order to feed his endless ego. As if all his supposed wealth wasn't enough to make him feel special? Once I was on the line he couldn't cut me quick enough. I need to get out of here before I stomp back to give the entitled jerk a piece of my mind.

The gondola engineer is engrossed in some sports game onscreen and barely notices me waiting for the small passenger cabin that's coming round on the track. The cabins aren't huge and it's a relief to have it to myself. I've been customer servicing for hours and this is only a respite before I get to the bar down in town and carry on fulfilling people's orders. Still hot and flustered, I toss my backpack onto the seat with too much force. It slips straight off and I groan in frustration as my things scatter everywhere. I slump on the seat. There's no rush to collect everything, I have over twenty minutes to pull it together.

I hear rapid footsteps and hope whoever it is will be polite enough to wait for the next cabin. But a big hand stops my door from sliding shut and the suspension car wobbles as he steps inside. There's a bumping sensation as the cabin moves over the pulley system. I don't love the gondola—being suspended high above the jagged edge of a mountain freaks me out a little. But right now I'm more freaked out about the view *inside* the cabin.

I stare at him in consternation—the entertainment who wasn't. The self-proclaimed billionaire property magnate. He takes the space on the seat beside me, the doors bang shut and then there's silence as he stares at my stuff scattered all over the floor.

'What happened?' he eventually asks. 'Did you have a tantrum?'

Stunned, I do nothing as he slides onto his knees in the small space in front of me. He retrieves the items one by one— my comb and a spare hair tie, headphones that I can't use now to avoid this conversation, coins, my favourite tinted lip balm and some pain relief. He passes each item for me to stuff back into my bag and meets my gaze every time.

It's immensely irritating that he's so handsome. That my body is literally melting. What's with his mixed messages?

'Thanks,' I mumble, embarrassed and confused.

The heated intimacy in his eyes bamboozles me. As much as I want to, I can't look away from him.

'Why are you skipping out early?' Having gathered all my gear, he gets up from the floor and sits beside me. 'Have you got a date?'

I feel myself flushing. 'Another job to get to.'

'You often double shift?'

Determined not to let him get to me more, I lift my chin. 'Triple.'

He doesn't take his gaze off me. 'You need the money.'

'Most of us mere mortals do.'

He nods as if he understands. But he can't possibly. What does he know of struggling daily for survival? Of responsibility? I've been responsible, not just for myself, but for my little sister, Ava, since I was eleven and she was seven. After Dad skipped out and Mum went down a spiral of bad choice after bad choice, I needed to ensure Ava got through school—I had to because she's gifted. Seriously super smart, but having to shift schools so many times when we were kids impacted her despite her insane IQ and the intense extra study she did. So I worked and when Mum wanted to make one move too many I said no. I took on Ava myself age seventeen and I was super happy to. I wanted her to have the stability she needed—that we'd never had. I still support her now, six years later. And once she's finished her studies, I'll focus on my own future.

'I should have told you I wasn't the entertainment,' he says after a long silence. 'But I was taken by surprise and the temptation to tease you was irresistible.'

'It was my fault for jumping to conclusions,' I say stiffly.

'It seems like you'd prefer I was a booty dancer to a billionaire.' His smile briefly quirks. 'Don't you like me now you know I'm basically made of money?' He actually shoots me kicked-puppy eyes. 'It doesn't usually work that way.'

'Doesn't it?' I murmur shortly, so easily provoked into outrage all over again. 'What? Don't tell me you're some poor little rich boy now seeking my sympathy?'

The curve of his mouth deepens. 'Right now I'll take anything I can.'

I shake my head. 'You've got enough from me already.'

'Oh, I disagree,' he counters softly.

I glare at him but at the same time I'm almost helplessly drawn to him. He's more good-looking than most. Honestly, he's more *everything* than most.

'I'm glad you've finished work early. Now I'm allowed to talk to you,' he adds.

'Allowed?' I echo. 'As if you pay attention to the rules anyone else abides by?'

'You really think you have me nailed, don't you?'

The most appalling flush swamps me. I'm so hot I can't even swallow. It's a replay of that moment in the storeroom when I stood too close to him and he held me against him and time stilled.

An ominous clunking sound breaks the searing spell between us and the cabin sways awkwardly. Startled, I glance out of the window. Usually the view is spectacular when the moon and stars cast a glow over the lake but tonight the celestial elements are obscured by clouds. That clunk is replaced by a sharp metallic screech.

I've no idea how long we've been in the cabin or how far we've descended but I know we have to be some distance from the bottom still. Meaning we're suspended above a rocky mountainside and if the cable breaks we'll smash down and likely won't live. Just then the sky lights up—yet illuminates nothing. The lightning just bounces back from the thick cloud. The storm has hit sooner than predicted.

'I—'

The cabin light flickers before cutting out completely.

'Um…' Dain pulls his phone from his pocket.

As he studies the screen I hear his smothered curse.

'We've lost reception,' he says.

'It doesn't seem like there's power in town,' I mutter, pointlessly peering out of the window.

I hear the wind whistling around us. How did I not hear it pick up so much during the descent? I've been too distracted by *him*. But this is a major problem. We're suspended in a tin can, high above a jagged mountain in a major weather event. My pulse skitters.

'You feeling okay?' His query is soft.

I nod, then realise he can't see me but even in this darkness he's sensed my rising nerves. I don't want to think about how far we could fall. How we'd smash to smithereens. 'Yeah,' I lie. 'Are you?' I squeak.

'I'm hanging in there.'

I smile weakly. 'Tragic attempt at a pun.'

He turns his phone's torch on, sits it between us and smiles at me. It's a gorgeous smile and it humanises him and with him half hidden in the dark he feels more accessible.

'I feel wobbly,' I say. 'Like the ground has vanished beneath my feet.'

My joke is even more feeble but it's better to challenge my brain to come up with puns instead of staying fixated on his attractiveness. But my brain does that anyway. Relentlessly.

There's another sudden jolt and the cabin sways in a way it isn't supposed to. I draw a sharp breath. Dain's phone slides off the seat and lands on the floor, lighting the corner instead of us. He doesn't move to retrieve it. Instead he puts his hand on mine. I'm so unashamedly grateful I twist my fingers to grasp his and cover his wrist with my other hand. Just like that I'm clinging and I don't care.

'It might take some time for them to get power back online,' I worry.

'There isn't a generator?'

'I don't know. I don't usually work up there. I was just helping out a friend.'

'You enjoy your work?' he asks calmly.

'I've been doing it a long time.'

'Your latte art was pretty cool. I've seen some done before but your bird design for Simone was excellent.'

'Thanks.'

'You must have practised a lot.'

I know he's distracting me. I welcome it. I drag in a breath and make myself focus. 'Yeah, but mostly I do it to put online. I have a social media channel for it.'

'You have an influencer side hustle?'

I swear I hear an element of judgement in his tone. 'I'm hardly at influencer status but my ASMR videos are really popular. And my how-to-do-it-at-home tutorials are increasingly getting clicks.'

'And that's the dream—to be an Insta-recognisable influencer?'

Oh, there's definitely judgement there.

'Actually, I'm going to have my own roastery one day. My own coffee label. And my channel is absolutely going to help with that.' I'm not trying to impress him. I'm just babbling. It's helping but not as much as his hand-holding is.

'You want to take on the big multinationals?' he asks.

'No, I just want a boutique label. I want to support coffee growers with ethical practices who provide a sustainable wage. There's room in the market for that and the world needs to change.'

'You're an idealist.'

I shake my head. 'A humanist.'

The light from the phone on the floor in the corner is just enough to let me see him, hopefully without him seeing how much I'm staring. *He's* the perfect distraction from the fear that I'm about to plummet hundreds of feet onto rocks. His

eyes are stunning. A deep blue, they glitter with a vitality
that makes me want to lean in to feel his energy. Okay, his
muscles too. I want to test out the length and breadth of him
for myself. It's the weirdest thing. I avoid men. But this isn't
like anything else. This is like a lightning strike and, yes,
I know that's a cliché, but it's the best my befuddled brain
can come up with right now. I guess the storm outside is a
prompt and all.

'They should have shut down the gondola,' I murmur. 'We'd
be safer up at the top even without power.'

'We'll be fine.' His hand tightens on mine. 'We're more
likely to be in a car accident.'

'You know your facts.' Who's he trying to reassure? Me
or himself?

'Several.'

'You're a one-per-center, though. You're already in a bunch
of minority sections. Top of your class. Most wealthy.'

Most gorgeous.

'And you think that makes me more likely to be killed in
a freak gondola accident?' He sounds amused.

'You're all kinds of special,' I mumble.

His hand tightens on mine. 'Look at me,' he says softly.
'We're going to be fine.'

'You don't know that.' But I breathe out slowly. I am not
going to lose it here. I never lose it. I stay calm even when a
situation seems dire. 'But there's nothing either of us can do
in this moment to make it better.'

'No?'

I pause, struck by a sudden frisson in the atmosphere between us.

'Powerless is not a position I'm used to being in,' he says.

I can well believe it. And, even though I mightn't have the
money he does, I do have my own drive. 'Me neither.'

'You were in charge of all the wait staff.' He nods. 'You're
usually in control?'

'Of everything front of house.'

'Yeah,' he mutters. 'You were more than efficient. You control everything else too. Multiple jobs—even how the milk spills into a cup...'

I loathe feeling as though I have no control over my life. My whole childhood was hostage to my mother's whims. Ava and I had no choice about where we lived or for how long. Mum made us pack up and move on in an afternoon. I left places and people I loved without the chance to say goodbye or explain why. That's not how I live now and it's not how *I'll* ever make anyone live.

'Two control freaks trapped in a stalled gondola in the middle of an electrical storm...what a nightmare.' I manage a smile.

He smiles back. 'It's not so awful.'

I shoot him a sceptical look. 'I can feel your pulse racing.'

'It is,' he says. 'But not because I'm scared.'

My pulse races. Not because I'm scared either. 'I guess there's nothing like a natural disaster as a great leveller. Your money isn't going to make any difference now.'

'Have I lost what little lustre I had?' He's mock mournful.

'You know I was never attracted to your billions, but your brawn could still be useful.'

'Brawn?' He almost chokes on a laugh. 'How so?'

Searing temptation takes hold of me and suddenly it doesn't matter that he froze me out the last time I tried flirting with him. This time he's intimately close—I can feel his pulse, see his smile, and it's intoxicating. 'I think my chances of survival will be higher if you cushion my landing.'

'What?' His jaw drops.

'If you're wrapped around me I'll be protected.'

'So I'll go splat and you'll be saved.' He smiles. 'From this height?'

Amusement shimmers through us both.

'I'm happy to increase my odds even if it's only by an infinitesimal amount,' I breathe.

He leans closer. 'Are you asking me to hold you?'

I can't answer. His grip on my fingers tightens and while he cups my jaw with his other hand he leans closer still. I stop breathing.

And my stomach rumbles. Loudly. I stifle a moan. As if it weren't mortifying enough to be so gauche in here with him.

'You're hungry,' he teases softly.

I'm thirsty too. Frankly I have all kinds of needs right now. 'I'll survive.'

But my pulse skips. If this is the moment before my death then I don't want to go without having ever kissed a man. And a man is right here with me and he seems like he might—

'Do you need distraction from that as well as the imminent disaster?' he asks.

'What kind of distraction are you thinking of?'

'Well, *you* did think I was the entertainment but I think a lap dance might make the car swing too much. I think we're going to have to take this gently and slowly.'

I stare at him warily, because when it comes down to it I can never trust anyone. 'You froze me out with your silence in the restaurant.'

'No. You stunned me into silence.' His expression softens. 'I was trying to stay in control. I couldn't do this there.'

'This?'

The brush of his lips is balmy, teasing. His tenderness takes me by surprise, as does the moment he takes to lean back and search my eyes. I realise he's seeking my consent.

I can hardly think. 'This is…'

'What I've wanted to do all night.' His gleaming gaze bores into me—intense and unwavering. '*You're* why my pulse is racing.'

I just topple right into his arms. He scoops me close and then his mouth is there again—on mine. And I melt.

It turns out that kissing is the best ever way to neutral-
ise panic. The best way to stay in the moment, to not give a
damn about anything else in life—not even imminent death.
Kissing is the best ever thing full stop. We kiss and we kiss
and we kiss.

I have no idea how long we've been stuck here and I no
longer care because there's this and this is the beginning, the
end, the everything.

He pulls me onto his lap, wrapping his arms around me.
So tight. So right. I actually quiver and his embrace tightens still more. I'm twisted sideways but I manage to free my
arms to wind them around his broad shoulders and we just
keep kissing. He's hot and his attention is lush and he carries me with him.

This is nothing but a moment in the middle of a storm.
He'll be leaving the country shortly. I'll never see him again.
So I'm not just here, I'm all in as a need I've long denied un-
leashes within me.

'What was it you said?' He growls, picking up on my restless hunger. 'She deserves a good night and I shouldn't make
her wait any longer…?'

His hands sweep over me as he plunders my mouth. I shiver
even though I'm hot. He palms my breasts then shapes my
waist. I feel his tension, the ridge of his arousal beneath me.
I moan as I realise he's as hot for me. I want it with him. I
want it all. He slips his hand beneath my dress. The trail of
his fingertips against my skin makes my moans earthier. I
can't retain control of myself. My hips rock to a rhythm that's
new to me yet is as old as time. He doesn't stop—he targets
his attentions. Because he knows what he's doing. He knows
how his touch sends me mad. Dissolving all thought, leaving
only feeling. *Need.*

'Sweetheart,' he mutters as he pushes my panties aside.
'All this wet is for me.'

I gasp and groan at the same time—torn between extreme arousal and embarrassment. It's not a pretty noise.

But he gives further encouragement. 'So sweet, I want to taste it.'

Oh. I melt even more because to my astonishment I want that too but there's no time. I'm not anywhere near naked nor is he but it doesn't matter because I start to shake.

'Oh, darling...' His tongue slides past my lips and into my mouth, invading my heat the way I know he wants to plunder that other part of me.

I ache with searing need. His hand moves more intimately against me and he slides a finger inside my virgin flesh. I gasp—his possession is such a relief but still isn't enough. I rock my hips. Riding him. He holds me firm while stroking me, gruffly purring encouragement.

'I want...' I can't finish my sentence.

'I know what you want.' He growls roughly. 'Come on me, Talia.'

It's so intimate I could die. But he orders me into a raw response with coarse, lusty words that make me hotter, slicker, wilder until at last I convulse. I tear my lips from his to shriek through the unbearable ecstasy.

It's good. Oh, it's good.

I squeeze my fingers into his shoulders as I shudder, gasping for big breaths to recover something of myself. I've just come apart completely. I've never lost control like this with anyone. But in *his* hold, it's not just empowering, it's addictive. Only the totality of that insane satisfaction lasts mere seconds. With a moan I kiss him with complete abandon. Showing him what I can't verbalise—I want *more*.

He groans and his hand cups my sex possessively. 'Talia...'

'Yes.' Unfettered, I pant between kisses. 'Yes, yes, yes.'

His whole body tightens beneath me. 'You want—'

'Yes!' But a sliver of sanity stirs and I lift my head. 'But I can't get pregnant or—'

'Your fellow control freak has a condom in his wallet.' His words are muffled against my neck as he suckles my skin. 'Kids aren't on my agenda.'

He's unapologetic but his obviously vast experience isn't a turn-off. I know nothing. He knows everything. I could learn. I *want* to learn. Especially with him. Here's my chance. I'm not afraid of anything any more. For the first time in my life I'm fearless—such is the power of that orgasm and the madness in this moment.

'Not mine either. Not yet for me.' I glance at him. 'Not ever for you, right?'

'Right.' He chuckles lightly. 'So let me get it.'

He wriggles to dig out his wallet. I just get more aroused all over again.

'Look at us. Capable people. In control,' he mutters.

'So in control.' I'm sliding towards oblivion again—*so* fast.

'Rational right to the end,' he insists with mock seriousness as he teases me even more.

'Stop congratulating yourself on your genius and put it on.'

'Right. Ms Impatience.'

'Of course I'm impatient.' I lean against him. 'We're hanging by a thread and who knows how long we have…?'

He laughs but it morphs into a groan. 'Quite.'

He lifts me to my feet, moving me only slightly away from him, and delves beneath my hemline again to slide my panties down and off. He doesn't bother taking off my dress. There isn't time. He balances me with one hand while hurriedly unfastening his trousers, lifting his hips enough to bare his thighs and free his straining erection. Then he pulls me back onto his lap with strength that awes me. This time I'm fully facing him, my legs straddle him. Even though I'm basically still dressed, I'm more exposed than I've ever been in my life.

He kisses me, unfastening the first few buttons of my dress with deft skill, pushing it so he can access what he wants— my tight, turned-on breasts. He traces hot kisses down the side of my neck and teases my nipples with his fingertips before fastening his mouth on one and feasting. I almost howl. I can feel the pressure of him at the apex of my thighs and all I can do is rock some more and moan. His hands work fast between us now. I hear the sound of the wrapper tearing, the hiss of breath as he rolls the protection down his erection. Am I really going to do this? *Hell yes.*

Nothing's ever felt like this. I don't think I'll feel anything like this again. My hunger just sharpens.

He pauses. 'Are you sure?'

I've never been more sure of anything. The wind whips outside and every so often lightning cracks but I don't care. I'm no longer scared. Impatient, I push forward, pressing onto him. But something isn't quite right and the sudden pain is intense. I freeze.

'Sweetheart?'

I chose not to tell him. I figured it doesn't matter. It's my business. But now I *can't* speak. I'm overwhelmed and all I want is for him to help me.

'You're so tight,' he mutters between clenched teeth. 'Has it been a while, darling?'

'Y-yes.' A half-truth isn't a lie, right?

I don't want him to stop. But right now I'm frozen because I don't know what I'm doing. I don't know how to get through this. It's a searing, tearing sensation.

'Let me help,' he grits.

'Yes, please.' I need it—him.

He pulls out. I whimper because that's not what I wanted at all. But he kisses me and he's so tender with my mouth. His fingers are tender too. Slow and teasing and he sweeps me back into that heat. I melt again and soften. He strokes, not just one finger inside me, but two, then three—pumping me, priming me with slow deliberation. It's so much and so good I almost come again. That's when he slides his fingers from me. I hiss in frustration.

'You're ready for me now,' he says, voice low.

'Yes…' I roll my hips.

He grips them hard and holds me still. I feel his broad blunt tip and heat surges within me. I slide as he thrusts so we collide and merge. I moan helplessly but this time the strangeness of the sensation is surpassed by surging pleasure. Pain hits then disappears as his guttural groan makes me slicker and I take more of him still. The sliding friction is easier—and exquisite. I take him to the hilt, feeling suddenly powerful, and squirm closer still.

Neither of us are quiet now. The sighs are from me. The grunts from him as he leads me into a rhythm that's intense and undeniable. My mind, my body, close around him.

'Dain,' I moan into the hot crook of his neck as I curl around him.

'Now you're there, darling,' he murmurs approvingly, cradling me closer. 'You did it, you've got me.'

'Yes.' I want him. *So* much.

He's big and he's strong and the dragging sensation as he moves inside me is mind-blowingly delicious. What began as an amusement—as funny and tender and little more than a tease—has become something far more intense. There was another thread beneath that lightness—a ribbon of deeper desire that's now pulled free. We move together. He smothers me with kisses. It's as if he's wanted to do this for all eternity and now he has the chance, he's consuming me.

'Oh, gorgeous,' he breathes against my neck over and over and over as I sway like a blossom in his hold. 'You're just gorgeous.'

I melt in the heat of his approval. My eyes water again for a totally different reason. This is nothing like I've ever dreamed. It's better. Hell, maybe I'm already dead and I'm in heaven because this is the best feeling in the world.

'I can't last much…' His voice is ragged and he's struggling for coherence and it's all the sweeter, hotter, dirtier.

All I can do is moan in reply. My eyes close. I feel enveloped—inside and out—in hot velvet and silky steel. The storm outside is forgotten. The swing of the car only adds to the sensation of fierce freedom. Of achieving an impossibility. I'm secure in his embrace yet it's the wildest moment of my life. Finally it overwhelms me. I cry out as I come so hard I don't know anything any more. There's total body annihilation. I hear his words—filthy and fierce—as he thrusts hard into me, harder than ever, and grips me to him. The moment is more sweet than I could have ever imagined possible.

I don't know how long it is later when I realise I'm slumped over him, my head resting on his chest. We're still intimately connected. I never want to move.

'Imagine if the cable breaks now,' he mutters. 'What a way to go though, right?'

'Embarrassing if people found us locked together,' I mumble.

He nudges me gently. 'Worth it? Not worth it?'

'So worth it.' I lift my head and smile at him.

In the dim light cast from his phone I see him smile back and—

A screeching sound startles me. The cabin jolts severely and suddenly descends a few metres along the cable. His grip on me tightens to stop me from falling from his lap. The cabin lights blink a couple of times and then return to full power and Dain's arms loosen. I scramble off him and quickly tug down my dress, refasten the buttons at the neckline and scramble for my panties. My cheeks burn. So do other parts of me.

There's no camera in the cabin—thank goodness—but there is an intercom and it suddenly crackles, emitting a calming pre-recorded message saying we'll be at the ground soon and not to panic.

Dain swiftly does up his trousers and retrieves his phone from the floor. His shirt is half unbuttoned, his face flushed. He looks more than dishevelled—dissolute. As he glances up at me his muscles visibly tighten. I almost liquefy into a puddle on the floor. Apparently I've discovered my inner nymph.

But I gulp air, striving for nonchalance. 'We should probably—'

His phone beeps with a series of messages. Then it actually rings.

He glances at the screen and answers immediately. 'Simone? You okay?'

I can hear his godmother's tone but can't make out what she's saying. My heart kicks. Family loyalty matters to me. Well, *some* of my family. I would never not answer an invitation or call if my sister Ava needed me.

'Fine. I'm fine.' His gaze is trained on me as he talks to her. 'Everyone up there okay?' He nods reassuringly at me as he listens to what she says.

I smooth my hair and sit back down, grab my backpack and hold it on my lap in front of me like a protective shield.

Dain ends the call with Simone. 'Talia—'

'No regrets,' I quickly whisper.

His phone rings again. I see his frustration at the interruption but I'm relieved and gesture for him to answer it. I don't want to talk about what just happened. I don't want to analyse it or ruin it in any way. He lives in a different country. He's a billionaire and I'm a barista. This is over.

We're at the bottom of the gondola before that second call ends, before I can believe it. I can't believe anything about tonight. As the doors slide open there are five huge guys in firefighting gear waiting for us. I take advantage of the crowd and chaos to escape.

'Talia!'

I ignore his call. I run into the night—taking control— because I don't want an awkward, embarrassing goodbye. There's nothing to say. This was a moment I'll never regret, a moment I'll always treasure.

But nothing will ever come of it.

CHAPTER FOUR

Dain

As MY PILOT brings the jet in to land I gaze at the mountain to the right. I'm not in the cockpit—my licence is more hobby than necessity—but if I had to take over the controls, I could. The mountains are snowy and majestic, the southern lakes sapphire, yet it's the gondola complex glinting in the sunlight snagging all my attention.

It's almost a year to the day since I was trapped in a suspension car with an annoyingly unforgettable woman. Almost a year since I last had sex.

Yeah, I can't believe that either. Trust me, I'm not happy about it.

My sexual appetite has simply…dried up. When I returned to Australia, I met other women but never took any home. Opportunities they offered, I ignored. I worked harder and longer hours until basically becoming a workaholic hermit.

In the decade before this last year I had many lovers and remained on good enough terms with most. I was upfront with what I offered—never more than a few nights' ultra-discreet fling—private islands, private hotels, no prying eyes. Definitely no cameras.

But Talia ran straight into that stormy night—leaving me. I had to stop and thank that rescue crew. It couldn't have been

more clear that she wanted to get away. I let her. I don't chase
women down.

I did, however, invest in Simone's project. And eventually
I did go back to that restaurant—two months after that searing night I braved that bloody gondola again. By then the entire hospitality staff had turned over. The chef—Kiri—had
been headhunted and moved north. No one on shift the day I
returned knew anything about who'd been on front of house
that wild night. I figured that was fate telling me to quit. I
wasn't about to walk around town going to every restaurant
and café on a quest to track down a barista called Talia.

Okay, I did do that. Briefly. It didn't work.

Now I'm back in Queenstown. We broke ground on Simone's apartment building two months ago and I'm here to
check progress. And okay, yes, I can't resist the possibility I
might see her.

I now know her name is Talia Parrish. Yeah, as much as I
loathe online platforms I fully social-media-stalked my way
to that information three months ago in a moment of fury
over my tragic existence of the last year. I found her channel.
I'm not one for sharing anything online but frankly I found
it a disappointment. All her recent videos are just hands and
coffee art—very clever art, to be fair, but we don't get to see
her face.

I can't forget her face. I've tried but she haunts me at night.
Every night. Worse, memories of that encounter hit at the most
inappropriate times. I've never been as unable to control my
own thinking. Hell, right now my body hardens the way it
does at the thought of her. Only her. Frustrating isn't the word.

I need to see her again. I need to put that haunting nymph
to bed for good.

Maybe it's just that feeling of unfinished business. The way
she slipped into that storm to get away from me grates. We'd
gone through something in that cable car—something more
than just a physical tryst—so her instant vanishing act felt like

a betrayal of the connection—the trust. Yeah, I'm a fool. The people *closest* to me kept the most terrible secrets from me, why am I so bothered by some random woman running off?

Twenty minutes after our mid-morning landing I'm walking along the main street of Queenstown. It's postcard perfect and there are crowds of ski and snowboarding lovers everywhere. I want to wipe them all out of my way.

'We'll be back soon!'

I freeze. I recognise a husky edge in that call. I turn even though my heart has yet to pump another beat. A bell jingles as the door of a warm-looking café closes. A woman is walking away from it—away from me.

I stare after her. She's wearing a woollen hat but there's a brunette plait hanging partway down her back. She's wearing an enormous black puffer jacket. From here I can see one seam patched with a piece of black duct tape. Even so a feather escapes. Because it's bulky I can't tell her shape but she's about the right height. What little I can see of her legs is encased in dark blue denim. Her boots are leather but, like the jacket, patched and old.

There's no way it'll be Talia, but I follow anyway. I'm compelled. She walks with a gentle sway that's almost hypnotic. Swallowing, I mock my foolishness. Her head is down and I haven't seen her face but I can't shake the conviction that it's her so I follow her journey all the way to the public gardens at the edge of the lake. She doesn't walk with both arms at her sides. She's holding one in front of her. Has she hurt it in some way?

In the gardens she pauses and I stop, hanging back by a tree so she can't see me. There's almost no one around now but the view of the lake and back to the small town is beautiful. It's not warm enough to be outside for long but she bends— somewhat awkwardly—to brush a dusting of snow from the park bench. Her bulky jacket still shields her body from me but as she sits on the space she cleared I glimpse the side of her face. It's her. It really is her.

My jaw drops but I say nothing. It's eerily quiet aside from a bird or something chirping. But it's not a bird. It takes me a beat to realise it's the cry of a small child. A baby. Talia fusses with a woollen scarf or something and tucks her head down. After a few moments the crying stops and it slowly dawns on me. She's not just cradling that baby. She's breastfeeding it.

Shock paralyses me. I stand there beneath the tree, staring like some deranged stalker while her earlier words to whoever was in that café come back to me.

'We'll be back soon.'

We.

I'm good at maths. Always have been. But right now my brain is only focused on the fact that sometimes—just some-times—one plus one can equal three. I don't know how old that baby is. I don't know what a roughly three-month-old baby would look like. But I'm guessing it wouldn't be big.

So she got pregnant—*when*? Oh, I know. I know *exactly*. My gut burns with intuition. It was late one stormy night when she was suspended metres high above a mountain. When she was in my arms. When we sought mindless bliss together.

It was almost a year ago. Which means it's almost a year that she's kept this from me. She's not just deceived me, she's *deprived* me. I'm devastated.

In the next second rage hits.

I already know how it feels to be shut out. When family deny you everything. That's why I'll never have one of my own. You can't trust anyone. But it's happened to me *again*.

I almost can't stand. I press my palm to the rough trunk of the tree I'm under. It's cold and gnarled and it digs against my skin. I breathe in the freezing air—slow and deep—until I'm cold again too.

She adjusts the way she's holding the baby. I don't hear her words exactly, but I do hear the loving tone. Something other than rage swamps me.

My controlled breathing was pointless. Now I'm burning inside—kicked alive—by instinct. Need. *Action.*

I walk towards her, letting my boots scrunch on the stones and the frosty fallen leaves. But she doesn't even lift her head. From the angle I approach them at I glimpse the baby. It's asleep. I see it's dark lashes flush against soft-looking chubby cheeks. Talia's eyes are closed too. She's pale but as beautiful as ever as she rests in the weakened sunlight. I stop only a few feet away but still she doesn't stir.

I'm so focused on her I've forgotten to blink. Shocked and disbelieving. My teeth ache from the cold. From the fierceness with which I've been clenching them.

'Talia?' My voice is raspy but I try again. 'Talia?'

Her eyes flash open. Her chin jerks up as undeniable and absolute horror flashes on her face. *'No!'*

CHAPTER FIVE

Talia

No.

My involuntary emotional outburst hangs in the air and I can't bite it back no matter how much I want to. I've long given up thinking he might appear at any moment and for a split second I hope I'm dreaming. But I'm not. He's here. And he's looking...

Furious. *Fine.*

Dain Anzelotti towers over me and, despite my terror, all I can do is soak in the sight. A year ago I thought he was handsome. I was wrong. He's jaw-dropping. He's not in a suit today but instead wearing that casual billionaire winter uniform—leather boots, well-cut jeans, form-hugging merino sweater, tailored jacket. The layers don't hide his lithe, muscular frame. The denim grazes his quads. The jacket emphasises his broad shoulders. But his blue gaze nails me to the bench.

I'm stunned into silence, into stillness. Yet as the seconds tick a tendril deep inside me stirs to life. I thought it dead, not dormant. The shocking lust that once led me to lose control completely. He says nothing but I feel utterly disadvantaged as he stares at me from above. I don't breathe as he, oh, so deliberately lowers his gaze to intently study his tiny son tucked against me. I fight the overwhelming urge to run. I know it would be futile.

I don't know Dain well. We were together for only a couple of hours. But I can tell he's leashed. But the emotion burgeoning within *me* is what's really scary. I lost all control with this man and it upended my life completely. I can't allow that to happen again.

'Who's this?' His voice is raspy.

I don't answer. I can't. Is he *playing* with me?

'Don't try to tell me he isn't yours,' he adds harshly. 'I can't imagine you'd breastfeed a friend's baby in the park.'

'You were *watching*?' I gape. 'How long have you been following me?'

'Twenty-four minutes. Since you walked out of that café.'

I'm stunned again. He followed me here. He stood and watched me feed Lukas. I feel exposed—it's such a personal thing. Ordinarily it would be natural for the father of my baby to watch me nurture our baby but Dain rescinded his right to that intimacy months ago. It's too late now. It *has* to be. I lift my chin and emotion betters my brain. 'What do you *want*?'

His blue eyes flash fire. 'What's the baby's name?'

Oh, please. 'I already told you in the messages I sent you months ago,' I spit my fury at him. 'Again in the photo taken when he was born.'

Dain stands very still. 'What messages?'

I glare up at him, refusing to believe that flare in his eyes. 'The emails.'

'Never got any.'

'Don't believe you.' But I'm quaking inside because I know, I *know* I didn't try hard enough. 'I sent them to every permutation of your email I could think of. I even sent them to the help desk listed on your company website.'

There were four actual messages sent to multiple addresses. All increasing in urgency. But I *stopped* sending them. I tried but then I quit after Lukas's birth. I gave Dain the shortest of chances. Because he never bothered to reply. I knew he wouldn't. He told me he wasn't a commitment kind of guy and I saw for myself that he wasn't and I decided I didn't need to chase harder. He wasn't interested. I don't want that for my child. I want to protect him. And myself. Because I know rejection. I know just how much it *hurts*.

Suddenly Dain's on his haunches in front of me and his tone is colder than the frosty air swirling around us. 'What's the baby's name?'

I stare into his blue eyes and am helpless to do anything but answer. 'Lukas.'

His indrawn breath is sharp. 'Spelt how?'

Yeah. Smart question. But I guess it proves that I did go on his company website. I did try to make contact a few times at least. Because Lukas was his grandfather's name. My throat tightens. 'You already know—'

'Humour me,' he says, too silkily. 'I think it's the least you can do.'

'Lukas. With a K not a C.'

Another sharp breath. 'And does little Lukas have a middle name?'

Hearing him say Lukas's name does something to me. I'm suddenly shaking inside—such a sentimental fool. I wanted my son to have a connection to his father even when his father didn't even want to know him. 'His full name is Lukas Dain Parrish.'

Dain's gaze slices through me. 'Parrish?'

'That's my name.'

'But he's my child.'

I brace and look right into his angry eyes. '*Our* child.'

I've already given him two of Dain's family names. It was for balance and frankly more than generous enough.

The image slides into my head again. The one I hate. I know Dain went straight from that liaison with me into the arms of another woman that night. Whether she was his girlfriend or not I don't know. I don't want to. The thought of being the 'other woman' sucks. The pictures I saw online that next morning made me feel sick. In fact I felt sick every time I so much as thought of him for weeks after. And I kept thinking of him. Kept feeling sick. Morning sickness, in fact. Because I'm an idiot.

'You didn't tell me.' His rage is less suppressed now.

'You ignored my messages. Why are you here?' I ask him again before he can deny getting them again. 'Why unannounced?'

Is it to startle me? Because if so, it's certainly worked.

He stands, towering again, embodying the huge, threatening shadow he's become in my life. 'You need to come with me,' he demands.

'I don't think so.'

'We need to talk.'

I'm suddenly furious. Does he think he can ignore my messages and then just turn up? I can't let him storm in and blow up my life when I've come through the worst days after giving birth. When I almost have a sustainable routine going.

'You've had plenty of time to talk to me. You've chosen not to.' I go stone cold inside. 'I messaged multiple times and you ignored them.'

But the blank denial in his eyes is so real, I falter. He's shockingly pale. His breathing is uneven. To my eternal horror I *know* this is all news to him. But I push on because now I'm terrified. 'Your chance to be involved has been and gone.'

His cool gaze slides over my face and drops to the baby again. 'Wrong. This is the first I've...'

I don't want to believe him. But I do. And now I feel atrocious.

'Then why are you in Queenstown if not to see us?' I whisper.

'Checking on a project.'

It's business.

I'm incredibly—stupidly—hurt. It's purely because of fate that he's found us. I shouldn't have gone for a walk today. I should have gone upstairs to feed Lukas. Then he wouldn't have seen us. Disappointment slices into me. It's the destruction of the last flicker of hope I hadn't realised I still had. But I'm still weak enough to be attracted to him even when he's ignored me till now. That I could be this crushed—again—is appalling. I'm as vulnerable as my mother and being that gullible—falling for a wealthy, good-looking cheater—was something I'd promised myself I wouldn't do.

I tear my gaze from Dain and look down at my baby. He's tiny, precious, so vulnerable and I'm overwhelmed by the need to protect him. I don't want him hurt. Not the way I was. I'll do anything to shield him from the wounds of being unwanted. I lean closer to him and breathe in his sweet baby scent. He has his father's eyes. The midwife told me that baby's eyes are often blue at first but that they can change, but that hasn't happened yet, and I don't think it will. He has Dain's dark brown hair too. And his ability to consume every inch of my attention.

'We don't need your help,' I mutter.

'No? Then why are you sleeping on a park bench in the mid-morning, like you're a homeless person?'

'We were just getting some fresh air.' But I'm overly defensive because if it weren't for my boss, Romy, we *would* be homeless. I live above her café. I know it's not ideal. I work in the kitchen in the very early hours—baking the muffins and pastries for the day. I'm still building my channel and film at night in the café when it's closed. But Lukas is a demanding baby and I can't care for him at the café and disturb the customers downstairs during the day. That's why I take him for long walks along the waterfront.

Now that I'd fed him I was letting him sleep for a moment before tucking him properly back into his sling so I could walk back. But I'm tired. I've done today's baking. I've done my own work overnight so I snatch sleep in short shifts whenever I can. I'm doing okay and working my butt off to do better. Because I adore Lukas and I'll do whatever necessary to provide for him. But it's hard. Even so, I definitely don't want Dain's help now.

'Talia.'

Bleary-eyed, I glance up at him again. He's *beautiful*. It's like a boulder landing in my stomach—immobilising me. He's also determined. And fiercely strong—physically and mentally. Panic sweeps, darkening everything in the world except for him—as if he's in the damned spotlight—he's all I can see. And what I feel is overwhelming.

I liked him. A lot. But he—like everyone—let me down. I know that the only person I can ever really rely on is myself. Lukas is relying on me too.

And I know giving in to whatever Dain is about to demand will be dangerous. If he wins now, he'll think he can win always.

'Let's go to your home,' he says. 'We'll talk there.'

I don't want him to see how we're living. I don't want any of this. We live in different countries. We have vastly different lives. So I have no idea what he's going to want or how it's going to work. But I will stay in Lukas's life and so I have to be calm and stay in control. I have to do my best for my son.

I don't answer Dain verbally. I simply stand and start walking, cradling my precious son, hating the heat that's coursing through my body as this tall, devastating man wordlessly falls into step alongside me. Well, he stalks really—like a barely leashed predator. For the first time in months I feel revitalised—fury fills me with the energy I've been lacking in so long. As we walk I lift my head and breathe deep and when we finally arrive…

I'm ready to fight.

CHAPTER SIX

Dain

I'VE HAD ONE serious concussion in my life from a skiing accident when I was fourteen. Back then I lost three hours but right now I'm more stunned and confused than when I woke up and found myself in a hospital hundreds of kilometres from the ski field. Today it seems I've lost *months*. I can't see straight, let alone think. My thundering pulse deafens me to anything—any excuse—she might try to make.

She's had a baby. My *son*. And this is the first I've heard about it and that's only because I happened upon them by accident.

I barely register the walk back to the café. She leads me through the crowded tables to the rear. Behind a door marked *Private* there's a narrow flight of stairs. Climbing them, I feel the echo of that small storeroom where we first met. The room at the top of these stairs is even smaller. The first thing I see is a narrow bed. A baby bassinet is pulled up beside it. Everything is clean and neat but spare—it's minimal in decor, devoid of luxury. Bare necessities only.

Anger churns but desire adds a vicious twist right at the most wrong of moments. I want her on that bed. With me. Which is ridiculous because it's nowhere near big enough for the both of us. Yeah, cognitive function is fully impaired and anger is the safest option.

'How long have you lived here?' I growl.

'I need to change Lukas,' she mutters.

I watch. She's efficient as she cares for the baby. Of course she is. She's done this hundreds of times. I wouldn't know where to begin. My anger sharpens as she picks him up again. The betrayal is intense and when she smiles at the baby I snap.

'You need to start packing,' I hiss and shove my hands into my jacket pockets.

'Packing?'

'You can't stay another night here.'

It's noisy. It's tiny. Which is probably why she has to go for walks during the café's busiest hours. It's appalling.

She stares at me with such mistrust it burns. What did I ever do to deserve it? But I rein my resentment in. I need her to agree with me.

'We can't talk properly here. Not with people trying to enjoy their coffee downstairs.' And not in front of the child. 'Did I ever give you reason not to trust me, Talia? Because right now I feel like I'm the one who can't trust you, given you never told me I have a son.'

'I *tried*—'

'Exactly where did you supposedly send all those messages?' I ask.

'Don't you believe I sent them?' she whispers furiously. 'Why don't you check?'

'Why do you think I'm asking?' I snap back. 'A forensic IT search is about to be launched.'

She looks down at the baby and I see her striving to steady her breath. 'There isn't a direct email for you listed on your company website. You have no phone number. Your social media profiles are non-existent. You're *very* well protected from the public.'

She's right. I push for as much privacy as possible. 'So you sent them to…?'

Coming from one of Australia's most wealthy families—
plus being single—provides challenges. All emails are filtered
but surely hers should have been flagged.

'I sent them to the information address.'

What did she say? How blunt was she? How many did she
send? I can't shake the feeling that it wasn't as many as possible. 'You should have tried harder.'

She lifts her chin defiantly. 'Perhaps I should have gone
to the *media*? Sold my story? Shamed you by saying we had
sex in the middle of a thunderstorm and that as a result...'
Her eyebrows lift.

I'm on fire inside at the thought of that—I'm too aware
of the ravenous public appetite for personal drama. I would
have *loathed* it but the truth would've got to me at last. 'Perhaps you should have,' I say more calmly than I'm feeling. 'It
would have got my attention.'

'And destroyed *my* reputation—my career—in the process.
I'd have become known as Dain Anzelotti's baby-mama. As
far as I could tell, you weren't interested. I needed to protect
my own earning potential.'

'You're a waitress.'

She glares at me but I'm unapologetic. 'No doubt you'll
think it arrogant if I suggest that your being linked with me
would only *enhance* your earning potential,' I add.

'You don't know anything about me.'

Not entirely true. I know some things. Quite a lot. I know
the sound she makes when she's so hot she can't stand it any
more. I know her scent. I know how tightly her hand can
squeeze mine. I know her taste. But I don't trust her. I don't
trust anyone.

'Right, and you know little about me—'

'I know plenty. I looked up who you were.'

I see condemnation in her eyes and my skin prickles. Has
she seen the past—some of those stories about my parents?

Is this why she's kept Lukas secret, because she's afraid I'll be as awful as my own parents were? 'And whatever you discovered put you off trying harder to contact me?'

'You don't want to settle down. You're used to getting what you want. Who you want. When you want.'

'And these are such insufferable qualities you think I shouldn't have any part in my son's life?'

She whitens.

But I'm angry with her judgement. Only at the same time she's right. I'm used to people doing what I ask them to. I'm used to being in charge of pretty much everything. Yet Talia Parrish only has to enter my mind and I lose control of my own damned body. I'm hard for her. I'm always hard for her. *Only* hard for her. And I hate it.

Stupid, *stupid* chemistry.

Once was not enough. That's all.

Memories flood my mind. That night was a set of circumstances where adrenalin was pumping and the satisfaction— a life-threatening moment made earthly pleasure extreme. I had to hurriedly get rid of that condom. There was no time to check it properly but I've often remembered her tension when I first entered her. Crazy as it is, I suspect she was a virgin. But surely not.

She lifts her chin. 'I don't want him confused by all the women in your life.'

I narrow my gaze. '*Neither* of us will parade lovers in front of him. I don't want him to have a revolving door of people he thought might care about him only to be disappointed.'

Her eyes widen. 'I agree.'

'Fancy that,' I say coolly. 'We might agree on more once we really get going.' I drag in a breath. 'I can adjust accordingly, Talia. I hope you're able to do the same.' Her assumptions about my character annoy the hell out of me. 'Why did you stop trying to reach me?'

She stands stiffly. 'It was clear you weren't interested.'

'I didn't *know*.' I bite the words.

She could have tried again. Tried harder. I'm furious with myself for ignoring that nagging feeling about her for so long.

'I want you to come to Australia with me.' I blurt, losing the ability for fine negotiations.

I need privacy and time to get my head around this and there's only one place I know where I'm sure I can get it. My place is a fortress.

'No.' Shock whitens her face. 'Not possible.'

I just stare at her.

'I don't have a passport. Nor does Lukas.' She squares her shoulders. 'That's why I couldn't travel to try to see you when I realised I was pregnant.'

She's determined to throw roadblocks up. She didn't have the money either. That's evident. Defensive as hell and I'm not coping with it as well as I should.

'We'll get them expedited.'

'That'll make them more expensive.'

'Hardly a problem for me.'

'Billionaire. Right,' she says scornfully. 'I'm not leaving New Zealand. My *life* is here.'

My gaze drops to the baby and I see her defensively tighten her hold on him. She looks scared.

'And *my* life is *there*.' I pause. 'Lukas belongs to us both.'

'So what are you suggesting? Should we chop him in two?'

I dislike myself intensely at this moment. She really didn't want me to know. She doesn't want my input with Lukas. That hurts. I'm independent. In control. I've had no control here in this. I grit my teeth at the realisation that I'm not going anywhere without her. 'I'll delay my return to Australia. We need time to sort this out. But I'd like you to stay with me so we can take advantage of Lukas's nap times to talk.' I look down at her. 'I'm trying to compromise, Talia.'

She hesitates. 'It'll take me a while to pack. Give me the hotel address and I'll meet you there.'

'I'll sit down and hold him while you get on with it.'

She doesn't expect that. Honestly, I've surprised myself too. I'm not exactly an experienced baby-handler and I give a mutter of thanks that one of the women in HR returned recently to show off her new baby and they made a deal of me cradling her baby. It means I've the smallest notion of what to do now.

Honorary fun uncle was the extent of what I was aiming for in life. I have no siblings, so real uncle was never going to happen. Nor was having a wife. That last one still isn't.

Talia doesn't move and I stare at her. Frustration surges at her obvious reluctance. I take a seat on the edge of that too small bed and hold my arms out. She finally steps forward. Our hands brush as she places Lukas into my arms. I look down at him and it's a good thing I already took a seat because my legs suddenly empty of strength.

He's a beautiful boy. Curling eyelashes. Unblemished pink cheeks. He's tiny and so light that I'm terrified I'll crush him—my *son*.

My heart stalls. I never wanted this—never so much as imagined it. But now he's here and in a split second of clarity I know I'll never, ever give him up. He's mine. I'm awash with a feeling unlike any other. Protectiveness obliterates all other emotion. I'll do anything to ensure his safety. He'll be with me. Always. Involuntarily I glance up at her and our gazes mesh.

So will she.

A whisper of equal clarity that I want to reject. Other feelings surge. I focus on the anger. I can't trust her but I need her—*Lukas* needs her. And I'm going to need defences to deal with her.

Her deep brown eyes are like pools—sombre and intense. 'Something wrong?' My voice has roughened to sandpaper.

'No.' Abrupt, she glances away.

It's a lie.

'Talia—' I raise my voice but break off as I remember. I look down at the innocent baby in my arms and then look back up at her. 'I'm not fighting with you in front of Lukas. Not ever.'

CHAPTER SEVEN

Talia

THERE'S SUCH SAVAGERY in his whisper I step back but I can't help looking at them again. He's still studying Lukas, intently absorbing every detail as if he's never seen a baby before. I'm unable to move—literally arrested by the sight of my son and his father finally together. Lukas looks tiny as Dain carefully cradles him. There's such a 'them' about this moment—an intimacy I'm intruding on. This should have happened three months ago. It should have happened the day Lukas was born.

Loss hits me, yearning and, yes, remorse. Each blow knocks the breath from my body. The regret isn't only for the delay in this, but the realisation that *we're* not a family. My son doesn't have that. I don't have that—a partner to offer not just support and security but love.

I remember the day of Lukas's birth. I missed Dain—I wanted to hold his hand through the delivery. I haven't let myself think about that since. But I cried, alone—and scared.

He's angry with me. He's right to be. I ran away from the conflict—the rejection—just as my mother always did. I already know I wouldn't fit into his world. Wealthy people like him live on a planet that has no place for me except as an employee. I've been told in no uncertain terms, repeatedly by one of the rich jerks my mother fell for and by his daughter, who I thought was my friend. But I was merely her charity case.

I turn away, angry with him too. For never replying. Never returning to Queenstown. For having other priorities in his life. But we were only ever supposed to have been a moment and it's unreasonable of me to have wanted otherwise.

I pack quickly. I'm used to taking only what I can carry so I'm pretty minimalist. It's the extra things for Lukas that slow me—his nappies and clothes, his few toys, his bassinet and bedding.

'You don't have a pram?'

I shove a toy into my backpack and answer shortly. 'I use a sling for now.'

I would've loved a pram or buggy to take him on walks but there's no way I could get a pram up the stairs and there's nowhere to store it in the café. Besides which, I couldn't afford it. It's less than five minutes before everything is stowed.

Dain carefully passes Lukas back to me. 'I need to make a couple of arrangements.'

It's a relief that he puts his intense focus onto his phone. He taps several messages before making a call.

'Do you have a car seat for him?' He interrupts his flow to ask me.

I nod, I was loaned one. I'm glad Romy isn't on shift at the café, so I don't have to explain anything to her in person. I'll leave a message for her in a bit.

Ten minutes later I carry Lukas and my backpack downstairs. Dain carries Lukas's bag and his bassinet. On the pavement, a driver waiting beside a gleaming black car hastens forward to assist. I don't know if I'll be coming back. Again, that's something that's all too familiar.

Bitterness wells and I blink back tears. I'm used to upheaval like this and I'm a survivor, but I didn't want Lukas to experience it ever. I want him to have stability and *security*. So I have to work this out with Dain.

I've never forgotten that night and part of me is still deeply attracted to him—the hormonal, basic breeding instinct part.

You'd think it would have been satisfied already. Yep, I'm a fool. It's not that I don't think relationships can ever last but a guy like Dain—rich and entitled—isn't a commitment king. Yet I went with him anyway—blinded by looks and charisma and the impetuousness sparked by that stormy night. And if it had been for just that one wild night I might've got away with it, but for my precious child.

It's a twenty-minute, awkward-silence-filled drive out of town.

I frown. 'I thought we were going to a hotel?'

Instead we pull up at a stunning mansion on a large section. Established trees shield it from the road, yet once we're inside I clock the amazing views of the vast landscape.

'This place belongs to a friend,' he says.

'Does she hire it out?'

'What?' He looks blank. 'No.'

I could kick myself. She's wealthy—another world where you can have a holiday home bigger than most people's houses and keep it empty most of the year round. I've no reason or right to be jealous yet the feeling rising within me is nothing but ugly. I make myself say something polite. 'It's beautiful.'

'We'll have privacy here,' he says crisply.

He cares so very much about privacy. I wonder what happened to make him value it so acutely. Is it simply the pressure of being a high-net-worth individual? That poor-rich-boy thing? That isn't happening to Lukas.

There was an image of Dain and his grandfather on the history section of the company website. Nothing of his parents. Dain looked about eleven in the photo.

'You don't need anything else for Lukas?' he asks as he carries in the bags. 'I thought there were all kinds of things babies needed, but this doesn't seem like much.'

Shame burns. I don't have the money for anything more than the basics.

'We'll get whatever else we need in Australia,' he says.

'Don't think that by repeatedly mentioning it, I'll suddenly agree to move.' I follow to see where he's taking Lukas's bed. 'I'm used to sleeping near him.'

'Sure.' He walks forward. 'While we're here, he's in the room between each of ours.'

Lukas is restless and needs some playtime. I lay him on the warm rug in front of the wood-burner that was lit before we arrived. I kneel beside him and pull out his favourite rabbit toy to play and let him kick out his legs.

Dain appears in the doorway but doesn't venture in. 'He'll be okay if we watch him from here while we talk?'

My stomach sinks. I feel as if I've been summoned to the principal's office. He's watching Lukas but as I approach his gaze lifts. Heat crawls over me. Suddenly clumsy, I almost trip over my own feet.

'What's the project you have in Queenstown?' I mumble to distract us both from my humiliating loss of co-ordination.

'The new apartments by the golf course. That's why I was here a year ago. Simone wanted my investment.'

I know the ones. According to the sign they're all sold already and they've barely begun building them.

'Why did you run off so quickly that night?' he asks bluntly.

'I had another job to get to.'

'Wasn't it cancelled because of the storm? Surely the bar was closed after the power cut? You could have taken two minutes to say goodbye.'

Because *goodbye* was all there should've been to say. I don't answer and he doesn't wait long.

'When did you find out you were pregnant?'

He's going direct. I've imagined this conversation so many times but I still struggle to explain. 'I'd been working long hours and just thought I was irregular. It wasn't till I started showing that I...' *Completely panicked.* 'That I did a test.'

'Were you taking care of yourself?'

I stiffen. 'I don't party, if that's what you're worried about.'

There's a rueful twist to his lips I don't quite understand. 'I'm more worried about the hours you work.'

I don't respond because ironically it's right this second that I realise how horribly tired I am. I've been filming late at night, baking early morning, caring for Lukas round the clock all while recovering from his birth.

'You knew the baby was mine?' His voice lowers.

My shrug is non-committal because I don't want to tell him that he's the only person I've ever slept with.

His gaze flickers. 'You didn't consider ending the pregnancy?'

Maybe he thinks I'm irresponsible given I'm in not in the best position to care for him? Once I was past that initial amazement I was elated. 'Even if I'd found out sooner, I wouldn't have done anything differently.'

'Including not trying harder to contact me?'

The truth is I'll do *anything* to keep my baby, but I can't tell him that because it will give him absolute power over me. Even though he'll likely have that anyway, given he has resources I can't compete with. I'll have to compromise.

'I love Lukas,' I say huskily, my heart aching. 'I tried to contact you. When you didn't reply I stopped.'

'Your family helped?'

I'm thrown. 'My what?'

'Did they support you through the pregnancy?' He frowns. 'Your parents?'

I'm so stunned I'm too honest in my answer. 'I haven't had parental support in years.'

'They're dead?'

'It's been so long since I saw my father he might as well be,' I mutter. 'My mother is around but…'

'You're not close.'

My mum's way of coping with anything bad is to uproot and ship out. Unfortunately bad stuff happens to her frequently and usually involves some jerk. She's been desperate for someone to depend on for my whole life and made way too many bad choices in that search. We had to move far too often, which impacted on my and Ava's friendships and our education—not that Mum cared about those things. Or us.

But I did. I'd already been working part-time for years to supplement what little money Mum made and I didn't want Ava to have to start over in yet another school. I dropped out and worked full time, that way I could afford a tutor to extend her. The school turned a blind eye to the fact no one turned up to parent-teacher interviews. But I don't explain all this to Dain, he's frowning enough as it is.

'I've been supporting myself since I was a teenager.' I lift my head proudly. 'I work several jobs and work hard.' It's never been easy but I've supported Ava for years and now Lukas too. 'My social media channel is building and income is trickling in from that. I don't want to lose momentum.'

'You don't need to make money,' he dismisses. 'You can delete the channel.'

'Pardon?' If I had hackles, they'd be on end. 'My career matters to me.'

'You never have to work again if you don't want to.'

'What? And be completely dependent upon you?' I'm appalled and a horrifying thought occurs to me. 'I don't want to be a kept woman. Certainly not your wife.'

Would he be that old-fashioned?

'Have I asked you to be?' he drawls.

Of course he hasn't. I'm not the society sort of wife Dain Anzelotti would have. The beautiful model with the famous family pedigree that he was photographed with minutes after being with me, however, she'd be perfect. I grit my teeth.

'I'm not interested in marriage,' he adds.

'That night you were unashamedly anti-kids too.'

'What's happened isn't Lukas's fault. I'll be there for him.'

'What does that even mean?' I ask smartly. 'Will you tolerate his existence? He won't be too much of an inconvenience?'

I step forward. If there's no commitment between us there's an easy escape for Dain and I already know no one can be relied on. 'You get one chance,' I mutter fiercely. 'If you ever walk out on Lukas then you're out of his life for good.'

'Right back at you.' He steps forward to go toe to toe with me. 'I don't believe in marriage.' He sneers through the word. 'We'll have an unbreakable, legally enforceable *contract*. It doesn't need to be difficult or emotive. We'll agree to terms and we'll get on with it.'

He means an access plan. He means a dictate on where we live and how long for. What school Lukas will go to. Which doctor. Every aspect of his life will be agreed in advance between us. I'm going to lose full autonomy and have to agree with a man used to getting his own way. He's watching me closely and the longer I remain silent, the bigger the storms grow in his eyes.

'My parents' marriage was a mess,' he suddenly whispers. 'I was weaponised. Victimised. Blamed. That's never happening to Lukas. We'll work everything out between us well ahead of time so he never has to feel—'

He breaks off and takes a sharp breath. He glances away from me to look at our baby on the soft rug.

He doesn't want to tell me more. Fair enough. There's plenty I don't want to tell him either.

'Okay, we'll work it out,' I agree softly. With no marriage. No dependency. 'We both want the best for him.'

The problem is we might not always agree on what that 'best' will be.

CHAPTER EIGHT

Dain

I NEVER DISCUSS my family, but this morning has been shock after shock and my new reality is so far from normal I'm spinning. I glance at Lukas to ground myself and remember the priority here. He has my eyes and colouring. But knowing that Talia stopped trying to contact me grates nerves already stripped raw. Instinct screams at me to scoop him up and squirrel him to the safety of my own home. But instinct doesn't eliminate ignorance—I've no idea how to care for a baby, how to create the safety I fundamentally crave for him. It's all emotion and no experience. I don't like it. I don't like any of it. Especially the fact that I can't do this without her. And I'm angry with her. Yet every damn time I glance at her every damn atom within me heats. I *can't* lose control. She hasn't allowed me any in all this and that's not something I can tolerate. Family drama upended my life before and I'll never let it happen again.

She says she doesn't want anything from me, yet I see that same heat I feel in her eyes when she looks at me. She can't hide it and I'm tempted to use whatever power I might have to engineer an advantage. But then I remember how quickly she ran that night. Was it me or is it something within herself?

It must be me. And it must be bad. Because it's unbelievable that not even my money was a motivation for her to try harder.

Lukas begins to cry. While I freeze, Talia steps forward to pick him up.

'I need to top him up and hopefully he'll sleep again.' She looks around for a chair to nurse him in.

I can't stand to watch that sweet intimacy again so I walk away. I check the rooms, fiddle with the heating, attending to the basics—shelter, warmth…food? I grab my phone, start a list and make an order. Gradually I feel calmer. I call my legal team then my primary assistant. There's a huge amount to arrange and not a lot of time to do it.

As I finish the fourth call I see a car pulling into the driveway. Relieved, I head out to meet the delivery guy and carry the bags back to the kitchen.

Talia appears in the kitchen just as I'm serving up. The shadows beneath her eyes have deepened since I first saw her this morning, plus she has a pinched look as if she has a headache. While Lukas is thriving, she needs replenishing. I clench my jaw to crush back my growl of frustration. 'He's asleep?'

She nods and I glimpse how bony her shoulders are.

I jerk a thumb towards the kitchen counter. 'Sit. Eat.'

She glares but mercifully doesn't argue.

Lunch is a simple spread—warm soup, crunchy bread, soft butter. As she eats, I watch colour slowly return to her cheeks. I eat as well. But it feels more dangerous to be around her without Lukas.

'You should rest,' I mutter as soon as she's done. 'You look like you need it.'

She looks startled, then indignant.

'Go,' I say gruffly. 'Take a break.'

She meets my gaze. Yeah, it's definitely more dangerous to be near her without Lukas. But apparently she feels the same because she scuttles away.

In the late afternoon my team get in touch. They've expedited the information I requested and I print the file they've sent. The space for the father's name is blank but the baby's name gives it all away. *Lukas Dain Parrish*.

Just as she said. It would have been easy enough for her to discover my grandfather's name. It's in the brief family history I allowed on the company website to sparsely furnish the company's 'story'.

An hour later I put the printout on the kitchen table in front of her. 'You didn't name me on the birth certificate. I understand that if I were named, then I would be a guardian. As guardian I'll then have some say in my own child's upbringing.' I breathe out but my chest is tight. 'My lawyers filed a declaration of paternity.'

Her hands tremble, and my teeth clench because I hate her obvious fear of me.

'I want to establish Lukas's legal rights as well as my own. If anything happens to me, Lukas inherits.' I try to explain my reasons. 'No question. No delay. Plus he gets everything he should have had from the start.'

'We don't need things.'

'*You* don't have to have anything from me,' I say pointedly. 'Lukas, however, is different.'

'You sure you don't want a DNA test?'

My skin tightens. She thinks I have any doubt? 'Eventually. My lawyers will insist on it but you and I already know.'

Her eyes widen.

'What's weird to me is that you wanted him to have a family connection yet barely tried to contact me. It's hard to understand.' Was money really no motivation? Because that's not how it usually works in my world.

She bites on her lip. 'I don't like having to rely on anyone.'

Trust issues. Yeah, we have those in common. I offer the faintest smile. 'You're still a control freak, then?'

'Leopards. Spots.' She drops her gaze.

'Born that way or forged?' I ask.

She freezes.

'I was forged,' I mutter.

'Your parents?' She jerks a nod, answering before I do. 'Ditto.'

Right, we have dysfunctional families in common too. 'What is it you don't like about me, Talia?' I can't believe I've asked.

'You're used to being in charge.' She doesn't deny it.

I bristle. 'So are you.'

Her glance is pointed. 'Not on the same level.'

Lukas cries and she goes to him before I can blink.

I make more arrangements. Sort flight schedules. Offload my over-full diary for the next couple of weeks.

Dinner is desultory. She glances at me a few times but doesn't break the silence. I glance at Lukas and don't know where to begin with him.

She takes him to bathe and get ready for bed and I don't interfere. Given I'm going to need time away from the office, I draft a tonne of instructions. It's late when I turn out the light and the house is silent.

Three hours later I'm lying there still wide awake when I hear him crying.

I get up and pull on my jeans. The house is warm enough not to bother with anything else. I step into the doorway and see her pacing around the small room with him. She looks exhausted. And beautiful.

'Is it like this every night?' I ask with clenched teeth.

'He's a little baby.' She defends him with quiet ferocity. 'He has no concept of time. And he's hungry. He's growing fast.'

There's a proud tilt to her head. I didn't mean to be critical, just curious. But we seem to read the worst into every interaction we have. I turn and stalk to the kitchen. Lukas can only keep growing like that as long as Talia is well rested and well-nourished herself. I grab a few crackers, slice cheese, slice an apple, make a milky hot chocolate and throw the lot onto a tray I find. It's hardly pretty but it's something.

I stomp—silently—back to the bedroom we're using as his nursery. Now Talia's curled up on the narrow bed and Lukas is in her arms. I clench my fists to ride out the urge to drop to my knees at her damned feet in awe and instead set the tray beside her so she can reach it easily.

'I don't need—'

'Don't,' I say sharply.

She glances at me—equally sharply—and says nothing more.

I lean back against the wall and glare at her. She sighs heavily, rolls her eyes and grudgingly picks up a cheese-topped cracker. My muscles don't ease any until she's onto her third. She sips the warm milky chocolate.

Eventually she puts him back into the small bassinet. He stirs and she rests her hand on him for a moment of reassurance. Then she straightens and silently steps out of the room. I follow her. Before I think I reach out and take her arm, turning her to face me. In the dim light of the hallway her eyes are huge. They draw me in—so rich and unfathomable.

Desire engulfs me. Paralyses me. She basically hid my son from me. Because of her I've missed out on so much. But her soft skin is beneath my fingertips and I can't resist stroking her lightly with my thumb. Just the once. I see her skin flush, hear her breathing race. Her response is instant—just like that night in the gondola.

I can't speak. I just stare at her and inwardly battle the overpowering desire to pull her close and kiss her and touch her everywhere.

'You don't have to get up every time he cries,' she mumbles.

Rejection. Denial. Again. It's as aggravating as hell that she won't let me help her.

'You do.' I flinch. 'You have. For months.'

As she stares up at me something changes in her expression. Her whole body seems to tremble. 'I'm sorry.'

The words I've been waiting for all day finally emerge from

her but weirdly I don't want to hear them. Not *now*. Because they make me feel something—*want* something—that I know in my bones is dangerous. I'm suddenly, sharply vulnerable. I cannot trust her. I cannot take her in my arms. But I'm so tempted. Frustration is an inferno.

'Go to bed,' I growl.

I release her too roughly. I almost push her away. I have to because in the next heartbeat I'd have hauled her close and damned myself.

Her swift steps are silent on the soft carpet. Her door closes with the faintest click. The speed with which she leaves me is both relief and agony.

I slowly uncurl my fist—holding back from grabbing her again has my hand cramping. I have no idea how I'm going to get through this.

CHAPTER NINE

Talia

I SLEPT BADLY and it wasn't because Lukas had woken more than once. Dain had been thoughtful—grumpy, but thoughtful—in the middle of the night. I wasn't able to get back to sleep at all because the reality of my position is very clear. It's taken less than twenty-four hours back in his presence and I'm willing to do almost anything he wants. I don't deserve his attention but I want it. And last night—for a moment—I had it. But he stepped back right at the moment I would've surrendered. He doesn't want me any more. Or maybe he doesn't *want* to want me. And he doesn't trust me.

But I'm going to go with Dain to Australia. I'm going to agree to almost anything he wants to ensure Lukas has the best from us both. Because Lukas comes first. But it's not only Lukas depending on me, I have Ava too and I have to do my best for her as well. If I leave she'll be alone. Which means taking a risk. Enraging Dain seems less terrifying now I've seen him with Lukas.

He's *interested* in his son and he wants the best for him. Yep, he might've had some tough times in his own childhood that he doesn't want to open up about, but he wants to protect Lukas from anything similar. Fine by me. It's awful to admit, but I'm actually a little jealous of the way he looks at Lukas, how carefully he held him. I need to get over that. And knowing I don't have his trust, I figure I might as well do the worst and hopefully ensure Ava is okay as well.

I find him sitting at the kitchen table. There's a coffee beside him and the remnants of an omelette on a plate. My heart thunders and I feel cold, but I do the thing I promised myself I never would.

'You said you're a billionaire.' My voice cracks. I clear my throat and make myself continue. 'Is it all tied up in assets or do you have access to cash?'

Surprise lights his eyes. 'I can access cash. Why?' He cocks his head and surveys me steadily. 'How much do you need?'

I don't hesitate. 'Quarter of a million.'

'Uh…' He does hesitate. Briefly. 'No more, no less?'

'Quarter of a million. Cash. Upfront.'

'Or…?'

I swallow. 'Or I'm not going with you. Nor is Lukas.'

It's a bluff but one I have to make.

To my astonishment he doesn't instantly get angry. He blinks but the smallest quirk tilts his lips. Surely he's not *amused*?

'How will you stop me from taking him?' he asks blandly. 'And you, for that matter. You know I could bundle you both onto my jet and—'

'You're not a bully. You're not a criminal. And you don't have passports for either of us yet,' I say.

'The passports are less than twenty-four hours away and if you think I'm such a straight-up good guy why didn't you try harder to let me know you'd had my son?'

I don't want to admit my shame. I take a breath. 'This is my price. I won't ask for anything more. Not for me. Ever. But I need all of it. Upfront. Before leaving.'

'You want it in unmarked dollar bills? Untraceable bags?' His smile deepens.

I purse my lips. I need to remain serious so he finally gets that this isn't a joke. 'Bank transfer will be fine.'

'Sure.' He keeps his gaze drilled on me as he pulls his phone from his pocket. 'I need your account details.'

He says it so matter-of-factly I just stare for a moment.

'You're doing it *now*?'

'You want the money, don't you?'

I fumble for my phone and pull up my banking app and read the numbers to him.

He taps his screen for a few moments then glances up at me. 'The money's gone through.'

I just gape at him. 'What?'

'Refresh your app,' he says. 'It should be there.'

I really don't want to believe him, but I do it. And there it is. I break into a sweat. My account has never seen so many zeros. There's a quarter of a million dollars—plus the meagre few hundred I had saved in there. I drag in a breath but still feel as if I'm suffocating. The sweat trickles down my spine as I tap the screen to forward the payment to Ava right away. I'll call her and explain it all later. I just want that money out of my account now. Because I feel bad about this. So bad. I'm barely aware that Dain's now standing beside me, silently observing over my shoulder.

But the payment doesn't go through. I frown at the 'transaction denied' message.

'I put money into that account all the time,' I mutter. 'Why won't they let me do it today?' I tap the app and try again. A big bright red alert message appears at the top. 'It's been "blocked for unusual activity".' I read it aloud in frustration. 'I have to phone them. Or go into a branch and take photo ID with me.'

'Your bank is right to query such a large transfer,' Dain says, way too calmly for me to handle.

'Because I'm usually so destitute an amount like this has to be some kind of fraud?' My eyes fill. I was so close and I'm frustrated. And I'm kind of blown away that he's just done that with no questions asked and I'm horrified with myself for asking him to in the first place. I feel as though I'm about to vomit.

Dain pushes me into the seat and hunches down before me.

'Breathe,' he instructs calmly. 'Just breathe.' Reaching up, he wipes a rogue tear from my cheek.

'How about you just tell me what it's for?' he says after a few moments. 'Are you in trouble—is it debt collectors?' He growls. 'I can help, Talia. I have a whole team of people who can help. It's not hard for me. I have an appalling amount of privilege. Let me help you with whatever the problem is.'

I stare at him and simply feel worse.

'Because there's obviously a problem,' he adds. 'Talia?' he prompts.

'It's for my sister,' I blurt.

His eyes widen. 'Sister?'

'Yes.'

'I didn't know you had a sister.'

I shoot him a look. 'Swapping life stories isn't a favourite pastime for either of us.'

'Right.' He almost smiles again. 'So she's in debt?'

'No. That's the point. I don't want her to be.' I breathe in slowly, frustrated because I'm explaining this backwards. 'She's a student. This is for her fees, her flat, her food for the next few years. She's in her second year of med school and she wants to specialise and—'

'That's a long expensive road ahead.'

'Exactly. She can't work while studying. She needs to concentrate fully. I don't want her to worry—'

'You've been supporting her for years,' he interrupts. 'Because neither of your parents help.' He suddenly rises and grabs his phone from the table. 'Give me her bank details.'

'What?'

He flips my phone around and copies the account number for Ava. I just stare at him, too sluggish and sickened to believe what I'm seeing.

A few minutes later he flips the phone back towards me. 'There's quarter of a million in her account now.'

As *well* as the quarter million in mine.

'Your bank lets you do that no problem?' I stammer. *'Twice?'*

The man had access to half a million dollars just like that? I feel even more nauseous. 'Now I have to transfer all that back to you. But I have to go to the bank to—'

'Leave it,' he says shortly. 'Doesn't matter.'

'You're not *buying* me, Dain.' Even though I've basically just asked him to.

'Never dreamed that would be possible.' He suddenly chuckles. 'You're the one who demanded payment before leaving.'

'I'm not keeping that money in my account. Only the money for Ava and I'll pay that back. Eventually.'

He sighs and rolls his eyes. 'Whatever will help you sleep.'

But I feel worse.

'You might want to phone her before she calls her bank thinking there's been some sort of mistake and asks them to reverse it.' He draws a breath. 'You'll want to see her before we leave the country. We can—'

'No!' I shake my head furiously and the truth spills out before I think to stop it. 'She doesn't know about Lukas.'

'You haven't told your sister you've had a *baby*?' He frowns. 'I thought you were close.'

'We are.' But I have to explain more. I want him to understand his money isn't going to be wasted. 'I didn't want her dropping out to help me.'

'Yet that's what you did for her.'

'I never dropped *in*. I always worked. I never...' I shake my head, frustrated that I'm not explaining this well enough to wipe that frown off his face. 'Ava's amazing. Like really, really amazing. I didn't want her jeopardising her future and that's what she'd do if she knew—'

'How much you're struggling.'

I glare at him. 'I've worked too hard for too long to get her into the position she's in now.'

He glares right back at me. 'Your sister should know you've had a baby. Just as your baby's father should.'

It hits. Hard.

'You really do like keeping everything within your very tight control,' he says.

I don't know why he's so bothered by this. 'I was doing it for *her*.'

His mouth thins. 'No, you were controlling. Not involving her in any decision to help you or not. She'll be angry with you for keeping this from her.'

'That's a price I'm willing to pay because *her* future is too important. I was going to tell her once I had things more secure.'

'Fortunately things are more secure now. We'll visit her before we leave.'

I stare at him.

It didn't occur to me that visiting her would even be an option. I'm used to packing up and clearing out without any chance to say goodbye. The moment my mother decided, that was it—all hands on deck to put our few things into bags before they were forgotten. We always left as if a killer were at our heels.

Dain misinterprets my hesitation. 'Surely you don't want to leave the country without seeing her?'

My heart's in my throat. I would *love* to see her. I've missed her so much in these months that I've kept away from her. 'Are you sure?' I ask hesitantly. 'You don't mind?'

His jaw drops. 'I'm not a monster, Talia,' he mutters bleakly. 'I'm not going to force you to pack up and leave the country without saying goodbye to your family or friends first.'

I hear the hurt in his voice. 'I… I just…'

'Think the worst of me.'

'Of most people,' I correct. My heart squeezes. It isn't only him.

'Well.' He watches me. 'You can ask me for anything.'

To my total mortification my face heats and I can't even mumble a response. The things I really want to ask from him are way too…way too…*wild*.

CHAPTER TEN

Dain

'YOU WERE ABLE to lean on me that night in the gondola,' I point out to her, trying to soften my tone. How can I be fascinated and furious with her at the same time?

'That was a life-threatening situation,' she mutters.

The tips of her ears are scarlet again.

What's it going to take to get her to trust me again in any small way? Because I'm trying here. She's just demanded an outrageous sum of money and I've not batted an eyelid and supplied it immediately—although admittedly my motivation was mostly to confound her. But I desperately want her to open up more. I know she's ballsy and bristly but when she laughs—which is too rarely for my liking—she's a delight.

It's shocking enough that she hadn't properly tried to contact me about Lukas, but that she hasn't told her own sister about him either is blowing my mind—even when she insists they're close. And it touches a wound of my own. Not being told my grandfather was terminally ill—on the pretext of protecting me—is something I've never forgiven my family for.

'My assistant found the messages you sent and forwarded them to me,' I say.

She watches me warily.

'Overzealous spam folders and weak double checks in play

there. There weren't as many as I'd thought. You didn't discuss the pregnancy in the first couple.'

'Of course I didn't, that was personal.'

Part of me appreciates her discretion. But her first two loosely worded messages—I need to get hold of Dain. We met one night—didn't pass the spam/stalker test. The last was too generic—I've had a baby—even with the photo attached.

'You could have tried harder,' I say. 'You should have.'

She could have tried to contact Simone. There were several avenues she chose not to go down.

'What were you so afraid of?' I ask.

Her skin pales. 'You have a lot more to offer him than I do.'

'You're his mother.'

'That doesn't always mean much.'

An element in her voice makes me wince. 'Do you struggle to accept help from anyone?'

'I took help from Romy.'

Minimal help that she paid back by working for her—making cakes and coffee. 'But you won't take it from me.'

'There are other complications between us.'

My gut twists. I'm tempted to sort those other complications out. I can't help wondering if there was any other man in her life after me. I shouldn't be thinking on it. I'm hardly about to tell her I've been celibate since sleeping with her. Besides, I have the feeling she won't believe me.

Too late I realise my glib display of outrageous wealth has backfired. If I make a move on her now she might not feel able to say no. She might think I've *bought* her. That's just *ick*. I was so determined to be flippant. To prove nothing's a problem. No demand too outrageous. I didn't think through the implications.

I can't allow her to kiss me as some kind of repayment. But all I want right now are her kisses. And isn't this just the way it is with Talia? Contrary. Confounding. My muscles bunch and twitch. I just want to tear her clothes away. Mine too.

It's a relief to hear Lukas's cry coming from the nursery.

I go to him immediately. I croon ridiculously as I pick him up and try to soothe him. I turn about the room and see she's followed and is watching me. The look in her eyes isn't worry. It's heat. She can't stop looking. Despite my edginess I keep talking nonsense to Lukas to keep him settled because to my amazement it seems to be working. There's a feeling I just don't recognise in myself when I look at him and even more when I then look at her. It's absolute awe. I glance to the ceiling and pull in a steadying breath.

'*Oh!*' Talia all but squeals.

'What?' I whip to look at her but she's staring in rapture at Lukas.

'He's smiling!' she says.

She's smiling too and she's beautiful and now I don't know where to look. I'm torn between the two of them.

'And?' I mutter weakly.

'He hasn't smiled before. This is his first smile.'

'Really?' I look back at Lukas then back at her and back again, and again.

'First social smile.' She nods. 'Happens between eight and twelve weeks and here he is…smiling at you.'

There are tears in her eyes and she's so effervescent there's no way she's faking this. I talk more nonsense to Lukas because it just bubbles out of me and he smiles again and Talia *beams*.

A chuckle escapes me. I want to do anything. Everything. I feel utterly alive—I want to keep them both with me and have them happy but in the same breath I feel a sudden helpless futility. Because this is something I can't ensure. I couldn't help my parents' happiness. Nor my grandfather's. I don't think I can do happy families. It goes wrong—it never lasts.

But I'm beginning to get her. She's done everything for herself—and her sister—for years. She's so determinedly independent I know the reasons why she doesn't want to rely on anyone are deep-seated. She's been let down before.

So I'll try to do whatever it takes to make sure she can't walk out on me again. Because I want this to work for Lukas. Somehow I need her to trust me. I need her to talk to me. Talia's withholding of information wasn't just about protecting Ava. It was about protecting herself too. Because people are selfish. They do things for their own reasons. Me included.

We sit together on the floor. Lukas is stretched out between us and we each have a toy in hand—waving them in front of him to tease another smile. The rabbit I'm holding is old. One of its ears is at risk of spontaneously severing. Possibly its head too. It's surprisingly easy to sit here with her. It reminds me of those tragic jokes we shared when we were in the gondola.

'Do you have siblings?' she suddenly asks.

'Time to swap life stories?' I shoot her a sardonic look.

Her shoulder lifts—half apology, half amusement.

'No siblings,' I mutter. 'For a while I wished I had them, then I was glad I didn't.'

'Because your parents fought?'

I nod. 'They used me.' I was alternately a weapon or a prize. 'Any sibling would have been an adversary. We'd have been played off against each other.'

She dangles her toy above Lukas. 'It was that bad?'

'Worse.'

'I was lucky to have Ava…' She sighs deeply and her worried expression make me tense.

It's obvious she has more to say but she's gone silent. I fake patience and waggle the ripped-up rabbit at Lukas. I should win an acting award, I really should.

'About Ava…'

I wait.

'I want her to believe I'm happy. That I want this.'

'You mean move to Australia with me?' There's a hit in there that makes my chest ache.

She puffs out a breath. 'I don't want her to doubt…'

'You want us to act like we're happy together. Is that what you mean?'

'Yes.' She swallows. 'I don't want her to worry about me.'

She's spent her life caring for her sister. Maybe her sister should have been more aware of how hard her big sister was working for her. But Talia wasn't honest even then.

It's a good reminder that she's a liar. She lies to the people who should be closest to her. I know how much that hurts the one lied to. Supposedly *protected*.

I almost tear the ear off the rabbit. I slide it into my pocket so Talia doesn't see. 'You want me to act the besotted boyfriend?'

She must have caught the anger in my expression because she turns away. 'Forget it.'

I reach out and turn her back. I run my hand through her hair and see that smokiness enter her eyes. Is *this* honest, Talia? I ignore her words and focus on the micro actions of her body that she can't control. The flush that builds in her cheeks. The quickening breath. The way she leans a bit close without even realising. I lean closer and she mirrors me so we're almost intimate, our baby content between us.

'Trust me,' I say softly. 'She'll understand what it is you *really* want.'

CHAPTER ELEVEN

Talia

THE NEXT MORNING we're driven to Dunedin in that fancy car with the so-silent-he's-almost-robotic driver. As every kilometre passes I get more nervous. This is crazy precarious. I desperately want to see Ava before leaving but I've no idea how I'm going to explain everything.

'She doesn't need to know we've been...'

Out of touch? Estranged? I can't even figure out how to talk about this to him, let alone my younger sister, who I've tried to be a solid support to.

Dain doesn't lift his gaze from the laptop he's typing on. 'It'll be fine.'

I knock on her door and wait while holding Lukas in my arms. I've an almost violent urge to run away—I don't want Ava to feel as if I've let her down in some way. As if I've made Mum's mistakes all over again. Dain slings a heavy arm around my shoulders, literally anchoring me in place as if he senses my urge to flee. He steps in close and almost presses me into his side as if sheltering me and Lukas from a cold wind.

'Stop worrying.'

His breath warms the side of my neck and I shiver and he cuddles me closer still. His heat seeps through my old down jacket and the anxiety inside morphs into something else. I look at Lukas in my arms to hide the sudden emotion sweeping through me. The door opens.

'Talia?' It's a stage whisper at first, then Ava's voice rises twenty decibels. *'Talia?'*

She stares from me to Lukas in my arms then up to Dain, standing tall beside me, then back to me and around the three of us again—a circle of movement and amazement.

'Surprise...' I say weakly.

'Oh, my...' Ava looks from Lukas then up at Dain again. 'Oh, *my*!'

'May we come in?' He floors her with his most charming smile.

Gaping, Ava steps back and we file inside her cramped student flat.

'You've been keeping secrets,' she hisses at me.

'I know. This is Lukas.' I pass my baby to his aunt. 'And his father, Dain.'

Ava melts as she stares down at Lukas. 'Talia, he's gorgeous.'

Yep, both of them.

'How did you—when?' Ava's eyes fill with curiosity and reproach. 'What's been going on?'

Emotion clogs my throat. At the sight of her displeasure I suddenly feel so guilty. I hadn't really thought this might hurt her.

'Talia didn't want to worry you,' Dain says gently.

'I met Dain in Queenstown,' I say. 'One thing led to another...'

'Sure did.' Ava smiles awkwardly.

'It was an instant thing,' Dain says.

He still has his arm around me. He's playing a part. I play my part too. Only for me it isn't a pretence. My legs really are like jelly, my heart isn't just racing, it's turbulent. The attraction that hit me the moment I first saw him rears from its slumber. But it's always been there. It never left me and now it's wide, wide awake.

Ava offers us tea or coffee and apologises for the tiny flat. I'm used to it but I see Dain's assessing glance around and stiffen. He sees me notice him and simply holds me closer. And that just makes me flustered.

'You look thinner in the face.' Ava studies me intently. 'Are you sure you're okay?'

I feel Dain's quick frowning look down. After what happened last night I don't need him being any more over-protective. 'It's just been busy. I'm fine.'

'You're able to feed him okay?' Ava checks.

'He's a hungry boy.'

'So you need to be eating enough to—'

'Stop it.' I force a laugh. 'You're a second-year med student, not a paediatrician already.'

'Maternal nutrition is—'

'Enough. I eat well.' I shush her. 'Dain's overprotective enough, you'll only make him worse.'

'Good.' Ava shoots him an imperious look. 'Make sure she eats properly. Little and often.' Ava glances at me again. 'Make that *lots* and often.'

I shake my head.

'You work too hard. You always have.' Ava leans close and her voice lowers. 'You should have told me.'

I feel queasy at her plaintive tone. I've hurt her when it was the last thing I wanted.

'You needed to focus on your studies,' I murmur.

I feel Dain tense beside me and I quickly glance at him.

'You've been sending me money all this time.' Ava suddenly clicks. 'Did you work all through your pregnancy?'

'Lukas was a little unexpected.' Dain steps in and fills the sharpening silence. 'I'm here to support both him and Talia now.'

The frown in Ava's eyes doesn't fade. 'You think you can get Talia to depend on you? She doesn't let *anyone* in.'

Ava blinks and her head swivels towards me. Dain watches me too and I feel as though I've let them both down. I'm weak and I go for the distraction he provides.

'Ava,' I say gently. 'Dain's helping with your fees now.'

'What?'

'Have you checked your banking app lately?' I ask.

Ava winces. 'Why would I—?'

'Have a look at it,' Dain suggests.

Ava passes Lukas back to me and pulls out her phone. Her face goes all blotchy when she opens her app.

'My accountant will be in touch,' Dain says quietly. 'There might be some tax implications, but she'll manage that for you.'

'Are you for real?' Ava looks at Dain and then at me. 'Is this for *real*?' She shakes her head vigorously. 'I can't accept this from a stranger. I *can't*—'

'You can accept this from *family*,' Dain interrupts firmly. 'And that's what we are now. Right, Talia?'

I've lost the power of speech. I'm still clamped to his side and he drops a kiss on the top of my head. It brings *everything* back—the scent of him, the strength of him, the sheer vitality of him that's so bewitching. I liquefy inside.

Ava's stunned to silence as well. Yep. Full Dain Anzelotti effect in action.

She looks at me. I feel the heat on my skin and know I'm blushing. I can't hide my response to him.

'Consider it a scholarship,' he says. 'You've accepted those before, right?'

Ava nods but she doesn't take her eyes off me. I'm trembling inside and I hold Lukas more carefully because I have to direct my energy somewhere.

Dain smiles but both his arms are around me now as if he

knows I'm close to spontaneously combusting and he's literally holding me together.

Ava's eyes soften. 'Oh, Talia,' she whispers. 'I'm so pleased for you.'

She isn't talking about the money. What she sees—or what she *thinks* she sees—is wonderful. It's what I ache for. And what I don't have. She believes the lie he's presenting, only right now it's truth for me—I'm in thrall to him and I absolutely want to go with him to wherever he chooses...

'I'm taking Talia and Lukas to Australia.' Dain's voice is gravelly.

'Australia?'

'Dain has a family home there,' I explain as Ava's eyes go huge. I've no idea if that's actually true but I know the impact the idea will have on Ava—the same impact it has on me. 'It'll be Lukas's family home too.'

Ava nods slowly. 'And yours. A permanent place to stay.' She sends me a small smile. 'Finally.' Ava blinks rapidly and looks down at Lukas. 'I can't believe I'm an aunty.' She breathes in shakily. 'I'm going to miss him and I barely know him.'

I glance up at Dain. There's a bleak expression in his eyes that he quickly blinks away when he catches my eye.

'We'll send lots of photos. Videos. Calls.' He turns his attention to Ava and promises.

He never got those. I never *sent* any—not after that one shot of Lukas as a newborn. I feel terrible. 'We really need to go now, Ava, I'm sorry. We have to get to the airport. Can't miss the flight.'

'Ava's like you,' Dain says bluntly as we pull away from the kerb. 'Bossy, untrusting.' He sighs. 'We didn't get far in the life-story swap yesterday. What happened with your dad?'

I shoot him a look. 'He walked out when I was eight and Ava was four. There were always other women and once he'd left for good he didn't want to know us at all. He just wasn't interested.' I grit my teeth. 'My mother didn't cope. She thought she needed someone, so she went from one jerk to the next. She had high hopes for every new guy she let into her life and when those hopes were shattered, we moved. Every time.'

'How many times?'

I shrug. 'I can't remember exactly.'

'Every year?'

'At least.'

His expression tightens. 'And you took care of Ava.'

I swallow. 'Of course. Now you've met her, you know why. She's wonderful.'

It only takes minutes to get to the airport but we don't head to the main terminal, but to a smaller building to the side. The driver and an equally discreet porter gather our belongings from the car while Dain lifts Lukas out as though he's been doing it for months. Yep, he's a fast learner. And even though we've left Ava and there's no need for any further pretence, Dain doesn't distance himself any. He wraps an arm around me and hustles me to a small counter, shielding me and Lukas from the few other people in the room.

'Are we leaving right away?' I mutter.

I'm more nervous now than I was about seeing Ava and it's not the actual flight putting the fear in me.

'You don't want to?'

'I wouldn't mind some lunch,' I prevaricate.

Because I'm about to be cooped up in a very small space with him for *hours* and I don't think I can trust myself. I don't even step away from him now when I actually can. Pretending for Ava has stirred me up—I can't help wishing that the tenderness in his touch were true.

'We'll eat on board,' he says.

That's when I glance out of the window and see the plane on the tarmac. It's sleek and has no commercial markings. The truth dawns on me. 'You have a *private* jet?'

'We would've flown to Dunedin from Queenstown, but the pilot went to pick up your passports. He's just finalising the flight plan for us now.'

My lungs seem to shrink. I'd forgotten about the passports. But they're here—turned around super quick because of his power and resources. 'You always travel on your own jet?'

'I like the privacy it gives me,' he says.

'Because you're secretive?' Maybe he doesn't want anyone to see Lukas and me with him—maybe that's why he's hurrying us out onto the tarmac.

'Not *secretive*,' he says coolly, guiding me towards the stairs. 'Private. There's a difference.'

CHAPTER TWELVE

Dain

I PAUSE, HOLDING Lukas as Talia regards the jet even more warily the nearer we get to it.

'Is it big enough to get us all the way?' she asks, drawing in a shuddering breath.

'I promise I'll get you all the way,' I mutter with a smirk. Yes, I'm all but waggling my eyebrows with the innuendo. I can't help myself.

She looks at me and the colour rises in her cheeks.

Yeah. I've spent the morning right beside her. Touching her. I've been inhaling her scent and feeling the warmth of her soft skin and all I want is to strip her and stroke her until she's slippery and supple and hot enough to take all of *me* again. I still want her and I can't hide it. The way she melted against me earlier tells me she's the same. That part of the pretence in front of Ava was no pretence at all. She still wants me too. But the complications—Lukas's well-being—are too much.

'I meant is it big enough to get us all the way to Australia?' she clarifies primly.

'It got me here.' I smile. 'You don't feel safe?'

'I never feel safe. Not entirely. I don't think it's possible to.'

My gut clenches. She's spent her life worrying the rug was about to be tugged from beneath her and it seems it happened time and time again. So no wonder she fights for control and is so determined to do everything herself. She's always had to. She never lets other people help—or not much at any rate, which infuriates me, even though I've learned she's been let down by the people she should have been able to trust most. Her parents. And that's something I can well understand.

'It's worse now Lukas is here.' She glances at the plane again. 'I'm horribly overprotective.'

Yeah, I know the feeling. 'I guess that's pretty normal,' I mutter as I glance down at him in my arms. 'He's utterly defenceless. He doesn't just need protection, he needs everything. He's completely reliant on you for survival.'

'On *us*,' she says softly.

Right. I have to pause for a moment as warmth bursts in my chest as if a damned firework's been ignited in there. That's the first indicator from her that we're a team and in this together. And even though she's the one who's prevented this, that she now acknowledges it brings a burn of satisfaction to me.

We board and strap in. There's a cot for Lukas but for take-off I place him in her lap and she uses a baby belt that's attached to hers. Despite what she's acknowledged, I know better than to offer to take him for this moment. I know she can't give him over to me yet. But I can be there for them both. Her face pales but I suspect that it's not just the flight bothering her but the enormity of this action. I don't dismiss how hard this has to be for her.

Once we're settled I reach across and take her hand in mine. She closes her eyes but doesn't pull away. I know she doesn't want to need me, but that she takes my touch soothes something inside me. I can't resist leaning closer on the pretext of looking at Lukas. Although I want to look at him too. As the plane accelerates down the runway her hand twists and she holds me back. Tightly. An electrical pulse charges between us and the only response I'm capable of is to hold her even more tightly. A shiver runs through her and she opens her eyes and looks straight into mine. Hers are an even deeper brown than usual and I don't think that emotion is fear.

It takes everything not to lean in and kiss her. Yet despite that keen frustration victory hums in my veins. Our physical compatibility is undeniable and right now I feel like a damned saint. I've been living like a monk for months. So not me. I work hard. I like reward. I like knowing I can get what I want. Her smile is what I want and her body is next on the menu.

Except it can't be. There's Lukas. There's all this complication.

I release my seat belt as soon as we've levelled out, and pull together a snack plate for her. Keeping myself busy is the only way I can get through this.

I take Lukas from her and settle him into the cot that's been installed in the plane. The cabin door is locked. I told the flight crew not to disturb us when we first boarded. I pass her the papers I printed early this morning before leaving the holiday home in Queenstown.

'Will you look through these résumés and let me know if you have a preference?' I ask. 'I'll arrange interviews for the top three as soon as we land.'

She looks confused. 'For what position?'

'I have a cleaner and a team who come and look after the grounds as well as a chef who's onsite for some of the week and leaves meals for the weekends. But this is the first nanny I've had to employ and I assumed you'd want to have input into that decision.'

'You want Lukas to have a nanny?' She's arctic and there's no way she'd take my hand now.

But I expected a spiky response from Ms I-Don't-Need-Anything-From-Anyone.

'You worked right through your pregnancy and continued the moment you left hospital after giving birth,' I point out calmly. 'You need a break. Lukas needs you to have a break. To sleep.'

'I don't need a break.'

'The dark circles under your eyes tell a different story.'

Her back straightens. Yep, just made her spikier. Too bad.

'The nanny isn't making any major parenting decisions.' I aim to inject a little levity. 'It's enough that the two of us will probably debate them intensely. I've no doubt we'll overthink our way around all sides of any issue and won't need any outside interference to make it worse.'

She shoots me a look but to my pleasure she can't hold her smile for long. She actually chuckles. 'I don't *want* to disagree with you.'

'Then don't,' I reply, as if it's the most obvious answer ever. But I feel a ridiculous level of relief and I smile back at her. 'You can't do it all by yourself, all of the time. You don't have to. Not any more. You can share the load.'

'Like you do?'

'I have plenty of people who support me—I just told you only a few of my home team. So let's get a nanny to tend to him for the late night feed. Just that one. We'll see how it goes and then assess. Okay?'

She doesn't actually know I'm being uncharacteristically reasonable here so she can't appreciate my effort in that regard.

'Okay,' she mumbles. 'Thank you.'

I can't resist teasing her more so I lean really close. 'Pardon? I didn't quite catch that.'

'Thank you.' But there's a defiant gleam in her eye as if giving me thanks is the last thing she wants to do.

And yeah, it's the last thing I want from her. I *do* want her time and attention. Her company. But somehow that has to be separate from all this and I can't see how that's possible so I pull back.

The flight drags. She reads every résumé cover to cover and puts them in an ordered pile of preference. Then she plays on her phone. I'm actually fidgeting because I want to talk to her but at the same time I want to control that urge. Just to prove to myself that I can. She suddenly reaches over and offers her phone. The screen is unlocked and there's a photo of Lukas in front of me.

'I thought...' She shrugs and worries her lip somewhat helplessly. 'I don't know if you want to see them but, if you flick through, there's every photo or little film I have of Lukas since he was born.'

Speechless, I take the phone from her and stare hungrily at the screen. I don't know how much time passes as I absorb every image, every small video, every glimpse into his little life thus far. He's only three months old but she has a hundred pictures of him and every last one is stunning. Maybe it's her social media work but the woman can construct a frame. Maybe it's that her subject is so completely perfect. He's so beautiful. Yeah, I'm smitten with him. I never imagined I could feel so much for something—someone—so small. I slowly scroll backwards through the pictures and at one I draw a sharp breath. It doesn't show Lukas. It's Talia. A very heavily pregnant Talia.

Talia glances across and leans over to see which picture has me so floored.

'Oh.' Her cheeks redden. 'Romy took some. She said I needed to record the pregnancy because it goes fast. So I posed a few times.'

She's looking embarrassed in the photo and even more embarrassed now. My heart pounds. I swipe back one more.

'Oh!' She gasps. The colour in her face instantly intensifies. 'That's terrible,' she babbles. 'I forgot it was there. I didn't mean...'

I don't let her take the phone back. It's a bathroom selfie. She's wearing a bra and panties and nothing else. She has to be almost at full term. She's so beautiful my heart basically bursts.

I just stare at it. At her. Raw yearning overwhelms me. 'I missed your *entire* pregnancy,' I mutter between gritted teeth. 'I never got to *see* you...not once...'

Not that night in the gondola cabin either. It was too dark. There were only glimpses of perfection when lightning lit the sky. And right now I'm almost overcome by the urge to tumble her to the floor and impregnate her again here and now and then chain her to me so I don't miss another damned second of it. Yeah. Shocking.

I don't, of course. But I do tap the phone and flag all the photos I've just been looking at.

'What are you doing?' she mumbles.

'I want a copy of them,' I almost growl as I pull out my own phone and wirelessly transfer the files. 'Okay?'

I'm too gruff and it's not really a question because I really don't want her to say no. And for a guy who—I fully admit— is fully paranoid about other people having photos of me, it's rough of me to just send copies of these direct to my phone.

'Even those ones?'

Yeah. The ones of her. I nod jerkily. There's silence and I slowly look up. I have to look her in the eyes to check I have her consent. Her bloody beautiful deep brown eyes snare me. I just drown in them. She's still for a while, not saying anything while she reads who knows what in my own tense expression.

'Okay,' she says softly.

I swallow and make myself build some humanity. 'Tell me about his birth,' I croak. 'Was it okay?'

She hesitates and now her gaze skitters from mine. 'I don't remember a lot of it.'

Liar. She's holding back from me. And suddenly I'm furious with her. I want to find out more. Disappointment merges with challenge. I want the entire truth from her. And that's when I accept I'm willing to do whatever it takes to get it.

CHAPTER THIRTEEN

Talia

I CAN'T HOLD his gaze. He's missed so much and I feel terrible. I should have pushed harder. Showing him the photos was a peace offering, the smallest of ways in which I could try to make amends. But I don't tell him about Lukas's delivery even though I should. I don't want him getting angry with me for going through that alone and I suspect he will. For a moment here on the plane things were good between us—we even laughed. Now there's a flash of that bleakness in his gaze as I pass off the question, but he says nothing. He holds my phone back out to me.

'Now you have my number,' he says dryly. 'No excuse not to stay in touch.'

As I take my phone the plane shudders. I stiffen. Before I can breathe his hand is on mine.

'It's just a few bumps. Give it a moment.'

Sure enough the plane settles as we zoom through the clouds but my pulse races on regardless. He hasn't released my hand and I haven't tried to pull away.

'What is it with you needing a comforting touch in life-threatening situations?' he teases.

'I think that's a pretty normal human response.' I bluff but it's nice to see his smile again. 'And you're the one who grabbed *my* hand.'

He chuckles. 'You're a good liar.'

I shoot him a startled look.

'You lied to Ava very easily about us,' he elaborates.

I press my lips together. 'Only because I didn't want her to worry at all. Not ever.'

'I guessed that was why.' He sighs. 'But it makes me wonder who you do ever open up to.'

I shoot him another startled look and pull my hand free of his. He doesn't try to stop me.

His low bitter laugh mocks me. 'Yeah, no one. I figured that.'

I'm irritated because I'm certain *he* doesn't open up to anyone either. 'And your point?'

He straightens in his seat and leans closer. 'I don't want you to lie to me. Not ever.'

He echoes my words. I swallow because while it could be considered a threat it's more of a warm invitation and it's utterly disarming.

'I'd like you to promise me that you won't,' he adds steadily. 'And don't hold back on all the truth either.'

Yeah, he knows I omit things. Because I just have and of course he knows it. But it's for good reason—or so I've always thought.

'I think you owe me that,' he finishes.

I realise the photos weren't enough. Nor was the apology. He needs the whole truth. He's done all the right things since finding out about Lukas. He's tried to give me time, space, he's taken me to see Ava and offered unquestioning support. I haven't. I need to be honest with him.

Not making more of an effort to tell him about Lukas was terrible. It's as though a fog has lifted from my mind. For me to hold his lifestyle against him—to be so *judgemental*—was wrong. I need to course correct. Now.

'You know that night at the gondola was out of character for me.' My throat clogs because this is personal and it's hard to say.

His eyes widen and he slowly nods. 'Yet you assume it wasn't out of character for me also?' His focus is even more intense now. 'What do you think you know about me?'

I bite my lip, embarrassed because I've been emotional. He wants to be there for Lukas. He wants to make everything work between us. He's trying. So I need to try too. I need to be honest even if it means more anger from him.

'I found a photo of you with another woman taken later on the night we were together.' The thought of it still turns my stomach. Was she his girlfriend? I hate to think I was the other woman in a cheating situation.

He sits up straight. 'You what?'

'I know you met up with another woman that night.' I hurry to tell him I know the truth. 'It's your prerogative, I guess, it's not like we were—'

'You—'

'Allowed my own prejudice to cloud my thinking,' I interrupt him because I need to get all this said before I chicken out. 'I made assumptions and I was wrong to and I'm sorry. And the thing is—if I'm really honest with myself it's not because I was being judgemental of your lifestyle. But rather I was jealous.'

His jaw drops. 'Of this other woman?'

'No.' I swallow. 'Of you.'

He looks mystified. 'For…'

'Having fun?' I shrug and finish weakly. It's so stupid and I've made bad decisions because of it.

I assumed he wouldn't be interested in being a father. None of the cheats my mother dated ever were. My own cheat of a father sure wasn't. I tarnished Dain with their brush.

He stares at me for a moment. I can't read his reaction as he rubs his mouth with his fingers.

'Show me the photo,' he suddenly orders.

'I can't. I don't have it.'

'There's Wi-Fi on the plane, search for it again and show me.' He's very businesslike.

Yep, instant regrets on being so honest. But I do as he asks.

'There are almost no photos of me online,' he says conversationally as I fumble with my phone. 'I have a team who keep it that way. That's partly why it was all but impossible for you to get in touch with me directly.'

Because he's a control freak who hates being in the press. Yep, I've got that. And I don't blame him now I know a little more about his parents putting him on the front page in their personal fight.

But it's the Internet and some things never die on the Internet. I find the picture and turn it so he can see. It was in a gossip-column piece from a small Queenstown paper that I followed on my social media. It popped up in my feed the morning after that momentous night. The photo showed him with a famous New Zealand model and I was appalled.

'I'm not identified in the caption,' he says thoughtfully. 'That must be why my minions didn't pick it up.'

'But it's *you*.' I brace as he studies the photo. He doesn't deny it.

'Is she your girlfriend?' I ask.

The corners of his mouth twitch. 'What makes you think we're *together*?'

Well, duh, you only need to look at the way the model is looking at *him* to know they're intimate. But Dain's eyebrows are raised questioningly and I can't tell him it's all in her eyes.

'We're not even holding hands,' he points out calmly. 'Not kissing. Not touching at all.'

I swallow. 'Because you're private.'

That he isn't named in that caption actually speaks to the power of his discretion. Maybe the photographer didn't recognise him and was interested in the model.

He regards me steadily. 'Okay, I'll give you that.'

So he was with her. My innards shrivel.

'But you didn't notice my hair apparently grew about three inches in less than a couple hours?' He watches me.

'What?' I stare at him then back at the photo.

'My hair was shorter when I was with you,' he says. 'Don't you remember tugging on it? Because I remember you tugging on it.'

A flame of heat rivers through me. With trembling fingers I study that photo again.

He's right, I didn't look too closely at the time because I was cringing—and I was too busy feeling inadequate looking at her. But now I do look more closely. And, yes, his hair is longer than it was that night.

'This photo was taken two years ago when I met Willow. I haven't seen her since then, though according to that caption she was back in Queenstown that weekend. But I never saw her and last I heard she was modelling in Paris.'

Willow is even more famous than he is. The gossip piece focused on her, not the man escorting her. And she suits the name, what with her endless limbs and, oh, yes, I am jealous. I clocked the location—a cool bar in Queenstown—and, given the date of the article, I assumed the photo was taken that night. That he went from a quick canapé—me—to the sumptuous feast that was her.

'So she wasn't your girlfriend?' I ask.

'Not the night we were together,' he says. 'I don't cheat.'

Now I feel even worse.

But Dain actually chuckles. 'You really screwed up.'

I really did.

He inhales. 'As penance I think you ought to be wholly honest with me.'

I glance up at him, confused. I've just confessed the worst.

'Were you a virgin that night?' he asks bluntly.

I shrivel—emotionally that is. If only I could *really* shrivel right out of existence. How did he know? Did he guess? I'm mortified. 'I...'

Can't even breathe the words.

But he just waits.

'Why does it matter?' I mumble as I eventually nod.

'Why didn't you tell me then?'

I swallow.

'You couldn't, right?' he says. 'You couldn't be that vulnerable.'

'I've never regretted it. Not for a moment,' I reassure him in an embarrassed rush. 'It was amazing. You were...' I trail off and look at him. 'Are you even more angry with me?'

'I'm feeling all kinds of things about you, Talia. But yeah, anger is one of them.' He looks thoughtful. 'And you're jealous of my supposed lifestyle?'

My lips are suddenly dry and I lick them. 'Do you deny your lifestyle is...uh...exciting?'

'I don't think it's as extensive as what you're thinking.' He looks right into my eyes.

I don't want to think about it too closely. 'Oh?'

His gaze is unwavering. 'I haven't had sex in about a year.'

My jaw drops. 'You mean...?'

No. Surely not.

He closes my mouth with a finger beneath my chin. 'Yeah. I do mean.' His gaze deepens. 'Let me guess, you don't believe me.'

'I...' *Am floored.*

'Yet it's *true*,' he says and he's somehow even closer.

'Why didn't you?' I blurt.

'Why didn't you?'

I can't answer.

'Here's the thing, Talia,' he says slowly. 'I won't lie to you either. If nothing else there has to be absolute honesty between us because we have to work together. For Lukas. So honesty always. Deal?'

I'm bamboozled by his revelation but I hear that caveat—*if nothing else.*

'Deal,' I breathe.

He doesn't look satisfied. In fact his expression tightens and he's somehow closer.

'You've worked hard to care for your sister for a long time. Worked hard to care for Lukas,' he says almost thoughtfully. 'You've never let anyone take care of your needs—not until that night with me, right?'

I can only stare at him.

'And not since then?' His sudden smile is saturnine. 'You should be indulged, Talia.'

'I should.' My spellbound agreement slides out on a whisper.

I can't turn away from him. I can't look away from the heat in his blue, blue eyes. I can't ignore this desire any more. I'm utterly still as he slowly moves closer. His smile is all I can see. His touch is all I want. And at last he's there—his mouth is on mine. I open to him on a moan and he echoes it with one of his own. The pressure is hot and escalates in seconds. I clutch his shoulders. I thought I'd remembered but I was wrong. This intensity shuts my mind down. I just want him. All of him. Here. Now.

He growls in the back of his throat and I feel his muscles bunch. He drags me across his lap and I tremble in absolute rapture at being in his arms again. I press against him and the kisses deepen. He teases me with his tongue. His hands hold me—hard and secure—and sweep down my body. I'm aching and ecstatic and I just pour it all into kissing him and lose myself in the bliss.

I pay no attention to the voice saying something from far away.

But suddenly Dain tears his mouth from mine. With a muttered swearword he lifts me back into my seat. Dazed, I can only look at him in confusion—and yearning.

'That was the captain speaking.' He half laughs, half groans. 'Seat belt on.' He fastens my belt before tending to Lukas. 'We're landing.'

But I'm still up in the clouds and I really don't want to return to earth.

CHAPTER FOURTEEN

Dain

IT WASN'T SUPPOSED to happen. I intended to do whatever it took to get her to trust me but also keep my damned distance. But somehow she's defused my temper and the damned endless lust I have for her has me so distracted I can't catch my breath. But she wants me just as much. Right back. And I'm all but feral inside.

We land in Brisbane and I dispense with my waiting chauffeur to drive Talia and Lukas to my house myself. I don't want my off-balance state to be obvious to everyone. Frankly I've yet to figure how I'm going to introduce them to my staff, how I'm going to explain their sudden appearance in my life to anyone. But it doesn't matter, I can delay most of that. Right now I just want to be alone with them both.

'This is a beautiful area…' She's wide-eyed as she looks at the leafy neighbourhood I begin to slow down in. 'You don't live in one of your own apartments?'

'When working in Sydney or Melbourne, sure. But this is my place to escape and I thought it would be a better place to bring Lukas. It offers total privacy.'

'It's huge.' She's pale as we drive through the massive security gates. 'How do you manage it?'

'I have staff.' I pull up outside the house and pause, not

understanding her wariness. 'You don't like it?' That I care so much about her opinion is just weird.

'Oh, no, it's amazing. It's just really huge.'

'With this space and privacy I can fully relax. Property is work. This isn't work. This is my paradise.' I get out of the car and breathe in the perfumed scent of the garden. Then I shrug. 'Like you, I moved a lot when I was a kid. I was shuttled from apartment to apartment and always being asked to compare them—which was bigger, which was better. I just wanted to stay in the one place and not have to decide and try to placate them. So this is wish fulfilment perhaps.'

'It's your *home*,' she mutters.

'Right.' I feel awkward. 'A garden and a pool and I can have my friends over to play without worrying World War Three is about to erupt in front of them.'

She smiles at that. 'You have your friends over often?'

Her smile pulls my own and I start to relax. 'I've been known to have parties.'

'Debauched dance parties with beautiful women?'

'That's what you immediately picture?' My mood lightens more and I laugh. 'You see me and think sexy dancing?'

She blushes delightfully. My smile just gets bigger and I'm half tempted to dance towards her right now. Her inexperience and unexplored desire and passionate curiosity intrigue me. Because I also know she's an extremist—it's evident in the hours she works, the lengths she goes to—misguidedly sometimes—to look after those she loves. She's either all in or she's all out.

In some respects I'm the same. Physically I want all in. But while the chemistry between us crackles I'm wary about dealing with it. Usually sex is uncomplicated. Desire is transient. Once it's sated I move on and I've stayed on good terms with many of the women I've slept with. Because emotional boundaries don't get crossed. I make sure there are no expectations, offer no 'relationship'—I've no interest in that burden. Because it is a burden.

So surely I could sleep with her again and us remain pleasant in parenting Lukas? The problem is she's untrusting too. She's been hurt by her past and I can't be sure she wouldn't turn and try to block me out once we're done. I never want Lukas to witness a war like that of my parents.

I think Talia believes in happy families as little as I do. So I've got to resist the temptation to touch her. We'll keep things calm and serene and safe. I'll never make her some impossible-to-keep promise. Because the only thing I'm certain of is the impermanence of any affair.

I step forward and lift Lukas from the car, carrying him while I take Talia on a quick tour.

'The parties are purely for business,' I explain. 'I need to be engaged with the community—keep the profile up. So there are charity balls, philanthropic events.' I can't resist walking near enough for our shoulders to brush. 'The beautiful and the wealthy attend. Future and current clients.'

To be honest I probably should have one soon. It's been a while since I have and it would be a way of revealing Talia and Lukas are in my life—at least to those I work most closely with. They're better off being informed directly by me rather than by the inevitable whisperings and speculation that will begin. But it doesn't have to happen this weekend or anything. We all need to settle in together first.

I lead her through the atrium and into the first of the living areas—the one with the view over the pool and tennis court.

'Do you play tennis? Swim?' I ask. 'There's a home gym, yoga room and sauna as well. Use any of them any time.' I want her to feel comfortable here. 'There's a home cinema too—'

'You have everything you could ever want.' She doesn't look comfortable. 'You never need to leave the place if you don't want to.'

'Right.' I tense a little. Because yeah, that was part of it. Full privacy.

'You know I want to keep working,' she says in a low voice.

'I know.' I inhale deeply. At that comment I can't wait any longer and can only hope my assistants have been as efficient as they usually are. 'On that, I have something to show you in the pool room.'

She shoots me a wary glance. I'm actually nervous, which is ridiculous. Still carrying Lukas, I walk past the tennis court and the pool to the low building at the back.

'This is the pool room,' I explain.

'It's a whole other *house*.'

I smile because that's actually true. It's a three-bedroom cottage.

'Do you want me to live in here rather than the main house?' she asks.

A flash of guilt makes me flinch. When I first thought about her moving here I considered that, but now there's no way. 'I think we both need to be near Lukas at night and he'll definitely be in the main house.'

I lead her to the large kitchen usually reserved for pizza parties and pool refreshments and let her walk in ahead of me.

'I've had my assistant set a few things up, but you can change the layout and of course you can exchange any items if there's another brand of equipment that you prefer.'

'Are you kidding me?' Her eyes are huge as she slowly turns on the spot.

I lean against the doorjamb and feel a smug satisfaction for the first time in days. I've shocked—and pleased—her. It feels good. I want to please her some more. I want to see her smile and her skin flush and hear her light laughter.

She runs her hand lightly over the gleaming chrome of the brand-new Italian espresso machine. It's a commercial one with so many levers I wouldn't know where to start, but she clearly does because she whispers its name beneath her breath with the reverence of meeting a deity. Watching her makes me smile harder.

Then she sees the double camera set-up—the rotating mount so she can film directly above the polished counter-top and get that bird's eye view, and the other camera on a free-standing tripod. There are diffusers and other technical gear so she can get the exact lighting she needs. There are smaller boxes that I told my staff to leave unopened because I thought she might like to enjoy unwrapping them herself—it's crockery and tools for any kind of coffee shoot she can think of. She's speechless but that doesn't mean I can't read her mind on this.

'I know your channel is important to you,' I say. 'This way you can keep making content while being here at home with Lukas. It will do for now, right?'

Her wide-eyed gaze turns troubled. 'You hate social media.'

'Well, I didn't think *I'd* be in your videos.' I smile at her.

'Right.' She almost smiles back but then she goes solemn again. 'I'll pay you back.'

I instantly chill. That's not a conversation that interests me, but I don't want to argue with her. I turn and begin walking back to the main house. 'I'll show you the nursery and your room now.'

She runs to catch me and grabs my shoulder to make me stop. 'Thank you, Dain.'

I stare down at her. Yeah, I wanted to please her but oddly I really don't want her gratitude. I don't want her feeling be-holden to me. I want there to be nothing like that between us again.

'No problem.' I'm gruff. 'Keeping you happy is important.'

She pulls back and I want to bite out my tongue even though what I've said is true.

I keep moving. I show her through the airy bedroom suites that have been arranged for them. There's a room for Lukas. One for a nanny next door while Talia's is further along. My bedroom is at the other end of the corridor but I don't make the mistake of showing her right inside that—my self-control has its limits.

'I need to do some work,' I say shortly once I've swiftly nodded whose is whose room. 'Will you settle Lukas into the nursery?'

'Of course, he's due for a snack.'

I carefully hand our son to her. It's torture being so close and getting a hit of her soft fragrance. I'm tempted to go into the nursery with her and sit with them while she tends to our baby. Except I need to get my head back together and I haven't done any real work in days.

Only half an hour later I can't stay away any longer. I go back to the nursery half expecting to see them both taking a nap. But while Lukas is bundled up fast asleep in his crib, Talia isn't there. I hear noises and walk along the corridor. Talia's in her bedroom—red-faced and frantic and rummaging through her bags.

'What's wrong?' I watch her tearing through her few clothes. 'You've lost something?'

'A toy Romy gave to Lukas.' She tips one bag upside down and keeps shaking it even though there's clearly nothing else to fall from it. 'I can't find it. It isn't anywhere. But I was sure I'd packed it.'

Her whisper is urgent and upset.

I freeze. 'Are you talking about that ripped-up rabbit?'

'Yes.' She whips her head up. 'Have you seen it?'

'It was almost decapitated—'

'I hadn't had time to fix it.' She's suddenly in a fury. 'You *took* it?'

CHAPTER FIFTEEN

Talia

'IT WASN'T YOURS to take.' Anger surges into me. 'What did you do with it?'

He's frozen. 'Talia—'

'You got rid of it? Threw it out?' I gape at him in horror. 'Because it was ragged?'

He walks out of the room and I'm so furious I follow him, not stopping to see where he's going, not stopping my tirade. He doesn't want to deal with my emotion? Too bad. 'Wasn't it good enough for your standards? Didn't it fit into this perfect nursery you've put together like magic?'

It was broken and it wasn't perfect but it was *loved*. But it wasn't good enough to stay here. I'm so hurt. This place is so perfect and I most definitely do not fit in. Because I'm like that toy too—worn out and worthless to a guy like him.

'Talia—'

'It mightn't have met your standards but it was given with love and—'

He bends down to the bag at his feet and turns back to face me, his hand outstretched.

I'm instantly silenced. I stare at his hand and slowly take the rabbit from him. His ear and head have been stitched back on properly.

'I wouldn't have thrown out a clearly much-loved toy, Talia.'

His breathing is jumpy. 'I assumed it was one of *your* child-hood toys. I didn't realise it had come from Romy. And I'm sorry if repairing it was the wrong thing to do.'

For a moment I struggle for air. Tears spring to my eyes as I study the soft little animal. I'm relieved. I'm touched. And I'm utterly embarrassed.

Swallowing hard, I run my finger over the neat stitching. 'You did this?'

'Yeah.'

'When?' I finally glance up at him.

He looks a little embarrassed. 'Before we drove to Dune-din.'

'You said you had work to do.' I try to smile but it doesn't really work. 'Did you lie to me?'

'This *was* work.' His shoulders lift. 'Of the unpaid paren-tal kind.'

My heart absolutely melts.

'I didn't know toy surgery was on your CV.' But then he has a bunch of skills and talents.

'I'm sorry if I overstepped,' he says quietly.

'You didn't. You were really thoughtful.' Guilt washes over me. 'I just haven't had the time…'

'Because you've been doing those important things like keeping him alive.'

I shake my head as a tear runs down my cheek even though everything's okay now. Better than okay, in fact. 'I'm hor-monal,' I mutter by way of an excuse as I brush it away.

He regards me with a smile that's both sweet and sceptical. 'I don't think it's hormones. I think you're tired and upset. Which isn't surprising, given how much you've had to pro-cess recently.'

But it's more than that. I've just blown up at him and he deserves to know why. Yet again he's shown me he can be trusted so he deserves to know that it isn't *him*.

'I don't have any toys from my childhood.' I rub the toy to

soothe myself as I speak. 'I don't have anything at all, actually. So I want Lukas to have the toys he's been given.'

He cocks his head ever so slightly and it's just enough to tempt me to keep talking.

'You already know we moved a lot,' I mutter. 'I've lived in every city, most small towns in the country. Mum would pick us up from school and we'd just leave. She'd have broken up with the latest, or been abused by the guy's wife.' I wince, remembering how the daughter of one guy once shredded me at school. 'Mum would've packed a few clothes for us but never anything else—never any toys or anything. None of those little silly things I collected as a child. Things that shouldn't matter.'

'But do.'

I nod. 'So then you just accept it. That you're not going to keep them. So I stopped collecting.'

He's still as he listens.

'What little I have now I've got for myself, and even now I tend not to hold onto them any more. If you have less, then you don't feel a loss.' I shrug. 'Because if you haven't had something to begin with you can't really miss it...' I have no idea if I'm making sense to him but it's easier for me this way. It's emotional safety. 'Things don't last anyway, you know? Nothing is for ever.' But I run my fingers over the toy he's restored. He's fixed it so it *can* last longer.

'Right.' He slowly nods. 'But you want different for Lukas.'

I stare hard at the rabbit. 'Yep.'

'I get it.' He takes a step towards me. 'Both of us have parents who disappointed us.' He sighs and his smile is a little twisted. 'I had so *many* toys. Didn't love any of them.' He shoots me a rueful look. 'Poor little rich boy, right?' He bows his head. 'My parents behaved badly—either spoiling me or neglecting me, purely to antagonise each other. So I'm not unscathed. I have scars and triggers. Like I react badly when I think someone thinks the worst of my intentions. I still feel the shame and humiliation of having any private business aired. Their infidelities were exposed and picked over by everyone—gossiped about. They used me—taking me from school to go to a sports game but tipping off the press, one upping the other in spoiling me. But only in public—it was evidence-gathering for the lawyers and if there were no points to be gained the outing was abandoned.'

That he tells me this steals my breath. 'I'm sorry, Dain.'

He glances away, breaking that searing contact. I glance around too and it finally dawns on me that we're in his bedroom.

It's every bit as beautiful as the rest of the house—everything is gorgeous, it's jaw-dropping quiet luxury. But he's so used to it he doesn't seem to have any idea of how sumptuous everything in his life is. And I mean everything—from the private jet and gleaming cars to the discreet staff who appear and do things without him needing to direct them at all before melting into the shadows, to this palatial, magnificent home with every last detail and smallest fixture the absolute finest. Maybe his apparent unawareness is what happens when you're born into a family that's been wealthy for generations.

He could've gone out and bought a million new soft toys for Lukas. But he didn't—despite being surrounded by all this perfection. Because for all that wealth he was poor in other ways. He fixed up this old rabbit because he sensed its sentimental value.

'I'm still not sure he really fits in here even with the repair,' I mutter.

That Dain even knows how to stitch it stuns me. Surely he never had to darn his holey socks or anything. He'd have been handed new ones.

'He belongs with Lukas,' Dain says gruffly.

I glance back up at him only to see he's watching me and his expression isn't masked. I see his hunger. I see it and feel it and match it. I move closer.

He swallows but doesn't step back. He's watching me the way a predator watches the thing it wants. Warily, quietly, intensely—waiting for it to wander within reach.

I get that he doesn't trust people because they always have an ulterior motive. People want things—generally money—from him all the time. I don't want any of these *things* from him. At all. What I want is far more basic than that. Far more reckless. And it is so impossible to resist. But I should. For Lukas I should. For myself.

But the blue of Dain's eyes vanishes in the black heat of his pupils and the yearning I see echoes my own.

'Talia...'

I don't want him to think I want him because he's been nice—because he's helped me in so many ways already. It's frustrating and somehow I need to make that clear to him. 'I understand why you're not interested in marriage,' I say.

He stiffens. 'I've never wanted any kind of wife, trophy or otherwise. I can't commit to something I can't believe in.'

'Good.' I step towards him. 'Because *we're* definitely *not* getting married.'

He seems to stop breathing.

'Never, okay?' I whisper.

He tenses even more. I know he's reserved but he's very clear about what he *doesn't* want. I wouldn't consider this if I thought he had other intentions but there's honesty between us now. There's also this chemistry—it burns ever more intensely, ever more out of my control. I ache for touch. I stroke the toy I'm still holding instead. The toy he's fixed. Another wave of emotion engulfs me. I've misjudged him. Again.

'Never,' he finally agrees huskily. 'There's no reason for us to do something we know would be damaging to Lukas and to ourselves. We just...co-parent. Quietly and easily.' He stands very still. 'Lukas needs you. And you need...less stress.'

'I thought you said I needed to be indulged,' I say softly.

The words escape before my brain catches up—control

slipping free of my hold, like water sinking through sand. But it's not a trickle, it's an unstoppable tsunami. I freeze but at the same time I really don't. I sway ever so slightly towards him. My body doesn't give a damn about the future. It's only interested in *now*.

'Talia...' he mutters a whispered warning.

I'm too far gone to pay heed. This passion between us is temporary. Such things are *always* temporary, right? This I know. All those men in my mother's life...

But I also know that *Dain* is not a cheater—I was wrong about that. He's reserved and private and wants to do his best for Lukas. He's gorgeous. And I can't resist this need any more. Because Dain will *always* do his best for Lukas—as will I. So I know he'll still work with me as best he can even after this chemistry fades. Neither of us wants Lukas to be caught up in arguing parents.

'So you want me to indulge you?' he says.

I lightly toss the toy to a side table so my hands are free. 'You wanted honesty, right?' I swallow. 'I still want you.' I touch his chest. 'I can't seem to stop wanting you.'

His hands span my waist and now I couldn't step back even if I wanted to.

I really don't want to. 'I don't want to complicate things but—'

'You can't get past it?' he interrupts with a growl.

'Right.' I nod. I can't *think*.

'Funny thing, nor can I.'

I'm so relieved my knees almost sag. 'We let it run...' I eventually say. 'Let it end.'

'And then move forward?' He's still but his hold on me tightens. 'For Lukas.'

'Yes.' I nod. 'We'll work it out for him. He'll always come first.'

'Right.' He leans towards me.

I truly do freeze now as his mouth drops towards mine. I shiver as he kisses me. And then I combust.

Throwing my arms around his neck, I kiss him back. He growls and moves swiftly, picking me up in his strong arms, dropping me onto his bed and tumbling on top. I moan in sheer relief. We're finally back on that page—the one we belong on together.

His hands sweep over me, swiftly stripping me. But suddenly he stops, a sharp drawn breath whistles between his teeth. I freeze and suddenly realise he's seen the red scar slicing across my lower abdomen. In the heat I've forgotten that I haven't told him.

'I had a C-section,' I whisper in hurried explanation. 'He was round the wrong way.'

My attempt to minimise it doesn't work. He rises above me to look me in the eyes and the expression in his eyes makes me squirm with guilt.

'Were you scared?' He stares right through my defences.

'The doctors were great,' I mutter.

'Were you scared?' He tightens his grip on my wrists and leans closer over me. 'You didn't have a friend with you. No family.'

'I was okay,' I say. 'Most importantly Lukas was okay.'

I see the anger in his eyes. The hurt. I know he wants to rail at me. I see the ripple of emotion run through his body and his muscles bunch. I'm totally at his mercy and I deserve his wrath. But after the growl of annoyance from the back of his throat I feel an intimate caress so tender I quake. That's when I realise the punishment he intends for me to take is that of unbearable pleasure.

His exploration is slow and torturous. He kisses my scar reverently and then continues his exploration south, worshipping my body.

'I hate that you were alone,' he says huskily. 'All this time.'

I don't want him to be this gentle. This tender. I feel as if

I don't deserve it. I shiver and try to pull back. But he grabs my hips and holds me still.

'I'm indulging you, Talia,' he whispers fiercely. 'You definitely should be indulged.'

'Even though I didn't tell you everything?'

'I've forgiven you.' He sighs roughly. 'Maybe it's time you forgive yourself on that.' He sits up and takes off his tee shirt in a wide, whipping movement.

I stare at him—made emotional by his words and overwhelmed by the sight of his body. Yep, I slither deeper into lust with him. That should be impossible. It should. I never realised I could want him more. But I do.

Neither of us were completely naked in the gondola. I've never actually been naked in front of a man before. But I'm not shy—he's always made this easy for me. And he's *stunning*. His lips curve as he sees me staring.

'I forgot,' he mutters. 'You like to look. You didn't really get the chance last time.'

He slowly strips the rest of his clothes for me. I'm so blown away by him all I can do is lie on his bed and stare.

He comes back to lean over me. 'You know you can touch if you want.'

I lift my hands and run them over his body but that's all I can do because he's back between my legs—teasing me so I'm only able to arch my hips closer and it's so erotic and so intimate I gasp.

'Let me indulge you,' he murmurs. 'Surrender to me, Talia.'

The sensations are so intense. I moan. Loudly.

He suddenly lifts away, rising up to kiss my mouth. Thoroughly. I stare at him questioningly when he lifts away to look into my eyes.

'Can't wake Lukas,' he murmurs in explanation. 'Don't want this interrupted before we've hardly begun.'

I've forgotten our son is sleeping in the room just down the hall—how terrible of me. He reads my mind and laughs again.

'You're allowed a little time for yourself,' he says. 'And you're definitely allowed a lot of time for *me*.'

That mix of arrogance and confident sensuality melts me. He moves back down my body and laughs again when he tastes for himself the effect his words have had on me.

'You're so deliciously responsive, Talia.'

That just makes me respond even more. I melt with his approval. And he works more than his tongue. He lets his fingers talk too. I gasp and bite down into the soft pillow to muffle my sighs and it's seconds, mere seconds, before I come hard.

I'm breathless but I know what I want—what I need—now. 'Dain.'

He glances up at me, a picture of hedonism sprawled between my legs. But as he sees my expression he frowns. 'Are you sure you're ready? It's not too soon?'

'It's not soon enough,' I mutter desperately. *'Please.'*

He flashes a tense smile at me. 'Okay.'

He leaves me for a moment and shoots me a rueful glance as he gets protection but, honestly, I'm too busy enjoying watching him get ready for me.

'I've also got protection of my own now,' I whisper, not wanting to hold anything back from him now. 'I talked it over with my doctors after Lukas's birth and they thought it might help regulate my cycle.' Which would make managing one thing a little easier.

'Two forms of protection is good,' he says gruffly.

'I think so too.' I smile at him.

He returns to the bed. I bite my lip—excited and a little apprehensive. He's big and strong and I'm neither. But he pulls me into his arms, sweeping a hand down my back, moulding me into his hard heat. I moan. He rolls, pinning me beneath him, and coaxes my legs further apart.

'You want me?'

There's a rawness to his question that pulls an equally harsh, honest response from me.

'Yes!'

He thrusts. Hard. He's inside me again and I'm a rippling, shivering, incoherent mess. Because it's good. He's good. He's in me, with me, and we're both so stunned it's a second before either of us can exhale.

'It's been so long,' he groans.

And then he moves. All I can do is wrap my arms around him because all I want is to keep him right here with me. I'm so close to him and I love it. This.

'You're as hot as you were that night.' His expression wild as he rears up and presses harder into me. 'So hot.'

He thrusts into me again and again and it's exquisite. I arch and cling, pushing to meet him with every wild movement. It's the best thing ever and once again it's shockingly quick. I go as tense as a wire. Next second my body is so crunched in ecstasy that my soul-piercing scream is silent.

I keep my eyes closed, because as I struggle to catch my breath I realise an alarming truth.

I'm never going to get enough of this.

I'm never going to get enough of *him*.

CHAPTER SIXTEEN

Dain

I CANCEL BUSINESS trips and make video calls instead. Even then I've cleared my schedule more than I ever have. I don't want to leave them. Not for fear she'll walk out on me. She's slept in my bed every night since I brought her here. She can't get enough of me and I'm the same for her. I don't dwell on that fact too long. It'll ebb. These things always do.

So I'll just enjoy the fact we now have a nanny for night time. Even so I'm trying not to be too demanding so Talia can catch up on some of the sleep she's been short of for months. But actually, despite my best intentions, she thwarts me—she's demanding and playful. I relish the challenge of keeping up with her. Her unexplored passionate side has been fully revealed and it's a seemingly bottomless well of want.

I go to Lukas in the mornings. I love 'talking' with him first thing. I scoop him up and change him and bring him to Talia. His smiles have developed to laughter and babbling. I don't recognise my own spontaneity. Since when do I work from home? Since when do I delegate meetings? But I'm a father playing catch-up with his firstborn. I don't want to leave them for hours at a time and go to work. I've lost so much time I don't want to miss a moment more.

I know Talia feels as though she doesn't fit. I know she has a fear of loss. But I can protect her here in my home and there's one more thing I can do to cement her security. I work with the lawyers via video link then take the paperwork to her at lunch.

'What's this?' She's instantly wary, which makes me tense up totally.

'It's Lukas's reissued birth certificate,' I say. 'Your contract. Plus some other papers.'

'My contract? For what? I don't need a contract.'

I glare at her. 'Can you give me just five minutes before interrupting with your rejection?'

She shoots me a mulish look. 'I don't understand what you're doing. Or why this is even necessary.'

'So that no matter what happens to me, or what happens between us, you and Lukas will have a home. Always.'

'I thought we'd agreed on that already,' she says shortly. 'I trust you.'

My heart stalls. 'Right.' I clear my throat. 'This is just the documentation to prove it.' And then some, actually, but I'm a bit thrown.

'What about this?' She points to one of the papers.

'My life insurance policy. It'll be worth it for you if I die.'

Her flushed cheeks are leeched of colour in a second. 'You think I'd want Lukas to lose a parent?'

'Talia…' I feel terrible. I just hit her with casually cruel words. My parents were so good at it. Knowing where and how to strike to inflict maximum emotional damage. I'm screwing up already. I could hurt her. Hurt Lukas. I don't ever want to. In part that's why it's important to me to get this paperwork squared away. So that if—*when*—things go south between us, everything is still sorted for Lukas. And her.

'I'm sorry,' I mutter. 'That was insensitive.'

She looks troubled more than hurt. 'You realise he needs *you*, not your money.'

I stare at her.

'*You're* worth far more than any amount of money,' she adds as if I haven't grasped it already.

I feel awkwardness heat my face.

'And *I* don't want your money.'

Yeah, I've got that message, actually. She's already given back the money that I put in her account. I understand why she did it. If our positions were reversed I'd have done the same. Even so, it annoys me immensely.

'You never have to worry about not having a home. Or not having enough ever again. You never have to worry about this being taken away from you or having to just up and leave.'

Her face pales and I know I've hurt her by reminding her of the past, but the point is she's through that now. 'You know it's nothing to me.' And there are no conditions.

'It's not nothing. You can't do things like this for everyone or you won't be a billionaire for very much longer.'

'You're not everyone,' I mutter through gritted teeth. 'You're the *mother* of my *child*.'

She stiffens, and somehow I feel as if I've said the wrong thing.

'I don't want a massive disparity between his parents' lives,' I try to explain, but I'm making it worse. 'I don't want him subjected to bitter comparisons—'

'You mean when we live separately.'

I hesitate. We haven't talked about the future and it feels like boggy ground to cover now. I don't want to go there. I don't want to think on it. Not yet. We're still letting that chemistry run. 'You let me give Ava money.'

'Yes, and that benefitted me. *That* was enough,' she says passionately. 'This, for *Lukas*, I understand. That you want to make his future secure no matter what. But this isn't what *I* want from you.'

There's suddenly an undercurrent between us that I'm wary of exploring.

What does she want? What does she really want from me?

I don't want to know. It's safer to retreat.

'If you don't want to touch the money, then don't,' I grit. 'Earn your own and save my unwanted amount for Lukas.'

'I will,' she says firmly. 'I'll do exactly that.'

'Great.'

She turns away from me. I'm not sure if I've angered or pleased her. I shake my head as I walk away. I really need to get to the office and get myself back on track.

I last less than three hours at the office. It's too soon to be there, right? I need to make sure they're okay. Talia's not in the main house and for a moment panic flares before my grounds-man quietly tells me she's at the pool house.

There I stop in the doorway, stunned at the scene. Those boxes are open but things are *not* organised. There are beans and froth and coffee grounds everywhere. A million lattes are scattered over the bench, each with intricate designs on the top. There's music quietly playing and randomly she's in a bikini. The whole thing makes me smile. My heart sings. My body has its usual reaction—on steroids. But as much as I ache for her right now I don't want to interrupt her and take her from her happy place. I step back but she catches sight of me.

'Hey.' Her smile is huge.

It's all the invitation I need. I step forward, warmth flowing through me already. 'What are you doing?' Duh. As if it isn't obvious.

'Making use of Lukas's nap time,' she says. 'We had a swim earlier hence…' She glances down at the bikini she's wearing. 'I got this from that drawerful in the wet room. They're all new. All sizes catered to.' She pauses. 'For your guests?'

I shrug but the possessive thread in her question makes me even hotter. 'Did Lukas enjoy the water?'

'Loved it until he got completely over-tired. The nanny took him inside.'

I wish I'd been here to play in the pool with them both. 'And you decided to do some content creation. In your bikini.'

'Of course,' she answers, with a nonchalance that's undermined by her sparkling gaze. 'You said this was my kitchen to do whatever I wanted in.'

'You're saying you're the boss in here?'

'Yes.' She caresses me, tugging at my suit. 'You're a little overdressed for such a warm day.'

Oh, another invitation I cannot resist. 'You think? What would you advise me to do?'

Her smile is positively wicked. 'I think you should strip.'

I laugh at the eagerness in her expression. 'You want me to dance for you.'

The tip of her tongue touches her lip. 'Would you?'

Her playfulness delights me. This is Talia at her best—confident and relaxed, doing what she loves and teasing me too boot. So of course—despite my inner awkwardness—I begin. But the way she watches, the way she breathes—any last inhibition vanishes. I'm confident in my body but this is next level. This is about seeing her glaze over.

Her hands are at my waist. Firm hands. She pushes and I let her spin me so I'm the one with my back to the kitchen counter. She steps forward and pushes me another pace so the wood is flush against my butt. She takes my hands and spreads my arms, placing my palms down on the counter behind me.

She's fast. And she's breathless. It's an effort for her to unzip my trousers. I grip the counter to stop myself taking hold of her. Taking over. That she's initiated this makes me harder than ever. Like that night in the gondola, when she was shy but forward, curious as hell. I ache to hear her little laugh again but I'm helpless to do anything now—I'm utterly in thrall to her next movement.

'What do you think you're doing?' I gasp.

'What do you think I'm doing?'

'Control freak,' I mutter. 'Always needing to be in charge.'

'And there's you, always needing to know every last little thing.'

Our lips brush but she pulls away playfully quick. Her breasts almost touch my chest. Desire whispers between us, a dangerous thread that's about to ignite.

She works down my chest. Licks my abs. Lust clouds her eyes as she takes me in hand and I get how much she wants this. I'm so damn grateful because I want it too. More than anything. I lose everything in this heat between us. I forget the impossible issues. The old anger that underlies my very existence. There's just this. I shake with sheer delight in a single stroke of her tongue and the playful scrape of her teeth devastates me. And when I see her eyes I really start to lose it. She's got this dreamy look and her cheeks are flushed and I realise she's loving doing this to me as much as I love being on the end of her dangerously provocative mouth. I want to stroke her. To make her come with me. I don't want to be alone in this—

'Dain...' she sighs. It's the sound of desire.

Yeah, I'm not alone. I gasp as I realise how aroused she is. I thread my fingers through her hair and she takes me deep into the back of her throat. I can't hold back. Her hand tightens and her mouth—her hot, wet mouth—pulls. I babble her name over and over, begging her to finish me—

It tears through me in a white-hot convulsion. She holds me through it, taking everything I release into her, until I sag back against the counter. Reduced to nothing. Barely able to stand. I blink hazily and watch my vixen rise to her feet in front of me. I'm all but catatonic as she licks her lips. Her eyes now sparkle and her cheeks are flushed. And then she laughs.

The resurgence of energy is instant and stunning. I was wiped out only moments ago but now I want to reduce her to the same incoherent, slick mess of arousal that she made me. I touch her with as much tenderness as I can muster and discover she's already there.

'Oh, you enjoyed me,' I growl with voracious delight.

Her eyes glaze. 'Yes.'

Sex usually brings me emotional oblivion. But this isn't oblivion. I'm *here* with her—more present than I've ever been in my life. I want to see her. Taste her. Please her to the point where she can't speak any more. Where she can't deny me anything.

'My turn,' I rumble.

She yelps as I lift her onto the counter. And then she laughs. She lets me have her body. In this realm she grants me permission for everything.

And I take it.

CHAPTER SEVENTEEN

Talia

HE SLIDES HIS palm up to hold me by the side of my neck, tilting my head back so my mouth is in place to meet his.

'You realise it's my turn to be in charge.' His eyes glitter.

He's hoarse and he's flushed and his muscles jump beneath my fingertips. He pulls my hands off him and presses them to my breasts.

'Play with yourself while I feast.'

My jaw drops. He grunts a laugh and kisses me. His hands cover mine, pushing my fingers to pinch my tight nipples. I'm already hot from having him at my mercy only minutes ago. From feeling him pump into my mouth. But now I'm his plaything and I obey.

'Good girl.'

I gasp as that edge of arousal sharpens.

He tugs my bikini bottoms. I quickly wriggle to help him. I'm so eager I ought to be embarrassed but he just praises me again and I liquefy on the counter before him. He drags his hot open mouth down my body—from plundering my mouth, to suck my neck and down my sternum—a direct line down my centre until he hits that sensitive part of me. He's not merciful. He's avaricious. He wants all of me—my absolute surrender. He laughs as I writhe, desperate for the release he withholds from me. His fingers flicker and invade, filling the aching void inside me while his tongue teases—rewarding me.

The convulsions overwhelm me almost instantly—wave after wave of an exquisitely intense orgasm that goes on for a mind-blowingly long time. I try to slow my breath. It doesn't work.

'You don't think you're done, do you?' He teases a finger up the inside of my thigh.

My mouth feels tender but I manage to smile at him. He sweeps my mussed-up hair from my face and smiles back. He's the sexiest thing I've ever seen.

He's hard again and just like that I'm ready again too. He pulls me so I'm on the edge of the counter and presses close. I cry out with guttural completion as he fills me. His powerful thrusts almost shunt me away from him. He grunts and tightens his arm around my waist to hold me closer and closer as he rams more deeply inside me. I curl my legs around his hips to help—to lock him to me. It's hot and fast and we're both slick so we clutch each other even harder and it's like nothing ever. I'm barely on the counter, he's taking almost all my weight and its so, *so* good that in the end all I can do is scream in supreme satisfaction.

It takes an age for me to blink my way back to reality. I turn my head to rest it on his sweat-slicked shoulder and that's when I see the tripod. And the little red light. Flashing.

'Oh!' I gasp. 'Oh, *no!*'

'What's wrong?' He eases away enough to look into my face.

I push him further so there's enough space that I can slip down from the counter. 'I'm still filming,' I mutter.

'What?' His eyes widen. 'You're what?'

'The cameras. They're on.'

He freezes. 'Not live streaming?'

Panic washes over me as I double-check. 'No.' Relief is

instant. 'No.' I stop the recording and release a shaky breath. 'Just recording.'

But that's bad enough. I flush from the top of my scalp to the tips of my toes. The things these cameras have just seen? Dain will be horrified.

But his mouth twitches as he watches me press my hands to my hot forehead. 'Have we inadvertently made our own movie?' He cocks his head. 'You should see your face right now...'

Yep, I bet. I'm an enormous beetroot.

Both cameras were filming as I worked on my latte art and then I saw him and just got distracted and all that time when we were on the bench doing...very adult things...there was a camera filming. Two cameras, in fact.

He catches my eye and to my amazement that twitch at the corner of his mouth becomes a full-blown grin and next minute we're both helplessly giggling like absolute fools to the point where I have to wipe tears from my eyes.

I guess it's the endorphin release—the lingering pleasure of those moments, followed by total panic and then sheer relief that the world hasn't just been privy to them.

Dain disappears into the other room and reappears in a robe, holding another that he wraps me in.

'We have to delete them...' I mutter apologetically as he fastens the waist belt of my robe for me. But I'm engulfed by a wave of heat as I recall just what's been captured on film. 'We should do that right away,' I add, stupidly flustered.

'Sure,' he says easily, but there's a devilish glint in his eyes as he studies my face up close. 'If that's what you want...'

'It is. Absolutely. That footage can't survive,' I immediately respond and then look at him. 'Don't you think?'

Of course he does. He's all about privacy and having as little online as possible. This would be a nightmare for him, right?

But he just raises an eyebrow at me. 'Don't you think we should watch it first?'

I gape at him and suddenly I'm awash with a hot flush even worse than before.

But he's flushed too, and he crowds me even though he's wrapped me in the soft silk robe already. 'You can see for yourself how beautiful you are when you lose total control.'

Oh. My.

'Dain...' I'm so flustered I can hardly say his name.

He chuckles. 'You don't think it would be fun?'

My heart races. Curiosity has me. As does the amusement in his eyes. He can be ridiculously fun. He reads my expression and his own lights up.

'I'll get the popcorn.' He turns to the nearest cupboard.

He makes me giggle again. I feel reckless and wanton and naughty and it is so liberating. He grabs the cameras in one hand and takes my hand in the other and leads me into the large comfortable lounge that overlooks that deep blue pool.

I had no idea who Dain Anzelotti was, that night in the gondola. The lifestyle he lives is so foreign to anything I've ever experienced. Things that he doesn't even notice take my breath away. The private jet. The people quietly attending to his every need. The fine silk perfectly tailored to skim a body sustained by meals whipped up by an award-winning private chef. But none of that is relevant right now. It's just him and me—teasing each other, being free with each other.

It's only because of one passionate whim, a wisp of recklessness in one moment, that we're together again. I know these are a fantasy few days and they're not for ever.

He splits the enormous smart screen hanging on the wall so the footage from both cameras plays simultaneously side by side. There's a bird's-eye angle from above us and a side-profile angle. He fiddles so we get the sound from only one of the cameras and it plays low on the speaker. There is music playing but I can still hear our conversation.

Dain takes a seat right behind me on the rug—encircling me. Neither of us eat the popcorn. I stare at the screen—riveted—half appalled. In the next moment I'm fully aroused. It was steamy at the time, now it's just smoking hot and I'm toast.

There's his dance. There's me dropping to my knees and—

This time I can see his face, not just feel his reaction. I can see the size of him, the strain of his body—arching towards my touch. The way he looks at me as I pleasure him turns me to goo. I can't sit still as I watch him then lift and spread me on that counter. Hearing his words—what he's going to do to me—then seeing him do it to me is as hot as the moment it actually happened. Which honestly ought to be impossible.

'What do you think?' His breath stirs my hair.

I can't look away from the screen but from behind he loosens my robe and touches me. He begins with my breasts but then one hand glides lower. I moan as I realise how wet I am in this instant but he tells me how good it is. How good I am. That he's turned on too and he can't wait to taste me again. And then I'm wetter still. And that just makes him double his words of approval because it means I'm ready to take him again and he really needs me to be ready—

'See?' He nips the side of my neck tenderly as he lifts me onto his lap and gives me everything I want in a slow, searing slide. 'You're so beautiful when you let me indulge you.'

I quiver in a mini release right away, because he's so big and so hard and it's just what I want. He groans as I take him to the hilt.

The action on the screen is fast and energetic, but his possession of me now is lush and lazy and total. He teases me intimately, so lightly with the tips of his fingers, so I grind on him harder, clenching within to lock him inside. He swears in earthy, guttural delight. I'm just utterly incoherent. Again. I don't watch the climax on screen, I'm too busy having another.

It's quite some time before I can speak again. He's stretched out on the rug and taken me down with him and is holding me close. I've never experienced physical intimacy or pleasure like this. He's playful and inventive and every time I'm left a shaking mess. It doesn't get easier. It doesn't lessen in intensity. It's always unbearably exciting. And I can't get enough.

As if he knows how raw I feel he caresses my back with long, light, tender strokes that slowly soothe my oversensitive soul. 'Still want to delete it?'

I lift my head just enough to see his face. He's flushed and handsome and like a pirate.

'I…'

Can't think when he smiles at me like that.

His smile is the most powerful weapon I've ever encountered. All I can do is smile back. 'I can't believe we did any of that.'

'Yeah.' He strokes my cheek. 'Shall we go back to the house—?'

'And see Lukas.' I finish his thought.

He smiles even more. Then he unplugs the cameras from the screen and puts them in my hand. He curls my trembling fingers around them so I don't drop them because I'm still so weak I'm butterfingered. 'You should keep the recording to remember. Or replay again some time. It's yours. Always. You decide what to do with it,' he says. 'I trust you.'

I can't believe he's given me this thing that is unbelievably personal. This is a man who loathes anything private being played out in public. A man who does the almost impossible to ensure any digital trace of him is erased. A man who values nothing more than his privacy.

'I could sell this for money, Dain Anzelotti…' I mutter. 'I could put this online.'

'You could. But I know you won't.' He smiles slightly. 'Your reputation, remember? You once said your career would be ruined by an association with me.'

'While you said it would be enhanced.' But I smile at him shyly. 'You trust me with this.'

I'm touched. His trust is a gift more precious than any *thing*.

I don't want to delete it. Ever. I don't want to lose anything from these days because I know this isn't going to last. But I realise this film isn't ever going to be enough. I want and need the real thing—*him*—again and again and again.

CHAPTER EIGHTEEN

Dain

I ADORE TEASING HER. It's so easy. She's so responsive. So satisfying. I race home early every day—well, the days I actually make it to work in the first place. Almost a week has passed in a fog of lusty laughter—it's light and crazy easy.

But it can't last much longer. The whispers have begun. It was inevitable—the leak wouldn't have been one of my staff but perhaps a delivery driver, or maybe someone saw us at the airport. Who knows? But I've had more calls to my private number in the last week than I've had in months and I can't continue to ignore their questions. While I try to maintain a low public profile, people pay attention. I'm worth a lot of money, plus I'm in charge of a lot of other people's fortunes. I have thousands of contractors counting on me plus high-paying customers, and we'll keep those customers only if the reputation of my company remains pristine. And I am my company. It's my name on the door. If my personal life becomes the story, then the company suffers. That's what happened with my parents and I won't let it happen again.

So I need to show my face at headquarters, do some site visits and restore balance—the pendulum has swing too far. I also need to own my new personal situation. The only way is to front-foot it.

I'll never bow to the external pressure to do that traditional 'right thing', the sexist instruction to 'make an honest woman of her'—it's old-fashioned and unnecessary. And it doesn't work. We won't make our parents' mistakes. We'll see this through then care for Lukas like the responsible adults we are.

I find her in the pool house and, confronted with her beauty, I can't resist kissing her so it's a few moments before I can speak.

'Unfortunately, despite my best efforts at total privacy, the rumour mill is rumbling.' I sigh. 'You need to meet my parents. We need to introduce Lukas to them first.'

'Your *parents*?' She pulls back, stunned. 'You're still in contact with them?'

Yeah, if I had more of a choice I wouldn't be. 'They're shareholders.'

Her jaw drops.

'*Minority* shareholders,' I clarify. 'Part of the divorce settlement and my buy-out when I took over.' I reduced their impact but couldn't cut them out completely and they still talk. So even though I rarely see them I know I need to include them in this. But in my own way. 'Confidence in the company—therefore in me—is essential. Curiosity has been roused. I need to take control of the narrative.'

'Of course you do.' She rolls her eyes.

I laugh as I tug her closer. 'Don't worry. They're too wrapped up in their own war to give a damn about you.'

'They're still fighting?'

She has no idea.

'They'll go to their graves fighting. The bitterness is next level.'

'I thought they divorced when you were—'

'Fourteen, yeah.'

'That's a while ago.' She draws in a deep breath. 'How will you introduce me? Am I a friend, casual acquaintance, captive?'

Oh, she makes me smile. 'We don't need to define anything. They can think whatever they want.'

'And how's that controlling the narrative?'

She's right but I don't like considering these details too closely. The complications my fractured family could bring stress me out. 'We'll fake it.' I snap decide. 'No reason they won't believe us. Like we did with Ava. You've only just agreed to come back with me. I've had to work at it. You took some convincing.'

'No one's going to believe that.'

'You don't think you exude cool indifference? That you're not an impervious, powerful woman?'

'Cool indifference?' She looks sceptical.

'Yeah. Infinitely capable and needing no one.'

'That's not possible. Everyone needs someone sometimes.'

I'm distracted by her. 'Do you ever need someone?'

She angles her head. 'Sometimes in a dark, dangerous, life-threatening moment I don't want to be alone.'

Her mouth mocks but her eyes flicker and I know she actually means it.

'You want someone's hand to hold?' I ask quietly.

She stares intently at me and her smile slowly softens. 'Brief me on how you want me to handle them.'

I feel a wave of gratitude for her attempt to make this easy for me and suddenly I don't hold back on the truth. 'They're coming tomorrow night.'

'Tomorrow?' Her eyes widen. 'Decisive.'

'Best-case scenario it'll be a stilted and uncomfortable Cold War situation. My mother will ask me directly for money. My father will have a business idea he wants to run past me after dinner. A quick pull aside. It won't be quick. They'll both be disappointed. They'll each blame me for being too much like the other. It'll devolve into an argument between them.'

Honestly, it'll be a timely reminder of everything I don't want.

'You don't want to invite them individually?' she asks.

'And have one outraged because they weren't the one to meet Lukas *first*?'

'That would happen?'

'Absolutely.'

She looks wary now. 'Do you want them to be a big presence in Lukas's life?'

'I need to show respect and let them know he exists, but he won't become a pawn between them. Ever.'

She nods but her tension doesn't lessen. 'Will they disapprove of me?'

My skin tightens. She's vulnerable. 'One will, one won't. Purely to disagree with each other so it doesn't actually matter what you do or say, they'll just take a side as soon as one stakes a claim either way. Don't worry about it and for heaven's sake don't take it personally.' But of course there's no way she won't take it personally. I'm hit with a tardy premonition that this is a bad idea. 'You know, maybe you don't have to be there…'

Now she looks even more tense.

'I don't want to stress you out,' I explain quickly. '*I* find it stressful enough.'

But to my surprise the pinched look slowly leaves her face and she lifts her chin. 'They're your parents, naturally it's more stressful for you.'

'I'm used to it.' I shrug.

'Well, now you don't have to face them alone.' She flicks her hair back like a diva. 'I've dealt with the rudest, most obnoxious customers. Your parents will be a cinch.'

It was worse than I'd predicted. *Stupid.* I don't want to discuss it. Don't want to meet her eyes. Can't believe I let her see it. *So stupid.*

She's silent and the staff have taken away the barely touched dinner plates. We're standing on the veranda in darkness, having watched my parents drive off in their separate cars.

'Can you not…feel sorry for me?' I mutter.

'You don't want me to feel for you?'

Something inside me twists. I'm lost for words.

'They treat you terribly,' she says. 'It's shocking.'

Her saying it aloud makes it worse. I regret inviting my parents here more than ever. Not because I can't handle seeing them, but I can't handle Talia seeing the truth. 'Don't—'

'I'm sorry you went through all that with them.' She ignores my quiet plea. 'At least I had Ava, but you were alone.'

'Not completely,' I murmur. 'I had my grandfather for a while.'

'Lukas senior.' She leans against the veranda railing and gazes across the gardens even though it's too dark to see much. 'You looked close in that photo.'

The one photo I allowed to remain on the company website. 'Right.'

I thought we were.

Silence again. I chance a glance at her. In the moonlight she's so pretty. I've mostly seen her with her hair tied up—a messy top knot or a high ponytail—but tonight she let her hair loose. It's long and glossy and now I can't take my gaze off her. I ache to snake my arm around her waist and feel that contact with her. I want it to be like the gondola when the rest of the world disappeared and there was only the two of us.

Her expression softens as she looks back at me. She doesn't say anything. She doesn't pry any further and I appreciate that restraint.

'I was sent to boarding school in my early teens. I appreciated it, to be honest. It got me away from the week about war with Mum and Dad. They were in separate houses by then and fighting over everything, including me. But neither really wanted me, I was just a useful weapon. Weekends and holidays were still a battleground, same with school events. They'd argue over who got to attend the sports day and then either they'd both show and cause a scene or neither would show up. That's when my grandfather stepped in.' I found solace with him for a time.

I don't know why I'm telling her when I can't stand the sympathy I already see in her eyes. But I can't stop myself babbling on because seeing my parents tonight brought it all back up. And being with Lukas and knowing I never, ever want him to feel anything like I did. Talia needs to understand why that is so we can be sure to work through this together. That's why she needs to know, right? For Lukas.

'He was my escape from them. I'd go there for every holiday and every other chance I could. I adored him and we bonded over the business. He taught me a lot about it—the history, his dreams for it. I knew it was tearing him apart to see my parents neglect it because they were too busy fighting each other. It became both our hope for me to turn it around in the future.'

'And you did.'

'Eventually, yeah.' After he died.

She nods and we're silent for a while.

'I wasn't told he had terminal cancer,' I mumble quietly.

She jerks and looks at me again.

Even though I now know the reasons why, it still hurts. 'It was weird at first. He stopped replying to my messages, didn't take my calls. I got through to his secretary and was told he was too tired to see me. It was so sudden I didn't know what I'd done wrong. But it had to be something.' My chest tightens. 'I wasn't to come home to his house from school. I was to stay and study because he was busy now and didn't have time to see me.'

'Are you saying your grandfather ghosted you?'

'Basically. Yeah.' I roll my shoulders, unable to ease the tension building inside. 'I didn't study though. I spent the semester wondering what I'd done to make him stop—'

I break off. I don't use the 'L' word. But that was how it felt—that he'd stopped loving me. He'd stopped letting me be in his life. Because I'd done something bad and I didn't know what.

'It was Simone who told me in the end. The media were about to break the story that Lukas, the Anzelotti patriarch, was terminal and there was going to be all-out war between my parents for the company majority. It was salacious and cruel. Simone came to the boarding school and smuggled me out, furious that I hadn't been given any warning.'

'Did you get to him?'

'My parents met me. It was the one time I saw them united. They said the truth had been kept from me to protect me. They didn't want me to be distracted from my schoolwork. They wanted me to do well in my exams.' My fingers tighten on the railing. 'This supposed concern from the people who'd been distracting me for *years* with their bitter fights.'

'That must have been really—'

'Shit? Yeah, it was. Because they'd done it at my grandfather's insistence. He'd said he would change his will if they didn't both toe the line on it.' I glance at her and can't get my voice above a whisper. 'It was *his* call.'

'Did you get to spend time with him before he died?'

'No.'

'Dain, that's… I'm so sorry.' Her eyes are bright. 'So when you found I'd kept Lukas from you—'

'Yeah, low moment.' I don't want to go there again. We're past it. I half regret saying anything at all.

'And you were angry about my not having told Ava,' she says.

'I felt for her.' I clench my gut. 'I know what it's like to be kept in the dark. It makes you feel…incompetent.' Rejected.

'No wonder you keep people at a distance.'

Her expression eases the ache in my chest but at the same time causes another to build. I ache to hold her. I ache for the balm of her soft body resting against mine. I've never needed physical comfort like this before. Sex is only fun. It's only a moment—a great release—then I walk away. But this isn't that. I freeze because I don't understand it. I don't welcome it. I don't *want* this change. I don't want to *need* anyone the way I need her right now. I grip the railing to stop myself moving to her. Only it hurts to resist the urge.

'Dain...'

My throat aches. I can't answer her. But I can't send her away either. And I can't take my gaze from her.

Her smile is sad. 'You're so guarded.'

Maybe. Yeah. I've never told anyone about my grandfather's decision. It was far too painful to utter aloud. I probably shouldn't have done it now. I make myself turn away and bow my head. I wait for her to leave. Expect her to.

There's silence. But then I feel her hand slide onto mine.

'I don't blame you for that,' she breathes. 'It's okay.'

On auto I release the railing and turn my hand to lace my fingers through hers. I lock them together. Us together. She wraps her other arm around me, her palm pressing flat just below my ribs, her stomach flush against my back. For a long time we stand linked like that. I'm silent, sandwiched between the railing and her, and it's oddly, overwhelmingly safe.

Compassion. It's an altogether different feeling from any I've felt with her. No less powerful. If anything, it's...*more*. I can't remember the last time someone just hugged me like this and the warmth and weight of her leaning against me is so soothing I don't ever want to move.

'Sometimes families just suck,' she whispers.

I half laugh and that horrible tension, the agony, that's been twisting me up all night finally eases. 'Yeah.'

CHAPTER NINETEEN

Talia

I DON'T SLEEP WELL. Dain brings Lukas early in the morning for me to feed him, then takes him to change and dress. Now they're engrossed in one of their endless nonsensical conversations. Dain's chattier with his son than anyone and I can hardly bear to look at them. Lukas is the sweetest thing I've ever seen while Dain's the sexiest. My heart twists at the joy they've found in each other. I don't want anything to come between them or to damage the relationship now building between them. Especially not me.

I leave the room and go to shower, still processing what I witnessed last night. It was a revelation. I don't think I was any help—*sometimes families suck*—I wince at my tragic attempt at comfort. But it's true, right? And wouldn't it be good to pick your own? If I could choose, I'd keep both these guys so close.

But Dain doesn't want that and after last night I really understand why. Dinner with his parents was worse than he prepared me for. He diverted conversation. Distracted. Deflected. He worked so hard I was exhausted just watching him. They were sad, selfish people who complained and contradicted each other from the moment they arrived. Over who got to hold Lukas first even—over everything. The constant point-scoring shocked me. Ultimately they just want things from

Dain—money most especially. He's never been valued for himself. No wonder he doesn't trust anyone.

He was still charming to them, but I saw glimpses of a child desperate to please, to placate, to make everything better and bring peace to his world. I get it, I'm the same. I'm only capable and efficient because I had to be. But Ava loves me, and Romy supported me, and Dain himself has been wonderful to me. But he didn't have that. No wonder his relationship with his family is fractured. No wonder he fiercely guards his privacy. No wonder he fights hard to retain control over everything in his life.

I realise now that he has walls that I can't breach. And even though I know they're awful people, their judgement of me was obvious. It doesn't just hurt. It makes me nervous. I know he and I have some things in common—lust for each other especially—but not enough of the *right* things.

I don't know that I can exist in his world. If I were on the staff, sure—but as his supposed equal?

'Want to come on an adventure with me?' Dain asks the second I walk into the living room.

'An adventure? Where?' Just like that I'm diverted.

He smiles at my immediate interest. 'You and me, only for a couple of hours. Lukas will be better off here than where we're going.'

Of course I can't resist. I kiss Lukas and leave him with the nanny. Dain guides me to the garage on the edge of his property. I've not been in there yet, and in the doorway I stop and blink. There are several cars lined up neatly inside. All of them are very fancy.

'You have a collection?' I tease.

'Only a little one. Of only the best ones.' He flashes a smile. 'Don't hold it against me.'

I don't. I chuckle. We have a very different attitude to *things*—I don't collect, he does. But now it's only things he truly appreciates. And I can appreciate that quirk of his today because the sleek two-seater convertible sports car he selects has heated leather seats and it's sheer luxurious fun to cruise with the top down and feel the wind in my hair.

It's so early there's surprisingly little traffic and we arrive at a marina in no time. An astonishing array of boats gleams on the pristine blue water.

Butterflies flutter in my belly. 'How many are yours?' I cover it with a joke.

'Only the one.'

'The biggest?'

He laughs and then looks at me with gentle understanding. 'You okay at the thought of going on the water? It's a beautiful morning. Calm, pristine conditions.'

'You're saying I'm going to be safe.'

'I wouldn't risk you,' he says softly.

I know. Because of Lukas.

'You can hold my hand if you want.' He holds his palm towards me.

I take it.

We board a gleaming white catamaran. I feel as if I've stepped into a film set, only it's real. The crew are lined up to meet me. They're dressed immaculately and are so polite, so well drilled in their job he doesn't need to issue orders. Everything is beautiful and perfect, it's like magic. I know it's not just that they're paid a mint to do it. I get the feeling they *want* to do a good job for him—same with the discreet staff at his house. They're loyal because they actually like him.

He's *not* as entitled as I first thought. Yes, he was born into wealth, but he worked hard to turn the family company around when it foundered. He's worked hard to get what he has. And he's working hard to please me now.

'Aren't you going to captain the ship?' I ask once the crew disappear to get ready to move.

'Not this time,' he says lazily. 'I'm going to breakfast with you.'

'But you can, right? You have your boat licence and a whole other bunch of licences, right?'

'Right now I'm hoping for a licence to eat,' he teases.

I follow him up to the large back deck and see the feast already set there.

'When did you arrange this?' I ask.

He just smiles. I blink repeatedly at the beautiful view—and I don't mean the bay. I'm too blown away by him to nibble on the fresh fruit and pastries.

'Nothing tempts?' He notices. 'The chef will make you something fresh if you want?'

Laughing, I shake my head. 'I'm too busy taking in the view. The water looks so inviting—'

'You want to swim?' His eyebrows lift. 'It's not too cold?'

'This is warm for me.' I smile. Even though it's technically still winter, it's much hotter here in Brisbane than back in the South Island of New Zealand. 'But no, I don't want to swim.'

'But you want to strip?' He teases.

I just want to stare. At him. Which I don't. I make myself look beyond him. We glide over the blue waters passing beautiful bays with gleaming gold sand. It's invigorating and my heart soars.

'I've never been sailing,' I chirrup thoughtlessly, turning to look at him again. I never imagined *ever* being on a boat like this.

Again he just smiles. He knows. Of course he knows that there are lots of things I've never done. I bow my head to hide the burn of embarrassment—I'm so *gauche*. But he lifts my chin, forcing me to meet his intense blue gaze again.

'There's no shame in never having gone sailing before,' he says softly. 'But now you can. With me.' He pulls me close. 'We'll come back—scuba when it's warmer.'

'I don't know how to scuba.'

'I'll teach you.'

'You're a qualified scuba coach as well?'

He chuckles.

My heart thunders. 'Why did you arrange this?'

He waves a hand. 'It's a beautiful morning.'

'You don't have work to do?'

'Maybe we both deserve a little break from work. You've been working your whole life too.'

My lips twist. 'You've got bigger rewards, though.'

He gazes towards the bay. 'I don't mind sharing with you.'

For a moment I'm speechless.

'Thank you for helping me with Ava,' I eventually say. 'Thank you for this. Thank you for everything.'

His expression closes. 'You know I don't want your gratitude.'

'Too bad.' I shrug. 'You'll get used to it eventually.'

His mouth twists. 'And maybe you'll eventually get used to getting what you actually deserve.'

CHAPTER TWENTY

Dain

I WATCH THE flush cover her face. She doesn't feel it, does she? *Deserving.* Given her parents' abandonment and selfishness, maybe that's not surprising. But she's spent years making her own way, caring for her sister without any help…she should feel *proud* of all that. Surely she's proved her worth to herself?

I really want her to have some fun and I've seen her in my pool throughout the week. It seems that, like me, she loves the water.

'What else can we add to the list?' I ask as I reach for a glass of fresh orange juice to ease the dryness of my throat. 'Stand-up paddle boarding in Croatia? Jet-skiing in Dubai?' I warm to my theme. 'Snorkelling in the Caymans? Water-skiing in—'

'I have been water-skiing,' she interrupts. 'Once.'

I'm instantly curious and lean close.

She reads my expression and laughs a little bitterly. 'It wasn't a good idea.'

'No? Why not?'

She presses her lips firmly together.

After a moment she sighs. 'I went with a girl from school,' she mutters. 'I thought I'd made an actual friend. She was wildly different from me—happily married parents, money, popular, pretty…perfect…'

'No such thing as perfect,' I mutter when she pauses too long.

'No.' She draws a big breath in. 'It was a day trip with her family. I thought it went okay. But it turned out my mother was having an affair with her father and when it came out the very next day she marched up to me at the cafeteria at school in front of everyone and said she'd only invited me because she "felt sorry for me". That I was her act of charity for the week because my clothes were ugly and I didn't belong there and everyone had been laughing at me for weeks. They all sure laughed at me then.'

I know how words can hurt and when they're thrown out in public they can hurt even more. And even if Talia rationalised this as merely retaliation from another hurt girl, it still stung. Shame still clung. I know it—I know that very particular burn.

'I was happy to leave town that time,' she adds. 'But that was the last time Ava and I did.'

'You stayed put in the next place until Ava went away to university.' I watch her. 'Why didn't you move with her then?'

She pauses. 'I wanted her to be free to focus on her study and not feel guilty about me.'

'Guilty?' I frown.

'She struggled with me working long hours for not much pay. It was better for her not to have to see that. Plus I could earn more in Queenstown—and there was a lot of work available there.'

'Enabling you to work three jobs at once.'

'Right.' She picks up the other glass of orange and takes a deep sip before shooting me a look over the crystal rim. 'Why are we talking about me again?'

I shrug innocently. 'I'm curious.'

'Well, I'm curious about you too,' she says softly.

I don't want to push her away. Her interest in me is a pleasure—I know it's not that she wants to *pry*. It's different. Given I want to know everything about her, it's actually a kind of relief that she obviously feels the same about me. Not just curious. Not just interested. *Fascinated.*

That night when she was upset thinking I'd thrown out Lukas's rabbit she eventually explained about having no things as a kid herself. I felt pleased that she told me. That she trusted me enough to tell me something painful and personal. She's just done it again now.

And again I'm honoured. It's a precious thing.

I needed to clear my own head after last night. Feeling the wind in my hair and the freedom on the water is my favourite way of doing that. I wanted to share it with her. But now I want to share more.

'I first sailed with my grandfather,' I mutter awkwardly. 'He taught me.'

Her expression softens. 'He taught you lots of things?'

'Yeah.' I put down my glass. 'Took me up in a small plane when I was only ten.'

'Is that even legal?' She shakes her head but laughs softly. 'Sounds like you were lucky to have him. And he was lucky to have you.'

I go tense inside.

'I'm sorry he didn't give you the chance to say goodbye to him,' she adds.

I glance at her sharply. But, of course, she'd been through something similar many times—with places, other people.

'It hurts,' she says. 'Even though he was trying to protect you, it hurts.'

I can't answer.

'And he didn't give you time to prepare.'

'Yeah.' I breathe out slowly. Not for the loss. I was so isolated and then his death was such a shock. 'It *sucked*.'

I take her glass and set it on the table beside mine. She's right. Having time to prepare for tough things is important.

'Phase one is complete.' I cup her face. 'Phase two is scheduled for tonight.'

Her gaze smoulders at my touch. 'What are you talking about?'

'Your introduction to my world.' I brace.

'Oh.' She grimaces slightly. 'What's phase two?'

'One of my famous parties.' I smile.

'Tonight?' Her eyes widen.

'Anzelotti Holdings is the primary sponsor of a new staging of one of Shakespeare's plays at the King's Theatre in town.'

'Okay...' She looks unsure. 'I thought you said party?'

I suspect she's never been to the theatre before. 'Beforehand, yes.'

'Before? So it's not going to be a wildly late night?'

'No, we're talking a pre-show function at a bar down from the theatre.'

'Not a debauched party at your place?'

'No.' I'm not ready to have anyone else at home yet. 'Time limited, guest-list limited. Risk limited.'

'Top-tier control freak right there,' she mutters.

'There'll be plenty of people watching. And there might be cameras.'

'You hate those.' She wrinkles her nose. 'Are you sure I need to be there?'

Yeah, I think it's important that we get on with her introduction to life here. To my life. 'You have to meet everyone some time. You have something to wear?'

Her gaze narrows. 'I'll figure something out.'

She doesn't want to ask me for help—that damn pride of hers again. I know she has a thing about *things* and about not holding onto stuff. She doesn't want to need anything from anyone. I fight to suppress the urge to challenge her on it now.

'Party.' She huffs a breath. 'Theatre. You take me out sailing, make me all warm and relaxed and now you're trying to kill my calm?' She pouts at me.

Yeah, an experience is different. An experience is something she *can* take from me.

'Oh, I apologise.' I lean close. 'But as it happens I know another way to make you all warm and relaxed again.'

I know our physical intimacy is only going to be temporary, but I don't yet have the strength to resist the power of it.

To resist *her*.

CHAPTER TWENTY-ONE

Talia

BACK AT THE house I feed and play with Lukas. From upstairs I hear a car arrive and it's so unusual I peek out of the window to see who it is. I see Simone step out of the sleek car and I'm instantly nervous. What's she going to think of Dain having a baby with a random barista?

'I've a good mind not to speak to you at all.' Simone's reproachful voice carries up the stairwell as I slowly descend. 'I only learned about Lukas and Talia when I came to Brisbane, Dain.'

She sounds hurt.

Dain's chuckle is that charming kind. 'You know I prefer to keep a low profile.'

'But not from *me*—'

'I know,' he placates her calmly. 'But I needed some time. It's important Talia feels comfortable—I want her to be happy here.'

What I've heard should make me feel good, right? But there's something off in that statement. He's mentioned it before—that I'm to be happy. He says it to Simone so *emotionlessly* that I start to worry that what he's doing for me is simply *duty*. It's like he's ticking off a checklist of things to keep me happy—putting me in a house to die for, giving me support in caring for Lukas, enabling me to regain full physical strength and energy, providing a workspace with every appliance imaginable to continue my career, taking me on trips on the sea. And, of course, sex. Fantastic, unbeatable sex to keep me satisfied.

Is it a formula he's following? Like the amenities he ensures are present in his luxury apartment buildings. Everything is perfect down to the smallest, finest detail. And good for him, right? How can I possibly judge him for trying so hard to please me? But I'm not judging him. I'm despairing. Because I'm worried it's not actually what *he* really wants or desires. I don't want him jumping through hoops trying to make me happy. That's too much of a burden for anyone.

And the problem with that fantastic, unbeatable sex? It doesn't keep me satisfied. It only makes me want more.

I brace and take the last few steps down.

'Hi, Simone.' I make myself smile, determined to show I don't need either of them to 'make me happy'. But at the same time I can't help wanting her to like me. 'Do you want to meet Lukas?'

Surely she can't resist our sweet son.

'Oh!' She holds out her arms and I place Lukas in them.

Simone beams. I glance to see Dain's reaction but he's looking at me. A small smile plays at the corners of his mouth, grateful pride warms his eyes and I know I've done the right thing in showing her Lukas. My heart swells and I flash a conspiratorial smile back at him. His widens in response and that deeply personal fire that burns between us flares inside me.

'How gorgeous…'

I turn at Simone's comment, expecting her to be cooing over Lukas but instead she's looking from Dain to me and back again. Her smile is bigger than either of ours. She walks to Dain and he takes Lukas from her with the protective gentleness he has for his son.

Now Simone looks positively rapt. 'I'm taking Talia out

for a late lunch, Dain,' she declares brightly. 'We'll be back in time for the theatre tonight.'

He stiffens. 'But—'

'Sounds lovely. Thank you, Simone,' I interrupt, because I've something I really need to do and Simone has inadvertently provided the opportunity. 'Lukas is due for a nap so—'

'So that's perfect.' Simone sweeps me out of the door before he can object again.

'Thank you for this,' I say to her a little nervously as her driver pulls smoothly away. 'I've not seen much of the city yet.'

'You haven't been out?' Her eyes narrow.

'We have, just privately.' I don't feel as if I've missed anything. I've enjoyed being wrapped up in our own perfect paradise. I don't want outside interference. Or judgement. To be honest I didn't think our seclusion was actually a deliberate strategy of Dain's, but of course it must have been—because he needs me to feel 'comfortable'.

That wedge of doubt within me widens.

I know he's intense about privacy, but maybe he doesn't really want to present me in public? Yet we're doing this theatre thing tonight. And I need to rise to the occasion.

Simone instructs the driver to take us past the city's highlights. She points out restaurants and cafés, informing me which are the best and most popular.

'I'm not going to ask you about Dain.' The older woman smiles coyly. 'I don't need to. It's obvious.'

I don't know how to interpret that and I haven't any spare emotional energy to try. I'm just glad she's not going to subject me to an interrogation. That doesn't mean I can't interrogate her though.

'Would you mind if we skip lunch and go shopping instead?' I ask. 'I don't have a suitable dress for the theatre tonight.'

Simone sparkles. 'Of course.'

She takes me to a lane lined with gorgeous boutiques. I glance through the dresses. It's a good thing I've spent so many hours serving at high-powered functions. I know the sort of style that I can get away with—even if it is only off the rack.

'Can you tell me about the guests tonight?' I ask casually.

Simone shoots me a sharp look but then smiles. As I try on a few clothes she talks me through Dain's senior management team. They all sound like highly articulate, highly educated over-achievers. Great. Nothing to feel nervous about, then.

I stand in front of the mirror and look at my reflection. The black gown hugs my waist and floats to the floor, setting off the dainty silver sandals the saleswoman encouraged me to try with it. The look is perfectly appropriate for the night ahead, though part of me wants to see Dain's reaction to the small cut-outs in the bodice.

'I'll take the dress,' I say to the assistant with a smile. My budget won't stretch to the shoes.

'Let me get the sandals,' Simone says.

I hesitate. Accepting gifts requires grace and I know from Dain that I'm not so great at that.

Simone nods. 'You'll almost be tall enough to look Dain right in the eyes.'

He's the reason she wants to help me. She's genuine and she cares for Dain and suddenly I don't have the heart to deny her.

'Thank you,' I mutter awkwardly, fighting my instinctive reaction to reject her offer. 'That's very kind.'

'I'm glad you're here, Talia,' she says as we drive back to Dain's house. 'It's a good thing.'

I leave her downstairs and hurry up to the nursery to feed Lukas. Then I shower and prepare.

Dain walks into my room just as I'm fastening the straps on the silver sandals. I straighten and try not to fidget in front of him as he looks me up and down.

'Will I do?' I can't help seeking his approval. 'Simone gifted me the shoes.'

'And you let her?' His eyebrows lift. 'Progress.'

He looks stunning in that perfectly tailored black suit. I'm desperate for the reassurance of his touch but he remains eight feet away.

'We'd better get going,' he mutters.

We don't take the little sports car he drove this morning. This time we're in a luxury sedan and there's a chauffeur to drive us.

In the back seat I can't help stealing glances at Dain. It's like the night at the gondola—he's simply breathtaking in formal attire.

He catches my eye and his own gaze ignites. He half groans, half growls. 'Come here.'

Yes.

I press against the restraint of my seat belt and kiss him desperately.

'I don't want to ruin your hair—'

I don't care and he runs his hands through it anyway. There's such urgency in my need for him. I'll never get enough. I realise this now.

'Talia?'

I just kiss him. I just want to be close to him and pretend this perfection is real. Right now it *is* real.

He kisses me back but he's gentle and tender and I want to provoke him to more because for me this need is *unbearable*.

'Talia.' He breathes hard.

His soft words ignite me.

We're *so* close. I don't care that there's a driver. I don't care that people can see into the car. I just want him. I *need* him.

But he grabs my wrists and pulls away. 'We have to stop.' He looks at me ruefully. 'Or I could send a message saying we've both got food poisoning and turn the car round right now...'

I laugh, but honestly I'd love him to do just that. I don't want to face anyone else today. My wariness rises. Insecurity completely has its claws in me. I want us to stay in our own world. Alone and intense. Because while I can put on an almost-designer dress and fancy shoes, they're only wrappings. I know I really belong on the service side of the coffee machine, not centre stage in the society he's the star of.

I struggle to catch my breath and stare out of the window as I try. The setting sun glints against the glass-fronted highrises of the city. I've never left New Zealand before. I had no idea Brisbane is such a big city. But I can't wholly appreciate its beauty. I'm suddenly scared. And for the first time since arriving in Brisbane, I'm cold.

The pre-theatre party is at a champagne and oyster bar. The gilt-tipped forest-green ropes discreetly inform the public that entrance to the venue is reserved for invited guests only, but there are other bars either side and they're full and noisy. The customers ensconced in them stare as the car pulls up right in front.

Dain exits first and slides his hand into mine once I've got out of the car. The contact strengthens me, stirs me, my pulse regulates to match his—albeit a touch faster than normal for us both. He pulls me closer against his side.

'Is it true you're a father, Dain?' someone calls.

Startled, I glance up. I spot a camera. Then another. Someone else calls his name. I look, but I'm aware Dain doesn't. He knows not to.

I'm shocked. I realise how galling this must be for him— he's so intensely private but his secret—Lukas—is known. And he's being forced to be seen with me. To present *me* in public. My pulse skitters but he keeps us both moving until we're inside. I desperately try to slow my breathing but it's impossible because there are people…so many beautiful people.

I blink. Swallow. Straighten.

The bar is sophisticated. Its decor features that luxurious

green with discreet gold trim in sumptuous curves and heavy marble countertops. A gleaming display showcases some of the oyster, lobster and caviar they serve. Bottles of champagne line the back wall. There's ice everywhere—the diamond kind as well as frozen water providing a bed for the ocean's delicacies. I freeze on the inside. I thought I was used to billionaire bashes from my time waitressing at exclusive Queenstown venues but this is next level. While it's intimate, there's a raft of people present, each one obviously very important, very sophisticated. They're the sleek elite. But they all revere Dain. They watch him, listen close, their bodies angle towards him—seeking his attention. I see it and understand it. Mine does the same.

And he's just swept in—effortlessly stalking past the press, effortlessly commanding the entire place.

We're offered champagne in fine crystal flutes. Dain introduces me but their names and faces are a blur in less than a second. Some are politicians. Some are society mavens. Some are models—at least they look it.

The noise of chatter renders words inaudible as I surreptitiously try to take it all in and note how they're all staring not so surreptitiously at me. I feel like a lamb who's been led into a wolves' den. But that's wrong, right? I'm just overwhelmed. Surely these people are nice and I'm being silly.

He doesn't relinquish my hand and, full disclosure, I can't help clinging onto him. But I don't want to rely on Dain for my confidence. Surely I can handle this myself.

Only I'm in awe of everyone's elegance. They're exquisitely vivacious, effervescent yet refined. They glitter gracefully and it comes so naturally to them. My stomach sinks. Dain's privileged and powerful and he should have a partner who doesn't only hold her own but is an *asset* to him. I've an awful feeling I'm a liability. Any of the stunning women here would be a better partner for him than me. They're all used to this scene and they don't just handle it, they shine.

I'm suddenly grateful there's a time limit because of the play. Dain introduces me to the director of the theatre and the head of fundraising and I really try to make their names stick in my mind. Mischa and Chloe. They ooze glamorous, effortless chic. We converse about nothing very much as perfectly attired waiters offer specially curated pairings of oysters and champagne. The shellfish have been prepared in several ways. The vibe screams understated, indulgent luxury but these people don't even blink. They're not just used to such rare and expensive nibbles, they're connoisseurs of them.

After a while Dain gets collared by a man wanting a quick quiet word. From dinner with his parents, I know what that means. The guy wants money. Dain glances at me apologetically but I send him a smile of reassurance. I can do this. I don't *need* him. I only have to listen and smile, right?

I talk more to Mischa and Chloe, but Chloe's gaze follows Dain. My spine prickles and I can't help looking her over. Her dress is beautifully fitted and clearly couture, her hair and make-up sublime, she's wearing a stunning emerald pendant and her hands are beautifully manicured. My nails are neat but only because they're seen in my videos. Hers are stunning. *All* of her is stunning. She catches me staring.

'Have you been to Dain's island?' she asks with a smile that makes me shiver a little.

'Um…no. Not yet.'

What island? I didn't even know there was an island.

'It's amazing.' She nods as if she's doing me a favour in telling me this. 'You're going to love it. Dain's done such a wonderful job rebuilding the house there.'

And she knows because she's been to stay? That's…great, and all of a sudden I'm reminded of the water-skiing day. I'm the charity case again—the one who doesn't really fit in.

'You *must* get him to take you,' she adds. 'I prefer the helicopter to the jet. It's faster.'

There's a helicopter as well? I don't ask. I just feel ignorant and increasingly out of place.

Our passion in the car on the way here was an ephemeral, false assurance. I shouldn't care what any of these people think about me. Talia of a year ago wouldn't have. But now I feel so very vulnerable. He's more powerful than I imagined and I don't think I can step up to this public plate and stand beside him.

'It's best when Dain is piloting.' Chloe looks at me with a smile that doesn't reach her eyes. 'Did he fly you here from New Zealand?'

I know I'm not handling this well, but I've been around people like Chloe before. I smile and swipe out with my claws, just a little. 'We were busy in the cabin.'

Her eyebrows lift ever so slightly. 'With a crying baby?'

'Actually, Lukas slept for the whole flight.'

'I bet he's very advanced for his age,' Mischa says with a genuine smile.

'Yes,' Chloe agrees with venomous enthusiasm. 'After all, his mother is *very* clever.'

She takes another sip of champagne. Inhibitions are down and tongues are looser than they were when we first arrived and even the best manners in the world can be lost.

'You make coffee, is that right?' Chloe asks.

I try to tell myself the snobbish tinge I think I hear is probably only in my head but her gaze on me is icier than that bed for the oysters on the bar and now the thoughts in my head are even more anxious and insecure. 'Yes, how did you hear about that?'

'Dain's father said you're a waitress and wannabe influencer. You do make little videos, don't you?'

So Chloe knows Dain's father and he's disparaged me. I feel for Dain. He had to live through his parents' divorce, he doesn't need his own private life being dissected in public like this. Not by a parent. And I'm not going to make it worse.

'Yes.' I lift my chin and smile directly at her. 'I make ASMR videos of latte art. Some people find them soothing.'

'It's a fad.' Chloe shrugs. 'You'll have to pivot if you want to grow your numbers.'

I nod peaceably enough but inside my pulse is skittering out of control. Chloe's right. She's also ruthless. Most of the people here are, I realise. This is a world *so* far from mine. It's *his*—hell, he's the king of it. I'm a waitress. I can make a good coffee. But who am I to hold my own with people who literally run the world? Who are beautiful and accomplished and confident? Short answer is I can't.

But I'm stuck here. I can never run away. The permanent home I long craved for is actually a prison—a gilded cage in which I don't belong and where I'm not *really* wanted. Yes, we have chemistry but, no, that's not for ever. I'm here only because of Lukas.

Two more people join us. I can't remember either of their names. I'm a good server—I can remember the dinner orders for parties of ten or more—but there are more than eighty people in this bar and I'm off balance. I'm worried about Dain. He's actually very *private*. He's worked hard to pull his company back from the brink and overcome the destruction from his parents' interference. Being the source of gossip now must be appalling for him but he's putting on a brave front. Yet he can't control their judgement of me. The undercurrent of bitchiness cements my understanding of just how out of place I really am.

I do not belong here.

My attempt to eat the freshly shucked *au naturel* oyster from its shell is awkward. They do it in unison, like a graceful ballet.

'Aphrodisiacs, I'm sure you're aware,' Chloe says, her gaze sliding to Dain again.

'I haven't been to one of these events in ages,' the new guy says.

'Dain's been too busy to host. Now we know why.' The woman raises her glass to me. 'Off the market at last.'

'Well.' Chloe gasps sharply. 'He's not put a ring on it yet.'

The entire group stares at my unadorned fingers. My not-good-enough manicure. I'm filled with shame. My self-control drowns in it and in a flash of anger I retaliate against the rudeness. 'Then I guess there's still time for one of you to make your move.'

Normally I can maintain a cool facade in front of the most demanding, rude customers but I can't keep my cool now. This is worse than when Dain and I deliberately misled Ava. Because I'm *crushed*. The life we're presenting is *everything* I want. But it's a front and never going to be real. I'm not right for it. I don't fit. I never will. I'm not good enough for him. At the worst possible time, in front of all these avidly curious people, I realise I *do* want that ring. I want it all with him because I'm in *love* with him. And while Dain has been doing everything he can to make this work, what I truly desire is the one thing he'll never give—his heart. That's not in play. And I'll never be enough for him to want to push past the hurt of his parents' break-up.

I'm devastated. I want to run. Right now. Just as my mother would. But I can't. I'm cornered like a stray animal who's wandered into that wolves' den and I lash out.

'Truly.' I shrug as if I don't give a damn. 'Go ahead. I'm the mother of Dain's firstborn. That's all.'

Even as I say it I know it's wrong. I bite my lip—offence is the best defence and I've struck out when I shouldn't have. I have to stop myself from making this worse. For Dain. For Lukas. It takes everything to pull it back together. But I'm jealous and hurt and hopeless and I just want to hide. I force a smile as if it were a joke, but they don't smile back.

I turn, leaving them with their mouths still ajar.

I'm burning with regret, embarrassment, shame.

I *need* a coffee. I'm never going to get through the next ten minutes, let alone through the performance of an entire play.

I don't see an espresso machine at the bar and I slide through the crowd, ducking my head to find the staff door. I know my way through a kitchen and find the back exit in moments, paying zero attention to the surprise on the kitchen hand's face. The back alley isn't some dank place where rubbish bins are kept, it's festooned with fairy lights and populated with an assortment of eateries. I walk into the first one that has a coffee machine visible through the glass.

I haven't had a real coffee in so long that the hit is instant—warmth, energy, clarity. I know those people's opinions of me shouldn't matter but I care about the impact on Dain. And *his* opinion is vitally important to me. Yep, it's true. I really am in love with him.

My head pounds, blinding me as what's been brewing over the last few days crystallises. It hurts. Unbearably. I'm literally losing vision in one eye. But at the same time I really see. I really understand.

And I die inside. I never should have said that to Chloe. Certainly not in front of all those people. I couldn't last an hour before letting him down. I was overly defensive and uncontrolled. I don't have their education. I'm not engaging enough to fit. I've just made myself a laughing stock. And Dain.

He'll be annoyed, maybe even angry. But maybe that's good. Because I'm never going to be what he really *needs*.

I suddenly know what I need to do.

CHAPTER TWENTY-TWO

Dain

THE EVENING IS going better than I expected. In fact, I'm almost enjoying myself. I suspected Talia was insecure about coming. She wanted to look good—as if she ever doesn't. I was going to give her the diamond necklace I bought earlier in the week on a whim I can't explain, but when I saw her in that black gown I abandoned the plan. She needed not a thing more. Besides, I knew she'd baulk at accepting it and that she'd let Simone get her shoes is progress enough for now. She straightened up and I could only stare, my mouth gummed. I thought I could stay in control but then in the car she looked at me with that desperate desire in her eyes and I lost my head.

At first in the bar she clung to my hand as if we were facing a life-threatening situation but it soon became evident she didn't need me. I don't want her feeling as though I'm supervising her every second as if I don't trust her. I want her to be comfortable, to have fun and actually *enjoy* a party for once—not have to carry platter after platter of canapés. So I talked to that soap actor wanting investment advice for a while, only to then be immediately bailed up by a political candidate who leads me somewhere slightly more private. He drones on for way longer than I like. I've only just shaken him off when Simone hurries over.

'Where've you been?' she whispers.

'What's wrong?'

'Why aren't you glued to her side?' she hisses. 'People are talking and you left her alone to…'

'To what?' I stiffen. 'Talia's perfectly capable of taking care of herself.'

'Quite,' Simone snaps. 'A little too capable.'

I frown because that makes no sense. 'What's happened?'

'She basically told Chloe that there's nothing between you.' Simone watches me closely. 'That you're still on the market.'

I blink. 'She talked about us?'

I've said *'us'*, which immediately feels dangerous. But then I'm taken aback that Talia's publicly denied that there's an *'us'*. I shut down the outraged feeling that immediately rises. Now isn't the time to feel *anything*. My teen years of suppressing emotion in public come in handy now.

'I thought you'd figured this out,' Simone whispers urgently.

'I have,' I say crisply. 'Things are good. They're fine.'

'Fine?' Simone stares at me. 'They should be *fabulous*. You have a wonderful woman and you're—'

'Fine. It's under control.'

'It clearly isn't,' Simone mutters. 'She said that she's merely the mother of your baby. That's all. That there's still time for one of them to make their move.'

Anger swishes inside—I'm an overfilled bucket about to spill. 'Talia can say whatever she wants.'

And it was a sarcastic comment, right? But one I don't want her to say. Not to any of these people. Not at all. Especially when she's not said anything like it to me *first*.

I visually sweep the crowded bar but can't spot her. Was this event too soon? Maybe she wasn't ready. Maybe she felt more pressure than I realised. Or maybe she's messing with me and I don't know why. I thought I had iron-clad defences and could handle this.

Are we my parents creating public drama? People will talk if you give them something to talk about. And of course there was always going to be talk about us, but she's inexplicably caused more. That she's merely the mother of my child?

Rot.

How could she say such a thing when minutes before we arrived she was pressed close, *begging* me to take her? She was barely able to control herself, supple and slick in my arms, her eyes like jewels, dazed and full of desire, uncaring that we were in the back of a moving car. I battle the urge to find her, pull her close and prove to everyone present just how much she isn't merely anything. Prove to *her* that she can't resist me.

But I can't stand a scene and we're already a scene just by being here.

I still can't see her in the bar and a suspicion chills me. Has she run away from the party? The bigger question is whether she's run away altogether. That emotion I thought I could suppress so easily? It burns and my control slips. While she *wants* me, she doesn't need me. She doesn't want to need me and I suspect she doesn't *want* to want me either.

I struggle to keep my breathing even. I thought things were going to be okay. But it seems I'm wrong and my only relief is that Lukas is too young to be aware of any of this. We need to sort this out properly before he gets any older.

As I walk through the crowd one of the barmen slips me a scrap of paper. I glance at the scrawled note.

She's feeling unwell. She's sorry. She's taken a taxi home.

She's so damned proud. So damned independent. So damned defensive. I have a love-hate relationship with those things about her. Right now it's more a hate thing.

I crumple the paper and shove it in my pocket. She thinks she's been discreet in arranging this message, instead she's given the bar staff something to gossip about as well as half the guests. But I refuse to let anyone know how irate I am.

'Talia and I won't be able to attend the play, please enjoy it without us.' I mention the pertinent 'facts' to a key group who I know will pass the information on. 'Lukas is unsettled.' I smile and act as if I'm not seething inside. 'Talia's gone ahead already but I need to be with them both.'

I ignore Simone's silent scrutiny and say nothing extra to her. I tell the bartenders to be liberal with the champagne. It might help everyone forget Talia's comment. Except I don't care about any of them or what they think any more. I just want to get out of here and home to her. I want to make sure she *has* gone home.

Fear slices through me. I need to talk to her. But I need to regain control first. Good thing there's a drive to endure. I count the seconds as my chauffeur speeds through the darkening streets but it doesn't stop my brain from racing from one horrible thought to another.

I finally arrive back at the house. It's dark. I grit my teeth and head upstairs hoping like hell she's actually here.

CHAPTER TWENTY-THREE

Talia

I'M SUPPOSED TO be sitting in some fancy theatre right now. Instead I'm pacing around my room. I can't lie still because of the pounding on one side of my head. The killer headache is my own fault. I hadn't drunk a whole real coffee in so long it really affected me. I doubled back to the bar from the café and got one of the barmen to pass a note to Dain before getting in a cab. Now I'm jittery and nauseous as hell and I can't think what to do.

But my gut knows. My gut's already made me take action.

He's inspired strong feelings within me from the first. I've been passionate, possessive, jealous—yep, a whole gamut of intensity. But now I know everything I feel boils down to the one base element. *Not* lust. It's much richer and deeper than that.

I'm in love with him.

And the longer I'm around him, the further in love I'm falling. Now I feel even more sick. I can't let myself drown. I can't want it all like this—because it's an impossibility.

I've never felt as overwhelmed in my life as I did in that champagne bar with the blinding smiles and brilliant jewels and scintillating talk of things I know nothing about. My inferiority? I've never known it like that. I'm just not on his level. And to prove it I screwed up in seconds.

The door opens. I spin around to see him step inside. The floor bottoms out on me. I've no idea how I remain standing. That sickness builds in the pit of my stomach.

'You didn't go to the play?' My mouth is so dry I croak the words.

'I had a message that you weren't feeling well.' He leans back against the door to close it.

'You still should've gone.'

He stares at me. His expression is unreadable but I sense his reproach.

'You're never going to believe that I might prioritise you,' he says grimly. 'Why didn't you tell me you weren't feeling well?'

'It's a migraine. It came on suddenly,' I mutter feebly.

'Oh? Do you know what caused it?'

Not the coffee. Not even that stupid interaction with Chloe. She was merely the catalyst for my frustration and fear flaring. But I can't entirely regret it because it forced this reckoning.

'I can't do this,' I whisper helplessly. I can't lie to him any more. Or to myself.

'Do what?' he asks silkily.

The shiver of danger emboldens me. It's good that he's angry, actually. It'll make this easier. I'm wrong for him on so many levels and I don't want him to be with me only because he's afraid I'll cut him out of Lukas's life. I could never do that.

I know he's used to that denial—of time, attention, love. So am I. We're both damaged. We've both been denied. But he's worked so hard to make this work for me. He wants to be in Lukas's life and even though he has all the money, all that power, he, like me, fears loss of control. That his family, any emotional support or connection, could be taken away at any time. That he'll be shut out. He's as insecure as I am. So he's done everything in his power to make life here perfect for me. He's pleasured me over and over and over again. And I'm devastated. Because he felt he *had* to. Not because he *loves* me. Sure, he likes sleeping with me and we even have a laugh together but at heart he's only doing what he feels he must to shore up his own defences and protect his son. I understand it completely. It's what I'd have done too. The exact same thing. Pleasing. Working so hard to keep him happy. But things have changed for me. I want the fairy tale.

But he doesn't. And if he ever did, it he ought to be with someone who's his match. Someone who fits in this world. Someone who he feels strongly enough for to reconsider his position on commitment.

He stares at me as I stay silent. 'You talked to Chloe. Did she say something that bothered you?'

I bite my lip. 'I made a flippant comment.' My stomach twists.

'Is that what you call it?'

'Maybe I was too honest with her.'

'Honest?' He steps towards me. 'Is that what it was? When you told her in front of everyone that you're merely Lukas's mother and that there's still time for one of them to make a move? When you publicly denied a relationship with me?'

I grip the back of a chair, even more horrified. Because put like that it sounds even worse than when it happened. I felt shamed and lost control—but it was *in front of others*, when he desperately *needs* privacy in his personal life. I've jeopardised that just by existing. I remember those people taking photos outside the bar tonight. Dain isn't going to get his minions to hunt out those pictures and have them taken down. He was presenting me because I'm Lukas's mother—even if our togetherness is only to be temporary—and I've completely undermined his effort.

I denied that we have a relationship. My heart thuds as I make myself nod in agreement. Because yes, it was honest. I *need* it to be true. I need to push him away. I need to protect him. And myself.

His gaze darkens. 'Have you forgotten that moments before arriving at that bar we'd been—?'

'Of course I haven't forgotten. That happening in that car is part of the problem.' I draw a breath, but I still feel giddy. 'I can't want you that desperately. *You* don't want that.'

He stops still. 'I don't?'

'You don't want commitment. You know our intimacy was only an interlude.'

There's another moment—a flood of silence.

'An interlude that you've decided is now over,' he says very softly.

I make myself nod again. 'We were just going to let it run, remember?'

His body goes taut. 'You'd have been happy for her to flirt with me in front of you?'

My headache pounds.

He stares right into my eyes. 'Do you really think I'd go from your arms to another woman in one evening?' He lifts his chin. 'That's what you thought I did a year ago. And apparently nothing that's happened in the last few days has done anything to change your opinion of me.'

I want to shrivel up.

'Does it mean nothing to you that I was celibate for a *year*?' he asks.

I try to shrug. 'That's normal for me—'

'But if you'd met someone else?'

'I didn't…' I whisper. But I had chances. Handsome men came through the café all the time. Both before and after I had that night with him. But I was drawn to Dain in a way I've never been drawn to any other person.

'Why are you still so willing to believe the worst of me?' he asks.

He's hurt. Really hurt. My emotions spin. I'm making everything worse. Handling this all so incredibly badly. He doesn't deserve *any* of this. He deserves so much more than

I can give and the least I can offer him now is that truth. He should hear it directly from me. Because I do know how much honesty matters to him.

'Tonight was a mistake,' I mumble. 'I lost control. It isn't really *you*...'

His pupils dilate. 'I—'

'No, actually it is you,' I blurt in confusion. 'I just really need to find a way to stop liking you.'

He stares at me. He doesn't get it.

I inhale deeply but it doesn't loosen that too tight, suffocating feeling in my chest. 'I want you to be *happy*. You deserve to be happy.'

'Wow—'

'I want you to be free.'

'We have a child together, Talia.'

'Yes, but that shouldn't stop you from doing what you want. Or being with whoever you want.'

'So you thought you'd speed up the process by finding someone else for me to sleep with?'

'Cheating is a hard line for me.'

'So it will make it easier for you if I sleep with someone else, is that actually what you're saying?'

I brace inwardly. 'Better still if you married someone else. But we both know that isn't going to happen.'

His jaw drops. 'This is about the most screwed-up, irrational thing I have ever heard. And I heard some messed-up shit between my parents, Talia. I sure as hell don't need your help in finding a new sexual partner.' Yep, he's wildly angry and I don't blame him.

'I thought you got that,' he says. 'I thought we had an understanding.'

Tears prick my eyes. 'Well, we need a new one.'

'And you've already thought of it.'

'Yep.' I barely hold back my emotion. I have to get away

from him now. I just have to. 'I'm going to move into the pool house.'

'Pardon?'

'It'll give us space,' I blurt, increasingly uncontrolled because my head is killing me and my heart is breaking. 'I should've gone in there in the first place. Lukas will stay in the main house if that's what you want.'

'How generous of you. You've thought all this through.' He inhales. 'You're this determined not to need me.'

'No. I'm this determined not to *love* you.'

He recoils. 'You what?'

I exhale and it all just explodes from me. 'I love you! I'm so in love with you.' I can't blame this on caffeine jitters. I promised I'd never lie to him. That I'd never hold back on the whole truth. So there's no bluffing. No attempt to pretend. There's just truth. 'And I don't want to be in love with you but it's only getting worse.'

In the next second I can't believe I told him that. So passionately. So painfully.

The horrified look on his face tells me everything. He's so gorgeous but beneath that charisma, that charming smile, there's a man who's been deeply hurt. Who doesn't feel worthy of love. Who doesn't want me to love him. Who doesn't believe me.

'You're so in love with me you're trying to enable my cheating on you?' He's bitterly sardonic. 'You're so in love with me you can barely take a thing from me?'

'I don't care about your money. I never have. I only care about you.' I see the flicker in his eyes. 'You're *more* than money. If you had none you'd still be fascinating to me.'

He shoots me a cynical look that's devastating.

'You don't believe that I'm in love with you.' It appals me to realise he doesn't feel valuable.

'Words versus actions, Talia. You have to admit you've a very weird way of showing your supposed love.'

I grit my teeth. 'I want to leave you enough space so you can live your life fully however you want to.'

'You mean so I can sleep around.'

'I mean be *free*.'

'That's what you want for yourself,' he says sharply. 'You're trying to give me what it is that *you* actually want. You want to be free of me.'

He's right. I do. Because I don't want this pain—I can't live with it now and it's only been an hour since I really realised. It's only going to grow. From the look on his face I know I'm doing the right thing. He doesn't believe that I'm in love with him or that I want what's best for him.

Maybe he thinks I'm trying to manipulate him in some way and maybe this is coming out of the blue for him, but it only reinforces that this is right. What did he think was going to happen? That we would continue to sleep together just casually? Would his interest wane and he just not want me as much any more? I can't wait around for that to happen. I know he loves Lukas and wants to be in Lukas's life. Always. And he will be.

So I lift my head and answer with raw honesty. 'Yes. I do. I want to be free of you.'

CHAPTER TWENTY-FOUR

Dain

IT'S JUST REJECTION. Pure and simple. She says one thing, does the opposite and I'm too stunned to even think. I just respond from my gut. 'You've really had enough.'

'I—'

'Fine, go, then.'

Because I don't want to hear it. I can't. I'm just…*incandescent*. I can't blink away the red mist. I can't breathe through it. I've let her in and I shouldn't have and I need her gone.

'Go. Wherever you want. I don't care. Just go now.'

She looks hurt. What, did she expect me to beg her to stay?

I don't need to be rejected again. Be told twice that I'm not who or what she wants. No, thanks.

Her eyes fill. I cannot handle tears. I step back jerkily.

'Dain…'

There is *zero* point in continuing this conversation a second longer.

'You want to be free,' I snap.

People do this. They push you away right when they shouldn't. When you think everything is finally okay. But it's never okay. Because they don't love you. That's the biggest, cruellest lie of all and for her to use that one on me is unforgivable. And I can't hold back the bitterness. I shake my head—rejection of my own. 'You *don't* love me and you never should have said that—'

'I do.' She stands tall and pale. 'But you don't believe me. Because you don't trust me.'

'Do you blame me for that?'

She lies. I know it and she knows I know it.

'I'm not lying about this,' she says softly. 'But you can't believe me because you don't feel worthy of love.'

I'm stunned to silence as she stares at me with intensity in her eyes.

In the end I can only mutter weakly, 'And you do?'

'I didn't before,' she admits huskily. 'But I do now. Now I know I should and could have it. So can you. But the thing is, you don't want that from me. And I didn't mean to make things even more awkward for you.'

Awkward. She thinks she's made things awkward. She's made everything utterly unbearable.

I walk out of the room, unable to say anything more. I walk out of the house, unable to stand anything any more. I just walk out and keep walking. I do the one thing I promised I wouldn't. I leave them.

But she's already given up on me. She's decided that this isn't going to work.

I don't like quitting. I don't like failure. But I'm so angry with her. I want to smash something. Instead I storm down the road and head to the river.

I already know relationships don't last but she's ending ours way before time. Why? Because she *loves* me?

It's laughable. The worst, cruellest joke.

I don't want to think. I can't. It's too painful. But with every step I take away from the house her words echo in my head. She's ripped me open and poured salt onto the wounds.

My parents excelled in playing out their personal issues publicly for point-scoring in their war. They used me over and over in that way. My parents also kept the most *impor-*

tant thing secret from me—together with my grandfather they kept his terminal cancer diagnosis from me.

But maybe Talia didn't mean to do that. She looked horrified when I accused her of going public and that was when she pushed me away totally. It was for *my* benefit, she argued. For my freedom.

I try to remember—try to work out where it went wrong tonight. I stood with her at the start, holding her hand. She was quiet but charming. I believed her capable. I thought I could walk away. I thought she had the security. I was completely wrong.

In that moment at the party with Chloe, Talia was trying to protect *herself.* She was wounded and she exploded. Which meant she was deep in an emotional storm—like the night she blew up at me when she thought I'd thrown out Lukas's toy rabbit.

I suspected she felt she wasn't a good enough fit for me or my lifestyle—but I thought I'd reassured her. Clearly I failed and something must've happened to upset her.

The crowd. Chloe. Maybe *me.*

Talia's always wanted to protect her sister—not wanting Ava to feel guilty that she had to work so hard to help her. I have the horrible feeling she's trying to do the same for me. Because apparently she loves me.

I suck in a scalding breath because I know she lies. But the truth is so do I. I keep my true feelings close so they can't be used against me. I don't let many people into my life on an intimate level. It's always seemed pragmatic. Really it's cowardice.

Talia used to be a coward too. She lied most to those she's closest to. To the people she doesn't want to hurt and who she doesn't want to hurt her—her sister especially. But she promised not to lie to me no matter what. She promised not to hold back any part of the truth from me either.

It hurts that she has.

But her declaration of love didn't feel like a lie. It felt like a truth *tormenting* her. Something she could no longer hold back. And it was that pain that I reacted to—as fundamentally, instinctively, emotionally as I always do. I pushed back on it. Pushed it away. *Her* away.

In Talia's world she really thought she was doing me a favour but I still can hardly make sense of it. Because if she really loved me, why would she want to walk out on me? *How* could she? Surely if she loved me she could never leave me? Because I realise now—stupidly and terrifyingly—that *I* could never leave *her*.

I stop walking and try to still my racing thoughts because I'm struggling to think straight. I can't ever seem to stop and think straight. Not about her. My rational brain is never bloody involved—only the animal brain is. The lust part. The fearful part. And it's always just pushed me to action—emotionally driven action that I can barely control. Mostly I've been compelled to reach out and touch her. To take her in my arms. I've been possessive as hell from the moment I first saw her.

I want her to be mine. Just as Lukas is mine.

I could never leave him. I love him. But she knows that latter. She understands it. But she doesn't know the first. My heart squeezes and breathing becomes really bloody difficult. Talia's never had stability. Ever. She needs it more than anyone. I thought she needed it to be tangible—the house, the workspace, the life insurance. I tried to let her know that no matter what happens she and Lukas will be okay. They'll always have everything they need. But she wants more. The stability she really craves is emotional.

Talia has long hidden her needs from the people she loves. Hid her problems from everyone as best she could. She tried to manage alone for years—as if she didn't think she had the right to openly ask for help or comfort or anything she really needs.

But that night in the gondola she didn't hide from me. She

admitted her fears and she voiced her needs and I gave her what she wanted. What she needed. Which was simply myself. My time. My body. My complete attention.

I'd do it again. I always will. I will give her anything and everything she asks of me. What's mine is hers.

I am hers.

But tonight she asked and I didn't hear her. She told me she loved me but she didn't want anything else from me. Nothing else. She tried to minimise herself. She shrank in front of me because she didn't think that *I* could ever offer her the same.

That's not the Talia I want to see. Ever. I want angry Talia. Feisty Talia. Resilient Talia who does what she wants and needs to. She can't shrink. She's my whole world and I do *not* want her vanishing out of it. Ever.

I want her to say it again. I don't want her keeping anything back from me. I want her to trust me. I ache for that. But admitting that I want her. Need her. That's scary.

But she *did* things for those she loves too—she helped Ava. She protected Ava by not wanting her to worry.

What she did tonight told me so much—I just needed the space to think it through. She pre-emptively pushed me away because she thinks I don't love her. Because she thinks I'm with her only out of a sense of duty. It isn't duty. It's an undeniable ache that's assuaged only when I'm close to her. When I laugh with her. When I lie in bed with her. When I'm near her.

It's heartache. And I'm in trouble.

CHAPTER TWENTY-FIVE

Talia

I WAKE AND BLINK. I'm in a room I don't recognise. Then memory bites.

I moved my backpack to the pool house last night. I don't know if or when Dain came home. I barely slept but heard nothing. I was too busy replaying that horrific conversation. I told him I love him. He tore me to shreds.

It hurts. I wipe the tears from my eyes but they keep spilling. Endless silent tears. It's very early but I need to see Lukas. I look an embarrassing mess, but the nanny won't say anything. She's the latest of Dain's utterly discreet employees—contracted and paid a fortune to keep silent on his personal business because he doesn't trust anyone.

I warily walk through the house. It's quiet and feels ominously empty and my heart skips—what if he's taken him? Surely he wouldn't. He loves Lukas. He wants what's best for him and he knows that means both of us in our son's life. I pass my bedroom door. It's open and it's obvious I didn't sleep in there last night. The staff probably assume I was in Dain's room anyway.

But Lukas's room is empty too and I reach for the wall for support.

'The nanny's taken him for a walk,' Dain says from behind me. 'He's already had breakfast.'

I jump and turn. My pulse spikes at the sight of him. He's in jeans and a tee. Not crumpled. Effortlessly elegant as always. The only hint of any strain is the stubble on his jaw and the shadow beneath his beautiful eyes. 'Oh. Then I'll go back...'

I can't finish my sentence. I can't keep looking at him. I drop my gaze to the floor and walk, talking myself through one step at a time. I just need to get away and I'll be okay. Eventually.

'Stop.' His voice is thready. 'Stay. Please.'

And now I can't move. I'm stuck in the corridor of his gorgeous home and I can't get past him. Literally.

He exhales heavily. 'You come into my life and give me a glimpse of everything I could ever want and the next minute you're gone. You leave me. I can't stand it.'

My anger lifts. 'Last night you told me to go.'

'Last night I didn't know what I was doing.'

I shoot him a startled look.

'I wasn't thinking.' He steps towards me carefully. 'I was upset.'

I swallow. 'I'm sorry I said that to Chloe—'

'I don't give a damn about what she or anyone else thinks,' he interrupts me roughly.

'But I'm sorry I said...'

His facade cracks. 'Sorry you told me you love me?'

I'm hurt. Really hurt by his bluntness. And I want to escape—to evaporate. Anything to get away because I can't cope with the look in his eyes. I can't believe what I think I see.

He holds his hand out to me. 'Talia.'

Pressing my lips together, I shake my head and fist my hands at my sides.

'Please. This is a life-threatening situation of another sort,' he whispers. 'My world is empty as hell without you already, Talia. Take my hand and let's do this together.'

'This?'

'Do the rest of our lives.' He steps forward and wraps his hands round my cold fists.

I don't pull away. I can't. He walks backwards, his gaze not leaving mine, taking me with him. Unerringly leading me to his bedroom. I can't resist him. Tears fall from my eyes and I can't wipe them away because he still has hold of me and I need him to let me go.

He twists a little just as we enter his room and kicks the door shut. 'Talia—'

I avert my gaze from the bed. 'You don't have to say anything. It's fine. I'm fine.'

'Well, I'm not,' he says gruffly. 'And you're lying.'

'Dain—'

'I didn't listen to you last night because I couldn't face it,' he interrupts me. 'I couldn't admit—' He breaks off recalibrating himself. 'I didn't answer honestly because I was shocked and I was scared.'

'Of me?'

'Yeah. And of my feelings for you.'

I stare at him, my heart pounding. 'And what are those?'

He cocks his head as he did that night in the gondola. The smallest smile curves his mouth but there's regret in his beautiful eyes. 'You infuriate me. You're annoyingly independent and ferociously capable. Sometimes I just want you to let me help you because I *enjoy* helping you, but you don't want to rely on anyone because you were hurt and that saddens me, but I get it because I was too.'

But his smile widens as his words come stronger and faster. 'You're loyal to a fault and you'll do anything for people you love, even if it isn't in your own best interests, and that generosity melts me. Your wit makes me laugh and keeps me on my toes because you don't put up with my arrogance and entitlement. You liberated the playfulness I'd forgotten I had, and I rediscovered the joy of spontaneity and silliness. And the sex I've had with you is the best of my life. I'll never sleep with anyone else. You bring *all* the feelings out in me, Talia. I can't stop any of them, but especially not the biggest and deepest. You hold my whole heart in your beautiful, clever hands.'

He breathes more heavily and lifts our hands between us. 'You could crush it. You could end me. But…' he clears his throat '… I know you won't because you're a kind, loving person. And amazingly you love me.' His grip tightens on me. 'But you need to know I love you too, Talia,' he confesses. 'How can I not love you?'

I can't move again. It's awful to be so paralysed, so afraid, but I am. I want to believe him but it's taking its time to sink in because it's just unbelievable… I can't believe him.

'I'm not like any of those people at your party,' I whisper, unable to stop my insecurities escaping. 'They're all cultured and elegant and well educated. I don't even have formal barista qualifications, let alone a degree—'

'Neither do I.' He shrugs and then chuckles. 'My grandfather died and I skipped study and went straight to work and learned everything by experience. Same as you. We both work hard. We're both curious. We both want the best for everyone around us…'

That's true.

'I never wanted any of those people. I never wanted anyone the way I want you. And it's only you I'll ever want. The night we met, you pushed a universal override on every defence I thought I had. And you were never blinded by the superficial things that surround me in a way that's sometimes suffocating.'

'Your poor-little-rich-boy trappings?'

'Trappings is right. I was a fool. I thought my value depended on the success I made of my family company.' His smile is rueful.

'It was the one stable thing you could control.'

'Right,' he mutters. 'But the night we met you saw something else in me.'

'I thought you were a stripper,' I mumble.

His smile explodes. 'And for you I can be,' he purrs. 'Any time you want. But only ever for you.'

Warmth spreads inside and what little grip I have left on my emotion slips. 'You were gorgeous. And funny.'

'Because you bring out my playful side. Only with you can I relax. I can let go. Because I trust you.'

Those words break me.

'You're beautiful and funny and I want you to stay with me. Always. I was too afraid to admit it,' he whispers. 'But I love you, Talia. I love you totally. I don't ever want to hurt you and I know you never want to hurt me either. But we hurt each other a bit last night.'

My lungs have shrunk. I can't get enough oxygen to my brain. 'I was trying to control the ending. I thought you didn't...' I start to sob but still try to speak '...wouldn't ever... want me always. Let alone...'

'Love you,' he finishes for me, and repeats what I still can't believe. 'I love you.' He lets go of my hands at last and cups my face. 'And I can't go through another night like last night.'

I blink but the tears still fall.

'Neither of us do well with uncertainty,' he says. 'So know this. I love you and I will never leave you. We're always going to be together.'

I finally smile even though I'm crying more than before and he pulls me into a hug and it's everything I need. I feel the emotion overwhelming him too—his breathing shudders and his body quakes with the intensity of relief. I clutch him and bury my face in his chest.

'I just want us to be together,' he mutters. 'Our little family. And it can be what we make it, right?'

I nod eagerly.

'I think we were doing pretty well with it, actually,' he says almost shyly. 'Not like my parents. Not like yours either. We're different people. I know I need to open up more.'

'It's hard to open up,' I mumble.

'It is. But it's also not. I like talking to you, Talia. I like trusting you. And I'm so grateful for Lukas. He's our miracle and I give thanks for him every day, especially now. He's helped speed everything up.'

I can't help my smile. 'You want to speed up now?'

'No.' He smiles back. 'I want to go very, very slow.'

Slow is torture. Slow is bliss. Slow is absolutely everything I need.

He kisses me with such reverence that I start to shake. 'Dain…'

'Shh. Let me love you. I want to love you.'

I understand. As impossible as it ought to be, this is even more melting than the indulgence he's given me before because this time the underpinning emotion is given full and free expression. His hands sweep over me and I feel him tremble with restraint.

'I love you, Talia.'

He's opened up and it's heaven. My bruised heart bursts open too and then it just grows like an unstoppable wave made of wonder and warmth and joy. I hold him—half crying, half laughing—admitting all my deep-held, deep-hidden truths too—all the things I adore about him. All the ways he pleases me. I hold nothing back. We're aligned in absolute honesty. It's always been fun, always joyous between us. But there's an essential facet that's been revealed—a foundation firmly cemented between us, within us. I believe in him and he believes in me. And it is *awesome*. I'm shaking and breathless and when he finally, fully claims his place inside me we both moan. It's exquisite and it's everything. We're together, as close as any two people can be.

'There's a lot to be said for slow.' I sigh as the gorgeous sensations stream through me.

He looks at me with nothing but love in his eyes. 'There's even more to be said for always.'

CHAPTER TWENTY-SIX

One year later
Talia

'WHAT IF WE made another movie?'

Startled, I glance up at Dain and feel my skin heating. 'Are you serious?' I squeak.

We still have that movie we inadvertently made in the pool house that time and, yep, we might've watched it together a few more times in the last year. It's always fire. Always.

'Absolutely,' he says, not taking his gaze from me.

'Now?' I glance out of the window and see Lukas and the nanny making castles in the sandpit Dain had installed a while back.

'Well, you might want a little time to get your outfit sorted first.'

'Outfit?' I'm a little stunned but *definitely* intrigued. 'You want to dress up?'

'Oh, yeah, definitely.' His eyes smoulder as he stares at me. 'I'd love to see you in a—'

'Don't you dare say maid's outfit.' But my mouth has gone dry because I'm down a rabbit hole of exciting outfits I'd quite like to see Dain in.

He chuckles and steps close. 'I was thinking more the sort of movie we can share with others,' he whispers. 'Bore them with, actually. But we can make another later if you like.'

I frown, confused and totally distracted by how close he suddenly is. 'You want other people in our personal movie?'

'Ava would like to be involved, I'm sure.' He brushes back a strand of hair from my face and his tenderness muddles my mind even more. 'Lukas will definitely need to be there.'

'What?' I'm hopelessly confused, and the way Dain's laughing isn't helping. But I can't resist leaning closer because I want to kiss him. The light in his gaze morphs into tenderness and he suddenly drops to one knee before me.

I stare and it slowly dawns. Is the movie he's talking about making a *wedding* film?

'Dain?' I'm so breathless I feel as though I'm about to faint. But I see the sudden vulnerability in his eyes and realise the full importance of this moment. 'You don't have to...' I whisper. 'We don't have to...'

He doesn't believe in marriage and I get why. He suffered so much in his parents' divorce. We don't need it. I have faith in him—in us—regardless. I know we'll be together always. 'I know—'

He puts his finger over my lips. 'I love you. I want to commit to you and promise that I'll be here for you always. I want to share my life, my bed, everything I am and have with you as my wife.' He breathes in. 'Will you please marry me?'

I stare at him and my eyes prickle with tears. There's no camera here now but it's so intimate and special the memory will be seared on my heart.

'I want to take that leap of faith with you,' he adds. 'Not for anyone else. Just for ourselves.'

He believes in me. In *us*. And there's only one answer I can give. 'Oh, *yes*!'

His smile explodes. So does my heart. He pulls me to the floor with him and we're a tangle of limbs and heat until he traps me beneath him and suddenly pauses.

'I haven't got you a ring yet... I wanted you to help choose. But I have something for now.' He pulls something from his pocket. 'I know you think things don't last, but these are dia-monds. And they will.'

I gasp at the gleaming rope of jewels he dangles above me. Given their size and number I'd have thought they were fake, but this is Dain so I know they're not. 'Dain—'

'I got it so long ago,' he mutters with a gruff laugh. 'I wanted to give it to you the night of that play we never saw, but I knew you had a thing about things.'

'A what?'

He looks at me ruefully. 'I figured you'd think I was try-ing to buy your favour or something.'

Back then maybe I would have thought he was trying to buy my favour. But now I know better. Because I want to do things for him and give things to him. Every*thing*. And I know he wants to do the same for me. I understand his motivation and I believe in him wholly.

'The *"or something"* is that you love me.' I take the jewels from him. 'Just as I love you.'

I drape the heavy diamond choker across my throat. 'Fas-ten it for me?'

But he fumbles. Swears. Abandons the attempt and lets the treasure slip to the floor beside us.

Because he devours me. Because *I'm* his treasure. Just as he's mine. We're everything and all to each other.

For ever.

* * * * *

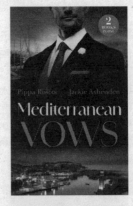

COMING SOON!

We really hope you enjoyed reading this book.
If you're looking for more romance
be sure to head to the shops when
new books are available on

Thursday 18th July

To see which titles are coming soon, please visit

millsandboon.co.uk/nextmonth

MILLS & BOON

MILLS & BOON®

Coming next month

ITALIAN'S STOLEN WIFE
Lorraine Hall

'I am very well aware of who you are, *cara*.'

His smile felt like some kind of lethal blow. Francesca could not understand why it should make her feel breathless and devastated.

But she had spent her life in such a state. So she kept her smile in place and waited patiently for Aristide to explain his appearance. Even if her heart seemed to clatter around in her chest like it was no longer tethered. A strange sensation indeed.

'I am afraid there has been a change of plans today,' he said at last, his low voice a sleek menace.

Francesca kept her sweet smile in place, her hand relaxed in his grip, her posture perfect. She was an expert at playing her role. Even as panic began to drum its familiar beat through her bloodstream.

'Oh?' she said, as if she was interested in everything he had to say.

No one would change her plans. *No one*. She narrowly resisted curling her free fingers into a fist.

'You will be marrying me instead.'

Continue reading
ITALIAN'S STOLEN WIFE
Lorraine Hall

Available next month
millsandboon.co.uk